PRAISE FOR

# The Lady Sherlock Series

"Loaded with suspense . . . a riveting and absorbing read . . . a beautifully written novel; you'll savor the unraveling of the mystery and the brilliance of its heroine."                                           —NPR.org

"Sherry Thomas has done the impossible and crafted a fresh, exciting new version of Sherlock Holmes."
—Deanna Raybourn, *New York Times* bestselling author of
*A Perilous Undertaking*

"Sherry Thomas is a master of her craft, and *A Study in Scarlet Women* is an unqualified success: brilliantly executed, beautifully written, and magnificently original—I want the next volume now!"
—Tasha Alexander, *New York Times* bestselling author

"Clever historical details and a top-shelf mystery add to the winning appeal of this first volume in the Lady Sherlock series. A must-read for fans of historical mysteries."          —*Library Journal* (starred review)

"A completely new, brilliantly conceived take on the iconic detective . . . A plot worthy of [Sir Arthur Conan Doyle] at his best."          —*Booklist*

"Readers will wait with bated breath to discover how Thomas will skillfully weave in each aspect of the Sherlockian canon, and devour the pages to learn how the mystery unfolds."
—Anna Lee Huber, national bestselling author of
the Lady Darby Mysteries

"I am breathless . . . Sherry Thomas is simply a genius—twisting classic Sherlockian memes into complicated knots and then gradually untying them so that we're left with a beautiful, seamless ribbon of an adventure tinged with romance."          —*Romantic Historical Reviews*

# THE HOLLOW OF FEAR

## SHERRY THOMAS

BERKLEY
New York

BERKLEY
An imprint of Penguin Random House LLC
375 Hudson Street, New York, New York 10014

Copyright © 2018 by Sherry Thomas

Library of Congress Cataloging-in-Publication Data

Names: Thomas, Sherry (Sherry M.), author.
Title: The hollow of fear / Sherry Thomas.
Description: First edition. | New York : Berkley, 2018. |
Series: [The Lady Sherlock series ; 3]
Identifiers: LCCN 2018018554| ISBN 9780425281420 (paperback) |
ISBN 9780698196377 (ebook)
Subjects: LCSH: Women private investigators—England—London—Fiction. |
BISAC: FICTION / Mystery & Detective / Historical. |
FICTION / Mystery & Detective / Women Sleuths.
Classification: LCC PS3620.H6426 H66 2018 | DDC 813/.6—dc23
LC record available at https://lccn.loc.gov/2018018554

First Edition: October 2018

Printed in the United States of America
1  3  5  7  9  10  8  6  4  2

Woman with shawl © Susan Fox/Trevillion Images
Winter background by Roy Bishop/Arcangel
Book design by Tiffany Estreicher

*For my agent, Kristin Nelson,*
*who is still making everything possible.*

## Prologue

"Hello, brother," murmured Charlotte Holmes to the man who helped her descend from the carriage.

The man, who had hitherto presented himself as Mott, groom and coachman to the Holmes family, half bowed.

They stood in the coach house behind the town residence that Sir Henry, their father, had hired for the Season. Charlotte's sister Livia had just been delivered to the front door. And the entire family, with the exception of Charlotte, would be setting out for the country in the morning, as it was nearly the end of July, a fashionable time to leave London.

"May I offer you some tea?" asked Mr. Myron Finch, her half brother, pulling off his driving gloves.

He seemed entirely unconcerned that she'd peeled back his secret. Then again, he had read the note she'd pressed into his hand when he'd helped her into the carriage earlier, requesting that he put the vehicle directly into the coach house after Livia stepped off. He might not have known that she wished to discuss his true identity, but he would have braced himself for *something*.

"Tea would be much appreciated," she said.

He showed her to a stool near an uneven-looking folding table. "I'm afraid I haven't any decent foodstuffs on hand. I'll be vacating the place as soon as I've taken your family to the railway station tomorrow morning."

*Her* family.

"Not to worry. I have just the thing."

She opened her handbag and took out a small wrapped package. Having briefly lived on the edge of hunger earlier in the summer, after she'd run away from home, she never left Mrs. Watson's house without a supply of comestibles.

The package contained three slices of plum cake. "Shall I serve you a piece, Mr. Finch?"

"Certainly," he replied, echoing her elaborate politeness. "Let me light the Etna stove."

The Etna stove, made for travelers, was said to boil water in three minutes flat. Charlotte was content to wait in silence; apparently, so was her father's illegitimate son.

He was an unremarkable-looking man: his features neither handsome enough nor odd enough to attract notice. But as with most other seemingly ordinary faces, a closer study yielded interesting details: fine-textured skin, long lashes, a strong jawline.

"How did you think to hide here?" she asked, after tea had been made and served.

She occupied the only seat. He stood against a brick column, a dented tin mug in one hand, a piece of plum cake in the other.

"When we realized the kind of danger we'd put ourselves in, Jenkins and I agreed to go our separate ways."

There was a pause before he mentioned Jenkins by name, the first hint of deeper emotions. Jenkins had been his friend from school, and the two men had served Moriarty, a man of dangerous aims. Years later, they had left Moriarty's service together.

But Moriarty rewarded deserters with death. Jenkins had already met his. Mr. Finch, as of now, was still in one piece. But for how long?

"It stood to reason that two lone men would be more difficult to track down than two men traveling and rooming together," he went on. "For me, it would be better to disappear into the bowels of London. But where in London would I be safest? Where would Moriarty's minions be least likely to look for me?

"Moriarty preferred to bring into his service young men born on the wrong side of the blanket. The subject of our fathers came up from time to time—and I'd always said that I would never introduce myself to the man who'd sired me. Not even if I somehow became Home Secretary—or rich as Croesus. He would need to come to *me*, hat in hand.

"They believed me, because I was—and am—sincere in those sentiments. I decided to take advantage of that and tuck myself away in the last place they would expect."

She had wondered what he had made of the Holmes family—and whether he had been disappointed in their father, even though he couldn't have expected much to begin with. To Sir Henry, Myron Finch had only ever been an abstract inconvenience addressed via family solicitors. How had Mr. Finch felt then, standing before the father who did not know what he looked like—nor had ever cared to find out? "We are not the easiest people to work for."

"You and Miss Livia are all right."

They met a minimum standard of decency and consideration. But their parents . . .

Charlotte nodded. "An excellent strategy. I thought you were more than you let on—but often people are. I didn't in the least suspect anything while I lived here."

"When did you realize? And how?" he asked, as if the questions had only then occurred to him.

In his nonchalance, this brother might be more similar to her than any of the siblings with whom she had shared an upbringing. "Very recently. When I went to your old school and asked to see photographs of cricketers from your batch."

"And what prompted you to do such a thing?"

"It's a long story."

She gave him a condensed version of the maneuvers, on the part of a Moriarty ally, to find him. The ally, who had known of both Charlotte's connection to Myron Finch and that she was taking consulting clients under the guise of Sherlock Holmes, had asked Sherlock Holmes to find the errant Mr. Finch. And the irregularities of the case had eventually led Charlotte not only to unmask Mr. Finch but also to expose the Moriarty ally.

He listened without interruption. And except for a widening of the eyes when she mentioned that she was Sherlock Holmes, he could have been nodding along to a stranger's account of garden pests.

But when she fell silent, he exhaled, a shaky breath—he was not free from fear, after all. "I knew that if they found me, I'd be dead. But I had no idea so much effort had been expended toward that end."

If he only knew. She had not told him that the Moriarty ally was none other than her friend Lord Ingram Ashburton's estranged wife, who had been passing along crucial information that she'd gathered from spying on her husband, himself an agent of the Crown. As a result of coming to Sherlock Holmes, her secret had been exposed. And she was now a fugitive, her children essentially motherless.

But Lady Ingram's fate was not Mr. Finch's concern. He had enough of his own worries.

"I understand you have taken something of value from Moriarty," said Charlotte. "But I imagine, theft or not, he must make an example out of everyone who deserts him—or his other minions might think they could abscond at will."

"Not many wish to. Then again, those who do choose not to express that desire aloud. Jenkins and I were unusual in that we knew each other before we pledged our fealty to Moriarty. Most others come into his service singly and alone."

"And his organization becomes the only family they know."

"Precisely."

She wondered, then, and not for the first time, what had compelled him to leave this "family". Had it been the culmination of years of ever-increasing urge? Or had he, like her, made up his mind within minutes, when his circumstances deteriorated abruptly?

She did not ask that question. She asked, "If you don't mind my curiosity, what did you do for Moriarty, exactly?"

"I was his cryptographer."

*Similarities.* "I had to solve a Vigenère cipher recently. It nearly broke my will to live."

He smiled and made no response.

Charlotte took a sip of her tea, a strong, brisk Assam, served without milk or sugar. "What do you plan to do now?"

"I think you know I plan to disappear again. But that isn't what you are asking, is it?"

"You are correct," said Charlotte. She nibbled on her slice of plum cake, which had held up well despite having spent the evening in her rather cramped handbag. "I am more interested in what you intend to do with what you stole from Moriarty."

"I didn't steal anything from Moriarty," said Mr. Finch.

Charlotte raised a brow.

He smiled slightly. "That is the official version. Moriarty will deny, to his dying breath, that anything has been taken from him in an unauthorized manner. I don't know how you came by your information, but it most certainly wouldn't have been one of his usual agents. To them he would have said only that we were traitors—and that would be reason enough to hunt down and eliminate us."

"I received my intelligence from people who call themselves the Marbletons. Mrs. Marbleton was once married to Moriarty. Or perhaps I should say, she still is, since she did not die, as is commonly believed."

"And which late Mrs. Moriarty is she?"

"Excuse me?"

"There are three late Mrs. Moriartys."

"*That* many?"

"First died in childbirth. Second in a skiing accident in the Swiss Alps. Third of an embolism of the heart."

"This would be the second Mrs. Moriarty—still alive after all these years. Then again, she might not be Mrs. Moriarty at all, if the first Mrs. Moriarty also turns out to be still alive somewhere. Is there a current Mrs. Moriarty?"

"Not that I know of. There is a mistress whom Moriarty seems fond of—but he is determined not to marry again, since he considers himself an agent of misfortune to any woman named Mrs. Moriarty."

"How thoughtful," Charlotte murmured.

"Anyway, please go on. The second Mrs. Moriarty is still alive and well."

"And it is from her associates that I learned that you may have something of value to Moriarty."

"I'm going to toe the official line and say that there is no such thing."

Because it would be better for her not to know? "The Marbletons want to meet you. They'd like to offer you a safe haven. In exchange, they desire to weaken Moriarty by exploiting the item you have not stolen and are not carrying."

"They have very rosy expectations."

"They claim—or at least one of them claims—that they are tired of running and hiding. They wish to be on the offensive. To better ensure their safety and well-being by making Moriarty fear *them* instead."

Mr. Finch rubbed a hand along his chin. "I'm not convinced about the existence of this Marbleton clan. You sign your own death sentence upon leaving Moriarty."

"According to one Marbleton, that they have managed to evade Moriarty for this long is precisely why you ought to join forces with them. They can help you stay alive longer than Jenkins managed to."

He was silent.

"I am only the messenger—the choice is yours. If you decide to accept their offer, you can call for a letter for Mr. Ethelwin Emery at Charing Cross Post Office. The letter will contain further instructions."

"I'll remember that."

"And I must warn you, the Crown is now also interested in your whereabouts. Agents of the Crown may not wish you dead, but if I were you, I would avoid crossing paths with them. I don't trust that they will have your best interests at heart."

"I have heard talk about Lord Bancroft Ashburton. I am forewarned." Mr. Finch cocked his head. "Did you accept his proposal, in the end?"

He had been present at the memorable occasion when Lord Ingram announced to a room of men there specifically to drag her back home that she was considering a proposal from Lord Bancroft.

"No."

"I'm glad."

She raised a brow. "Why? Do you think a Lady Bancroft would have as dire a rate of survival as a Mrs. Moriarty?"

"Of that I haven't the slightest notion. But you yourself said, when Sir Henry asked why you hadn't accepted Lord Bancroft, that you weren't enamored of the idea."

"Is that all?"

"Is that not reason enough?"

Most people would be outraged that she, in her state of disgraced exile, declined a perfectly good proposal to please herself, when there were so many parties she could have better pleased by becoming Lord Bancroft's wife.

Was Mr. Finch truly so liberal in his thinking?

Before she could say anything, however, he pushed away from the pillar against which he stood. "Someone's coming."

The furrow in his brow conveyed the unwelcomeness of this visitor. Charlotte, too, rose. The lamp on the wall flickered. One of the carriage horses snorted, its tail swishing. Her hand clenched around the edge of the folding table, its surfaces pitted and rough beneath her skin.

Knocks came, three taps in rapid succession, followed by two louder thumps spaced farther apart.

She had thought it possible that it was Livia, coming to speak a few words to Mr. Finch on the eve of her departure, since she had relied on and trusted him to help her, without knowing that he was their brother. But this was not Livia.

The knocks came again, in exactly the same pattern.

The letters S and M in Morse Code.

"I might know who this is." Charlotte drew out her double-barrel derringer, which she'd carried on her person ever since the day her father attempted to abduct her. "You hide behind the coach, just in case."

He did as she asked.

Charlotte opened the door of the carriage house a crack and in slipped a woman. No, not a woman: Stephen Marbleton in a dress and a purple summer cape.

She'd last seen Mr. Marbleton a week ago, when he and his injured sister had stayed overnight at 18 Upper Baker Street, to avoid being captured by Moriarty's minions. Then he had sported a full beard; but now he was shaven, and his features possessed a delicacy that was further emphasized by the enormous pouf of violet-and-cream ribbons on the velvet-lined traveling hat that completed his disguise.

"Mr. Marbleton. Did you follow me?"

Immediately she knew that hadn't been the case. When they'd last met, she'd just discovered that he had been impersonating Mr. Finch. They'd had no idea then, either of them, who or where the real Mr. Finch was. "You were following my sister."

Did he flush? It was difficult to tell in the barely adequate light.

"I have not been following you, but I believe others were. If you are meeting with Mr. Finch, he had better leave right now."

Mr. Finch came out from behind the carriage. Mr. Marbleton's eyes widened. More proof that he had been following Livia: He recognized the coachman who drove her around town.

"Where are they stationed now," asked Mr. Finch, "the men who have followed Miss Charlotte here?"

"One in front of her parents' house. One at either end of the carriage lane."

Mr. Finch returned Charlotte's derringer and indicated a knapsack he carried, which earlier had been hanging on a peg beside one of the stalls. "I have a loaded revolver in here. I should be all right."

"Wait a second," said Charlotte. She turned to Mr. Marbleton. "Where were you? Did those men see you come in here?"

"I was in the house next door—the tenants have already left town. And more likely than not, the men in the carriage lane saw me. But that couldn't be helped."

"No, it's good that they saw you. There might be a way for Mr. Finch to reach safety unseen, but I will need your help, Mr. Marbleton."

He grinned. "Will you put in a good word for me with your sister?"

"Absolutely not. But if you wish to prove the sincerity—and capability—of the Marbletons to Mr. Finch, there is no better way."

Mr. Marbleton glanced at Mr. Finch, then back at Charlotte. He grinned again—he really was quite attractive with that seemingly lighthearted expression. "Well, then, what are we waiting for?"

"Mr. Finch, will you be disappointed not to use your revolver?"

"Not at all. I dislike both blood and loud noises."

"You will be pleased with my plan, then," said Charlotte. "First, let us disrobe."

Livia sneaked down the stairs and tiptoed toward the back door.

Only when she was outside, closing the door behind her, did she remember—how stupid of her—that Mott wouldn't have returned yet from driving Charlotte to Mrs. Watson's house. She glanced down at the small gift in her hand. She supposed she could place it by the door of the carriage house, but what if he didn't see it before he took the Holmeses to the railway station tomorrow and then left their employ forever?

The light in the carriage house was on. Had he come back, then, so swiftly?

She was still hesitating when the light in the carriage house went out and its door opened a few inches. It was hard to see in the dark, but could that be the corner of a summer cape, not unlike the one Charlotte had been wearing?

Charlotte was still *here*?

Livia's heart flooded with wild hopes.

They had spoken about Charlotte's plans to poach Livia and Bernadine from their parents, but Livia had understood it to be intentions for a too-distant future. What if she was wrong? What if Charlotte meant to put everything in motion tonight, right after she'd spoken to and perhaps bribed Mott?

But as Charlotte fully emerged from the carriage house, she

didn't look quite right. When did she change her cape to a dark one? Not to mention—no, no, it wasn't Charlotte at all, but Mott dressed in women's clothes!

She stared at him, her jaw somewhere around her feet. He saw her and raised his index finger to his lips, signaling for silence. After looking in both directions, he crossed the completely deserted carriage lane and let himself into the small rear garden of the house next door.

She rushed to the low fence that separated the gardens. "What's going on?" she whispered. "Where are you going dressed like this?"

He looked indecisive for a moment. "I'm in some trouble—some bad people I was mixed up with before I entered service. They are after me now, and Miss Charlotte is helping me to get away. I'll wait in this empty house until the coast is clear. You go back inside and don't come out again. If anything should happen to you, Miss Charlotte will have my hide."

If anything should happen to Livia? What about Charlotte?

As if he'd heard her question, Mott said, "She has a gentleman with her, someone you both know. Please, Miss Livia, go back and stay inside."

She still hesitated.

Mott's voice grew more urgent. "Hurry. There's no time to lose."

Her knees shook. How she hated to be so useless when Charlotte was headed toward danger. But Mott was right. She would help no one by not knowing what to do.

With another glance at the carriage house, Livia did as she was told.

⁂

"You would have made a pretty girl," said Charlotte to Mr. Marbleton, now wearing Charlotte's evening toque and her bright yellow silk cape.

He smiled cheekily. "Thank you. I take pride in passing for a comely woman, at least at first glance. You as a man, on the other hand, would not have attracted ladies by the gross."

Charlotte glanced down at Mr. Finch's mackintosh, which reached past her knees. Underneath that she wore a pair of his rough woolen trousers over her own pantalets. "Maybe they'd stay away before they learned of my genius. But afterward . . . I would need to beat them off with a volume of the *Britannica*."

Their lighthearted words did nothing to dispel the tension in the carriage house.

"Ready?" asked Mr. Marbleton.

She nodded tightly.

He helped her up to the coachman's perch on the town coach and opened the carriage house doors, before getting into the vehicle. She eased the carriage into the lane and inhaled deeply.

At this point, the most likely place for them to be stopped was right here in the carriage lane. She shook the reins and urged the horses into a fast trot, much faster than was strictly safe.

Houses began to rush by. She was a competent enough driver, but she was much more accustomed to handling one-horse carts on sparsely traveled country lanes. While the night was getting late, this was still London during the Season. The major thoroughfares would be heavily trafficked and she had never driven under similar circumstances.

And she wouldn't, if she couldn't even get out of the carriage lane.

A man stood at the end of the lane, waving his arms, signaling her to slow down. She drove faster. The man waved more exaggeratedly. Over the pounding of hooves—and that of her heart—she could vaguely make out him shouting orders.

The houses blurred. He leaped out of her way. She yanked the horses into a hard right turn, followed by one more, and would have collided with another carriage if it hadn't swerved.

Still she drove as fast as she dared, weaving between other carriages, cutting in front of fancy broughams with inches to spare, to the vocal displeasure of their coachmen.

Mr. Marbleton knocked from within the coach. She looked ahead and saw a large omnibus parked by the side of the street. She slowed and pulled as close to the vehicle as her skills allowed. The moment she passed the omnibus, Mr. Marbleton jumped out, so accomplished at these sort of things that he somehow managed to slam the carriage door shut behind himself.

When she glanced back again, he had already disappeared into the night.

---

She was almost at her destination when another, far more thorough attempt was made to stop her.

She complied immediately.

A man came up to the carriage. "Mr. Finch, we'll need you to come with us, please."

She recognized him: Mr. Underwood, Lord Bancroft's right-hand man. "I'm not Mr. Finch."

Mr. Underwood's eyes narrowed. "Miss Holmes, I see. You are dressed as a man."

"Much safer this way, don't you think, to be driving at night?" she answered, climbing down from her perch. "And I must confess, Mr. Underwood, I'm not sure why you think my brother is involved in this. I'm only rendering some assistance to our family groom, who has served my sister faithfully over the summer."

"Is that so?"

"Yes, his name is Mott. He told me just now that he was in trouble with some unsavory people and needed to leave, and if I would please return the carriage to the company my father hired it from. I promised him I would see to it." She cocked her head to one side and smiled. "Would you mind if I went on my way, Mr. Underwood?"

Mr. Underwood considered her. "It's late, Miss Holmes. Why don't you let us do that for you? I'll see you home."

Plainly he didn't believe her. In that case, he—and Lord Bancroft—must understand that she would play no part in their hunt for Mr. Finch.

"I happily yield the carriage into your care, Mr. Underwood. But do not trouble yourself to accompany me. I am well equipped for a stroll."

She let him see her double-barrel derringer—not exactly a show of force but not a subtle gesture either.

"Well, then," said Mr. Underwood. "Good night, Miss Holmes."

———※———

London after dark was not pleasant for an unaccompanied woman. Even if she traveled on streets lined with parks and fine town houses, she could still count on men assuming her to be a light skirt and therefore fair target for everything from lewd whistles to unwanted touching.

But a woman dressed as a man, though she still had to worry about actual criminals, was at least spared casual insults and crude insinuations.

No small freedom, that.

Charlotte remained preoccupied with the events of the evening. She had no means to contact Mr. Finch, but she hoped that he would send her a message once he reached safety. And to think, she had very nearly compromised that safety tonight—

A carriage drew abreast of Mrs. Watson's house at the precise moment Charlotte did.

She had not been particularly worried about being followed by Lord Bancroft's underlings—he already knew where she lived and worked—but still she had paid attention on her journey home. And she was sure this particular carriage hadn't been behind her at any point.

Where had it come from, then?

A light rain drifted down, the drops as insubstantial as mist. The coachman, like Charlotte, was covered by a large mackintosh, his features invisible. The door of the carriage opened.

"Miss Holmes? Miss Charlotte Holmes?"

She approached the carriage and its single passenger, largely in shadows. "And you are . . . ?"

"Pleased to make your acquaintance at last, Miss Holmes," said the man. His fingers tapped against his walking stick. His voice, soft but confident, betrayed a hint of amusement. "My name is Moriarty."

# One

SEVERAL MONTHS LATER

Inspector Robert Treadles accepted hat, lunch, and walking stick from his wife with an approximation of a smile. "Thank you, my dear."

Alice smiled back and kissed him on his cheek. "Good day, Inspector. Go forth and uphold law and order."

She'd been saying that for years, upon bidding him good-bye in the morning. Lately, however, those words set him on edge. Or perhaps it wasn't the words, per se, but the feeling that from the moment he got up, she'd been waiting for him to leave.

Near the end of summer, her brother, Barnaby Cousins, had died. As he had been without issue, in accordance with their late father's will, Cousins Manufacturing, the source of the family's wealth, had devolved to Alice.

She had told Treadles quite firmly that it would not change anything between them. And she was right, but not for the reason she gave—that she would still be the loving spouse he'd known and that he would not feel the least diminishment in the care and affection he received from her.

No, the reason nothing had changed was that everything had already changed before her brother's death. Treadles had learned that she had always wished to run the family business and only her father's firmest refusal had turned her gaze from that path.

He still couldn't completely articulate to himself the turmoil this had unleashed in him, except to conclude that until that moment, he had believed them to be a unified whole. Afterward, they were only two individuals who lived under the same roof.

She saw him out the front door with another smile. He started in the direction of Scotland Yard. But once a week or so, on his way to work, he stopped around the corner to look back. Each time her carriage had drawn up precisely a quarter of an hour after his departure.

And the woman who entered the carriage, smart, gleaming, and coolly self-assured, was a stranger.

No, that wasn't entirely true. She had always known her own mind and been competent at everything she did. And he had always taken great pride in her—when she'd been the feather in his cap, the envy of his colleagues, a woman who, despite the elevated circumstances into which she had been born, had found in him everything she needed.

Except that had never been true, had it? She'd always needed more. And now she had it.

He walked faster, suddenly as impatient as she must be, to put distance between himself and his marital home.

His day, however, did not improve when he reached Scotland Yard. The Farr woman was there again, harassing Sergeant Mac-Donald.

"I understand, Mrs. Farr," said Sergeant MacDonald patiently. "But you see, ma'am, I checked all the reports for unclaimed bodies first thing this morning, and we still don't have anyone who matches your sister's description. And without a body, we can't declare this a murder case. We haven't the slightest evidence, in fact, that your sister is deceased."

"But if she were alive, she would never have missed her niece's birthday—at least not without any word."

"Sergeant, I have work for you," said Treadles as he walked past.

The Farr woman raised her head. She was blind in one milky blue eye, her other eye a dark, almost periwinkle blue. She might have been good-looking once, but all she had now were a few lines and angles that, like the ruins of a palace, hinted at yesteryear's grandeur.

She regarded Treadles steadily, expressionlessly. But he sensed the scorn she chose not to show. What was it with those less-than-respectable women who somehow felt superior enough to hold *him* in animosity and contempt?

As he marched off, he heard Sergeant MacDonald say, in a lowered voice, "I have to go, Mrs. Farr. Think about what I said. Sherlock Holmes."

———❦———

"What did we tell you?" said Lady Holmes triumphantly. "What did we tell you?"

Livia gaped, unable to believe her own eyes.

She had expected the worst. The *worst*. Her parents did not possess good judgment. They were, furthermore, profligate and nearly bankrupt. When they had informed Livia, after returning from a mysterious trip, that they had found an exceptional place for their second-eldest daughter, Livia had not believed in the least their description of this earthly paradise.

Bernadine did not speak, nor did she respond when spoken to. She rarely left her room and spent her days spinning spools that had been hung on a wire. She had never been able to look after herself, and Livia had no hope that she ever would.

In fact, Bernadine's very existence filled Livia with despair.

What if she outlived everyone in the family? Who would look after her? Would she escape to the woods and become feral, the kind of creature around which adolescents spun eerie tales to give younger children nightmares?

Yet upon being told that Bernadine would soon depart for an institution that took in women with similar conditions, Livia had been outraged, especially at her parents' delight in the reasonableness of the fees.

Bernadine didn't bite the maids or disturb the neighbors. She never needed new clothes and barely required any food. Yes, she was a burden to her parents, but so was Livia, and all the other unmarried daughters in the land. That she must be looked after was no reason to send her off to *bedlam*.

But if this was bedlam, then Livia could only wish she herself was the one taking up permanent residence.

The ivy-covered house boasted wide bay windows on the ground floor and deep, cushioned window seats perfect for reading book after book. The gardens were not too big or formal, but as trim and comfortable-looking as the house, with hydrangeas and delphiniums still in bloom. Her favorite was the narrow walkway that led out from the back, passing under a long arching pergola and disappearing beyond a wrought iron gate. The lane probably ended someplace excruciatingly ordinary, a kitchen garden or a caretaker's cottage. But Livia was free to imagine that it was a magic path that led to a different beautiful and exciting destination each time she set foot upon it.

The inside of the house was as pretty and cozy as she'd hoped it would be, with an air of contentment rather than ostentation. Even the residents didn't seem particularly lunatic. To be sure, there was a woman spinning slowly in the corner of a parlor; another sitting on a large Oriental rug, gazing at her bare toes; and a third stacking books on the opposite end of the rug with the intent and seriousness of the builder of the Colosseum, only to knock the stack down and start all over again.

Livia eyed the fourth woman in the room, expecting her, too, to do something bizarre. The woman, in a large starched cap and a long black dress, stood close to the rotating woman, her back to the visitors. Only after a while did Livia realize that she must be a minder employed by the institution, there to make sure the spinner didn't fall and hurt herself.

Livia's parents had already moved on, pulling along an unhappy Bernadine. Livia hurried after them. In the next room, a combination of a library and a small picture gallery, two women sat at adjacent desks, both writing. The scene appeared normal and serene, until Livia realized that one woman was simply drawing lines again and again across the page and the other's paper was full of crude, grinning skulls.

Would Bernadine really be all right, surrounded by all these other women with their conditions?

But Bernadine, apparently, had found her true home. Against the far wall of the room stood a large rack of rods. The rods threaded through dozens and dozens of objects, not only spools but gears and what looked like the sails of miniature windmills.

Bernadine, usually slow and shuffling in motion, crossed the room with the speed of a comet. She slid onto the bench that had been provided and immediately began to spin the objects nearest her. She wasn't alone. Next to her sat a woman in a turban, who spun gears—and only gears—with just as much focus and interest.

"That is a perennial delight for some of our patients," said Dr. Wrexhall, nodding with approval.

He was also a surprise. Livia had expected an unctuous quack. But Dr. Wrexhall was a man of dignified bearing and measured words.

"Which one of the patients is the benefactress's daughter?" asked

Lady Holmes, always curious about the wealthy and the very wealthy.

Dr. Wrexhall had explained to Livia, who had not made the previous trip with her parents, that Moreton Close was financed by the widow of an extremely successful industrialist. They had only one child, a daughter. She had wanted the girl to make her debut in Society and marry into one of the finest families of the land. Alas, the girl's condition had precluded that from ever happening.

But at Moreton Close, the daughter was and would always remain in the company of other young women from the finest families of the land.

Livia had thought it a stretch to elevate the Holmeses to such stature, but her parents apparently considered it their due. Sir Henry strutted; Lady Holmes, for the first time since Charlotte had run away from home, wore a smug expression. Here at last they were being accorded the deference due their station. And even better, no one seemed to know anything about the disgrace attached to their youngest child.

They preened in Dr. Wrexhall's respectful attention until Livia reminded them that they must hasten to the railway station. At their departure, Bernadine paid them as little mind as her parents paid her. Livia was the only one to hesitate a minute. She almost put a hand on Bernadine's shoulders. But whereas Charlotte had learned to tolerate a sister's touch, Bernadine would have immediately pushed Livia's hand away.

In the end, she said, to the back of Bernadine's head, "I'll come back and see you when I can."

As if she hadn't heard anything, Bernadine set another two gears to spin.

Dr. Wrexhall walked them out. "I trust you will understand, Sir Henry, Lady Holmes, that we do not publicize our work here. The villagers are still under the impression that this is a family residence. Everything we do, of course, is based on the latest scientific methods and the most humane of principles; but I'm afraid there are and will always be those who would not understand and who would not wish to coexist peacefully with us in their midst."

Livia could think of two such people listening to him right now—her parents would have been outraged had there been such an establishment near *their* residence.

"But of course," said Lady Holmes. "We understand perfectly."

"Excellent, ma'am. You may expect weekly reports."

"We eagerly anticipate them," said Sir Henry.

*Liar.*

He wouldn't bother with them at all, and neither would Lady Holmes. At last they had achieved their hearts' desire: They had got rid of Bernadine in a manner that was more or less acceptable and they need never think of her again.

But Livia would keep a close eye on the reports. She would visit whenever she could. And she would not allow Bernadine to be forgotten.

Otherwise, how would she ever face Charlotte again?

❖

Usually Livia looked forward to her annual visit to Mrs. Newell's. Mrs. Newell was Sir Henry's cousin, and whatever entrée to Society the Holmes girls had possessed was due more to her popularity than to any stature their parents could claim, based on either lineage or connections.

In recent years, Mrs. Newell had tired of town. But she still liked to keep in the know. Besides a voluminous correspondence with everyone who was anyone, she also hosted house parties after the end of the Season.

Sir Henry and Lady Holmes were almost never invited—Mrs.

Newell did not care for their company. But she had a soft spot for Livia and Charlotte. This year, for the first time, Livia would attend alone.

She had dreaded the possibility that her parents would not allow her to go, which Mrs. Newell had prevented by sending a railway ticket, already paid for—and her own maid to accompany Livia on the journey.

But her absence from home meant that she would not be on hand when the first two reports arrived from Moreton Close. And there was no guarantee her parents would save them for Livia's return, even though she'd specifically requested that. Lady Holmes was liable to throw them into the grate out of pique that she herself hadn't received an invitation to Mrs. Newell's. As for Sir Henry, Livia wouldn't put it past him to destroy those reports as they came through the door—he who had long been revolted that he'd produced a child like Bernadine.

She would not be surprised if he was now erasing all traces of Bernadine from their lives.

As she boarded the train, however, foremost on her mind wasn't Bernadine, but gratitude that Mrs. Newell's maid had produced a ticket of her own and would not be sitting with Livia.

That—and a stomach-churning anxiety about the small package in her handbag.

Sir Henry didn't bother with the mail—which too often contained such unpleasantness as notices from creditors—until midday. Lady Holmes was a late riser due to frequent intimacy with her supply of laudanum. Livia, then, was usually the first person to sort through the morning post.

This morning, she had risen unusually late, having stayed up packing the night before. As soon as she'd seen the two items addressed to her, she'd heard Lady Holmes stomping down the stairs. There had been barely enough time to hide them under her skirts.

And she'd remained at the table an eon so that she could leave without anyone seeing them.

After that there had been only enough time to dress and leave. But now, finally, some blessed privacy.

But no sooner had she given thanks for that solitude than a local squire's wife and her daughter entered the compartment. Livia was obliged to engage in pleasantries. The squire's wife was horrified that Livia, after what had happened to Charlotte, was traveling alone—her protestations about the maid that had been sent to accompany her fell on deaf ears. These mere acquaintances declared their intention to forego their own plans and chaperone Livia all the way to Mrs. Newell's, with the further insinuation that Livia might not be, in fact, headed to a respectable relation's house.

She almost wept with relief three stops on, when the maid came to check on her. That happened to be her would-be rescuers' stop, and they detrained rather reluctantly. At last alone in her compartment, it was several minutes before she was calm enough to take out the letter and the package.

The handwriting on the letter she didn't recognize, which most likely meant that it was from Charlotte, who could write in different hands. And they had devised a system whereby Charlotte sent her pamphlets, with a letter sometimes concealed inside glued-together pages.

But as exciting as it always was to receive word from Charlotte, the one Livia had been dying to open was the small package.

She had become better at not thinking about the young man who had arrived in her life like a surprise present—excitement, allure, and more than a hint of mystery. They had met three times. Two had been delightful, *joyous* occasions; and then came the fateful third encounter, during which he'd revealed himself to be Mr. Myron Finch, her illegitimate half brother.

And she had been shattered by the revelation—and nauseated to have felt a great deal of incestuous sentiments for this bright, personable young man.

Only to collapse in relief when Charlotte had sent a message that he was *not* their brother.

All that had happened near the end of the Season. She had met Charlotte only one time afterward, the night before the Holmes household left London. And she had, very deliberately, mentioned neither their illegitimate half brother nor the man she had fallen in love with who wasn't, thank God, Mr. Myron Finch.

Her intentional lack of inquisitiveness meant that she'd failed to learn what Charlotte knew about him. But Livia had harbored other hopes: Shortly before that meeting with Charlotte, he had sent her a beautiful, hand-illustrated bookmark of a woman in white reading on a park bench, which had been exactly how they'd met.

It hadn't seemed overmuch to expect that he would write to her at some point. But the bookmark had signaled the beginning and the end of their correspondence.

He had disappeared, and she had no idea whether she ought to wait or forget him altogether.

Or rather, she knew she ought to forget him, but she had not succeeded—she couldn't even be sure she had tried.

Maybe she never needed to: This package bore his handwriting.

Her heart palpitated. She opened the package and, with shaking fingers, teased apart the top of the velvet pouch it contained.

Inside the pouch was a cabochon. Of moonstone. One of the two books they had discussed, upon their first meeting, was titled *Moonstone*. The other, of course, was *The Woman in White*, as represented by the bookmark.

It *was* him. But what did this mean? Was it a significant signal, or the beginning of another long stretch of silence? Of nothing but her lonely and useless yearning?

Perhaps she ought to speak to Charlotte. Why had he tried to pass himself off as their illegitimate brother? Who was he? And what exactly were his intentions toward her? A bookmark was an acceptable gift from a male friend. A cabochon, on the other hand . . . Had it been mounted as a ring or set as the centerpiece of a pendant, it would have been outright improper: A man who wasn't married or related to her could not present her with jewelry.

As it was, smooth and polished but not ready to wear, the cabochon fell into a gray area, so gray one might as well call it charcoal.

She held the cabochon for a long time, then she returned it to its pouch and placed the pouch carefully in an inside pocket of her handbag.

Summer was long gone, but winter had not yet arrived. This was a time of the year when weeks of dreary rain alternated with rare crisp, clear days. Outside the train the sky was blue and the sun shone.

Livia had met her nameless young man under precisely such a blue sky, such a shining sun.

She shook her head and reached for the letter.

*Dear Miss Holmes,*

*I have news of your sister, Miss Charlotte Holmes.*

Livia recoiled. Who was this? She looked for the signature. *Caroline Avery.*

Lady Avery!

Lady Avery and her sister, Lady Somersby, were Society's leading gossips. They had been after Livia for news of Charlotte's whereabouts ever since Charlotte ran away from home. Livia, of course, had never divulged to a single soul that Charlotte was now living in a fine house facing Regent's Park and conducting business as Sherlock Holmes at 18 Upper Baker Street.

What did Lady Avery know? And how had she obtained that knowledge? Her heart constricting with a sense of foreboding, Livia read on.

*It came about in a most indirect and surprising manner. I was recently at Cowes, on the Isle of Wight. The day before my departure, my own maid being unwell, I engaged a maid from the hotel to help me pack.*

*As I supervised her in the wrapping of some frangible items, she claimed, upon coming across a picture in the months-old newspaper, that she had seen the gentleman. As it turned out, the subject of the photograph was Lord Ingram Ashburton, taken on the occasion of his last polo match of the Season. The maid was certain that she had not made a mistake, her reason being that one did not so easily forget a man such as Lord Ingram.*

*She told me that during the Season she had worked at a tea shop in Hounslow, not too far from the heath. And one Saturday, still in the height of the Season, he had come in with a lady to whom he appeared devoted. This piqued my attention, since the woman could not possibly have been Lady Ingram.*

*I asked her to give me a description of Lord Ingram's companion. These were her exact words:* She could be on an advert for Pears soap, if she lost half a stone. Or maybe one stone.

*My mind immediately turned to Miss Charlotte Holmes. Of course, given my reputation for accuracy and reliability, I couldn't base my claims only on the girl's account, as tantalizing as it was. Instead, I went home, fetched an album of photographs, and returned to the hotel in Cowes.*

*I showed the girl a picture that had been taken two years ago at Lord Wrenworth's house party. There were some forty guests in all, and she had no problem identifying Miss Charlotte as Lord Ingram's companion.*

*I made sure to ascertain that this sighting happened after Miss Charlotte's scandal. The girl assured me that earlier in the summer she had not been working at that particular establishment and so could only have seen them in July, well after Miss Charlotte had left home.*

*If this is unknown to you, I am pleased to be the bearer of good news: that your sister is alive and well. Or at least she was at the time she was last seen with Lord Ingram—and I cannot imagine that he would allow her to come to harm. If this is known to you, I should be obliged if you would either corroborate or correct what I have learned thus far.*

*Yours truly,*
*Caroline Avery*

# Two

Ninety minutes after breakfast, Miss Charlotte Holmes was on her second slice of Madeira cake.

The cottage Mrs. John Watson had hired for their country sojourn gave onto a lovely panorama of green hills and gentle valleys. But its interior was faded, with small and oddly placed windows. As a result, the parlor, even on a sunny day, was underlit, almost gloomy. And Miss Holmes, in her creamy dress the sleeves of which were abundantly embroidered with green vines and magenta flowers, was the brightest object in the room.

She hadn't spoken since she sat down half an hour ago. Not speaking was her natural state and Mrs. Watson had learned to savor Miss Holmes's silences. To think of them as something similar to the quietude of a slope covered in wildflowers, or the restfulness of rolling pastures dotted with new calves.

Since the night Miss Holmes helped her brother escape, however, the sense of tranquility had disappeared from her silences. Lately, sitting near her, Mrs. Watson thought of London fogs, thick and all-obscuring, of maritime brumes, the kind that made ships sail straight into rocky cliffs, and even, occasionally, of quagmire and quicksand, seemingly innocuous surfaces waiting to entrap hapless travelers.

Even her delight in the consumption of sweet, buttery goods felt . . . less joyful. She ate more—Mrs. Watson scarcely came upon her without seeing a biscuit or an entire Victoria sponge parked by her side. But the woman across from Mrs. Watson demolished her slice of Madeira cake with not so much pleasure as a mechanical neediness, the way a tense man would light one cigarette after another.

In the days and weeks immediately following Mr. Finch's narrow escape, Mrs. Watson, too, had been frantic with worry. She and Miss Holmes had conferred frequently and at length concerning the various scenarios that could arise, and what their countermeasures must be in any given situation.

But months went by and nothing happened. Mrs. Watson, as fretful as she could be, began to relax. Sooner or later everyone made a mistake. Even the otherwise unflappable Miss Holmes must overreact from time to time.

"My dear," she said, "we've been here three days and you've scarcely gone out. What say you we make a tour of Stern Hollow today?"

Stern Hollow was Lord Ingram's estate. They hadn't hired a house in the area for his sake. They'd come because Mrs. Newell, Miss Holmes's first cousin, once removed, lived nearby—and Miss Holmes's sister was expected at Mrs. Newell's for the latter's house party.

But Mrs. Watson was confident that Miss Holmes did not mind at all that Lord Ingram also happened to be close at hand.

"We needn't call on the master of Stern Hollow. We could simply apply to see the house. And he could come upon us as a coincidence, à la Lizzy Bennet's visit to Pemberley."

Miss Holmes eyed a third slice of Madeira cake, but did not

reach for it—possibly because she was approaching Maximum Tolerable Chins, the point at which she began regulating further helpings of cakes and puddings. "Is that a literary reference?"

"You haven't read *Pride and Prejudice?*" cried Mrs. Watson, scandalized. "How is that possible?"

"My sister is the great devourer of fiction in our household. As a girl, I found novels difficult to understand—I found people difficult to understand. From time to time I would read a story or two, if she absolutely insisted. She did not insist on *Pride and Prejudice.*"

"Well, I might need to, in that case. The scene I mentioned, Miss Bennet and Mr. Darcy coming upon each other by accident, is so very—" Mrs. Watson barely managed to swallow her next word, *romantic*. "Well, it makes for riveting fiction."

Though perhaps not the best analogy for the situation between Miss Holmes and Lord Ingram. Miss Austen wrote with humor and perspicacity, but she also wrote with tremendous decorum. What would she think of Miss Holmes's current situation as a woman no longer received in any polite drawing rooms—or the fact that Lord Ingram was still a married man, absent wife or not?

"Anyway," she hastened to add, "do let us make a point of touring the place. It is most attractive, from what I understand. And in any case, Lord Ingram might very well already be at Mrs. Newell's for her party."

"He wouldn't leave his children to attend a house party, however nearby."

"Oh, you don't know? Well, of course you couldn't have heard yet, since I only learned it myself this morning. His children left with Lord Remington weeks ago."

Lord Remington was the third Ashburton brother, the youngest besides Lord Ingram. Even so, there was an eleven-year difference between the two.

Miss Holmes, who had been studying a plate of almond biscuits, looked up. "Lord Remington is in England? The family's black sheep?"

Lord Remington had spent nearly the entirety of his adult life abroad. Mrs. Watson had a soft spot in her heart for him, but even she had to concur, somewhat at least, with Miss Holmes's assessment. "I might call him the grayest of the flock. Currently, that is. When they were all young—and Lord Ingram barely out of the womb—Lord Bancroft was, in fact, considered the actual black sheep."

"Really?" Miss Holmes's question emerged slowly and seemed to linger in the air.

"You would have been an infant then. But he was notoriously spendthrift. The old duke broke canes beating him."

"Hmm."

"I know. How people change. One should never be judged on one's adolescence. Now where was I? Oh, Lord Remington. From what I hear, the children were smitten with their uncle, and when he asked if they wanted to come with him to the seaside, they absolutely could not be held back."

"I guess in that case, there is no reason for Lord Ingram not to be at Mrs. Newell's," said Miss Holmes.

She took hold of an almond biscuit, then, remembering herself, set it down and instead picked up the correspondence that had come for Sherlock Holmes.

The consulting detective had stated in adverts that he would be away from London for some time. As a result, the previous month, Mrs. Watson and Miss Holmes had run themselves into the ground seeing to a torrent of clients motivated by this upcoming scarcity to request a consultation in the here and now.

But of course, there were always those who didn't read the adverts carefully. And Mr. Mears, Mrs. Watson's faithful butler holding down the fort in London, had forwarded a batch of letters that had arrived in Sherlock Holmes's private box at the General Post Office.

Miss Holmes quickly opened and scanned all the letters; then she read one letter again and handed it to Mrs. Watson.

*Dear Mr. Sherlock Holmes,*

*Sergeant MacDonald at Scotland Yard told me to write you. Do you still help with murders?*

*Sincerely,*
*Mrs. Winnie Farr*

The handwriting was boxy and all in majuscule letters, done by a dull pencil that had been wielded with enough pressure to cause a cramp in the writing hand. The paper had not been made from any virgin material but of fibers that had been repulped. And the envelope took advantage of the blank side of a handbill for the latest miracle tonic, with the General Post Office as the return address.

"I'm sure you have deduced that this woman might not have seven shillings on hand for a consultation," said Mrs. Watson. "I take it you think she wouldn't have written to us if she didn't think she had something of value to offer us in lieu of payment?"

The handwriting, despite its lack of ease and prettiness, had a proud, almost haughty quality.

"That is, of course, the hope," said Miss Holmes.

"And if we should be mistaken in that hope?"

Miss Holmes planned to remove her sisters from the family home, with payments of one hundred quid a year to their parents. As the only consulting detective in the world, she didn't lack for clients. But the reasonableness of her fees, and the fact that most of her clients presented problems that, however perplexing, also happened to be minor, meant that even with Mrs. Watson's ability to raise those fees at the least sign that a client could afford more, they were still fifty pounds short of that goal.

Not to mention that Miss Holmes, almost as soon as her income had become regular, had insisted on remitting weekly sums for room and board to Mrs. Watson, in addition to the latter's share in Sherlock Holmes's proceeds.

Miss Bernadine Holmes required someone to keep an eye on her. Miss Livia, who required only food and a roof over her head, was ostensibly less expensive. But Mrs. Watson knew that Miss Holmes also wanted to give Miss Livia books and trips abroad. And for Miss Bernadine, not just a harried maid but a nurse with experience and compassion for her care. Altogether, the obligations she planned to take on were fearsome for a young woman who could rely on only her own abilities.

And however extraordinary those abilities, she didn't have more hours in the day than anyone else. To give her time to Mrs. Farr could mean forgoing more solvent clients.

"It isn't a certainty that we will hear more from Mrs. Farr, or that hers will be a situation for which we can render any aid," said Miss Holmes.

"I should write back for more information, then?"

"If you would, please," murmured Miss Holmes. "Now, about our plans to visit Stern Hollow, ma'am."

Livia clutched at the moonstone as if it were a talisman that could fend off all the evils of the world.

Or, at least, all the curiosity from the guests who would, just beyond Livia's hearing, be making endless conjectures about Charlotte and Lord Ingram.

She knew what conclusion everyone would leap to, as soon as

Lady Avery's news spread: that Charlotte hadn't disappeared, but had become Lord Ingram's mistress.

This would be, of course, profoundly distressing—Charlotte had proved capable of keeping herself; and Lord Ingram would never have demanded such a tawdry exchange for his help. But it shouldn't be any more distressing than what Livia had already put up with during the Season, with tongues always wagging just beyond—and sometimes just within—her hearing.

And yet she was almost nauseated by anxiety. The sense of foreboding that had descended when she first read the letter had only grown stronger. Which was ridiculous. The story wasn't common knowledge yet. And even if it should become so, it would simply be an extra serving of unpleasantness in an already unpleasant world.

Lord Ingram's estate was nearby, was it not? If she sent him a note, he would call on her, wouldn't he, and assure her that whatever Lady Avery could unleash would only be a passing nuisance, soon dismissed and soon forgotten?

As if the universe heard her plea, Lord Ingram descended the front step of Mrs. Newell's manor just as Livia's carriage pulled up.

He wasn't classically handsome but turned heads anyway, the kind of man who sent a jolt of electricity through a crowd by doing nothing more than stepping into the room. When he remained still, he made her think of a cobra about to uncoil. In motion he put her in mind of a large panther, stalking silently through the jungle.

He handed her down from the carriage. "Miss Holmes. I'm glad to see you."

Usually she found him intimidating, but today his aura of assurance was exactly what she needed. Already she felt a little less panicked. "That sentiment is most certainly reciprocated, my lord. How do you do?"

"I am well. Mrs. Newell informed me that she is expecting you."

"She has been most kind to extend an invitation. And Lady Ingram, I hope she is much improved?"

His wife's decampment to a Swiss sanatorium would have been a much bigger topic of gossip had it not happened so close to the end of Season. When she hadn't received the ladies who had called on her, as was customary after a ball, it was assumed that her bad back must be bothering her again. It took will and effort for her to appear graceful in movement, and an entire summer of such pretense exacted a severe toll.

It wasn't until Society had dispersed to Cowes, Scotland, and hundreds of country houses all over the land that her friends received letters informing them that her health had deteriorated suddenly and it had been deemed prudent that she remove herself to the Alps where she could be properly looked after by a team of German and Swiss physicians.

Livia, like everyone else, hadn't learned of this development until after she had left London. She had written Charlotte about it, in the course of their surreptitious correspondence, since Charlotte had, earlier in the summer, asked Livia out of the blue what the latter thought of Lady Ingram's romantic past, and had even tasked Livia to extract what ladies Avery and Somersby knew of that particular topic.

At the time, distracted by what she had believed to be catastrophic romantic leanings on her own part, Livia had not paid particular attention to Charlotte's inquiry. But in light of Lady Ingram's departure, Livia asked Charlotte in her letter, was it not likely that Charlotte had been correct and Lady Ingram had at last decided to run away with her erstwhile sweetheart?

Charlotte had replied that they ought not to speculate. Livia, however, grew only more convinced over time. And to think, she had begun to thaw a little toward that woman. How abominably she had treated her husband.

"Her physicians assure me that her condition has stabilized," said Lord Ingram, in response to her question about his wife's health, "but she is still in need of their expertise."

*Did that mean she truly wasn't coming back?*

"I am glad to hear that," Livia said. "I hope she continues to improve."

"Thank you, Miss Holmes. I'm sure she appreciates your kind thoughts." For a moment she feared he was about to wish her good day and take his leave. But he glanced to his left and asked, "By the way, have you seen Mrs. Newell's new fountains?"

Thank goodness. It wouldn't do for them to hold a conversation standing on Mrs. Newell's front steps. Nor could they disappear into some cranny in the house or on the grounds. The fountains were perfectly visible from both the house and the drive and would give their conversation every appearance of propriety, without letting the actual exchange be overheard.

"A glimpse and only a glimpse, I'm afraid," she said. "Do let us study them in some detail."

As soon as they were out of earshot, Livia went to the crux of the matter. "I received a detestable letter from Lady Avery. I don't suppose you were so fortunate as to be spared a similar missive."

He smiled wryly. "I wasn't."

"I have no idea how I ought to respond. I was going to write you as soon as I'd settled in here. Have *you* replied?"

"I have—and told Lady Avery that it had been a chance encounter."

Livia had learned from Charlotte that she and Lord Ingram had been in contact—of course Charlotte wouldn't have left him in suspense as to her fate—but Livia hadn't expected them to be out in public. "So you did meet at the time and place Lady Avery specified?"

"I'm afraid so."

And now Lady Avery had his confirmation in writing. "People will draw all kinds of unsavory conclusions!"

They'd walked twice around one fountain; Lord Ingram guided her to the other. "That cannot be helped. Fortunately, their conjectures cannot materially injure Miss Charlotte."

True. As a fallen woman, Charlotte's reputation couldn't be besmirched any further. "What about you, my lord?"

"Me?" There was a trace of amusement in his voice. Or was it irony? "For what it's worth, I will not be barred from Society for having met with Miss Charlotte in broad daylight."

This Livia knew. He could have done far worse and not be punished in remotely the same way. Roger Shrewsbury, the man who had compromised Charlotte, was still accepted everywhere he went. "All the same, I hope it won't prove a nuisance."

He touched her lightly on the elbow. "It will be a nuisance, but you mustn't worry, Miss Holmes. It'll be forgotten by Christmas. And life will go on, for both Miss Charlotte and myself."

His attentiveness, his confidence, his matter-of-fact approach to the upcoming brouhaha—Livia could not have hoped for a kinder or more fortifying reception. Basking in his presence, she felt downright silly about her undue agitation, making a Matterhorn out of a molehill. Indeed, by the time he took his leave, she was smiling.

But the moment he disappeared from sight, uncertainty came rushing back, accompanied by a cold, hard dread. *It will not end well,* said a voice in her head.

*It cannot possibly end well.*

# Three

M rs. Watson approved wholeheartedly of Lord Ingram's estate. To be sure, she was inclined to approve wholeheartedly of his every deed and utterance. But when it came to Stern Hollow, she couldn't help but believe that her opinion must be shared by everyone who had ever laid eyes on this blessed expanse.

The entrance was unassuming, the scenery at first no different from that of the surrounding countryside: verdant pasture, groves of beech and poplar, crofter's cottages surrounded by well-tended land.

But as the drive meandered, Mrs. Watson caught glimpses of delightful vistas. Here, a pair of swans framed in the arch of a small stone bridge; there, a statue of Artemis next to a footpath, her hand on her bow; and in the distance, a white, slender Greek folly, perched above a waterfall that splashed into a sunlit stream.

They crested a ridge. In the shallow, sheltered valley below rose an immaculately proportioned Palladian house, nestled in acres of gardens and fronted by a spectacular reflecting pool that shone in the afternoon light.

Mrs. Watson placed her hand over her heart and sighed.

Miss Holmes, however, displayed no sign that she was feeling remotely similar to Miss Elizabeth Bennet at Pemberley: superbly impressed and duly regretful that she had let go of this man instead of fighting for him tooth and nail when she'd had the chance.

But Mrs. Watson did not fail to notice that Miss Holmes's blue-and-heather-gray promenade dress sported an enormous and entirely superfluous bow in the back, a downright flirtatious feature, in Mrs. Watson's judgment.

Presently Miss Holmes glanced at the map of the estate they had been given at the gatehouse. Mrs. Watson stopped talking and allowed her young friend to concentrate on driving. But as they came down into the valley and skirted the first herbaceous borders, she couldn't help exclaim, "Are the gardens not marvelous?"

Any halfway decent gardener could make his plot flower riotously in spring—it was the nature of the season. But to present an autumnal tableau worthy of a sonnet, that took talent, planning, and meticulous execution. Here, Japanese maples formed a backdrop of rich golds and vibrant reds, against which a profusion of dahlias and chrysanthemums still bloomed.

"It is pleasing to view, but a marvel it isn't. With the amount of money, expertise, and manpower that must have been expended, Lord Ingram ought to be dissatisfied with anything less."

Trust Miss Holmes to strip the romance from any scenario and see only the brute, barebones facts underneath.

"Well, he can't possibly be dissatisfied with this—with perfection."

Miss Holmes glanced about. "Yes, I suppose this is perfection."

The reluctant compliment gratified Mrs. Watson, until she realized that it was no compliment at all, but an indictment.

While Mrs. Watson wandered in the gardens, Charlotte made her way to the back of the house.

A proper country house did not reign in isolation. Behind the formal grandeur of the manor existed a collection of lesser buildings: the kitchen, of course, a complex of its own; the stables, usually some distance away; miscellanies such as the dovecote, the hen house, and the kennel; not to mention a number of greenhouses, the precise number depending on whether the master of the house required his own supply of strawberries at Christmas and pineapples in January.

Lord Ingram's godfather had been one of the wealthiest men in the realm. And one of the shrewdest: In correctly forecasting that the difficulty of keeping young people in service would only increase, he had chosen not to acquire for himself too extravagant a country property.

But that he had not bought the equivalent of a Blenheim Palace or a Chatsworth House didn't mean his seat was modest. Mrs. Watson no doubt yearned to see the inside of the house. But Charlotte was far more interested in the ancillary structures, where the work of the estate went on.

"Charlotte Holmes—I thought I might see you here."

The voice belonged to Lord Ingram, but slightly raspy, as if he were under the weather—or recovering from a night of hard drinking. She turned around slowly. "Hullo, Ash."

A complicated pleasure, this man. In fact, it was their sometimes fraught friendship that had taught her the meaning of complicated pleasure, a gladness pockmarked by not only irreversible choices but also staggering incompatibilities.

All the same, such a sharp, sharp, almost painful pleasure.

They shook hands. She couldn't be sure whether he held her hand a fraction of a second too long, or she his. When they let go, abruptly and at the exact same moment, despite the glove she still wore, her fingertips tingled.

"You are well?" he asked, as they walked toward the gardens.

"Well enough." Most of the time they were regular correspondents. But he had not written since they'd last met in person, months ago. And she, not sure whether he hadn't wished to hear from her, or if he needed something that she didn't know how to give, had also refrained. "You, on the other hand, look as if you haven't slept properly for a few days."

He was in tweeds, and boots that had seen plenty of service—the very image of the quintessential English country squire. If the latter had stayed up late then got up at the crack of dawn, that is.

"I met your sister at Mrs. Newell's earlier today," he said, making no comments on her observation.

"How is she?"

"Worried about you getting into trouble."

"I prefer to think of them as adventures. The adventures of Charlotte Holmes, consulting detective."

"What is this I hear about trouble and adventures?" said Mrs. Watson.

She and Lord Ingram greeted each other warmly. The last time the three of them had been together in the same place, Mrs. Watson had been in disguise as Mrs. Hudson, a member of Sherlock Holmes's household, and Lord Ingram had been full of disapproval over Charlotte's choice to take up with a former actress.

Today they were themselves, longtime friends and allies.

Mrs. Watson praised the gardens. Lord Ingram related his head gardener's struggle to secure epic quantities of Peruvian bat guano. Mrs. Watson laughed; even Charlotte's lips twitched a little.

In recent years their private interactions were often silent and tense; sometimes she forgot this other side of him. But he was a man who had no difficulty being charming and amiable in public, who could appear as outwardly perfect as his painstakingly maintained estate.

As they exhausted the more inconsequential subjects, however, his expression turned sober. "Unfortunately, I do have some actual trouble to report."

"Most vexing!" Mrs. Watson exclaimed, after he had recounted the contents of Lady Avery's letter and his reply.

"Given that I have, on more than one occasion, consulted their encyclopedic knowledge and been glad of it, I can scarcely be outraged simply because their attention has turned to me," replied Lord Ingram. "That said, most vexing."

Charlotte had not expected this particular wrinkle. The meeting in question had taken place months ago, well outside spheres frequented by members of Society. "Is my sister disturbed?"

"Yes."

He glanced at her. "You, on the other hand, aren't remotely discomfited by this news—not for yourself, in any case."

"That is the benefit of infamy," she said with some semblance of modesty. "One of them, at least."

He shook his head, but his lips curved. "Well, ladies, now that you've heard the bad news, may I interest you in a conducted tour?"

—✳—

The tour was of only the grounds. Given the minor scandal brewing, the last thing they wanted was for news to spread that Miss Holmes had also been seen in Lord Ingram's manor.

In truth, Mrs. Watson reflected ruefully, they ought not to have been anywhere near him at all. But since they were already on his property, they might as well enjoy themselves.

Miss Holmes might sniff at Stern Hollow's sheer perfection, but Mrs. Watson remained thoroughly charmed. The streams teeming with tiny silver fish, darting about in unison; the pretty swing dangling from a gnarly bough; and oh look, a secret alcove behind the waterfall they had seen earlier, accessed via a set of hidden stairs from the Greek folly itself.

The conversation was just as pleasant. She recounted several of the cases Miss Holmes had handled in the weeks before they left London. She also relayed greetings from her niece Penelope, who had resumed her medical education in Paris. "She and her friends are planning to visit the catacombs very soon—the thought makes me shudder, but she declares herself in a state of fervent anticipation."

"For someone who has already partaken of dissections, a few million grinning skulls crammed together in dark underground tunnels might prove a disappointment," said Lord Ingram dryly.

"But the part of her letter that had Miss Holmes in a lather was the description of her daily breakfast. She has taken to the French manner and consumes only coffee and one croissant in the morning."

Lord Ingram glanced at Miss Holmes, a seemingly casual look that was nevertheless potent enough to raise the ambient temperature. "And Miss Holmes is no doubt vexed at Miss Redmayne's restraint. Why only one croissant when she can have three instead?"

"You know me too well, sir."

Miss Holmes appeared distracted, as if she were in fact picturing warm, flaky croissants. Oh, that girl. Mrs. Watson was giddy merely from being in the vicinity of the desire that smoldered beneath Lord Ingram's tweed-clad decorum. Miss Holmes ought to feel a maelstrom of butterflies in her stomach, at the crosscurrent of so much physical attraction.

"You should have married my brother, then," said Lord Ingram, rather archly. "Bancroft has in his employ my late godfather's pastry chef, who is said to be a prince among pâtissiers."

Having been turned down once by Miss Holmes while she was still eligible, Lord Bancroft had done the extraordinary deed of asking for her hand again, *after* her fall from grace. To Mrs. Watson's relief, he had later withdrawn that proposal of marriage. Lord Bancroft had always made her uneasy, and she was a woman who, on the whole, enjoyed the company of men.

"Rest assured my regret is as deep as the sea," replied Miss Holmes, her tone breezy.

A small silence fell. Mrs. Watson rather fancied that had they been alone—and had Lord Ingram been less in command of himself—Miss Holmes would have been set against the nearest tree and ravished with a kiss.

"How are your children?" asked Miss Holmes. "Have they been well?"

Much of the heated charge in the air dissipated.

Mrs. Watson had avoided asking after his children. Pleasant as their chatter was, no one could be unaware of what had not been mentioned: Lady Ingram's absence.

Lord Ingram did not answer immediately. Ahead the house came back into view, so exquisite that, like the Taj Mahal, it seemed to float. Mrs. Watson's heart pitter-pattered.

"The children are well. Enjoying themselves with Remington," he said at last. "When they return, I would be pleased to bring them to call on you—with your permission, of course."

"We would be delighted!" Mrs. Watson enthused.

She had only ever met them at the park in London, during the Season, when Lord Ingram took them for their Sunday outings.

"I'm not sure we will be here that long," said Miss Holmes, pouring cold water on fervid plans in that measured way of hers. "The cottage is ours for only another fortnight."

The duration of Miss Livia Holmes's stay at Mrs. Newell's.

Lord Ingram glanced again at Miss Holmes—a quick turn of his head. Then he looked to where they were going: his house, which a moment ago Mrs. Watson had yearned to admire up close and in person.

But now she saw it as he must, a wilderness of solitude. Miles of echoing corridors, acres of empty rooms, long, hushed days, and longer, even more hushed nights.

"You should spend more time in the country," he said quietly. "Nothing in London this time of the year but rain, fog, and the odors of industry."

"And Sherlock Holmes's livelihood," Miss Holmes pointed out, her logic cutting through his sentiments with the sharpness of surgical implements.

"My oversight," he acknowledged after a moment, clasping his hands behind his back. "That is, of course, an overriding consideration."

The silence that followed made Mrs. Watson squirm. She endured it for no more than a minute before blurting out a question about the condition of his trout stream.

Conversation resumed.

———✳———

Mrs. Watson asked to be introduced to the head gardener so that she might compliment him and in turn receive advice about her own future horticultural endeavors.

Lord Ingram had known her since he was a child. In all those years, she had never evinced the slightest interest in the cultivation of anything with roots. As far as he could tell, her entire interest in botany began and ended with the arrangement of flower bouquets.

He managed not to raise a brow at her sudden fascination with the composition of soil and the best way to divide bulbs. If Mrs. Watson was so naked in her desire to leave the young people alone, then they must not let her effort go to waste.

"You were behind the house when I first saw you," he said to Holmes. "I assume you were looking for the kitchen garden?"

"I was indeed. May I have a tour?"

He gestured. "This way."

Her abiding interest in what would end up on a dining table, hers or anyone else's, for that matter, used to strike him as completely at odds with the cool ferocity of her mind. To his younger self it seemed that a person ought to be one or the other, a thinker or a gourmand, but not both.

He had pointed that out to her once, as he removed encrusted dirt from the handles of an amphoriskos he had dug up. She, sitting a few paces away, had listened attentively, a book in one hand and a jam tart in the other—the fourth consecutive one she'd eaten from the small picnic basket she'd brought. When he'd finished speaking she'd looked at him for some time, then gone back to reading and eating, as if he'd never taken the trouble to voice his opinion aloud.

It was the first time he'd told anyone how they ought to *be*. It also happened to be the last time: He had been beyond mortified that she'd treated his considered commentary as if it were an ant that had crawled onto her jam tart.

Years later, in the early days of his marital courtship, when the future Lady Ingram had seemed sincerely interested in and impressed by his every last utterance, he had experienced what he'd believed to be a profound gratitude. But it had been less gratitude than smugness: At last he'd met a woman who knew how to be a woman; the hell with Charlotte Holmes and her insufferable self-sufficiency.

He'd known nothing then.

Alas, he knew nothing now—but at least now he was aware of it.

The walled kitchen garden occupied a sizable lot and supplied all the fruits and vegetables the estate consumed, either fresh or preserved in jars, during an entire year. Her gaze immediately went to the fruit trees that had been espaliered against the inside of the stone walls: apples, pears, plums, peaches, and cherries, each a different variety.

"Your kitchen must produce legendary quantities of jams and puddings," she said, her voice wistful. "And there are fig trees, too. Does anyone here know how to make a fig tart? Did you ever replace the pastry chef Lord Bancroft poached from you?"

Speaking of Bancroft . . . "What happened between you and my brother?"

That courtship had been excruciating for Lord Ingram. Given

her situation, he couldn't possibly advise that she reject Bancroft's offer. Had she accepted, however, it would have been a phantasmagoric horror.

When she'd related that Bancroft had withdrawn the suit, it had been all he'd needed to hear. The train had stopped at the edge of the precipice, no further details necessary.

Now he was no longer so sure.

"Nothing," she said with perfect equanimity. "A grand total of nil."

"He hasn't been the same since you declined his second proposal."

They were walking down the central path of the garden, lined with ornamental flowers grown for the house's many vases. She caressed a crimson chrysanthemum the size of a large pom-pom. "I didn't decline—he rescinded his offer."

"Semantics."

"You give Lord Bancroft too little credit."

"And you give yourself too little credit for your ability to cause turmoil in a man."

This earned him a considering look—of course he'd given away too much of himself. "You say that because you are a romantic. You would be deeply disturbed to have *your* suit be unsuccessful twice in a row. Lord Bancroft is not remotely similar to you."

"I haven't been a romantic in a very long time."

"Being disappointed in love does not change a man's fundamental nature. You are more cautious, you wonder whether *you* can ever make a good choice, but you do not question the validity of romantic love in and of itself. And you still first assume that others, such as Lord Bancroft, love as you do, deeply and protectively"—she held up an index finger to forestall his objection—"before the voice of experience reminds you otherwise."

The woman was a holy terror: the sweetest face, the pillowiest bosom, and a perspicacity that stripped a man naked in seconds.

Fortunately, today at least, she didn't seem interested in further dissecting his fundamental nature. "And when did you see Lord Bancroft? Were you in London?"

"Can't you tell whether I've been in London at some point in the past three months?"

She didn't often turn her deductive powers on him. But ever since the day she'd taken one look at him and casually commented, *I see you've lost your virginity*, he'd been half convinced he couldn't have a single thought without her knowing everything about it.

"Well, from merely looking at you," she said without looking at him, her gaze on a patch of cabbages, "I can tell only that you have been extremely preoccupied and that you do not wish for me to guess at this preoccupation. But I shall venture to say that no, you haven't been in London, except perhaps to change trains when you brought the children back from the Devon coast at the end of summer. So Lord Bancroft visited you here—a rather unusual occurrence, wouldn't you say?"

To her statement on his virginity or lack thereof, he'd replied, with all the haughtiness he could summon, *I will not deign to address that.* The momentary satisfaction of embargoing the subject, however, had led to years of wondering how Holmes had fathomed what she couldn't possibly have known.

He chose to spare himself that futile speculation today. "Why would you think I'm more preoccupied than usual? My circumstances practically mandate a degree of preoccupation."

Now she inspected him, a head-to-toe sweep and back again. "Your valet was gone for a few days and returned day before yesterday, in the evening."

"Yes?"

"You prefer to shave yourself when Cummings is away, rather than entrust the task to another manservant. And you've always been competent at the task. I saw you in Devon, less than two days after Lady Ingram's departure. Cummings wasn't there. You shaved that day and you didn't nick yourself.

"But looking at you now I can see at least three places where your shaving blade had broken skin. They are all at different stages of healing, which tells me that not only have you been preoccupied to a remarkable degree, it is a preoccupation that does not let up.

"The nicks stopped with the return of your valet. But you, upon meeting my sister and realizing that I myself was likely to be in the vicinity and might arrive unannounced upon your doorstep, what do you do? You came home and, instead of changing back into the clothes you'd been wearing before you called on Mrs. Newell, you put on a different set of tweeds, a suit you haven't worn for a while—it still smells of the lavender sachets with which it had been stored. Not only that, but you also erred on the side of a fresh shirt and a pair of boots that haven't been outside since they were last cleaned, brushed, and shined.

"You have never dressed to impress me. And most likely you realized that I would notice your choice of attire. But you opted for it anyway: You'd rather that I guessed at the preoccupation than at the nature of it."

She did not look to him for confirmation—she knew she was right. He could only be thankful that she hadn't pointed out that he could have remained inside the manor and avoided her altogether.

He would rather be seen through, as uncomfortable and mortifying as that always was, than not see her at all.

"You are right about London," he said, exhaling. "I haven't left Stern Hollow since I came back from Devon. It has been a parade of brothers this autumn—even Wycliffe came."

Her brow lifted an infinitesimal distance, which for her implied grand astonishment. "Wycliffe came *here*, instead of summoning you to Eastleigh Park?"

"I know. I couldn't believe it either. My steward almost had an attack of nerves."

The current Duke of Wycliffe, Lord Ingram's eldest brother, had graced Stern Hollow only once before. A few days after Lord Ingram had inherited the estate, he'd arrived without notice, ordered Lord Ingram to accompany him on an inspection of house and grounds, and departed immediately afterward, saying only, *A fine holding. Look after it.*

"Did they all come because Lady Ingram is ostensibly in Switzerland for her health? Surely Lord Bancroft didn't tell the duke the truth?"

Wycliffe's duty was the continuation of his bloodline and the well-being of his dukedom. Unlike his three younger brothers, he had never sullied his hands with the work of the Crown.

"I'm not sure what Bancroft told him. Wycliffe was almost . . . solicitous."

She nodded slowly, apparently as dumbstruck as he had been.

She hadn't been the only person opposed to his marriage. Wycliffe had objected just as strongly, though primarily on the basis of his then extreme youth. He had expected a reckoning, an if-you-had-only-listened-to-me tirade. But Wycliffe's silence on the matter had been, if anything, far more excruciating.

He had never felt as colossal a failure as then—when Wycliffe pitied him too much to scold him.

"And Lord Remington, he didn't sail all the way from India just to make sure you were all right?"

"No." And thank goodness for that. The last thing he wanted was for an older brother to come halfway across the world because he had been incapable of managing his own life. "He left Calcutta before . . . everything happened."

"I still can't believe that you sent your children off with him. That you let them out of your sight."

Had it been Mrs. Watson making the statement, *I still can't believe* would have been a figure of speech. But this was Holmes. And *she*, by those words, meant exactly that. She didn't believe it.

He chose to answer as if she were Mrs. Watson. "Remington has always been the pied piper. Children adore him and never want to let him go. When he asked if they would like to go with him to the seaside, they jumped at the opportunity."

"Which seaside?"

"My cottage on the Devon coast. But they have departed for Scotland. Remington has plans to see Cape Wrath. Perhaps even the Orkney Islands. He assured me the weather should still be tolerable this time of the year."

She knew that Remington was his favorite brother. She knew that they were close despite the difference in their ages and Remington's long years abroad. Yet as they made their way past plots of artichokes, cauliflowers, and vegetable marrows, her incredulity was evident—at least to him, long accustomed to scrutinizing her face.

Next to the cold frames at the northwest corner of the garden she asked, "With the children away, why haven't you gone on a dig yet?"

He almost always went on digs in autumn—arranged for them well before the beginning of the Season. After Lady Ingram's sudden disappearance, with the children now his sole responsibilities, he had given up his earlier plans.

"I haven't made new arrangements. And frankly, at the moment, I don't wish to. See that hexagonal structure?"

The walled garden sloped toward the south, so that everything within benefited from maximum sunshine. From their vantage point, they had a clear view of the lavender house, which had never been used for making dried flowers in his tenure, or even his godfather's.

Several of his menservants were coming out of the lavender

house, one holding a broom and a dustpan, two pulling a large handcart. They locked the door and walked away.

"I'd ordered some more expedition equipment, but when they came today I didn't even want to look at them. They are being stowed as is, in their crates."

She allowed that answer to stand, which could mean she believed him. Or that she didn't but already knew everything she wished to know.

He let silence take over. They walked along the walls of the garden now, for her to inspect the espaliered fruit trees that had taken her fancy. After a minute or so, he glanced at her. Sometimes he could read her silence as well as he could a newspaper. Right now her thoughts were not about him. It was possible they did not even involve the whereabouts of his children: Her silence wasn't simply distracted; there was something unnerving about it.

He felt as if he stood on the prow of a ship, watching the captain scan the horizon for signs of impending disaster only the latter could recognize.

Then the sensations of ill omen dissipated into the ether, like so many coils of cigarette smoke. His breaths quickened. He was well acquainted with *this* particular strain of silence—the heat, the hunger, the coercive need to touch.

"You mentioned earlier that you'd like to see me remain longer in the country," she murmured. "You could bribe me to that end."

"Oh?" he heard himself say. "How much per extra day?"

"We could discuss that. Or you could pay me a call one of those days, when Mrs. Watson takes her afternoon nap."

*Yes. Would tomorrow do?*

He clasped his hands behind his back. "You did not write for three months and you think I would be amenable to perform such services at your beck and call?"

She scoffed. "*You* did not write for three months. And you think

I would be mollified with anything less than such services at my beck and call?"

He couldn't help but smile.

Mrs. Watson came into the walled garden then—she had probably run out of questions to ask the head gardener—and exclaimed at the extent and vibrancy of the place, this late in the season. He showed her the glass houses and, when she asked how those were heated in the coldest months, explained in some detail about the boiler room just beyond the north wall, where all winter long one of two boilers, sunk deep underground, would provide heat via hot water forced through a network of pipes.

The ladies took their leave not long after that. For discretion's sake, he did not accompany them to the front of the house, where their pony cart was parked, but bade them good-bye just outside the walls of the kitchen garden. Mrs. Watson extended a warm invitation for him to call early and often at their hired cottage.

"We will be most delighted to see you"—she turned to Holmes— "won't we, Miss Holmes?"

"Of course," she said, all limpid-eyed innocence, as if she hadn't propositioned him again. "We will await your arrival with bated breath."

He watched her walk away and felt, for the first time in a very long time, something like happiness.

## *Four*

L ivia had always had dubious luck. Nothing catastrophically bad—at least, nothing apart from Charlotte's banishment from Society—but a daily, sometimes hourly cascade of vexation. Doors closed on the hems of her dresses. Of all the picnic sandwiches in a basket, hers would be the one soaked by the contents of a leaking canteen. And if a magazine published a serial she enjoyed, she could count on the certainty that at least one issue would go astray, leaving her with a hole in the story.

But this was the first time she'd had to evacuate a country house party because the house itself flooded from the top down. Several cisterns had been built into the attic of Mrs. Newell's manor, so that gravity could supply running water to baths and water closets. On the second day of Livia's visit, two cisterns ruptured.

Fortunately, no one was hurt. Mrs. Newell, after a few minutes of dismayed incomprehension, declared herself grateful for everyone's safety. Her guests were corralled into the library, which had escaped the inundation, and served rich cake and strong spirits. In the meanwhile, grooms rode off in every direction, seeking aid at nearby establishments.

The village inn only had a couple of rooms to spare. The nearest house was shuttered, its owner abroad. But the third groom to return brought welcome news: The master of Stern Hollow had put himself and his abode at Mrs. Newell's disposal.

Everyone sighed with relief. Of course Lord Ingram would offer his assistance. Whatever rumors circulated about his parentage, his conduct had always been thoroughly admirable.

By dinnertime the entire party was in Stern Hollow, ensconced in comfort and style. Livia gasped when she saw her room. By now she had become inured to odd and frequently inferior guest rooms— rooms with ceilings barely higher than her head, rooms that looked onto a wall three feet away, rooms that were never more than six feet wide at any point *and* bent to fit around an awkward corner.

But this room was exquisite. It was sufficiently large to be airy and spacious but not so enormous as to dwarf the furnishings. Light green silk printed with lotus flowers covered the walls; a soft jade counterpane draped the bed. The window overlooked a knot garden boasting, at its center, a simple but graceful fountain, a basin held aloft on a slender fluted column.

Best of all, there were flowers everywhere: a bouquet of blush roses on the mantel, a pot of orchids on the writing desk, and, on the night stand, an arrangement of sweet peas, in such riotous colors that she really ought to disapprove—instead she mooned over their rambunctiousness.

She drifted about, caressing bedposts, curtain ties, and painting frames, her eyes stinging with abrupt tears. She had not been assigned this room at random—Lord Ingram had asked that she be put up in the manner of an esteemed guest, because she was Charlotte's sister.

This was what it felt like to be valued.

A housemaid arrived to deliver tea and help her unpack. Livia, flustered by her attentiveness, accepted the tea and asked her to re-

turn later. Now she needed to be by herself, to wallow in such loveliness and, above all, such care.

To think, Stern Hollow could have been her home, if only Lord
Ingram had married Charlotte instead . . .

How much sweeter Livia's life would have been, had she spent
the past six years here, instead of at home, with her unkind, unloving parents. How much she would have treasured every hour of
every day, always quietly celebrating her vast good fortune.

No, she reminded herself, Charlotte would not have accepted
Lord Ingram's suit—that much Livia knew for certain. And need-
less to say, Lord Ingram had been in love with another woman. Alas,
their choices had both turned out disastrously, so if only . . .

If only.

But there were second chances in life, were there not? A missed
opportunity in the past could, in the future, be embraced with both
arms. With Lady Ingram out of the way, Lord Ingram and Charlotte could arrive at a marital arrangement that suited them both:
As a friend, he would want to restore her to her proper place in
Society; and Charlotte, as persnickety as she was in such matters,
might agree to it for Livia's sake, if nothing else—without Charlotte she was beginning to wilt, a sun-loving plant forever stuck in
the shadows.

Her imagination took flight, lifted to ever greater heights by
thoughts of peaceful days and lively evenings, of security, freedom,
*and* respect. She would write—her words would flow beautifully
here, she was sure—and she would take long walks, rain or—

Her castle in the sky crashed to earth, scattering dream shards
far and wide, when reality intruded. Whether Lady Ingram had run
away with an illicit lover or been confined to a Swiss sanatorium,
she was only absent, not dead. Lord Ingram was as much a married
man as he had ever been, in no position to offer Charlotte anything
both permanent and legitimate.

And Livia would be headed back home again, all too soon, to the embrace of no one.

But how real it had felt, her imagined happiness, how infinitely bright and tangible.

—❈—

A quarter hour before dinner, all happiness, real or imagined, fled.

The guests were assembled in the drawing room. Mrs. Newell, acting as the hostess, went around informing each gentleman which lady he was to take to dinner. Livia observed the proceedings with her usual tightening in the stomach. Her dinner partner the night before had been obviously more interested in the lady on his other side; she hoped to have a more considerate gentleman this evening.

The next moment, the identity of her dinner partner lost all importance: Two bejeweled, beplumed women marched into the drawing room. Lady Avery and Lady Somersby, Society's leading gossips, had descended upon the gathering.

Given the antipathy Livia felt toward the two women, it was difficult to see how they could ever be welcome anywhere. But they were greeted with open arms at any number of gatherings, holding, in fact, standing invitations to a good many house parties—Mrs. Newell's, for one—that they didn't always have enough time to attend.

At any given point in time, only a small subset of Society was discussed in drawing rooms across the land. There was the louche Marlborough House set, of course, though Livia was personally bored by the Prince of Wales and his progression of mistresses. There were couples like the Tremaines, or Lord and Lady Ingram, whose wealth, glamour, and staggering marital infelicity made them perennial favorites for dissection, as cautionary tales, if nothing else. And there were the scandals du jour, such as Charlotte's, generating brief but intense bursts of notice.

Or at least the brouhaha surrounding Charlotte would have

been a lot briefer had she allowed herself to be exiled to the country, never to be seen again.

The point was, unless one originated a scandal or was close enough to one to be systematically hunted down by ladies Avery and Somersby, their arrival at a function generated excitement rather than dread. Livia herself had, on more than one occasion, tried to sneak as close as possible to the gossip ladies, especially when they discoursed among married women, to whom they gave the truly juicy stories that were considered too indelicate for maiden ears such as her own.

Livia glanced toward Lord Ingram, but he had his back to her. She didn't know how she managed to keep talking and smiling; she barely had any idea on which gentleman's arm she walked into the dining room.

At the head of the table Lord Ingram was as gracious as ever, though he did seem tired and tense. The dread that had never truly left since she first read Lady Avery's letter flooded her veins and intensified every time one of the gossip ladies looked toward him. She repeated to herself, ad nauseum, that the worst had already happened, that no titillating tidbit disseminated tonight could diminish either Charlotte or Lord Ingram in the long run. But her innards churned with ever greater ferocity, forcing her to give up any pretense of eating.

Almost as soon as the ladies had risen from dinner and removed to the drawing room, Lady Somersby accosted her.

"You have received my sister's letter, I presume, Miss Holmes?"

Livia answered stiffly that she had. "I have not had time to reply. I spent much of yesterday traveling—and much of today relocating to Stern Hollow."

Lady Somersby waved a hand. "We weren't anticipating any useful intelligence from your direction, in any case. It was more kindness on our part, to let you know that your sister had, at least as of July, been getting on quite well, all things considered."

Livia managed not to grind her teeth before she said, "How thoughtful of you, my lady."

"Indeed, we do think of everything." She leaned forward conspiratorially. "But this does complicate matters, do you not think?"

*Oh, when did you realize? Before or after you decided to tell everyone something they didn't need to know in the first place?*

Livia held on to her tongue, though she was sure her smile must have degenerated to a rictus. "Is that so?"

"Oh, rather. Think about it, Miss Holmes. You know of Lady Ingram's abrupt departure at the end of the Season, I'm sure?"

"I've heard it mentioned."

"Word was that her health took a tumble. My sister and I always regarded that with a grain of salt—or a pillar as large as the one Lot's wife turned into, if you will. We were at the ball that night. She did not look out of sorts at all. A bit impatient for her guests to leave, perhaps, but in no worse physical condition than most other people near the end of a Season.

"And then, all of a sudden, she was so badly off that she had to be shipped to Switzerland. How likely is that, I ask you?"

Livia had heard Lady Somersby ask that question before, at a different house party to which the Holmeses had been invited. Those were happier times—Lady Somersby hadn't implied that anyone except Lady Ingram herself had been involved in the decision to decamp for the Alps.

"Sometimes things deteriorate with catastrophic speed."

"I'm sure they do. But if she was in a terrible way, what was wrong with English physicians? They exist in great abundance in London, and our schools of medicine are not in the habit of producing quacks. Not to mention, why a sanatorium? It is not a place for stowing the desperately ill. And last I inquired, she wasn't suffering from polio, asthma, tuberculosis, or any other chronic disease for which a sanatorium offers suitable treatments."

Livia saw where this was going. "Everybody knows about her bad back," she retorted, her voice acquiring a nervous squeak. "And Switzerland has thermal springs for rheumatism."

"No one needs to disappear overnight to soak in hot springs," Lady Somersby pointed out. "She could have taken proper leave of her friends and acquaintances."

"Perhaps she didn't wish to. Perhaps she was fed up with Society and her back hurt and she just wanted to be away. This was your conjecture earlier, remember?"

Lady Somersby waved her hand again, brushing away her own erstwhile theory as if it were a wasp at a picnic. "Or perhaps she learned about her husband's involvement with your sister and was so upset that she simply had to run out."

Livia's grip on her fan tightened—would that she could whack Lady Somersby and get away with it. "That is farfetched, my lady. First, Lord Ingram and my sister are friends of long standing. Second, if Lady Ingram knew her husband at all, she would know that he would not abandon a friend in need. And third, let's suppose she assumed the worst, that Lord Ingram wasn't only helping my sister but keeping her, how would that make him any different from any other man in Society? Even if they weren't severely estranged, how many women have you known to become upset enough over a husband's indiscretions to leave *children* behind?"

"Well," said Lady Somersby slowly, "there *is* sense in what you said. I concede that particular theory might be flawed. But it is highly odd, isn't it, the entire situation with our host and his absent wife?"

"Whatever their situation is, ma'am, I can assure you that it has nothing to do with my sister."

Lady Somersby soon moved on. Livia slumped into a chair, feeling as if she'd wrestled a bear. If only she had any confidence that she had been the winner of the contest—or at least a survivor.

---❋---

"Miss, the carriage is ready to take you to the village," said the butler to Livia as she left the breakfast parlor the next morning.

Livia *had* been thinking, rather intensely, of getting away from Stern Hollow for a bit. She still loved her room, of course, and she longed to explore the grounds. But the current atmosphere, with the gossip ladies in residence and all the other guests whipped into a frenzy of curiosity, was hardly conducive to her peace of mind.

"I haven't ordered a carriage."

Her luck was such that if she didn't point this out but tried to take advantage of the butler's mistake, he would realize his error just as she was about to climb into the carriage, and she would be left on the front steps looking like the fool she was.

"His lordship ordered it for you, Miss Holmes."

Livia had to swallow past a lump in her throat—she was not accustomed to being looked after so thoroughly. "Do please thank his lordship for me. Tell him I'm beyond grateful."

As it turned out he was there in front of the house when she arrived. Her smile faltered, however, when she noticed his bloodshot eyes—it was as if he hadn't slept at all.

She cursed the gossip ladies. "Are you all right, sir? You look a little under-rested."

"I'm well." His voice, too, sounded scratchy. But his hand was steady as he helped her into the carriage. "Take as much time as you need in the village."

It was only as the door of the carriage closed that she realized he had left a folded note in her gloved palm.

*From High Street, make your way to Rampling Cottage on foot, a twenty-minute walk. You will be warmly received there.*

---❋---

"Oh, Charlotte," Livia murmured. "Charlotte. Charlotte. Charlotte."

She must have held her sister for a solid two minutes, but it wasn't enough. It would never be enough.

Reluctantly, she let go, and only because Charlotte did not enjoy sustained contact. "Is your Mrs. Watson here?"

"She went out for a walk. Usually I go with her. But given what happened at Mrs. Newell's, I thought chances were good Lord Ingram would point you my way as soon as possible."

Livia resisted the urge to enfold Charlotte in another long embrace, but she did cup Charlotte's face and kiss her on the forehead. Her sister had taken all this trouble to station herself nearby, just so they could meet. "You should have told me."

"There's always the risk that my letter goes astray. Mamma and Papa can't do anything to me, but they could keep you at home and not allow you to go anywhere. Which would not have been a desirable outcome."

Charlotte showed Livia into a plainly furnished sitting room, where a tea tray had already been set out. Charlotte put a kettle to boil on a spirit lamp. Then she set a plate laden with finger sandwiches and sliced cake before Livia. "You haven't been eating properly."

"When you're not there, nobody cares whether I eat or not."

"I'm here now, so tuck in."

A sandwich in hand, Livia told Charlotte about Lady Avery's letter. Charlotte, however, was more interested in the flooding at Mrs. Newell's house. And when Livia had given a satisfactory account, she asked, "How long will her guests stay at Stern Hollow?"

Some of Livia's delight at her reunion with Charlotte was already draining away. "Word is we will be there no more than three days. Obviously, Mrs. Newell's party ended the moment the cisterns broke and we are at Lord Ingram's not to continue the revelry but to make other arrangements without being too rushed or uncomfortable."

She didn't want to go home yet. She never wanted to go back home.

"Poor Lord Ingram. He didn't look well this morning. Can you imagine, having to host Lady Avery and Lady Somersby, who are going about pondering—right under his roof, no less—whether his wife left because she discovered that he'd been keeping you?"

Charlotte tsked. "For gossips of their distinction, they should know that Lord Ingram has far too many scruples to keep me. That man can be frustratingly hidebound."

Livia's brows shot up. Surely Charlotte didn't mean she found out for herself that Lord Ingram wouldn't take her for a mistress? No decision on Charlotte's part, however outlandish, should surprise Livia anymore. But she *was* surprised at this possibility—perhaps even a little shocked.

"Anyway," murmured Charlotte, "he and I are only friends. Let people think what they will. It can't hurt me. Nor will it reduce his standing in the long term."

Clearly Charlotte, like Lord Ingram, was minimally concerned with the information ladies Avery and Somersby were currently disseminating. If Charlotte, with her extraordinary perspicacity, didn't see anything to worry about, then Livia had absolutely no reason to go on agonizing.

Or at least every reason to ignore the misgivings that refused to go away on their own.

A question occurred to her—she didn't know why she hadn't thought of it before. "Do *you* know why Lady Ingram left so abruptly?"

Charlotte shook her head. "No."

Livia sighed and took a bite of a finger sandwich. "I guess I'd better tell you about Bernadine, then. She's no longer at home."

Half an hour later, Mrs. Watson returned from her walk.

Had she not been so sincerely amiable, Livia would have been roundly intimidated by her beauty and confidence. As it was, her delight in meeting Livia melted away not only Livia's feeling of being overawed but also her remaining wariness toward a woman of the demimonde, even one who had been so instrumental to Charlotte's success and independence.

Charlotte had mentioned that occasionally Mrs. Watson dressed with unnecessary splendor to warn "proper" ladies that she wasn't one of them. Such must not have been her objective today. While her dress did not lack flair, it still possessed an elegance that made Livia sigh with aesthetic longing.

And she was so warm, so maternal without being in the least limiting, that Livia found herself confiding about her recent difficulties with the second half of the Sherlock Holmes story. Charlotte had told her that she could do it, but Mrs. Watson made her believe that she indeed *would*. Being encouraged by her felt like those rare occasions when Livia threw aside her parasol and simply lifted her face to the sun.

As reluctant as she was to leave the cottage, she returned to Stern Hollow with a smile on her face and floated up the grand staircase. Now she would sit in her beautiful room and luxuriate in memories of the outing: Charlotte's sweet face, Mrs. Watson's beautiful soul, and the renewal of hope in her own heart.

Perhaps she would even take out the moonstone, cup it in her hands, and—

Lady Avery was in her room, hastily closing a nightstand drawer.

Livia stared at her, unable to believe what she was seeing. "Ma'am, wh—what are you doing?"

Lady Avery's eyes darted to the space behind Livia, as if wondering whether she'd been discovered by more than just insignificant Olivia Holmes. But there was no one else in the passage.

Livia stepped inside and closed the door. "Lady Avery, why are you in my room?"

Her voice was unsteady—she was not accustomed to demanding answers.

Lady Avery studied Livia, her gaze more calculating than wor-

ried. "Well, I don't mind telling you, Miss Holmes. My sister and I
received intelligence that there is to be a very grand act of indiscretion here at Stern Hollow, among the guests Mrs. Newell brought
from her house."

Livia's eyes bulged. "And you think *I* am to be the perpetrator of
that indiscretion?"

"No, no, quite the opposite. You have never shown the slightest
proclivity for breaking rules. But we must be thorough, you see, and
not overlook anyone simply because they seem unlikely. Yours is, in
fact, the last room I checked and as expected, I found nothing of
interest."

Livia's heart thumped with both fury and furious relief: She had
brought two of Charlotte's letters on this trip—and had carried
them on her person instead of leaving them behind for nosy house-
maids to discover.

And that precaution had saved her from the gossip ladies.

"Do please leave."

"Of course."

Lady Avery paused upon reaching the door, then turned around.
"I have a proposition for you, Miss Holmes. How would you like
to hunt for this grand indiscretion alongside my sister and myself?"

Livia blinked. "I— What? You want me to search other guests'
rooms for you?"

"No, no, that's all done. You are an intelligent and observant
young woman. You will be an asset in uncovering this major indiscretion."

Livia often berated herself for being stupid, but she immediately
grasped the nature of Lady Avery's offer. "You're afraid that unless
I join you, I'm going to tell Lord Ingram that you are transgressing
on his hospitality and browsing the belongings not only of his
guests but possibly of himself."

"Don't be ridiculous, young lady—Lord Ingram's rooms are secured with devices quite beyond our ability to tamper with. But yes, you are right about the rest of it."

Lady Avery sighed softly. "We are feared by those with something to hide and welcomed by the rest—but that welcome is conditional. As long as we have plenty of gossip, doors will open for us. The moment we can no longer provide the latest on-dits, we'll be just another pair of annoying busybodies."

"So you resort to underhanded tactics."

Lady Avery held up a finger. "Hardly ever. We rely on listening more than anything else—and when necessary, close questioning and record-checking. But this has been a frustrating summer. First your sister goes missing and we can't find out what has happened to her. Then Lady Ingram bolts to Switzerland and we are in the dark as to her reasons. If this goes on much longer, people will begin to wonder whether we've lost our knack."

Livia had trouble keeping her lips thinned in disapproval, when her reaction was more astonishment than anything else. It had never occurred to her that ladies Avery and Somersby might worry about their places in Society: They'd been such permanent fixtures that she'd assumed they'd always remain permanent fixtures.

"So we must uncover this major indiscretion. Of course, we didn't *want* to search the guests' belongings."

Except they had.

Elsewhere Livia might hesitate to expose them, but here she would not worry about not being believed. And should Lord Ingram choose to inform Mrs. Newell—after all, the gossip ladies were her guests—his accusation would land precisely where ladies Avery and Somersby were most vulnerable.

They were already figurative snoops of such renown, it would take very little to convince Society that they also happened to be literal snoops. While they were more than welcome at many stately manors when it was thought all they brought was titillating entertaining, a hostess would think thrice about inviting them into her home, should it become known that they *would*, in fact, riffle through every room, looking for incriminating evidence.

Amazement descended upon Livia. She, who was so powerless in almost every respect of her life, was, for once, the one with the advantage. Over someone like Lady Avery, no less, someone who had always seemed as powerful and indestructible as a swarm of locusts.

But she was able to savor that feeling of might for only a fraction of a second. If only she'd interrupted Lady Avery before she'd blabbed to everyone about Charlotte and Lord Ingram's encounter in the tea shop! Had such been the case, she'd have been able to save Lord Ingram some unpleasantness.

Beyond that, she had no idea how she could possibly make use of the situation.

What she did know was that she shouldn't let her advantage slip away, simply because she hadn't worked out how to exploit it.

"Lady Avery, I'm afraid I cannot possibly help you and your sister. We are in very different positions in life. You were respectably married and in widowhood you enjoy a generous dower. I, on the other hand, have no money and few prospects. And the sister whom I had counted on to be my companion in old age is nowhere to be found. I am in no position to pursue anyone else's indiscretions, when what I wish for the most is that no one had hunted down my sister's and ruined all our lives."

She opened the door, dramatically yet firmly.

After a moment, Lady Avery walked out.

## Five

The breeze was pleasant on Livia's cheeks—she'd been going uphill for the past ten minutes. Had she been standing still, it would have felt a little frosty.

The unseasonable balminess of the past two days couldn't last. Somewhere nearby a mass of cold air was on the move, its vanguard encircling Stern Hollow.

The imagery made her shiver a little, as if winter had already arrived.

She tried to dwell on the remaining warmth of the afternoon, the quiet serenity of the woods, and the sun that was still some distance above the horizon, generously shedding its light. But without quite realizing it, her mind turned to a different autumnal day, a different pretty estate.

Moreton Close. Bernadine, her sister who, if she hadn't been rail thin, would have resembled Charlotte a great deal. Her life at home had not been ideal, but it had been safe enough and stable enough. Who could vouch for the new place where their parents intended to stow her for the remainder of her natural life?

Charlotte had been quiet after Livia had spoken of Moreton

Close, of its disarming coziness and its seemingly content residents. And then she had said, "I'll take a look myself."

"But you won't be able to," Livia reminded her. "They don't let anyone in who's never been invited there before."

"Wait until you meet Mrs. Watson. No one will refuse to open a door when she stands on the threshold."

And Mrs. Watson had indeed possessed that magical quality, and Livia had felt a burden lift from her shoulders. Between Charlotte and Mrs. Watson, they would see to it.

But now anxiety returned.

Ferreting out the truth about Moreton Close would take time, even if they could finagle an invitation. After all, Livia had been inside—and hadn't found any cracks in the façade. What would happen to Bernadine in the meanwhile?

What if Dr. Wrexhall, who seemed so competent and reasonable, turned into a monster like the evil Mr. Hyde when all the visitors had left? Who would protect Bernadine then? Who would make sure that she wouldn't be—

"Miss Holmes, are you lost?"

Lady Avery and Lady Somersby, the vultures themselves.

After the confrontation with Lady Avery, knowing that the gossip ladies were in fact after a different and much bigger target, Livia's sense of foreboding had eased somewhat. Let them chase their mirage. May it take up all their waking hours and leave them no time or energy to remember Charlotte and Lord Ingram.

"No, thank you," she said coolly. "I am not lost."

But she had wandered off the path into a grove of aspens. As sunlight slanted through, the slender tree trunks were almost white. And the undergrowth had turned the same golden hue as the shimmering canopy of leaves high overhead.

"Will you head back with us? The temperature is dropping fast now," said Lady Avery.

Livia almost declined by reflex. Then she remembered that she had caught Lady Avery riffling through her room. Their offer wasn't an order but something closer to an apology.

She supposed she could be magnanimous while she held the upper hand. "Certainly."

They walked for some time in silence, then Lady Avery said, "We spoke to the servants."

"And did they shed any light on this 'great indiscretion' you are seeking?" Livia wasn't magnanimous enough to keep her tone free of snideness.

Lady Avery exchanged a glance with her sister. "We have discussed this and we have decided to tell you the truth. The part about the great indiscretion I made up on the spot. What we are investigating is not an indiscretion but an injustice."

"Injustice?" Livia couldn't help her incredulity. "What do you care about injustice?"

"From the very beginning we have cared passionately about injustice," said Lady Avery in all seriousness. "We move in Society and must speak its language and accumulate its currency—so we are fluent in enmities, liaisons, and financial entanglements going back several generations. Indiscretions and whatnot are amusing, we will not deny that. But along with an interest in sin, we have always been determined to unearth injustice where it exists and do what we can to remedy the situation."

Livia almost tripped over a stone that poked up from the ground. What was the woman going on about?

"You are probably not familiar with employment agencies for domestic service," Lady Avery went on. "But we always pass along what we know—if the master of a house takes advantage of the maids, or if the mistress works them too much and docks wages unfairly.

"We warn mothers of young ladies, or young ladies themselves, if we think they can handle such intelligence, when we know certain alarming things about young men they might consider marrying. Sometimes they marry them anyway, because they refuse to believe us or because their parents exert undue pressure. But we do what we can.

"Anyway, our point is, we try to prevent or expose injustice. Often we can't speak aloud—the culprits hold too unassailable a position or the consequences are too adverse, should it be found out who had passed on the information. But we do speak quietly, and we do inform as many people as possible, especially those who must brush up against their spheres of influence."

Livia stared at Lady Avery. She had never thought of the women as being in any way *helpful*. To anyone. She wasn't sure she believed Lady Avery, who admitted that she'd made up the bit about the "great indiscretion." Might this not be another gambit to make sure Livia didn't say anything about their having gone into every guest room at Stern Hollow?

The next moment a huge premonition slammed into her. "And what, exactly, is this injustice you are so interested in just now?"

"I mentioned that we spoke to the servants," said Lady Somersby. "They are a loyal lot, down to the scullery maids, and didn't consider it our business to ask after their master and mistress. But we both received the impression that while they are reluctant to say anything, they are as puzzled about Lady Ingram's departure as we are.

"Neither of the coachmen drove her to a railway station. No one in the house, in fact, saw her on the night of her birthday ball, after about half past midnight or quarter to one. The children and their governess aren't here right now, but we learned that even the children didn't get to say good-bye to her. The entire household, with a few exceptions, was ordered back to Stern Hollow the very next day, while Lord Ingram himself took the children to the seaside—neither of which had been in the plans earlier."

"Plans always change," countered Livia, even as her stomach

once again twisted with dread. "And wasn't it said that it was a sudden collapse? They had a houseful of guests. Given Lady Ingram's private nature, wouldn't it be like her to leave, since she must, with as little noise and drama as possible?"

The ladies did not escalate the debate. Livia was beginning to wonder whether her argument carried more weight than she thought it did, when Lady Avery said, "This is our first visit to Stern Hollow. I take it, Miss Holmes, that the same is true for you?"

"That is correct," Livia answered warily.

"What do you think of the estate?"

Their path turned and the house came back into view, quite close now, serene and lovely, nestled in its sweet green dell. "I find it enchanting."

"*We* find it a little chilling."

Livia's fingertips tingled with alarm. They were about to speak of Lady Ingram again.

"There is no imprint of Lady Ingram upon this place," Lady Avery continued. "Not at all. We spoke to all the senior servants, the majordomo, the butler, the housekeeper, the chef, the head gardener, et cetera, et cetera. It would seem that any and all alteration or improvement originated with Lord Ingram. Your room, for example, had been redecorated to his specification within the past year or so. The nursery. The library. The addition of certain fruit trees to the walled garden. It has all been Lord Ingram. It was as if——"

"As if Lady Ingram has no interest in houses or gardens," said Livia heatedly. "Such women do exist."

Charlotte was one. She appreciated a beautiful house, but she wouldn't lift a finger to help make one. And any interest she had in horticulture was tied directly to whether the species in question could be made into a good pudding.

"I don't doubt the existence of such women. But that is a terribly innocent interpretation on your part, Miss Holmes. Lord Ingram could very well have forbidden any input from his wife with regard to her own home."

"That is a preposterous statement to put forward, Lady Avery. Lady Ingram has one of the largest allowances in Society. And her husband has thrown a lavish ball to celebrate her birthday every year, even after he learned that she married him only for his money. He has been more than generous to her at every turn and does not have it in his character to practice such meanness."

"Being generous to his wife and undertaking extravagant gestures are choices that reflect well on *him*. They reflect especially well on him when it is believed that she does not deserve either. But think back to their rupture. I have investigated it, and everything rests on the word of one then-new under-housemaid, who told the other servants, who in turn passed on the gossip to servants they knew in other households. The story filtered upward to the ears of their masters and mistresses, and eventually a picture emerged that was wholly uncomplimentary to Lady Ingram."

Livia threw up her hands. "Because the *truth* was wholly uncomplimentary to Lady Ingram."

"We will allow for that possibility. But then you must also allow for the possibility that the truth might not be as complimentary to Lord Ingram: He *could* have orchestrated what the public was allowed to learn, in order to tilt the narrative heavily in his favor, and then practiced intimidation at home to isolate his wife and cow her into silence."

This was ludicrous. "No one could have cowed Lady Ingram into silence."

"Appearances are often deceiving," said Lady Somersby, who until now had been happy to let her sister do all the talking. "You should trust us on this, Miss Holmes. It has been our vocation in life to see beneath the surface. Women who appear perfectly happy sometimes live in fear of their lives. And men who give every impression in public of kindness and amiability can be monsters in private."

"And you believe Lord Ingram—*Lord Ingram*—to be such a man?"

"No one is above suspicion on such matters, because in private no one is entirely what they seem in public."

But wouldn't *Charlotte* have known if he was a monster? Wouldn't she have honed in on all the clues?

Then again, as remarkable as Charlotte was, she was still only human. He was her faithful friend; his wife remained barely an acquaintance. Would her opinion have been swayed, as Livia's most certainly would have been, by that unspoken hostility on Lady Ingram's part?

"Only last night you were telling me, Lady Somersby, that Lady Ingram might have run away from home. Now you portray her as a prisoner in her own marriage."

"Both are possible. We searched the manor not to look through anyone's things but to see whether she might have left behind some clues to her fate."

"Her *fate*? What do you think has happened to her?"

"What would your parents have done to your sister if she hadn't run away?" asked Lady Somersby.

Livia felt her jaw unhinge. "You think Lady Ingram has been shoved into the attic like Mr. Rochester's wife?"

"Who is this Mr. Rochester?" asked Lady Avery. "Why have I never heard of such infamy?"

"Fictional character, Caro. Dreadful mad wife in the attic, and with her there he tries to marry someone else." Lady Somersby turned back to Livia. "At least Lord Ingram won't be able to commit bigamy with your sister, since we all know he's already married."

Livia could barely keep her voice from rising an entire octave. "Why do you keep bringing everything back to my sister?"

"Everything comes back to her because she is an understandable motive. Think of this, what if Lady Ingram had something to do with her downfall? What if, instead of Mrs. Shrewsbury, it had been Lady Ingram who organized that mob who marched in on her and Mr. Shrewsbury? And what if Lord Ingram, in punishing his wife, thinks of himself as having righted a wrong perpetrated against Miss Charlotte Holmes?"

"Ladies, I begin to weary of declaring your ideas preposterous. It isn't so simple to hold someone prisoner!" Livia had tried writing something like that in her Sherlock Holmes story and the problems had immediately become apparent. "How does he feed her? Who empties her chamber pot? How does he prevent her from screaming without suffocating her in the process?"

A scream pierced the peaceful afternoon.

Livia started. The ladies looked at each other in confusion. The scream came again, a man's scream. The three women picked up their skirts and ran.

The path led downhill. Soon Livia saw the man. The boy, rather, an adolescent dressed in a dark jacket and dark trousers. A servant of the house.

He was on his knees. When he saw the women coming toward him, he rose unsteadily to his feet and attempted to speak.

"She's—she's—" He swallowed. "She's in there. She's *in* there!"

He pointed to a grassy mound to their left.

"Who is in there?" demanded Lady Avery.

But the boy trembled, as if he'd come down with a case of palsy, and couldn't get another word out.

Livia peered at the mound. "Is that the icehouse?"

"I believe so," said Lady Somersby grimly.

They found the entrance on the north side of the mound. The heavy door hadn't been locked but had shut by its own weight. With some effort, Livia pulled it open.

What in the world was she doing? She should be staying with

the poor, traumatized boy. Why was she headed for a destination that had made him run out screaming?

And who was *she*?

They passed through three antechambers, each chillier than its predecessor. The second one smelled of a badly kept latrine. Livia grimaced. Why should there be such a disagreeable odor in an ice-house?

The third antechamber was quite large. The lit taper that had been set into a wall bracket illuminated shelves built to either side, holding all kinds of foodstuff that benefited from cold storage. A wheelbarrow lay sideways on the floor, which was wet from a pail of milk that had been knocked over.

And fortunately here the air smelled mostly of milk and cold, nothing foul.

They skirted the puddle and headed for the last door.

Which opened to greater brightness than Livia anticipated— the lamp just inside had two lit tapers and a mirrored back. The ceiling domed above the ice well, the lip of which rose a foot from the floor.

Nothing, as of yet, looked out of place.

"So . . . he left his wheelbarrow outside to open this door and light the tapers," Livia heard herself say.

She had not advanced farther toward the ice well. She felt as if her blood was congealing, the warmth in her veins draining away.

"Once they were lit," said Lady Avery, her voice almost a whisper, "he would have gone to the edge of the well to take a look at the ice level."

Her sister took over. "Then he rushed out so fast he knocked over the wheelbarrow. For all we know, he might still be screaming outside."

Livia shivered—and not only from the fear that seemed to crawl out of her very marrow. The ice well was at least ten feet across in diameter and probably just as deep. How much ice did it hold? Two tons? Three? Her breaths emerged in visible puffs.

"Shall we"—Lady Avery swallowed audibly—"shall we step forward together?"

They did, inch by inch, as if they were approaching the edge of a cliff. The first thing that came into view was wood shavings on the far side of the ice well, providing insulation for the ice underneath.

And then an outstretched hand.

*Her* hand, whoever she was.

Livia whimpered. She, too, wanted to turn around and sprint away. But her feet kept carrying her forward.

At last they stood at the brim of the ice well and stared down onto Lady Ingram—Lady Ingram's body—lying on top of the wood shavings.

Someone patted Livia's hand—she'd been clutching at Lady Somersby's sleeve, with fingers that had been chilled to the bone.

"Well," said Lady Avery, her voice low yet harsh, "I guess this place *is* as cold as Switzerland."

# Six

*Six*

M rs. Watson was disappointed. Two days had passed since their visit to Stern Hollow, and Lord Ingram had not called. Granted, he had a houseful of someone else's guests. But still, he should have been able to get away for an hour or two and come to pay his respects.

"Really, he ought to know that I, at least, would have been anticipating his presence."

She fully expected Miss Holmes to make no comments. But Miss Holmes set aside the newspaper she had been perusing and said, "It is rather odd."

And that, apparently, was all she would say on the subject, for she picked up and glanced through the mail that had just arrived. "Mrs. Farr wrote back."

Mrs. Watson had to think for a moment to remember the name. Mrs. Winnie Farr, who had been given the idea to write Sherlock Holmes by Sergeant MacDonald, Inspector Treadles's subordinate.

"What did she say?"

Miss Holmes scanned the letter and handed it to Mrs. Watson.

*Dear Mr. Holmes,*

*Thank you for your kind letter.*

    *My sister, Miss Mimi Duffin, has been missing for almost three weeks. She is a grown woman and leaves London sometimes. But ten days ago my daughter Eliza turned seven. Mimi loves Eliza as her own and has never skipped her birthday before.*

    *When she didn't come—or send any word—I worried. Her friends hadn't seen her. Her room was already let to someone else, because she hadn't paid rent.*

    *Her landlady told me that when she saw her last, Mimi was in high spirits because she was about to take up with a fine gentleman who was going to keep her in style. If I can find this gentleman—if you can help me find him—maybe I will learn what happened to Mimi.*

    *I hope she is alive and well, but I don't believe it.*

*Sincerely yours,*
*Mrs. Winnie Farr*

"It would be a difficult search," said Mrs. Watson. "And most likely fruitless."

"True," said Miss Holmes. She tapped a finger against her chin. "Mrs. Newell's guests will depart Stern Hollow soon. Should Lord Ingram call upon us afterward, I might mention that we are headed to some of London's rougher districts."

Oh, that was genius. "He will insist on accompanying us. We won't wish to trouble him, of course, but who are we to keep saying no to such chivalry?" enthused Mrs. Watson. "Should I write back and arrange for an appointment with Mrs. Farr for, let's say, three days hence?"

Before Miss Holmes could reply, the doorbell rang. This being the maid's afternoon off, Mrs. Watson answered the summons herself. A young man who identified himself as a groom from Stern Hollow greeted her.

"I have an urgent message for the ladies of Rampling Cottage, mum."

Mrs. Watson had taken off her reading glasses before she came to the door—oh, the vanity. Now she found it difficult to make out the exact letters on the envelope—at least without holding the letter as far from her eyes as her hand could reach and squinting unattractively.

"An urgent message for us from Stern Hollow," she said when she returned to the sitting room. "I wonder if it's from Lord Ingram. Drat my old eyes."

Almost immediately Miss Holmes said, "That's my sister's handwriting."

"Oh? What news does she have?"

Miss Holmes took the letter. Her expression changed—changed so much that even someone not at all acquainted with her would be able to tell that something dreadful had happened.

"My goodness, what's going on?" cried Mrs. Watson.

Miss Holmes did not answer. She turned the letter over and read it again from the beginning, much slower this time, as if committing every word to memory. When she was done, she set it down on the tea table and pushed it across to Mrs. Watson.

*Dear Charlotte,*

*I hope my hand will stop shaking long enough for me to write.*

*Although what I really want is for what I'm about to tell you to never have happened at all.*

*Lady Ingram is dead. Her body was discovered in the icehouse by a kitchen helper. The poor boy ran out screaming. Lady Avery, Lady Somersby, and I, who happened to be passing nearby, ran to his aid. We* then went into the icehouse to see what had so frightened him, when he couldn't say anything beyond, "She's in there. She's in there!"

We saw her in the ice well. I'm not sure what happened afterward. I think one of the ladies tasked me to inform Lord Ingram, because the next thing I can remember is insisting to the house steward that I must see his master without delay.

When he received me, I found myself as inarticulate as the kitchen helper. "We—we were near the—the icehouse," I stammered, "the icehouse, you—you see."

Then I stared at him, as if he could divine what I could not bring myself to say. He looked back at me steadily, but with such weariness that my heart broke.

At last the words came. "Lady Ingram—Lady Ingram is in the icehouse. And she is no more."

Now it was he who stared at me, as if I were a chair that had spoken. His lips moved, but no sounds emerged.

"I think you will wish to see it—to see her—for yourself," I managed.

An eternity passed before he said, "Lady Ingram? Lady Ingram in the—in this icehouse?"

I nodded helplessly, wishing I'd never agreed to be a harbinger of evil tiding.

"Are you absolutely sure?" he asked, his voice so quiet I had to strain to hear.

I could only nod with unhappy certainty.

He rose, poured a measure of whisky, and pressed the glass into my trembling hands. "I'll have Mrs. Sanborn send up a tea tray to your room. It has been an awful shock. Please go and take some rest."

I did not need to be encouraged twice.

But now, with the tea tray beside me, my cheeks scald as I recall my utter uselessness. He'd remembered to see to my well-being but I didn't even possess the presence of mind to comfort him. To declare my belief in *his innocence. My faith that the universe would not be so cruel as to saddle him with the blame for Lady Ingram's death.*

*Alas, all I did was babble something incoherent. Worse, as I left, I wished him good luck.*

*I should have at least told him that you would get to the bottom of the matter. That he was not alone in this dire misfortune. But at the time I fled with an unholy haste, only to moan and shiver in the tranquil loveliness of my room, no longer able to hold on to any illusion of sanctuary.*

*Please, Charlotte. You must help him.*

*Please.*

*Livia*

———

Someone was whimpering, pitiful, wounded sounds.

Mrs. Watson. She clamped a hand over her mouth, her mind a battlefield of fear and chaos.

Miss Holmes stood by the secretary, sealing a note. "Ma'am, will you kindly hand this to the messenger?"

Her request pulled Mrs. Watson out of her paralysis. Yes, disaster had fallen. And no, it was not the time to hide in a dark corner, rocking herself.

"Of—of course." She'd forgotten entirely that the messenger was waiting for a reply.

She did not forget to tip the boy. When he'd left, she rushed back to the sitting room, where Miss Holmes already had two fingers of whisky waiting for her.

"Oh, thank you, my dear." She finished the entire glass in one continuous gulp, her eyes watering from the fiery eau-de-vie.

"Are you all right, ma'am?"

"Please don't worry about me. I am most awfully unhappy but I

shall be fine. We must think only of Lord Ingram now. And goodness gracious, those poor children of his."

It was a moment before Mrs. Watson could go on. "And you,
Miss Holmes, are you all right?"

"As of yet, nothing has happened to Lord Ingram," said Miss
Holmes quietly. "I will be busy in the coming days. And I will require a great deal of help. May I count on you, ma'am?"

"Of course!" said Mrs. Watson, almost shouting.

Had Miss Holmes some floors to scrub, Mrs. Watson would
have attacked them with religious fervor, if only to keep herself
from sinking further into this pit of anxiety. A "great deal" of work
to help her help Lord Ingram? Mrs. Watson would have climbed
over a mountain of fire to pitch in.

"Excellent. You'll need your notebook to write everything down."

Mrs. Watson leaped up to retrieve her notebook. The more
tasks, the better.

Miss Holmes dictated for the next forty minutes. Some of what
she needed would have occurred to Mrs. Watson herself; others she
couldn't even guess the purpose of. Why, for instance, did they need
to hire two houses in London, in two very different districts?

Miss Holmes gave no explanations and Mrs. Watson asked for
none. When they finished, Miss Holmes rose. "Mrs. Watson, will
you help me dress?"

It was only a while later, when Mrs. Watson was alone in the
sitting room again, that she had the sense that something else was
wrong. She paced for several minutes before her gaze fell on the tea
tray: They had been about to have their afternoon tea when the
messenger had arrived with Miss Livia's note.

And in all that time since, Miss Holmes hadn't touched anything that had been laid out: Slices of butter cake, plum cake, and
Madeira cake lay neglected on their respective plates.

Before the immensity of Lord Ingram's misfortune, Miss Holmes, with her otherwise constant and unfailing adoration of baked goods, had lost her appetite.

The dread in Mrs. Watson's heart froze into terror.

❧

Lord Ingram gazed at his wife.

He had not believed Miss Olivia Holmes. Seeing her petrified bewilderment and feeling the tremor in her hand had not shaken him from the belief that it must all be an enormous misunderstanding.

And *only* an enormous misunderstanding.

His wife's dead eyes killed that particular belief.

*Alexandra*, her name came to him unbidden. He had not thought of her as such in a very long time. Had referred to her, even in the privacy of his mind, only as his wife. And not with the pride and possessive zeal of a new husband, who had held her and whispered, *My wife.*

*My wife.*

*My wife.*

*My wife.*

*My heart*, he had meant then, *my sky, the center of my universe.*

He had been all goodwill and shining innocence. A man incapable of imagining that someday *my wife* would signify *my error, my shame, my ineluctable punishment.*

"My deepest condolences, my lord. It is a terrible misfortune."

Slowly he turned his head. Lady Avery stood beside him, peering up.

"A terrible misfortune indeed," he echoed woodenly, returning his attention to the woman in the ice well.

She looked . . . ungainly. After the birth of their second child, she had never moved as easily or gracefully as she had earlier. But even so, she would have been displeased, had she seen herself thus: her chin jutting out, her lips slack, her feet inelegantly splayed.

The urge rose to do something so that her posture would have met her own standard of acceptability.

Instead he tightened his fingers into a fist.

Her face, during the years of their marriage, had become squarer, harsher. Despite that, she would have remained lovely for at least another decade, before settling into middle-aged handsomeness, her erstwhile incandescent beauty something for others to reminisce about, and perhaps sigh over.

But death had robbed her of something essential. Her features were very much as he remembered, yet she looked a stranger, and not exactly an attractive one.

Dimly it occurred to him that he didn't want his children to see her like this. Let them remember the mother they loved as living and beautiful. Let them never witness the corpse that had nothing of her left, bad or good.

"We didn't know Lady Ingram had returned from Switzerland," said Lady Avery, her voice an artillery boom in the silence.

He turned to her again, still in a fog of numbness. "Neither did I."

"How do you suppose she came to be here?"

"I am as bewildered as you are, my lady." The deep-seated cold of the icehouse enveloped him, seeping in from every pore. He willed himself not to shiver. "Ladies, you will be much more comfortable in the manor. I will wait here for the police."

"We will wait with you," said Lady Avery, without a moment's hesitation. "We don't mind a little cold."

"And we are not bewildered," added her sister. "Only outraged."

*Outraged.*

He supposed he ought to be, too. But he couldn't summon enough outrage, not when Lady Ingram's choices had led to the deaths of three agents of the Crown. Not when he could have told her that her own untimely demise would be the most likely outcome, once she lost her place at his side and could no longer supply intelligence to Moriarty.

Those who betrayed Moriarty faced execution. And those who became useless—a slightly gentler riddance?

He couldn't tell how she had died. She wore a promenade dress, which seemed stiff with newness. There were no visible wounds, no markings on the throat, or telltale streaks of blood on her clothes.

He stepped onto the lip of the ice well, intending to get inside and take a closer look.

Someone grabbed him by his coat. "I don't believe you should touch anything, sir."

He stared at Lady Somersby. This was his wife. His estranged wife, yes, but his wife nevertheless.

It occurred to him at the end of a very long moment, during which Lady Somersby's eyes blazed like Lady Justice's, with her blindfold ripped off, that she meant to prevent him from tampering with the site.

*Him.*

Fear snaked down his spine.

The gossip ladies believed that *he* was responsible for his wife's death.

That she had never been sent to Switzerland but had instead been murdered in cold blood.

Here in her own home.

# Seven

*Dear Livia,*

*I'm sorry to hear of your ordeal.*
*Please convey Mrs. Watson's and my deepest condolences to Lord Ingram, as well as our sympathy for his children.*

*Charlotte*

This was not what Livia had hoped for from her sister. She needed a muscular, cavalry-coming-over-the-hills message. She craved for Charlotte to declare, *The finest mind of her generation assures you with every solemnity that the culprit will be discovered in the next twenty-four hours. That Lord Ingram will emerge unscathed. And that all will be well, including you yourself, dearest Livia.*

A knock at the door startled her, but it was only a servant informing her that the guests were being assembled in the grand drawing room. Would Miss Holmes please go down as soon as possible?

Livia reached the open doors of the grand drawing room as the din of excited curiosity abated to a sober, almost fearful silence.

Lord Ingram stood by the fireplace, his hair windswept, his eyes hollow. "It is my great unhappiness to inform you that Lady Ingram has been found . . . dead on the property. The police have arrived to begin their investigation."

Silence. A cacophony of disbelief. Silence again as Lord Ingram raised his hand. "I do not know what happened—this has been a great shock. I do know that local constables will have some questions for you. Tomorrow an inspector from Scotland Yard might ask to speak to you again. Until then, please remain at Stern Hollow."

Again, a roar of incredulity and dismay.

Lord Ingram waited. In the morning, he'd looked as if he hadn't slept all night. Now, he appeared as if he'd never known a full-night's rest in his entire life, his weariness etched into every feature.

When the guests had quieted, he said, "Dinner will be served at the usual hour. I regret to say I will not be able to perform the duties of a host this evening. Forgive me. My staff will see to your needs. Ladies Avery and Somersby will answer your questions as best as they can."

He walked out of the drawing room, the crowd parting to let him through. Closing the doors, he held on to the door handle for a moment, as if not trusting that he would remain upright were he to let go.

All at once Livia understood that he was afraid, so afraid that he couldn't let anyone see it, lest everything he feared came true.

Not wanting to be seen by those inside the drawing room, she had taken a few steps back, out of their line of sight. Now she rushed forward and took his hands.

"It'll be all right, my lord! Charlotte won't let anything happen to you. She'll find out the truth."

He looked as if he was about to say something but changed his mind. "Yes, I'm sure everything will be fine. I hope this has not been too distressing for you, Miss Holmes."

Livia had no idea what she said next. They spoke for a little longer before he excused himself and headed in the direction of the library. She squared her shoulders, took several deep breaths, and yanked open the doors of the drawing room.

Lord Ingram had not named her to answer questions for the guests, but she intended her voice to be heard tonight. Ladies Avery and Somersby did not know what happened to Lady Ingram any better than Livia did, and she'd be damned if she allowed them to besmirch Lord Ingram's good name with insinuations and irresponsible conjectures.

Days of premonition had not prepared her for what awaited her in the icehouse, but she no longer had the luxury of cowering in her room and hoping someone else would ride to the rescue. By God, she would defend him or go down trying.

---

Lord Ingram received the police sergeant in the library. The trio of constables he had brought would make a tally of guests and servants and question every last one. But Sergeant Ellerby had reserved for himself the initial interviews with the four witnesses who'd stumbled upon the body—and the master of Stern Hollow.

Lord Ingram had met county inspectors who had spent decades dealing with the darkest underbelly of London, world-weary men who had seen every variant of greed, cruelty, and criminal ingenuity. Sergeant Ellerby was not such a man. He was visibly affected by both the opulence of the house and the possibility that the offspring of a duke had slain his own wife.

Mrs. Sanborn, the housekeeper, entered behind Sergeant Ellerby, carrying a tea tray. She poured for the men and left quietly.

"Cream? Sugar?" Lord Ingram inquired, his voice suitably courteous.

"Neither, thank you."

"I'd offer you something stronger, Sergeant, but I imagine that would be frowned upon."

"Indeed it would. But please, my lord, take what you need. This is a day that calls for potent spirits."

Lord Ingram filled a glass with whisky. He didn't love intoxicants a quarter as much as Charlotte Holmes relished baked goods, but his capacity for spirits rivaled hers for cake. And tonight he intended to put that capacity to use.

A hard-drinking man was less likely to give the impression of being calculating.

He took a large swallow of the amber liquid, wincing as his throat burned. "What may I do for you, Sergeant?"

"The two ladies at the site, if you remember, sir, asked to speak to me."

He remembered very well. Lady Avery and Lady Somersby had all but grabbed the sergeant by the ear and demanded that he listen. Lord Ingram had left them to it and departed first. It would not surprise him if the ladies had spoken so much and at such a furious pace that Sergeant Ellerby's head spun.

"Lady Avery and Lady Somersby are Society's premier gossip historians. They must have had a great deal of useful particulars to impart."

His words appeared neutral; they were anything but. Sergeant Ellerby might be an intelligent man who was good at his work, but he was not accustomed to the forceful personalities of the gossip ladies and might very well have been resentful of the way they attempted to educate him of everything they deemed he must know and understand.

Out of deference to their age and rank, he would have tried to suppress his irritation at being told how to do his work. But when Lord Ingram pointed out that the women were known primarily for gossiping, he gave Sergeant Ellerby the excuse he likely already wanted to dismiss their theories.

Lord Ingram knew that Lady Avery and Lady Somersby were meticulous. They knew they were meticulous. But Sergeant Ellerby did not. Between the master of this impeccable estate and two matrons of middling attractiveness who wouldn't shut up, Lord Ingram had a very good idea whom the sergeant might believe more.

But that was true of a hypothetical county sergeant. There was always the possibility that *this* man had listened closely to the gossip ladies and realized what an invaluable source of information he had stumbled across. He might also view the master of this impeccable estate with commensurate suspicion, because a man whose home was perfect to the last detail was unlikely to give anything of himself away, except by design.

"Ah, no wonder they went on and on," said Sergeant Ellerby, clarifying for Lord Ingram where he stood on the spectrum, which was not very far from where Lord Ingram preferred him to be.

"I have heard from my staff that since their arrival, they have been inquiring into my wife's whereabouts—and the details of the night of her birthday ball, when she was last seen."

On that night, he had confronted her—and told her to leave. And then he had waited twenty-four hours before informing Bancroft of her crimes, so that she would have time to run far, far away.

Not far away enough, as it turned out.

"Did the ladies' meddling disturb you?" asked the sergeant.

"Yes, but not for reasons they would consider likely." Lord Ingram downed another draught of whisky. "I had hoped the truth would never come to light, because what happened to me is something I would not wish on my worst enemy."

Sergeant Ellerby had his notebook out. "And what exactly happened to you, my lord?"

❧

"Mr. Walsh, there is a gentleman by the name of Holmes to see you, sir," said the young footman to Stern Hollow's steward.

Within the past hour, Mr. Walsh had fended off, on his master's behalf, two men from two different county gazettes, a vicar and a rector, and three local ladies who had been acquainted with Lady Ingram and thought it their duty to call on her bereaved husband. Tragedy brought out the worst in people, he was now thoroughly convinced—and was very much in the mood to have the latest caller forcibly ejected from the house.

Preferably on his rear.

"And what does this Mr. Holmes want?" asked Mr. Walsh, scraping together what remained of his forbearance. "Any relation to our guest Miss Holmes?"

"I don't know, sir. He says he's been sent from Eastleigh Park."

Eastleigh Park was the seat of His Grace the Duke of Wycliffe, Lord Ingram's eldest brother. Mr. Walsh felt a tremor underfoot. Had the duke sent an emissary to berate his brother? Surely, tonight could not possibly be the time for it.

And how long could Mr. Walsh stall the emissary, if it came to that? How long could he protect Lord Ingram from this wrath from above?

"Where is he now? Still in the waiting room?"

"Yes, sir."

"Have tea sent to my office immediately."

Mr. Walsh put on his haughtiest mien and marched into the waiting room. If the duke had sent a flinty-eyed agent, let him see that Lord Ingram was not without foot soldiers of his own, willing to brave the front lines.

The young man in the waiting room sported a thick but well-groomed beard, topped off with a meticulously pomaded handlebar mustache, the ends of which curled up nearly an inch.

At Mr. Walsh's entrance, he rose. "Mr. Walsh, I presume? Sherrinford Holmes. I take it from your steely expression that you believe His Grace sent me."

Mr. Walsh blinked. "Do you mean to imply, Mr. Holmes, that you haven't been sent by His Grace?"

"No." The young man smiled slightly. "Not to say he won't dispatch someone, or perhaps even himself, in the coming days. But I have been tasked by Her Grace the Duchess of Wycliffe to see to Lord Ingram. Difficult days are ahead and she believes that he should have an ally at his side."

Relief and gratitude inundated Mr. Walsh.

Briefly.

It was all well and good to send an ally, but this Mr. Holmes . . .

He was barely medium height and surprisingly portly for his age, which, despite his abundance of facial hair, couldn't be more than twenty-five or twenty-six. Notwithstanding his rotundity, he was dressed nattily, his clothes of good material and superior workmanship. In fact, there was a great deal more than nattiness here: Mr. Holmes was dressed *extravagantly*.

The gold-and-sapphire-striped velvet waistcoat; the complicated, multi-tiered knot of the necktie; the boutonniere of three round, bright yellow craspedia flowers arranged against the iridescent eye of a peacock feather. From his watch fob hung an enamel peacock feather that matched the real one on his lapel. As he drew his watch out to check the time, he also extracted a monocle and screwed it into the socket of his right eye—a monocle the rim of which was actually, when Mr. Walsh looked closely, a serpent eating its own tail.

In his most desperate hour, Lord Ingram had received, for his only ally, a raging dandy.

"And you are just the person I wish to see, Mr. Walsh," said the dandy. "I will need to speak to the outdoor staff first thing tomorrow—and will depend on you to take the arrangement in hand. But tonight, the indoor staff are my object.

"You will please send me, one by one, those who have already spoken to the police. Any lists you have of their names, ages, positions, et cetera, would be profoundly appreciated. I shall need to borrow a corner of the domestic offices, preferably a quiet and secluded one, to conduct these interviews. And if Mrs. Sanborn would kindly make ready a room on the nursery floor, so I will be out of the other guests' way, she would have my eternal gratitude."

Mr. Walsh blinked again. "Would that be all, Mr. Holmes?"

"I should like to take a quick look at his lordship's and her ladyship's apartments before I speak with your underlings. Would you be able to accompany me there?"

Mr. Walsh hesitated.

"Is Lord Ingram speaking to the police at the moment?" inquired Mr. Holmes.

"Yes."

"If you need to, please ask him right now whether he will permit me into his rooms. Otherwise time is of the essence."

Mr. Walsh acquiesced. The tour of Lord Ingram's rooms was quick. That through Lady Ingram's, even quicker.

When Mr. Holmes had taken a seat at Mr. Walsh's desk and poured himself a cup of tea, he said, "By the way, even though Her Grace is more than capable of holding her own with His Grace, there's no need to mention my presence to him or anyone he sends."

"How should I tell the rest of the staff who you are, then?"

"You may say that I am a friend of Lord Ingram's, here to do a friend's duty."

He smiled as he spoke, a rather ironic smile at that, but his tone was firm to the point of severity. Mr. Walsh took note: Mr. Holmes's arrival in Stern Hollow was not to be breathed to anyone from Eastleigh Park.

"Do you think, Mr. Holmes, that anything we do can be of the slightest help to Lord Ingram?"

The question wiped the smile from Mr. Holmes's face. He sighed. "It is not a good situation, Mr. Walsh. There will not be any direct evidence linking Lord Ingram to Lady Ingram's death, but circumstantial evidence will be profuse and, almost without exception, unfavorable."

Mr. Walsh swallowed.

Mr. Holmes looked him squarely in the eye. "But I am here, now. And I am his last, best hope."

## Eight

It was eleven o'clock at night when Charlotte finished speaking to the last of the indoor staff. She jotted down a few notes from the final interview and looked over the list of men and women to whom she had spoken.

Normally she wouldn't need notes. But normally she did not meet forty strangers in a row.

A knock came at the door. "Enter," she said, expecting Mr. Walsh, back to conduct her to her room.

Lord Ingram walked in. He looked drained. But as he saw her, a glimmer of light returned to his eyes.

She leaned back and crossed her arms in front of her chest, her elbows resting comfortably upon the padding that formed Sherrinford Holmes's paunch. "Hullo, Ash."

"I thought I heard the sound of cake disappearing from the—" He glanced at the tea tray, back at her, then at the tea tray again. "What is this? Did Mr. Walsh replenish the cake plates recently—or did you not touch anything?"

Sweet things placed before her usually disappeared: Hunger wasn't necessary; cake tasted just as good accompanied by preoccupation, concern, or even boredom. The moment she'd read Livia's letter, however, it was as if her stomach had turned into stone. The refreshments Mr. Walsh had laid out might as well have been made of wax, for all the interest they stirred in her.

But did she want Lord Ingram to know that—yet?

She covered half of her face. "You must not think, sir, that this is a common occurrence. I . . . I don't know what happened. I assure you that the vast, vast majority of the time my appetite is as stiff as a flagpole and just as sizable. I am as shocked as you are by this inexplicable inability to perform."

Different gradients of incredulity flickered across his face, as he no doubt tried to decide whether she truly was comparing her lack of appetite to an instance of impotence.

"Did you have a particularly plentiful tea at home?" he asked after a while.

He was not getting off the subject; she hadn't thought he would, either. "My sister's note came just as we sat down to tea. So . . . no."

He peered at her, his brow furrowed. When he spoke again, his voice was low and tight. "Don't tell me you last ate more than eight hours ago. You are scaring me."

She exhaled. "You should be terrified. I am."

She had gone into the village to hire a trap at the railway station to ferry her to Stern Hollow. And had stood outside the station for a quarter of an hour, not because there were no carriages to be had but because she needed to pull herself together.

He gripped the back of the chair behind which he stood. Two seconds later he let go. "Come. I told Mr. Walsh I would take you to your rooms. There's supper waiting, too."

She rose, rubbing a sore spot on her back, only to remember that her padding went all the way around. "You aren't as good at feeding me as Lord Bancroft, but in a pinch, you'll do."

He gave her a severe look but did not dispute her claim.

Rooms had been assigned to her on the nursery level, as she'd requested—but they were nicer than she'd anticipated. Usually extra chambers this high up were seldom used and extremely plain, even in the grandest households. But hers was an apartment, sitting room, bedroom, dressing room, *and* its own attached bath and water closet.

"I used to stay here, when I came to visit my godfather. It suits Sherrinford Holmes's purpose, I take it?"

"It does."

"There's a safe in the wall. I'll give you the combination before I leave. And I've told Mrs. Sanborn that you hate disturbances in the morning. No maids are to come in to sweep the grate or relight the fire while you're still sleeping."

"Thank you."

She half expected him to leave, but he only stared at her, leaning against the door. As the silence was about to become too taut, the corners of his lips quivered.

"I will have you know that Sherrinford Holmes cuts a dashing figure," she protested. "Or at least he believes he does. And you will not go around injuring that poor man's feelings."

He cleared his throat. "I apologize."

Immediately his lips quivered again. Then he burst out laughing—and kept laughing.

He had the most attractive laughter.

"Poor Sherry will never forgive you!"

But still he couldn't stop, until she sighed and ripped off both her mustache and beard.

He straightened and cleared his throat. "I do apologize."

"You had better not do that when we are in front of other people."

"I won't." He looked down for a moment. "Thank you."

"You knew I would come."

"I meant, thank you for your ridiculous yet sublime disguise. When I understood that I would most likely be accused of Lady Ingram's murder, I thought I would never smile again, let alone laugh like a loon."

She hadn't seen him laugh much even otherwise—these had not been the best years of his life.

He pushed away from the door. "The skin on your face is a bit red."

She patted tentatively at her cheeks. "Mrs. Watson warned that the glue might be irritating. I'll have to work fast, so that I don't do irreparable damage to my otherwise beautiful visage."

"How fast can you work? Can you clear my name before I head to the gallows?"

"I'm sure Lord Bancroft will arrange for an escape, should your trial go ill."

All traces of mirth disappeared from his face. "But you think there will be a trial?"

"If you were someone looking at this case from the outside, what conclusions would you draw?"

He crossed the sitting room to where supper had been laid and pulled out a chair for her. "I already know what everyone else will think. But what about the great Sherlock Holmes? What unique light can he shed on the situation?"

"You saw the body. Was it really Lady Ingram?"

"I didn't go over every inch of her with a magnifying glass, but I'm afraid so."

Charlotte sighed, sat down, and removed the domed lid from her supper tray. Underneath was a small raised pie and a slice of charlotte russe, with beautifully striated vanilla-and-chocolate layers of Bavarian cream.

She picked up her knife and fork and cut into the raised pie. "Neither Sherlock Holmes nor his brother, Sherrinford Holmes, who is just as brilliant but not inclined to go around solving strangers' problems, can fathom why Lady Ingram lies dead in the icehouse."

Lord Ingram sat down opposite. "Even as I stared at her, I couldn't stop thinking that it was a ruse on her part to have me hanged for her murder so that she could then sweep back in and reclaim the children."

"Maybe that's exactly what this is. Maybe that's her secret twin sister in the icehouse. And the real Lady Ingram is waiting in the wings, cackling with anticipation."

"If she had a secret sister, whom none of us had ever heard of, I doubt that she is cruel enough to have the poor woman killed so that I could be framed for a crime I didn't commit." He raised his chin at her. "And don't just push food around on your plate. Eat."

She lifted a forkful of the pie, which had a game filling with a quail egg at its center, to her mouth. "What if the secret sister died of natural causes, and Lady Ingram simply made use of a convenient corpse?"

The game pie was delicious and she did not want another bite.

"Come to think of it, I couldn't tell how she died. She was fully clothed, and ladies Avery and Somersby wouldn't let me into the ice well." He shook his head. "No, we're speaking nonsense. This had to be Moriarty's doing."

"But from his perspective, it makes almost as little sense."

"Why so little? She was no longer useful to Moriarty. And she was hunted by Bancroft. Moriarty could very well decide to rid himself of such a liability. And then he could decide to make me pay, for disturbing his cozy little arrangement."

"First, I disagree that Lady Ingram became useless when she could no longer spy on Lord Bancroft. She was beautiful, intelligent, and ruthless. Such a woman would be an asset in many situations.

"Second, while Lord Bancroft is a dangerous man to cross, his reach is finite. Correct me if I'm wrong, but his agents have other missions they must see to, do they not? I imagine that at any given moment, only so many of them can be spared to hunt down Lady Ingram, and perhaps none at all."

He did not correct her; she went on. "Third, personal enmity exists only between you and Lady Ingram. I am almost certain Moriarty feels no particular animosity toward you—or Lord Bancroft, for that matter—much in the way that a clever criminal is wary of the law but does not hate every constable he encounters.

"To make you pay, as you say, would require him not only to kill a potentially valuable agent but then to concoct an elaborate scheme to transport her body to your estate just when guests, whom you had not planned on having, would be on hand to stumble onto said body. What does that gain him, professionally?"

"Not much," admitted Lord Ingram. "I have no interest in hunting down Lady Ingram, so that cannot be a reason for eliminating me. And if Moriarty thinks to injure Bancroft by sending me to the gallows, then he doesn't know Bancroft at all."

He reached forward and broke off a piece of the game pie's hot-water crust.

"You didn't have dinner?"

He shook his head.

"So I not only brought back your sense of humor, I also restored your appetite."

"Time restored my appetite. You happen to have food in front of you."

This made her smile slightly. His gaze lingered on her face a second longer than was entirely appropriate.

She pushed the substantial pie toward him. "Have it. But don't touch my charlotte russe."

"I make no promises."

"Then I had better eat it all before you finish the pie."

They were silent for some time, he eating steadily, she less so. He must have noticed, for he asked, "Why are *you* terrified?"

She had swept a dollop of Bavarian cream from the charlotte russe onto the plate and was playing with it. She stopped and looked him in the eye. "Where are your children, Ash?"

"With Remington—you know that."

"After what happened with Lady Ingram, I could have sworn you would never let them out of your sight again. What changed your mind?"

"Your sister once told me that you didn't speak until you were four and a half. I'm sure you were under great pressure to say something, anything, from the moment you could walk. But you waited until you were ready and not a moment before.

"Children are people. They have their own minds. I have never been the kind of parent to impose my own will at any cost. Lucinda and Carlisle wanted to go with Remington, and in the end they got their way."

Charlotte dabbed a napkin at her lips. Did she believe him?

In the middle of her first major case, Lord Ingram and Mrs. Watson had "met" at 18 Upper Baker Street, Mrs. Watson's property that had been staged as Sherlock Holmes's residence. Mrs. Watson had attired herself as the landlady, Mrs. Hudson, in a padded dress, a gray wig, and wire-rimmed glasses. Lord Ingram had looked upon her with unease and mistrust. And pointedly asked Charlotte whether, if it were anyone else, she wouldn't have considered it too good to be true that she had randomly encountered a demimondaine who not only took her in but enthusiastically supported her powers of deduction.

When he himself, as Charlotte would later discover, had sent Mrs. Watson to assist her—Mrs. Watson, his trusted friend, whom he'd known for longer than he had known Charlotte Holmes.

He had been so good an actor, so convincing in his display of rigid displeasure, that she, despite her powers of observation, had believed entirely in his disapproval of Mrs. Watson. Had not in the least suspected that he had conspired with the latter to provide assistance to her, in those desperate days after she'd run away from home, when she was perilously low on both funds and choices.

Across the table he took a slow bite of the game pie, studying her as she studied him, his gaze steady, opaque.

He had told her before that she was the best liar he knew, a prodigious, possibly generational, talent. She had not thought the same of him—perhaps because their interactions had been characterized by so much silence. But when she had confronted him, after finding out that he had been friends with Mrs. Watson all along, this had been his response: *I have said a great many things to you that are convenient, rather than truthful.*

What was he telling her now, the truth, or something more convenient?

"You've met with Sergeant Ellerby."

He narrowed his eyes at the change of subject. "Yes."

"You told him as much of the truth as you could, I take it, since lying at this point would lead only to further incrimination."

"Correct."

"You spoke calmly and conducted yourself with a dignity befitting your station, no doubt. But at the same time, you let him see your fingers tremble when you picked up that glass of spirits. From time to time, you stopped speaking to pull yourself together. And of course, you made yourself sound increasingly hoarse as the interview wore on, a man buffeted and battered by the unkindness of the universe."

His grip tightened on his fork and knife. "He was the first person I needed to convince of my innocence."

"Precisely. Why didn't you expend any effort to convince *me*, just now?"

"You can speak to anyone on the staff—Remington was here and he left with the children."

"I don't propose to dispute what everyone *saw*. What I need is the reason for their departure."

"I told you—"

"Be careful what you say to me. I have not in the least eliminated the possibility that you are the one who killed Lady Ingram, accidentally or intentionally, when she came to abduct Lucinda and Carlisle."

———※———

"Who is that?" murmured Alice, leaning into Treadles's dressing room. "Are you headed somewhere?"

Treadles buttoned his jacket. "Chief Inspector Fowler. He wants me to accompany him on a case."

Alice blinked. She had already been abed, probably asleep when the commotion of the late-night caller arose. "It must be a major case, then, if they've put him on it. And if he's asked you for help."

"It is a major case." He straightened the knot of his necktie and did not look at her. "Lady Ingram."

She gasped. "What?"

"Apparently everyone believed her to be overseas, but she was found dead this afternoon on the grounds of Stern Hollow."

He hadn't known anything about Lady Ingram's whereabouts—he hadn't written Lord Ingram since before the end of summer; nor Lord Ingram him. And without that correspondence, he had few means of obtaining Lord Ingram's news—they moved in very different circles and shared no mutual friends.

Except Sherlock Holmes, once upon a time.

"Doesn't Chief Inspector Fowler know that you are acquainted with Lord Ingram?"

Treadles stuffed a folded handkerchief into his pocket, only to realize he already had one. "He does. I expect that's why he has chosen me, because I'll be able to help him assess Lord Ingram."

Which could constitute the entirety of his duties on this case. Chief Inspector Fowler had strong ideas on how subordinates ought to behave. Treadles might be an inspector in his own right, but with Fowler in charge, he suspected his own role would amount to no more than that of a stenographer.

Not to mention, he would need to be careful in both speech and action so that he didn't come across as an advocate for Lord Ingram.

"Surely they don't suspect *him* of complicity in her death."

"I don't know enough yet," he lied.

*In cases like this, it's almost certain that the husband is responsible,* Chief Inspector Fowler had once told him on a different but similar case. And he would not have sought Treadles if he didn't already believe that he had a plum of a target in Lord Ingram.

Alice clutched at the lapels of her dressing gown. "Lord Ingram is our friend."

"And I am a policeman." He lifted his always-ready travel bag. "If he is not guilty, he has nothing to fear."

"But Chief Inspector Fowler is the Bloodhound of the Yard. They are not sending him out if they think the butler did it."

The handkerchief in his other hand he shoved into his pocket, only to realize it was the same extra handkerchief from earlier.

She took it from him—and wrapped her fingers around his hand. "Robert, are you all right?"

*No. I'm afraid for Lord Ingram and I don't know what to do.*

He gave Alice a perfunctory kiss and left before he could betray the depth of his fear.

❈

Lord Ingram shot out of his chair. He paced in the room, a caged animal barred in every direction. Dimly he was aware that Holmes watched him, her otherwise blankly limpid eyes not without a measure of compassion.

He braced his hands on the mantel. A fire roared in the grate and he couldn't feel the heat at all. The chill of the icehouse had crept inside his spine, its arctic dominion spilling vertebra by vertebra.

She came to stand next to him. "I'm sorry."

"It's not your fault," he said, barely able to hear his own voice. "But what am I to do?"

The forces arrayed against him were legion. The cold had spread to his lungs. A little more and his courage would fail altogether.

She spoke and he tried to listen. But her words rode over him like an advancing glacier, annihilating and endlessly cold.

When she finished speaking, she slipped away. He was bereft—and afraid in a different way. With Holmes there was always the possibility that she would leave him alone to pick up the pieces.

But she came back—and wrapped an arm about his middle. This was unlike her. She had kissed him twice, more than ten years apart, and propositioned him from time to time; yet he maintained a distinct impression that she found touching to be an odd and sometimes discomfiting experience.

*Charlotte doesn't like to be hugged*, Miss Olivia Holmes had once said, rather sadly, in his hearing.

But Holmes did not disengage. In fact, she placed both arms around him, and rested her cheek against his back.

It had been a very, very long time since a woman had embraced him. As his astonishment receded, her warmth seeped into his rigid frame.

He felt less chilled.

Less isolated.

Every day he moved among people, dozens, sometimes hundreds of people: family, friends, neighbors, classmates, archaeological colleagues, fellow agents of the Crown, and this was not accounting for his staff and ranks upon ranks of acquaintances. But he had been alone for a long time and had reinforced that loneliness even as he had despaired of ever being anything but alone.

Her touch, however, unleashed a monstrous need, so immense and chaotic he couldn't be sure what he hungered for, or even whether he wished to take—or to give. He held still, terrified of this need, and just as terrified that she had already taken its measure, she who saw too much and gleaned everything.

But as her warmth poured into him, as she remained where she was, not leaving him to cope on his own, his hand lifted to rest against the back of hers, his fingertips brushing against the cuff of her sleeve.

It dawned on him that she was no longer wearing her jacket, waistcoat, and paddings. A man's shirt was far more modest than the bodice of a ball gown—and he had seen her in plenty of those. But underneath the shirt she wore no corset, and through the layers of his own clothes he discerned the shape of her, pressed into his back.

Twenty-four hours ago he would have considered this impossible, that he and Holmes would be in each other's arms—and that he wouldn't immediately pull away. He had not written her since summer because even though Lady Ingram was never coming back, he remained a married man with nothing of value—at least in his own view—to offer her.

But everything had changed in a single day. He was no longer a married man. And at any moment he could lose his freedom—and possibly his life.

He did not move again. Not because he might startle her—she had ever been imperturbable in these matters. But because *he* was startled. He had thought he knew everything there was to know about his desire. Had considered it, so long fettered and trammeled, as tame, or at least manageable.

When it had always been feral. Primal.

Her lips touched his nape, just above the rim of his collar. He spun around, cupped her face, and kissed her on the mouth, a kiss that he might never be able to stop.

She was the one who eased them apart—and combed her fingers through his hair. "You are welcome to stay."

He rested his forehead against hers. He wanted to. Badly. But not with his wife's body still in the icehouse. "Tomorrow."

"Then get some sleep. You must be exhausted."

He'd taken a nap in the afternoon—and had slept like the dead until he was awakened to meet a frantic Miss Olivia Holmes. Still, he found himself swaying on his feet.

"Good night," he murmured, kissing her on the cheek. "Scotland Yard arrives in the morning."

Her lips curved, a barely there smile. "Let them come," she said. "And let them do their worst."

# Nine

Ironic that Treadles entered Lord Ingram's home for the first time not as a friend but a policeman.

It was also the first time that he investigated the death of someone he had met.

A few months ago, in the course of a different investigation, he had walked past Lord Ingram's town house in London. At the same time, Lord Ingram had emerged from the house and Lady Ingram from her carriage. The greeting between the two had been so aloof that Treadles, who had never seen Lady Ingram before, had almost mistaken them for strangers who happened to cross paths. There had been none of the smoldering tension that one sometimes encountered between former lovers, only a void, a complete absence of affection.

On that day he'd understood why Lady Ingram never attended her husband's lectures or accompanied him on his digs. On that day he'd also understood that he'd never be invited into Lord Ingram's home, as long as Lady Ingram, who took no pleasure at all in meeting him, drew up guest lists and seating charts. Not that he'd expected or even wished for such an invitation, his station in life being so far inferior. Nor would he accuse her of any particular snobbishness; her dislike of him had been impersonal, indifferent, a mere reflection of the vast distance between her husband and herself.

It was the first and last time he saw Lady Ingram alive. He had left the encounter deeply saddened, but without the slightest premonition that tragedy would strike within months. Or that suspicions would fall squarely upon Lord Ingram.

"Lovely," murmured Chief Inspector Fowler, when the manservant who greeted them had gone to inform the master of the house of their arrival. "As immaculate as the grounds."

The entrance hall was white-and-gold marble. Fluted columns soared forty feet to a blue cupola. An avenue of statues led toward a grand double-return staircase.

"That is a Rubens. Those two are Rembrandts, if I'm not mistaken," said Fowler, squinting through his wire-rimmed spectacles at paintings on distant walls. "And the three over there should all be Turners. We could be looking at a spectacular collection, Inspector."

Although Treadles had acquired a decent education in the history of art through his wife, he ventured no opinions of his own, beyond an "I'm sure you are right, Chief Inspector."

Fowler might appear friendly, even genial at times, but Treadles had learned not to trust that seeming affability. There was something predatory about him, a too-strong enjoyment in the nabbing of suspects. It was likely the man had no interest at all in justice, but only in the exercise of power.

And now he had Lord Ingram in his sights.

The manservant returned to lead them to his master. Beyond the entrance hall they crossed a picture gallery, three-stories high, glass-roofed, and dense with oils and sculptures. Fowler shook his head in admiration, whether at the abundance of artwork or the soaring architecture, Treadles couldn't be sure. Perhaps both.

Treadles had known that Lord Ingram was well-situated in life. But well-situated could mean a prestigious title and not much else. He'd had no idea of the depth and extent of his friend's wealth.

If he had, would that have prevented him from forming this friendship? Would he have been too conscious of his own ordinary origins?

They were brought to a two-story library that must house a collection of at least ten thousand volumes. Books lined all four walls. And the ceiling had been painted with a trompe l'oeil mural that made it seem as if the shelves reached up all the way to a bright blue sky, where chiton-clad philosophers from Classical Antiquity looked down in benign amusement.

On this cold morning, all three fireplaces in the library had been lit. By the largest fireplace stood Lord Ingram, somehow not at all dwarfed by the scale and magnificence of his home. He didn't look very different from how Treadles remembered him, but there was a grimness to the set of his features, a resolve that implied not so much confidence as a willingness to endure.

Treadles had debated, before boarding the late train, whether he ought to cable Lord Ingram. He'd decided against it—he would be arriving at Stern Hollow in an official capacity. And Lord Ingram would have already been told to expect Scotland Yard.

As Lord Ingram's gaze landed on him, however, he felt a rush of self-reproach, as if he had sneaked in and been discovered.

Nothing to do now but be the policeman he was.

Lord Ingram nodded with perfect correctness. "Good morning, Inspector Treadles. A pleasure to see you again."

"Likewise, my lord. May I present Chief Inspector Fowler?"

Fowler half bowed.

"Welcome to Stern Hollow, Chief Inspector," said Lord Ingram. He gestured at a man who had been studying what looked to be a large map of the estate when the policemen arrived. "Gentlemen, this is my friend Mr. Sherrinford Holmes. Holmes, Chief Inspector Fowler and Inspector Treadles of Scotland Yard."

At the sound of "Holmes," Treadles glanced sharply at the rotund, dark-haired young man, all monocle and exaggerated mustache.

Mr. Holmes bowed with a flourish.

Small talk was exchanged, on the policemen's journey, the weather, and the general efficacy of local constables.

"A county sergeant who knows enough to immediately send for Scotland Yard is, of course, always a praiseworthy one," said Mr. Holmes, smiling.

"Oh, I shall not disagree with that," said Fowler, with an unforced heartiness.

Treadles, on the other hand, wondered whether he heard something in Mr. Holmes's tone—not snide, merely amused.

Finally, Lord Ingram stated the purpose of the gathering. "I understand, gentlemen, that you would like to see the body."

Fowler did not immediately answer. Instead, he studied Lord Ingram, who met his gaze steadily. Treadles held his breath. Mr. Holmes, however, didn't seem the slightest bit concerned—Mr. Holmes who had never seen Chief Inspector Fowler at work.

After what seemed an interminable interval, Fowler finally said, "Yes, we would. Thank you."

"I will show you to the icehouse," said Lord Ingram with the evenness of a man with a clear conscience.

Or so it sounded to Treadles. Would Chief Inspector Fowler hear in that levelness of voice a clever murderer who had every confidence he would emerge unscathed?

"I have asked Mr. Holmes to accompany us," Lord Ingram went on. "This is a difficult time and I find myself in need of support, both moral and practical. I hope you will indulge me in this, gentlemen."

His words had the gloss of a request, but they were, in fact, an announcement. Mr. Holmes was coming with, and that was that.

"Certainly, my lord," answered Fowler, with apparent generosity.

Mr. Holmes paired up with Fowler; Treadles had to walk alongside Lord Ingram. Behind them Mr. Holmes answered Fowler's questions in a pleasantly baritone voice, though his enunciation wasn't as clear as Treadles expected, almost as if he spoke with a piece of boiled sweet in his mouth.

*Indeed, his lordship and I have been friends since we were children.*

*Yes, I knew her ladyship, too. What a sad and terrible fate for such a beautiful woman.*

*Oh, I happened to be in the neighborhood and thought I'd put myself at his lordship's disposal. Between you and me, Chief Inspector, I suspect he's letting me help more to be kind than because he believes I'll be of any actual use.*

There was something odd about Lord Ingram's friend, which had little to do with his almost coxcomb-ish appearance. Something contradictory yet strangely riveting. Despite the gravity of the situation, Treadles found himself wanting to stare at Mr. Holmes until he figured out what it was about the man that snared his attention like an itch in an unscratchable place. Failing that, since Mr. Holmes was currently behind his back, he listened to the latter's conversation with Fowler with far more attention than necessary.

Mr. Holmes began to question Fowler on the latter's customary practices at cases out of town. Treadles became aware that he hadn't spoken at all to Lord Ingram, and the length of his silence must border on unseemly. "My condolences, my lord," he said hastily, reddening.

"Thank you, Inspector."

"And the children, are they all right?"

"They are with my brother, and they have not been told yet." Lord Ingram exhaled. "So as of the moment, they are all right. But they are living in a soap bubble, and a storm of needles is on its way."

"I'm very sorry for their loss."

Lord Ingram exhaled again.

What had happened? How had everything gone so wrong? Not long ago Treadles had looked upon his friend with wholehearted and limitless admiration—that is, before he had learned the truth about Sherlock Holmes.

He caught himself. So often these days his thoughts began and ended with *before he had learned the truth about Sherlock Holmes.* And it was only recently that he had become aware of each instance.

Sherlock Holmes was not the First Coming. No one ought to reckon their days from her emergence on the scene. Not to mention, Lord Ingram's alienation from his wife had begun years ago. Treadles should have perceived sooner that all was not well.

But he had liked the idea that the great manors of the land housed harmonious families who embodied all the virtues that should naturally be present in lives so far removed from the strife of poverty and the narrowness of commerce.

Sometimes he *needed* that to be true. He encountered so much greed, stupidity, and ugliness. All that was base and tainted in human nature begged for a counterpoise in nobility and loftiness of character.

Before he had learned the truth about Sherlock Holmes, he had thought he had found such an ideal in Lord Ingram.

He winced at the direction in which his thoughts had once again strayed.

"Ah, that must be the icehouse," said Fowler.

Treadles was not intimately involved in the management of his household, but he knew that in warmer months, ice was delivered in blocks and kept in an ice safe. His late father-in-law, though a wealthy man, had not, as was often the case of those making a fortune in the Age of Steam, acquired a country house.

He had, therefore, no firsthand knowledge of how an estate dealt with the large amounts of ice required for its operations. Even after Fowler had pointed out the proximity of the icehouse, it took Treadles a moment to realize that he meant the grassy mound they were approaching.

He understood, from speaking to Sergeant Ellerby, that the previous day had been unseasonably warm. But overnight there had been a hard frost and the turf was encased in a crystalline membrane of ice that crunched audibly underfoot.

They rounded the mound, which wasn't the perfect hemisphere it appeared from the south, but more the shape of a pear, sliced in half along the length and tapering to the north. The entrance was located at the slenderer end, guarded by a police constable jumping in place to keep himself warm. At the approach of Scotland Yard, he saluted.

Chief Inspector Fowler didn't enter the structure immediately but made another slow tour of the exterior, Mr. Holmes in his wake. Treadles consulted a diagram that had been provided by Lord Ingram. The icehouse was built on a gentle slope to facilitate drainage, and the surrounding earth had been raised to insulate the most critical section, a brickwork, double-walled conical shaft with an interior diameter of ten feet at the top.

According to the diagram, at the bottom, the ice well narrowed to an opening two feet across, stoppered by a reed-covered grate, through which the melt seeped into an underground channel that conducted it, past an air trap, to the estate's own small dairy, keeping milk, cream, and butter cool.

The chamber that contained the ice well was finished with a double-walled domed roof, which was then blanketed by turf, making the icehouse appear a part of the landscape to anyone who didn't know what to look for.

When Fowler was ready, the constable unlocked the door.

"I'll wait for you outside," said Lord Ingram.

"And Mr. Holmes?" asked Fowler.

"Oh, I'm coming with," Mr. Holmes answered brightly. "Cheerio, Ash."

The first antechamber was a small, narrow tunnel, barely high enough for a grown man to stand straight. To Treadles it didn't feel perceptibly cooler than outside—in fact, shielded from the wind, it was more pleasant in temperature, if less fresh in the quality of its air.

The second antechamber was colder but not remarkably so.

Chief Inspector Fowler sniffed. "Doesn't smell much like a latrine, does it?"

"No," said Treadles.

Apparently the three ladies who had come through the icehouse all reported a foul odor in this particular antechamber—so foul that Lady Avery and Lady Somersby, while waiting for the police, had decided to wedge all the doors open to let the stench out.

The kitchen boy hadn't reported any odors. Then again, he'd suffered from a stuffed nose and hadn't been able to smell anything at all.

"I wonder about the reek the ladies noticed," murmured Mr. Holmes. "Curious, isn't it?"

When they reached the third antechamber, the cold bit into Treadles's face. He wound his muffler tighter about his neck.

The space, which functioned as a cold larder, was both wider and higher than the two previous ones. To the left hung game birds, sides of beef, and other butchered carcasses that he, not having spent much time in the country, couldn't readily identify. To the right, neat shelves held fruits, vegetables, and cheeses. Overhead, cured hams and sausages swayed gently from Fowler's exploratory touches.

In the middle of the antechamber lay an overturned wheelbarrow, the handle of which had fallen in such a way as to tip over a bucket of milk. Or so Scotland Yard had been informed—Sergeant Ellerby had allowed for the spill to be cleaned up.

The entire structure was windowless. At the opening of each door they had to light tapers. Inside the domed space that held the actual ice well, several lanterns had been brought in to add to the luminosity of the wall sconce.

Treadles lit all the light sources and then hastened to put his gloves back on. The cold of the ice chamber grew denser and sharper with every passing minute.

The initial report gave that Lady Ingram was lying atop a layer of wood shavings. Treadles had expected to find her halfway down the ten-foot-deep ice well; instead she was only eighteen inches or so below floor level, a great deal closer than he had anticipated.

"This is ice from last winter? Did it not melt at all?" he marveled.

"The construction here appears superb. And the bigger the volume, the longer the ice stays frozen," said Fowler. "Icehouses are usually built to hold enough ice for two years, in case any single winter is too feeble for proper replenishment."

"You are knowledgeable about icehouses, Chief Inspector," said Mr. Holmes.

"My father was in service, a member of the outdoor staff. It was among his duties to cut ice from the pond and resupply the icehouse." He indicated Lady Ingram with his walking stick. "At least ten inches of wood shavings on top, I'd expect. A good thing for us, or her ladyship would be stuck to the ice and we'd have a devil of a time getting her out.

"In fact, even less ice has melted than you suppose, Inspector.

Some should have been removed for use." Fowler turned to Mr. Holmes. "Would you agree, sir?"

"I would indeed. Although recently the need for ice has been minimal. The family—and a good portion of the staff—left for London shortly after Easter. Normally, upon their return, there would be guests. But this year, given Lady Ingram's absence, there have been none. Until now."

Mr. Holmes gave an absent-minded pat to his ample stomach. "I spoke to the staff. Before yesterday, the last time anyone came to fetch ice was when Lord Bancroft visited, some five weeks ago."

Treadles jotted down a reminder in his notebook to ask the servants to confirm this. Even though he wanted Lord Ingram cleared of any wrongdoing, he did not entirely trust Mr. Holmes,

"My wife enjoys perusing fancy housekeeping books," said Fowler. "If you listened to her, you'd think that in manors like this one, iced puddings and fruit ices are served year-round."

"It's expected that when a dinner is given, in town or in the country, that some kind of ice—or a number of them, depending on the scale of the occasion—will be served," answered Mr. Holmes. "And that is what 'fancy' housekeeping books concentrate on, those instances intended to impress others. But when people dine en famille, it's a different matter.

"In the case of Stern Hollow, Lady Ingram grew up in a household where ices were seldom served and never developed a taste for them. Lord Ingram is in general not particular about his food. As for the children, ice cream—or ices of any kind—is an occasional treat rather than an expected item in the nursery."

"The boy came yesterday to fetch the ice needed for last night's dinner," said Fowler. "But Lord Ingram's guests arrived in Stern Hollow the day before. What about that dinner? Did no one come to the icehouse in preparation for that occasion?"

"According to the cook, when the exodus from Mrs. Newell's

house came, in one of the luggage carts they brought the slab of ice that was already in their ice safe, so that it wouldn't go to waste. That slab was broken up, the resultant crushed ice put into freezing pots to facilitate the churning of various fruit ices for dinner. Therefore, there had been no need to visit the ice well the first day the guests were here."

Mr. Holmes made no mention of Lord Ingram's guilt or innocence, but it did not escape Treadles's attention that he had mounted a forceful argument for the latter: If Lord Ingram had killed his wife and kept her in the ice well, confident that no one would go there, then why hadn't he removed the body the moment he'd realized that large amounts of ice would be required for the guests abruptly thrust upon him? He would have had twenty-four hours to accomplish the deed.

Fowler said to Treadles, "Shall we take a closer look?"

The company climbed down into the ice well.

Lady Ingram was not frozen solid. Her clothes and the thick layer of wood shavings that covered the ice had kept her body at the ambient temperature, which, according to a thermometer on the wall, hovered a degree or two above freezing.

"No marks on her throat," noted Fowler.

After death, blood obeyed the law of gravity and pooled in the lowest part of the body. A supine corpse such as Lady Ingram's developed bruise-like discolorations on the back. But blood in the front of the body could be trapped by an injury to the flesh, depending on the nature of that injury.

"Was she lying in this exact position when she was found?" asked Mr. Holmes.

"Sergeant Ellerby reports that he turned her over briefly and then returned her as best as he could to the way he found her. And before that she had not been moved."

"Would it be logical to assume whoever had put her here carried her until they reached the lip of the ice well and then dropped her straight down?"

Chief Inspector Fowler, still crouched over the body, played with the small brush of a beard on his chin. "That would probably not be wrong."

"It will be difficult to judge when she died, I take it, given this inadvertent method of preservation," said Mr. Holmes.

"And you would be correct again, my good sir. Unless we are able to match the contents of her stomach to a known last meal."

Lady Ingram lay flat on her back but her head had rolled to one side, her nose close to the edge of the ice shaft. Fowler turned her face. "Hmm," he said, "didn't she have a beauty mark in her photographs?"

"Yes, sir," answered Treadles.

"I see only an excision here."

Treadles brought a lantern close and saw that the beauty mark had been scooped out, leaving a small dent where it had once been. The wound had healed but still looked recent.

"A pity," said Mr. Holmes. "It was one of her distinguishing features."

"Ah, look at this."

Fowler had rolled up Lady Ingram's sleeves and a small puncture wound was visible above her wrist. The otherwise ice-pale skin around it was discolored—the discoloration extending upward in a faint line, disappearing after approximately two inches.

Likewise on her other arm.

"Intravenous injections," said Treadles.

"The pathologist might be able to tell us exactly what the substance is. Or the chemical analyst," said Fowler.

"Do either of you smell the odor of alcohol?" asked Mr. Holmes.

The policemen exchanged a glance. Now that Mr. Holmes mentioned it, Treadles could indeed detect the faintest whiff in the air.

"If memory serves, Lady Ingram was a teetotaler—it was debated whether she even touched the champagne served at her own wedding. A shining paragon in so many ways, our dearly departed," said Mr. Holmes, and smoothed the ends of his mustache with what seemed to Treadles an unnecessary amount of enjoyment.

Such an odd chap.

Lord Ingram seemed drawn to people who were at least somewhat misaligned with the world.

"But alcohol, in sufficient quantities, is most certainly a poison," Mr. Holmes went on. "Assuming that she'd been injected with absolute alcohol, would that prove to be an irritant to the blood vessels?"

Again, a skillful argument put forth for Lord Ingram's innocence: He would not have killed his wife with injections of absolute alcohol, knowing that she did not imbibe on any regular basis.

Fowler frowned. "A rather diabolical way to kill, is it not?"

"But a relatively clean one, from a certain point of view. No need to visit a crooked chemist, as would be the case with arsenic poisoning. And the body could be passed off as having resulted from a natural death, if one wished to move it without arousing too much suspicion."

This was a body that came from elsewhere, implied Mr. Holmes, transported in a coffin.

Fowler, frowning more deeply, performed a systematic search of the pockets—very few, given that ladies didn't care for that sort of thing—and found nothing more than a handkerchief. He then slipped off her boots.

"Aha, what have we here?"

Something made a crinkling sound inside her woolen stocking. The removal of the stocking revealed a folded-up piece of paper that had been placed inside, against the sole of a blue-tinged foot.

Unfolded, the paper was full of writing. Upon closer inspection, however, it turned out that a single line of text was repeated nearly two dozen times, each iteration in a different hand.

*Vixen Charlotte Holmes's zephyr-tousled hair quivers when jolted in fog bank.*

Upon seeing that name, Treadles's gut tightened.

"What in the world is this?" exclaimed Fowler.

"A pangram," said Mr. Holmes. "A sentence that contains all twenty-six letters of the alphabet."

"And who is Charlotte Holmes?"

"Are you related to her?" Treadles asked at almost the same time.

"She is a friend of Lord Ingram's, a young woman with a peculiar bent of mind. I would not be surprised if she came up with the pangram herself," answered Mr. Holmes, unruffled. "And we are not related."

Fowler cast Treadles a look, before turning back to Mr. Holmes. "You say she is a friend of Lord Ingram's. Not Lady Ingram's?"

"Not in my understanding."

"Then why would Lady Ingram have in her possession something like this?"

Mr. Holmes hesitated. "That is a question better answered by Lord Ingram."

"Then let us speak to Lord Ingram," said Fowler, straightening. "The constables can arrange to have the body transported to the coroner."

"Gentlemen, would you mind if I looked around a little more?" said Mr. Holmes.

Fowler considered Mr. Holmes with a wariness that echoed Treadles's own. Mr. Holmes was no doubt acting on behalf of Lord Ingram, the prime suspect in the case. But Lord Ingram was also the brother of a duke, and a man of wealth and influence in his own right. It would not help Scotland Yard to antagonize him—at least, not yet.

"Go ahead," said Fowler, after a meaningful pause.

"Thank you. Much obliged," replied Mr. Holmes.

Mr. Holmes examined Lady Ingram's feet, her stockings, and her boots. Then he inspected the surface of the ice, pushing aside piles of wood shavings as he did so. Both the policemen watched him closely, but he worked with a singular concentration, seemingly oblivious to the scrutiny he himself was under.

"What are you looking for, Mr. Holmes?" Treadles asked, despite his intention not to do so.

"I haven't the slightest idea, Inspector. Anything out of the ordinary, I suppose."

"Do you see anything?" Fowler asked.

"A few strands of hair."

"Where?"

Mr. Holmes pointed at a spot some six feet removed from where Lady Ingram lay. The two policemen hurried forward to check. And there they were. Fowler took off his gloves, felt the strands, then approached Lady Ingram and touched the latter on the head. "Similar color and texture."

"Hers?" asked Treadles.

"We can only assume so," said Fowler, his eyes narrowed.

Once Mr. Holmes had finished with the ice well, he climbed out and proceeded to study the rest of the space. On their way out, he examined each antechamber, paying especially close attention to the doors and their locks. But when Fowler asked whether he'd seen anything else, he only shook his head.

Outside, Lord Ingram stood fifteen feet away from the entrance, a cigarette between his fingers.

"How did she die?" he asked.

The question was addressed to his friend.

Mr. Holmes fetched a pipe from inside his coat. "You've a match, Ash?"

With a somewhat disapproving look, Lord Ingram handed over a box of safety matches. Mr. Holmes lit his pipe with practiced ease and took a puff. "We'll see what the pathologist has to say, but my guess would be poisoning, by an injection of absolute alcohol."

Lord Ingram winced, an expression of fear and revulsion. And pity. He took a long drag on his cigarette, and then another. "Did you observe anything else?"

"Nothing the gentlemen from Scotland Yard haven't remarked. Her shoes do not fit her feet—probably the reason we were able to remove them so easily. And her stockings are far too cheaply made to have been her own purchase. A few pieces of straw among the wood shavings. Coal dust on the floor of the antechambers, up to the second one but not in the ice well itself. Some bits of metal filing right near the threshold of the entrance, still new and shiny."

Treadles hadn't seen the straw among the wood shavings, but judging by Fowler's self-satisfied look, he'd taken note of everything Mr. Holmes mentioned, and probably more.

"But enough of that for now. Let's go back inside and warm up," said Mr. Holmes. "I'm frozen down to my bollocks."

*Ten*

A plentiful tea awaited the party back in the library.

Treadles hadn't expected much of an appetite, but the cold of the icehouse and the wind-buffeted walk led him to gulp down two cups of tea and three tartlets. Chief Inspector Fowler, who appeared to have no interest in sweet things, heaped praise on the finger sandwiches. "Flavorful *and* substantial—not like eating air and bubbles, as is so often the case."

Lord Ingram, who again took up a position next to the fireplace, did not touch anything except a cup of black tea. Mr. Holmes, who didn't touch even that, sat sprawled in a nearby padded chair, legs splayed, head tilted back, eyes half closed.

Treadles stared at him. How many friends named Holmes did Lord Ingram have? And how many did he trust to find out the truth behind his wife's death?

"As you might have expected, my lord," said Fowler, "we will need to ask you some questions."

Lord Ingram appeared resigned. "Certainly."

Fowler glanced at Mr. Holmes. "Some of these questions could prove uncomfortable in nature."

"I have no secrets before Mr. Holmes," said Lord Ingram.

Was there an edge of reluctance to his tone, a wish that he *had* been able to keep a secret or two to himself? All the same, it was very much the master of the house who had spoken—and let it be known that Mr. Holmes wasn't going anywhere.

Mr. Holmes appeared not to have heard this tussle over his presence. Presently he poured himself a cup of tea and eyed the variety of refreshments on offer.

There was something oddly familiar about the way he contemplated cake.

"Mr. Holmes is a privileged friend indeed," said Fowler, pulling out a typed transcript of the interview between Lord Ingram and Sergeant Ellerby.

Treadles readied his notebook, even as his face heated from secondhand mortification. He had read the transcript, a story only the power of the Crown could make a man divulge, let alone repeat.

A sound came like grains of sand thrown against the window— it was raining, high wind driving a storm into Stern Hollow. In the grate, fire hissed, but otherwise the library was silent. Fowler continued to scan the transcript, each flip of the page as loud as the cracking of a whip.

Treadles braced himself. No one was better at winding up a suspect than Fowler. Make them wait. Make them guess. Make them wonder how much they'd already given away.

"The apple cake looks rather appealing," said Mr. Holmes to Lord Ingram, his words so incongruous Treadles almost laughed. "The apples come from Stern Hollow's kitchen garden?"

"Indeed, they do," replied Lord Ingram with the sort of grave courtesy appropriate to a question of pastry.

When a man *wasn't* the prime suspect in the murder of his wife.

Mr. Holmes bowed his head slightly. "I must try a slice then."

Chief Inspector Fowler did not glance up from the transcript but he looked irritated. Mr. Holmes's little aside had broken the tension, cracked it like a spoon to an eggshell. And there was no guarantee he wouldn't do it again, were Fowler to re-escalate the silence—and the pressure.

*Support, both moral and practical,* Lord Ingram had said about his friend's purpose at Stern Hollow. Was Mr. Holmes here to sabotage Fowler's effectiveness?

"Lord Ingram," began Fowler, "you allege that your wife ran away from home on the night of her birthday ball."

It would have been a stronger opening had it come at the end of a prolonged silence—and if Fowler had been able to pitch his voice slightly lower. Still, the statement arrived like a battering ram upon the gate of a castle.

Lord Ingram left the mantel to pour himself a glass of whisky. "She did."

"There is talk of her childhood sweetheart. But I find it difficult to believe that a woman of Lady Ingram's station would abandon everything for a love affair. It is my understanding that, in the upper echelon of Society, affairs are conducted under civilized rules. Why would she have run away when she could have indulged in a liaison, while retaining all the comfort and prestige to which she had become accustomed?"

Lord Ingram considered his glass, as if wishing he could down its entire contents in one draught. In the end he took only a sip. "Civilized rules require a state of civility, which was not a characteristic of my marital union."

"You mentioned a curtailment of affections but did not give a reason."

"I would prefer not to discuss it."

"I understand your reluctance. And I deplore intruding on another man's privacy," said Fowler, evincing no such reluctance whatsoever. "But your wife, whom no one had seen in months, was found dead on your land. Reticence, which I otherwise admire as a manly virtue, will not work to your advantage here."

This time Lord Ingram did pour back half of the whisky. Treadles winced inwardly. In happier times, he had shared meals and animated conversations with the man, and Lord Ingram had never imbibed except in exceedingly modest quantities.

He knew he should view his friend as the prime suspect, but he couldn't help a surge of sympathy. And a scouring of misery, that he himself, viewed as enviably married, was also, on the inside, in anything but an enviable state.

Putting down his glass, Lord Ingram walked to a window and stared out. The wooded slopes behind the house had turned red and gold, a beautiful tableau. Treadles wondered whether he saw anything at all.

"Immediately after the reading of my godfather's will, I told Lady Ingram that I would receive five hundred pounds per annum instead of the preponderance of his fortune, as was, in fact, the case."

The words emerged slowly, as if they were dragged across knife and fire.

Fowler set his chin in the space between his thumb and forefinger. "Does this imply you already harbored doubts as to the validity of her affection?"

Lord Ingram's hands clasped behind his back. "I knew when we met that her family was poor. I was more than happy to be their knight in shining armor. At the time it had seemed highly romantic, that our paths should cross when she came to London in search of a well-situated husband.

"I was young and vain—and likely believed myself a prize even without the attraction of my future inheritance. That the woman I loved perhaps wouldn't want to marry me . . . Such a thought never crossed my mind.

"That Season she stayed with a cousin in London. I didn't meet her family until after my proposal had been accepted. The lack of warmth she evinced toward her parents—and even her brothers—should have put me on alert. But I was blinded by love and freely discarded what I did not wish to see.

"In time I came to understand that a similar distance existed between us. I thought we had everything we needed to be happy—health, security, beautiful children. But she grew only more distant, more unreachable.

"That was when I learned that she had loved another, a man rejected by her parents because he was in no position to help her family. Everything began to make horrifying sense. She despised her parents because they refused to consider her personal happiness. She was remote toward me because she did not love me. Because she never would have married me, except for the fact that I was rumored to be my godfather's heir apparent."

Treadles dared not put himself in Lord Ingram's place. He didn't even want to imagine disillusionment of this magnitude.

"I didn't want it to be true. But I also needed to know. My godfather died soon thereafter and I made up my mind. If she loved me, then she would be disappointed that I would remain only a moderately well-off man rather than become a very rich one, but it would not be a fatal disappointment. If she did not love me . . ."

He'd been speaking faster and faster, as if hoping simple momentum would carry him through the worst part of the story. But now he came to a stop. His head bowed. His fingers gripped the edge of the windowsill.

When he spoke again his voice was quiet, barely audible. "Her anger was beyond anything I could have imagined. My godfather was Jewish, and it is rumored that I am his natural son. She told me, in exactly so many words, that without this inheritance, she had married me for nothing. And her children had Jewish blood for nothing."

Outside, wind howled. A sheet of rain pelted the windows. Inside, the silence was excruciating. Treadles didn't dare breathe, for fear of betraying his presence. He wanted Lord Ingram to believe that he was speaking to an empty room—it would be the only way he himself could have managed to relive such painful memories.

"There was no attempt at reconciliation, then?" Fowler was unmoved, his question cold and inexorable.

"As ruptures go, ours was thorough—and as final as an amputation. I imagine the truth came as a relief for her, an end to all pretenses."

"And for you?"

"On my part, I at last perceived her clearly—and I saw the greatest mistake of my life."

Another silence fell. Fowler polished his spectacles with a handkerchief. Mr. Holmes picked up the slice of cake that had been sitting beside him and gave it a quarter turn on its plate.

For a moment, something about him again seemed strangely familiar.

And then he looked in Lord Ingram's direction, his expression entirely blank.

Treadles almost cried out. That expression, as if he viewed the pain and suffering of others from a great remove, as if he himself never expected to experience such frailties—Treadles had seen that expression before.

On a woman.

On Charlotte Holmes.

Despite the foppishness of his appearance, Mr. Holmes did not look . . . feminine. He didn't even look effeminate. And certainly not at all pretty. While Miss Holmes was very pretty and extravagantly feminine—Treadles still remembered the endless rows of bows on her skirt the first time he met her.

But now that the idea had come into his head . . .

Sherrinford Holmes's girth might be a way to disguise Miss Holmes's buxom figure. His facial hair needn't be real and the dark hair on his head could be a wig. The wearing of a monocle subtly distorted one's features—but didn't account for all the differences between Sherrinford Holmes's face and Miss Holmes's.

Ah, of course, his less-than-perfect enunciation. At the time Treadles had thought he sounded as if he might have a piece of boiled sweet in his mouth. But he could very well have something else inside, something that altered the shapes of his cheeks just so.

Dear God, had Charlotte Holmes been among them all this time?

"Marital disharmony is a terrible cross to bear," said Fowler, setting his glasses back on his face and yanking Treadles's attention back to the interrogation. "But many do bear it. Lady Ingram did so for years. What compelled her to suddenly abandon her entire life?"

"This summer, not long before the end of the Season, Lady Ingram called on Sherlock Holmes."

What? Lady Ingram calling on Charlotte Holmes? But she *knew* Charlotte Holmes.

"Sherlock Holmes? The fellow who helped you on the Sackville case?"

Fowler's question was for Treadles.

Treadles could only hope his face was not a disarray of tics and convulsions. But there was no time to think. "Yes, sir," he said. "Lord Ingram, in fact, was the one who introduced me to Sherlock Holmes."

Fowler's attention shifted back to Lord Ingram. "Lady Ingram did not know that the two of you are acquainted?"

Treadles let out a shaky breath.

"I had never mentioned the name to her," said Lord Ingram.

"I see. Please go on."

"Before we do, gentlemen," said Lord Ingram, "you should know that Mr. Holmes here is Sherlock Holmes's brother. But he did not assist Sherlock with Lady Ingram's case and therefore cannot tell you much about it."

Had Treadles not realized Sherrinford Holmes's true identity on his own, his shock at this moment might have been too great to conceal from Chief Inspector Fowler.

"I dare say I'm just as good at this deduction business," said Charlotte Holmes. "But unlike Sherlock, I cannot be bothered about strange knocking sounds in old ladies' attics."

Fowler looked from her to Treadles.

"I have only met your sister," said Treadles to Charlotte Holmes, feeling ridiculous. "Is she well? And your brother?"

"My sister is well. And my brother fares tolerably."

"Mr. Holmes," said Fowler, his voice clipped, "you didn't think to mention sooner that you are related to the man who helped Lady Ingram search for her lover?"

Charlotte Holmes regarded him, her monocle flashing as she cocked her head. "With Lord Ingram in the same room, Chief Inspector, you think I should have brought that up before he did?"

Fowler blinked—and cleared his throat. Treadles winced with second-hand embarrassment for his colleague; the misstep was unlike him.

"My apologies, my lord," said Fowler tightly. "Please carry on."

"Very well," said Lord Ingram, his voice remarkably neutral. "Sherlock Holmes theorized that Lady Ingram must have come across the article in the paper about his willingness to deal with minor mysteries and mere domestic oddities. Certainly she arrived on his doorstep very soon after the publication of the piece, looking for help locating the man her parents forced her to give up.

"Apparently they had a standing annual appointment before the Albert Memorial. This year, he did not come. She posted notices in the paper. And when she still had no news of him, she called on Sherlock Holmes."

"And Sherlock Holmes agreed to help, knowing what Lady Ingram wanted?" demanded Fowler. "Knowing full well that—that he would be assisting your wife in an endeavor you would not have approved of in the least?"

"Geniuses must be allowed their eccentricities." Lord Ingram turned around at last. "Sherlock Holmes had never paid heed to conventional ideas of acceptability. Why start with Lady Ingram?"

Charlotte Holmes shook her head, as if she genteelly deplored such nonsense.

A door opened and closed softly. Everyone looked up at the gallery, which went all the way around the second story of the library. From where Treadles sat, he couldn't tell whether a servant had opened the door by accident or whether someone had come in.

Lord Ingram downed what remained of his whisky. "According to Sherlock Holmes, Lady Ingram was impatient to find this man, and then suddenly she no longer wanted to look for him. That was when Holmes spoke to me of the matter and warned me that it was quite possible that Lady Ingram hadn't changed her mind but had found him on her own.

"I, in turn, remembered that Lady Ingram had lately consulted a book on matrimonial law at home. With the revelation from Sherlock Holmes, I began to wonder what she would do, knowing that if she gave in to her heart's desire, I would have grounds for a divorce.

"She had always been a devoted mother. But in a divorce she would lose the children. What would she do if she had to choose between her children and the man she loved?

"Then a third, far more terrifying possibility occurred to me. What if she did not intend to give up either? What if she intended to run away with the man, my children in tow, so that she never needed to worry about being parted from them?

"With that in mind, I studied the cipher with which they communicated, and sent her a note in the same cipher, telling her that the night of her birthday ball would be a good time to take the children and leave, given that I would be distracted by my duties as the host.

"A little before one o'clock that night, she opened the door to the nursery, only to find it empty of all occupants, except me. I confronted her about her plan to make off with the children. And she, who had too long been accustomed to dealing with me without pretenses, was again bluntly truthful. I told her to go and not come back. She understood then that the children were now beyond her reach, that even if she stayed I would never trust her to see them again. And she must have decided that the only thing she could salvage from this misadventure was her lover and that she might as well leave with him since he had already cost her dearly.

"My primary concern had been to keep my children from being taken—to prevent that from ever happening. To that end, Lady Ingram's departure appeared a highly favorable development. It wasn't until I'd calmed down somewhat I realized the difficulty I was now in.

"Lady Ingram was a prominent member of Society. She had friends, acquaintances, and, however distant, a family. She had dozens of servants from whom her absence could not be concealed for any length of time. Not to mention, a ball in her honor was still in full swing.

"I had to brazen it out, but etiquette was on my side. Guests are supposed to slip out discreetly, without saying good-bye to the hosts, if they leave before the end of a ball. Those who stayed until carriages came knew better than to inquire of *me*, at least, as to the whereabouts of Lady Ingram. They would have assumed either she was seeing to other guests or that the strain of the long night was more than her bad back could take—the same assumption the servants would have made. And she had dismissed her maid for the night at the beginning of the ball, rather than making the latter wait until the small hours of the morning.

"Given all that, I didn't need to announce her departure until the next day. And then, only to the senior servants. I told them that her health had taken a catastrophic turn in the later part of the ball and that she'd needed to leave immediately. And then I asked them to carry on as usual, except that we would depart from London as soon as possible.

"To her maid, Simmons, I spoke separately. I told her that Lady Ingram had decided to leave her behind, as Simmons is not fond of either overseas travel or cold climates. Simmons once worked for my mother and was well-positioned to retire. She was distressed to be let go unceremoniously, after six years of service. But she is a kind-natured person and was more concerned for Lady Ingram than for herself.

"To the children I gave the same story. They were saddened but believed me when I said that she would return when she was well. I took them to the seaside to distract them—and to be somewhere my wife could not readily guess at, for I still feared that she would come for them.

"But there had been no sign of her in all the months since. Until yesterday, when I was told that her body had been discovered in the icehouse."

It was the same account he had given Sergeant Ellerby, only in greater, unhappier detail.

Fowler considered Lord Ingram for close to a minute, then extracted something from his pocket. "We discovered this in Lady Ingram's stocking. If you don't mind taking a look, my lord."

Charlotte Holmes leaped up, took the folded-up piece of paper from Fowler, and delivered it to Lord Ingram, still at the window. Lord Ingram smoothed out the paper and stared at it, his expression odd, as if unable to believe his own eyes. Miss Holmes gave him a few more seconds before retrieving the evidence and returning it to Fowler.

Treadles's eyes were on Miss Holmes the entire time, but could not detect on her face anything other than an eagerness to be of service.

"That is a sheet of my handwriting practice," said Lord Ingram.

Fowler leaned forward. "All these different hands, they are all done by you?"

"It's a hobby."

Treadles's heart sank. A man who could write as if from many different people? This was not a helpful skill for the police to discover, especially when they already suspected him of murder.

"And this . . . pangram"—Fowler turned to Mr. Holmes—"is that the correct word?"

"Quite so, Chief Inspector."

"My lord, why did you choose this pangram to write repeatedly?"

"I didn't. Miss Holmes came up with a number of pangrams. *Don Quixote jokes flippantly at windmill, vexing Bach and Mozart. Volcano erupts liquidly, spewing marzipan, pâte à choux, and breakfast jam.* So on and so forth. I used them all at some point."

"Nevertheless, this is the one Lady Ingram kept. Do you think she resented that you wrote another woman's name two dozen times on a single page?"

"Lady Ingram would have had to feel a sense of possessiveness toward me in order to harbor any twinges of jealousy. No, I don't believe she had ever viewed Miss Holmes as a romantic rival."

"And yet according to Mr. Holmes here, Miss Holmes was not a friend to both yourself and Lady Ingram, only to you."

"A woman can dislike another for reasons having nothing to do with a man. I daresay Lady Ingram's antipathy toward Miss Holmes stemmed not from her friendship with me but her ability to resist the pressure to accept a proposal of marriage."

Fowler's eyes narrowed. "I am not sure I understand."

"Miss Holmes's background isn't all that different from Lady Ingram's, a penurious respectability. But whereas Lady Ingram buckled under and married after her first Season, Miss Holmes long held firm on her disinclination to marry and turned down any number of proposals.

"Lady Ingram prized strength above all else. From the beginning, she sensed in Miss Holmes a strength greater than her own, both of mind and of character. That was what she was jealous of. That was what prevented any possibility of friendship: Simply by existing, Miss Holmes made her feel inferior—and angry at herself."

"Miss Holmes's name is beginning to ring a bell," mused Fowler. "I remember someone by this name connected with the Sackville case. Are we speaking of the same Miss Charlotte Holmes, who disgraced herself last summer and is now no longer received in polite company?"

"That would be the very same Miss Charlotte Holmes," said Lord Ingram.

Nothing at all had changed about his tone, yet Treadles felt as if his answer had been a rebuke.

They had never spoken of Miss Holmes, not openly, in any case. But Lord Ingram's steadfast support of and admiration for this fallen woman—Treadles did not understand it. And it made him realize that he did not understand Lord Ingram either. Not at all.

Fowler gave Lord Ingram a speculative glance. "To return to the subject of your ability to write in many different hands, sir, why do you suppose Lady Ingram would have carried that piece of paper with her?"

"I haven't the slightest idea. But it behooves me to tell you now that I have written letters in Lady Ingram's hand to her friends and our children."

Oh, this would not look good at all to a jury. Or in the court of public opinion.

"You had no choice, of course," said Miss Holmes gently. "Her disappearance would have been that much more incomprehensible if she hadn't written from her Swiss sanatorium."

"Do you have any of those letters that had been written to your children?" Fowler, for all his experience and sangfroid, sounded excited at this question.

Treadles's heart sank further. Anything that excited Chief Inspector Fowler was bound to be bad news for Lord Ingram.

"The children took the letters when they left with my brother—they wished to hear them read every night. But I have one that I had been working on, before all this happened."

Lord Ingram went to his desk, opened a locked drawer, pulled out a portfolio, and handed it to Fowler. When opened, the left side of the portfolio held a menu and the right side, a half-finished letter, which read,

*My Dearest Lucinda and Carlisle,*

*Thank you most kindly for your loving thoughts, as penned by Papa. I am slightly better, but alas, still not well enough that the doctors are willing to release me.*

*It is turning cold here, much colder than at home. But I find the cold tolerable, since the air is dry and the weather clear. From my balcony I can see a lake halfway down the mountain, surrounded by soldier-straight fir trees, with a tiny island at its center and what looks to be an even tinier chapel on this island.*

*You asked about the food that is served here. Well, that depends on which cook is on duty, the one from the German-speaking part of Switzerland, or the one from the French-speaking part.*

Fowler pointed at the menu. "And this is an example of her ladyship's handwriting?"

"Correct."

"You do an excellent imitation."

Lord Ingram made no reply.

The next few questions concerned Lord Ingram's whereabouts during the past forty-eight hours—and the past fortnight. "Given her state of inadvertent preservation, it might be impossible for us to determine her time of death with any accuracy," said Fowler.

Lord Ingram, blank-faced, pulled out an appointment book and answered accordingly.

"I understand you are a busy man, sir, so I will not take much more of your time. But there is one question that I must ask: Do you know of anyone who wished to harm Lady Ingram?"

Lord Ingram shook his head. "She did not instill widespread devotion, but neither did she inspire enmity. Her death benefits no one."

"I hate to ask this, but it must be done, so I beg your forgiveness in advance. Are you certain that her death benefits no one? Are you certain that you yourself do not stand to reap rewards?"

Lord Ingram raised a brow. "By being suspected as responsible for her death?"

"Nobody would have suspected anything if her body hadn't been found. If she had died somewhere else—overseas, for example— would you not have then been rid of an unloving wife, and would that not have been an advantage?"

"I have long coexisted with an unloving wife—were she to live to a hundred it would not have further injured me."

"But it would have prevented you from marrying someone who does love you. With Lady Ingram no more, in six months' time you will be able to marry again. This Miss Charlotte Holmes, for example, and rescue her from her disgrace."

Miss Holmes appeared unmoved; Lord Ingram, equally so.

"I will not take umbrage on my own behalf, Chief Inspector—it is your professional obligation to suspect everyone. But you are operating under an entirely mistaken assumption of who Miss Holmes is. She has no use for a husband and would not have accepted any proposal from me, should I be so thoughtless as to tender one."

Fowler waved his arm in an expansive gesture. "She wouldn't wish to be the mistress of all this?"

"If she wished to be the mistress of a fine estate, she could have achieved that easily. Half of the largest landowners in England had proposed to her."

"Really?" Fowler sounded almost impressed.

Treadles was confounded. All those fine proposals—and she threw away her respectability over a married man?

"Or perhaps it was one-quarter of the largest landowners." Lord Ingram turned to the subject of the discussion. "Does that sound about right?"

"Even one-quarter is a highly exaggerated figure," said Miss Holmes. "It's true that she received proposals from two gentlemen with considerable landholding, but one was deep in debt and the other elderly and in search of a fourth wife. On the other hand, there had been an industrialist, who, if he had been accepted, would have been able to purchase for her an establishment equal in scale and refinement to Stern Hollow, without feeling too great a disturbance in his pocketbook."

Lord Ingram gave his friend a baleful look. "I have never heard of this industrialist."

"They met during your honeymoon, from what I understand."

"Huh," said Lord Ingram.

"Very foolish girl, that Miss Charlotte," said Miss Holmes, with wry amusement.

"Huh," repeated Lord Ingram. He turned to the policemen. "And there you have it, gentlemen."

Fowler, however, was not so easily satisfied on the subject. "The last time you were an eligible man was a long time ago, my lord. That Miss Holmes wouldn't have entertained an offer of marriage from you then doesn't imply she wouldn't have changed her mind during the intervening years."

"Whatever the state of her mind, I didn't propose to her then and I will not propose to her now."

"Why not?"

"*Why not?*" Lord Ingram chortled, a derisive sound. "First, I am deeply disenchanted with marriage in general. Astonishing, isn't it? Second, I am not bold enough to wed Miss Holmes, even if she were to prostrate herself and make an impassioned argument for our union."

The woman in question whistled softly. "Now that's a sight I'd pay good money to see—Charlotte Holmes on her knees, begging you to marry her."

*Eleven*

Before the policemen were shown out, they made clear, albeit with great politeness, that the entirety of Stern Hollow was subject to search.

Lord Ingram indicated his willing cooperation and made a request of his own. "One of the three ladies who went into the icehouse, Miss Olivia Holmes, is of a much more sensitive temperament than Lady Avery and Lady Somersby. Coming upon Lady Ingram has been a great shock to her. If you gentlemen could speak to her first, so that she can put this behind her as soon as possible . . ."

Treadles's eyes widened. "Would this be the same Miss Olivia Holmes who is Miss Charlotte Holmes's sister?"

"Correct. She was Mrs. Newell's guest—and consequently now my guest."

"A small world, this is," said Fowler, his tone gentler now that the interrogation had finished—for the moment. "It will be no trouble at all to see her first."

"Thank you, gentlemen. Most kind of you."

The head footman arrived to show Scotland Yard to the room where they would conduct the rest of their interviews. When they were gone, Lord Ingram glanced up at the gallery, then at Holmes.

Their eyes met. She rubbed her bearded chin. "By the way, Ash, you bowdlerized my pangram. I'm devastated."

"I don't know why you believed I would have ever committed the original in writing, in any of my scripts." He took a deep breath. "Will you come down, Bancroft, or should we join you up there?"

Bancroft descended a spiral staircase and approached the fireplace. He was a slender, finely built man who usually appeared much younger than his actual age. But he had lost some weight, which emphasized the delicate lines that webbed the corners of his eyes. And his gait, otherwise smooth and graceful, gave an impression of jerkiness. Of agitation.

"How did you get here so fast?" Lord Ingram asked.

"I was at Eastleigh Park. You almost gave Wycliffe an apoplectic attack with your note. I talked him out of coming here himself, but that meant I had to act as his emissary."

"Why were *you* at Eastleigh Park? Since when do you visit Wycliffe?"

Bancroft was the most remote of the four Ashburton brothers. During the London Season he occasionally accepted invitations to dine at his brothers' houses, but rarely issued any of his own. Lord Ingram seldom met him except to discuss the more clandestine concerns of the Crown.

"I am obliged to account for myself to His Grace the same way you are—he doesn't order me to do it as often as he orders you, but it happens. And I thought it would be better for me to call on him now, so as to be spared a family reunion at Christmas."

"Excellent thinking, that," said Holmes.

Bancroft gave her a chilly look and said to Lord Ingram, "You weren't planning on making introductions?"

"This fine gentleman here is Mr. Sherlock Holmes's brother, Mr. Sherrinford Holmes."

Bancroft's eyes widened. He studied Holmes from head to toe, more than a little astonished. "I see. I should have expected an envoy from Sherlock Holmes, given the nature of the case. How do you do, Miss Holmes?"

"I'm very well, thank you, my lord. Should we ring for a fresh pot of tea?" asked Holmes. "You'll approve of the cake."

The cake that she hadn't touched. Granted, the modified orthodontia she wore to alter the shape of her face did not make eating easy, but the Holmes of old would have found a way.

"No tea for me," said Bancroft. "Tell me what you have found out, Ash. Is it really Lady Ingram's body in the icehouse?"

"I wish it were otherwise."

Bancroft ran his fingers through his hair. "Why? Why did it happen?"

Lord Ingram couldn't remember the last time his brother sounded so baffled—or so perturbed. "I wish I knew. If Moriarty is playing a game, I fail to understand the game's objective."

"And the police? Do they know anything?"

"Do you remember when you sent your man Underwood to fetch Miss Holmes from that tea shop in Hounslow?"

"Yes, you were with her at the time."

"Our meeting has been reported to the greater world by ladies Avery and Somersby—and the police are entirely seduced by the obvious. If this keeps up for much longer, I will need to become a fugitive."

"What about your children?"

This question earned Bancroft a sideways look from Holmes. Bancroft was hardly one to be concerned about other people's offspring, even if the children in question were his niece and nephew.

"Wycliffe will claim them, no doubt, and raise them to be stiff, pompous younger versions of himself."

Bancroft nodded slowly. "It hasn't been a smooth year for you, has it?"

Lord Ingram laughed softly. "Not altogether, no."

"I'll see if I can view the body. Anyone interested in joining me?"

Both Holmes and Lord Ingram shook their heads.

"Very well, then. I'll leave you to your work." He hesitated a moment. "I'm sorry I can't do more. It is imperative that we not breathe a word about Lady Ingram's betrayal of the Crown."

When he had gone, Holmes said, "He does look a bit worn down. Perhaps my powers over the males of the species are more legion than I suspect."

Lord Ingram rolled his eyes. "Your powers are exactly as legion as you suspect—you've never been one for underestimating yourself."

She smiled slightly and touched him on the arm. "Frankly, I'm a little disappointed that Lord Bancroft came, instead of the duke— I was looking forward to one of His Grace's deadly lectures. But now we must carry on."

———✣———

Treadles wished he had some time to think. Charlotte Holmes's presence was hugely problematic. As a potential material witness, she needed to be interviewed. But Treadles couldn't simply point Chief Inspector Fowler to Sherrinford Holmes and tell him to proceed.

Or could he?

It would be the right thing to do. The proper thing to do. But it would require him to admit that Sherlock Holmes, whose help had been instrumental in several of his biggest cases, was not only a woman, but a fallen one unwelcome in any respectable drawing room. The very thought was enough to make his head throb.

Perhaps it was a good thing then that he had no time to think. They had scarcely settled themselves in the blue-and-white parlor, bedecked with pastoral paintings, when Miss Olivia Holmes was shown in.

"Miss Holmes, thank you for taking the time to speak to us," said Fowler in his most avuncular voice.

Treadles hadn't known what to expect, but it was not this stiff, unsure woman. She might be pretty enough if she smiled, but as she sat down, smiling appeared very much beyond her. She studied Fowler, her eyes devoid of trust. And they remained devoid of trust as she provided one terse answer after another.

After Fowler had inquired about every facet of the icehouse discovery, he said, "I am interested in your opinion, Miss Holmes. You were acquainted with Lady Ingram. Can you think of anyone who might have wished her harm?"

"I had been *introduced* to Lady Ingram," said Miss Holmes, drawing that distinction with a trace of impatience. "So I could have claimed an acquaintance, I suppose, but I knew her very little."

"I thought Society was small."

"It isn't big. But it would be akin to asking a constable in the street what he might know of you, Chief Inspector."

"I see. But I understand that your sister Miss Charlotte Holmes is a good friend of Lord Ingram's. Would that not have earned you a place in Lady Ingram's circle?"

"Not in the least. A man's wife is the one who issues invitations to functions that they host together. And Lady Ingram had never invited my sister—or myself—to any of her events."

"Why do you suppose that was the case? Was she jealous of the friendship between Miss Charlotte and her husband?"

"I didn't know her well enough to speak to that. If she was jealous, then it was over nothing. My sister and Lord Ingram have always conducted themselves with the greatest propriety."

Treadles couldn't help interjecting himself into the interview. "Yet I understand that Miss Charlotte has been banished from Society because of an act of impropriety with a married man."

Miss Holmes stared at him, her expression at first dumbstruck, then furious. She took a deep breath. "And that man was *not* Lord Ingram."

"Thank you, Miss Holmes," said Fowler, his tone soothing, "for your time and cooperation."

Miss Holmes nodded curtly and rose. But instead of walking out, she stood in place. Fowler and Treadles, who had also come out of their chairs when she got up, stayed on their feet and exchanged a look.

"Did you remember something, Miss Holmes?" asked Fowler.

"No, but there is something that bothers me. I found Lady Avery searching my room yesterday. She later told me that she and her sister, Lady Somersby, were looking to see whether Lady Ingram might have left messages behind as to her whereabouts."

"Yesterday, after Lady Ingram was discovered dead?"

"No, well before. Even her confession came while the icehouse was still in the distance."

Fowler appeared to ponder this new information. "Where did ladies Avery and Somersby think Lady Ingram might have gone?"

"They weren't sure, but they weren't above suspecting Lord Ingram of keeping her under lock and key, possibly somewhere on this very estate."

"Given that she was found dead on this very estate, perhaps that was not such an outlandish charge after all."

"You are wrong, sir. Lady Ingram's body in the icehouse makes their assertions more outlandish, not less."

Miss Holmes stood straighter now, her voice stronger, a fiercer woman than Treadles had first given her credit for. "People thought it was a little odd—perhaps very odd—that Lady Ingram had left for Switzerland without any notice. But they didn't worry about her. No one worried about Lady Ingram, ever. Not even in the immediate aftermath of the rupture between her and her husband, when everyone learned that she had screamed that she'd only married him for his money. They didn't worry about her because they knew him. They knew that his character was above reproach."

"We do not always know people as we think we do," said Treadles.

"We do not. But in Lord Ingram's case, Lady Ingram lost absolutely nothing for confessing that she was a cold-hearted fortune hunter. She didn't lose her pin money. She didn't lose her accounts at London's leading dressmakers. She didn't even lose the yearly birthday ball in her honor. He continued to extend to her every courtesy and privilege that came of being his wife—and that was the only reason she was able to keep her place in Society. Because he didn't withdraw his support."

"Perhaps he was planning, even as he maintained a façade of gentility, the ultimate revenge," suggested Fowler.

"And then he chose to make his wife disappear on the night of a crowded ball, in a way that could only ever lead to unsatisfactory answers? You think Lord Ingram couldn't have done better than that if he had indeed been scheming?"

Fowler had no good answer for that.

"Regardless, this is not the first time I encountered Lady Avery and Lady Somersby since the end of the Season. I can tell you with complete confidence that when I last saw them before this gathering, they weren't remotely concerned with Lady Ingram's fate. Lady Somersby said it was her feeling that Lady Ingram had had quite enough of Society, something deeper than mere end-of-the-Season weariness. Her sister questioned whether it wasn't something to do with a latent animosity many felt toward her."

Fowler raised a brow. "Latent animosity?"

By now Scotland Yard had received the impression that Lady Ingram had not been beloved, but there was a stark difference between the absence of universal acclaim and the presence of widespread ill will, however subterranean.

"There are very few heiresses among the women jockeying for eligible gentlemen on the marriage mart. And the cost of failure is high: lifelong dependence on disappointed parents and indifferent brothers, perhaps even the necessity of becoming a lady's companion or, worse, a governess. No one would have thought any less of Lady Ingram for marrying the richest man she could find, certainly not when he happened to be both striking in appearance and sterling of character. Her success was a fairy tale, something to aspire to.

"And if that fairy tale was to gradually lose its potency, well, such is life. What was not supposed to happen was her brutal honesty. The unspoken rule has always been that if a woman marries for money, she keeps that to herself and maintains an appearance of interest in her husband. Because that is what his money paid for. She is never supposed to not only confirm that she has never loved him but also denigrate him in the same breath for his said-to-be half-Jewish blood."

"I didn't know Society ladies cared that those of Jewish roots should not be taunted for that fact," said Treadles.

"What? No, they didn't care about that. They cared that Lady Ingram didn't just tear the fairy tale in two but spat on it. They cared that this sent a shiver through all the *men* of Society. If a paragon such as Lord Ingram couldn't find a wife who genuinely loved him, what chance did the other gentlemen have? That lesson made them more cautious. Which, in turn, meant that unmarried women found it more difficult to land good husbands—and to keep up the illusion once they had."

Fowler blinked. "That is an extraordinarily cynical observation."

Yet highly riveting.

"That was Charlotte's analysis—she dissects things differently. *I* think people didn't like Lady Ingram because they admired Lord Ingram and felt he'd been treated badly. And then there were others who simply disliked her demeanor. When she made her debut, she appeared more genial. But as time went by, she became more and more unapproachable—and women don't like women who are too haughty.

"In any case, that was ladies Avery and Somersby's position ear-lier this autumn, not that anything had been done to Lady Ingram but that *she* might have taken the initiative to put herself out of reach. But here at Stern Hollow they have been consumed with po-tential disasters that might have befallen her.

"Ask them what brought on this concern, so strongly that they were willing to risk being caught poking into other guests' rooms. I don't know enough to make concrete guesses, but my sense is that something is rotten in the state of Denmark."

With that, Miss Holmes nodded again and left.

"Well," said Fowler, "I always enjoy a case more once witnesses start quoting Shakespeare, don't you?"

—◦✦◦—

Livia was still shaking as she climbed up the grand staircase. The house felt deserted, even though Mrs. Newell's guests were still on hand. But the shooting, the games of charades, the play that would have been put on—dear God, to think that she'd rather hoped she might be considered for the part of Desdemona—everything that had been planned lay by the wayside, like so many dandelions tram-pled by a party of riders.

Instead, the gentlemen played endless games of billiards, making quiet remarks between echoing clicks of cue stick on ivory. The la-dies slipped in and out of one another's rooms; fear, suspicion, and speculation swept along torrents of whispers. And the servants, al-ready unobtrusive in a well-run household, seemed to have disap-peared altogether.

In the beginning, there had been knocks at Livia's door, too. But she'd steadfastly refused to answer, not wanting to see the gossip ladies or anyone else who might either wish to commiserate or glean clues from what she could tell them—certainly not in the wake of all the speculation about Lord Ingram and Charlotte! Now no one came to call and she felt both relieved and spectacularly left out.

At the top of the grand staircase she met Lord Ingram, dressed as if he were about to go for a ride.

"Miss Holmes," he said gently, "you already spoke to Scotland Yard, I take it? I hope it wasn't too taxing."

"Oh, I dare say I'll—"

She bit back the last word. She'd live. But would *he*? Or was he already headed for a rendezvous with the hangman?

"I'll forget about it by dinnertime, I'm sure. Are *you* all right? Has Charlotte been able to find out anything?"

Although what Charlotte could do from her cottage, even Livia couldn't say.

"I'm well. And I'm sure Miss Charlotte will be instrumental in putting everything to rights again. Now, is there anything I can do for you?"

"No, you have so much—"

"You are mistaken there, Miss Holmes. Other than letting the police deploy as they will, there is absolutely nothing I can do about anything related to Lady Ingram's death. But if there is some service I may render you, it will take my mind off the situation. And that would be a welcome respite, however brief."

"Oh," she said. "If—if that is the case, then there *is* something that's worried me recently."

When she had time to worry about anything besides him.

"Please. Allow me to be of service."

"Well, I don't know whether Charlotte has ever mentioned her, but we have an elder sister who has never moved in Society."

Bernadine was thirty years of age and it had been a quarter century since she last stepped out of the house. As far as Livia could remember, her name had never crossed anyone's lips in a polite conversation. When Livia arrived in London, she was presented as simply Miss Holmes and not Miss Olivia Holmes, indicating that she was the eldest unmarried Holmes daughter, and completely erasing Bernadine's position. Even Mrs. Newell, who otherwise remembered everyone, always referred to the Holmes girls as a trio and not a quartet as they were in truth.

She could only hope what she was about to reveal wouldn't come as too much of a surprise to Lord Ingram.

"Miss Bernadine?" he said. "Yes, I know of her."

Thank goodness. Livia gave a brief account of Bernadine's change of surroundings, from the Holmes household to Moreton Close, the private institution for women from notable families who suffered from conditions similar to Bernadine's. "I don't trust my parents on important matters. I'm not sure I trust my own judgment on this, either. Charlotte has promised to investigate Moreton Close, but she can't be spared right now."

"I will direct my solicitor to make some inquiries, under the guise of representing the prominent family of a young woman who might benefit from their services. That way, we can perhaps gain entrance to the place."

"Will you? That would be wonderful!"

Lord Ingram smiled, as if her relief had gladdened him. "Consider it done. But please know that it might take some time."

"Thank you, my lord. Thank you!"

"No, thank you, Miss Holmes. And that reminds me, I have been tasked to give you a message." He glanced behind himself. There was no one around, but still he lowered his voice. "Please visit the nursery. A mutual friend wishes to speak to you. Good day, Miss Holmes."

---❖---

The nursery was cheerfully decorated but silent and empty. Livia paced for a good ten minutes before a knock came. She rushed to answer—Charlotte, it had to be Charlotte.

But when she'd opened the door, a round, peculiar-looking man stood outside, all boutonniere and coiffed mustache, an ornate monocle screwed into one eye socket.

Disappointment and suspicion snuffed out Livia's eager anticipation. "May I help you?"

"You may indeed, Miss Holmes," said the man gravely. "I came to inquire after your progress on the Sherlock Holmes story."

Only three people in the entire world knew that she was working on a story inspired by the Sackville case: Charlotte, Mrs. Watson, and the nameless young man who had recently sent her the moonstone cabochon.

Could this be *him*, in disguise?

Taking advantage of her astonished inaction, the man came in and closed the door. "I see Mrs. Watson and I are not the only ones you told, Livia."

This time, he spoke with her baby sister's voice.

Livia's jaw fell. "Charlotte!" she managed in a vehement whisper. "Charlotte! What—what— Good gracious— I—"

She gave up and stared.

The man—Charlotte—smiled. "You would cut a more dashing figure dressing as a man, Livia. The only way to accommodate my bosom is to create a considerable paunch."

"Your mustache . . . and beard . . ."

"I know. All very good. Mrs. Watson knew where to get the best."

Livia pulled herself together. "So how long have you been here?"

"Since last night. I'm staying on this floor, where there are no other guests."

"Have you found out anything? Do you know who killed Lady Ingram?"

"Alas, even Sherlock Holmes cannot solve everything at a glance."

"But you will find out who did this, won't you? You won't let . . . you won't let anything happen to Lord Ingram."

Even with all the disguise, Charlotte's expression was somber. "I will do what I can."

*Don't forget, I'll look after you,* Charlotte had told Livia at one point this past summer, not long after she'd established herself as oracle to Sherlock Holmes, fictional sage. The certainty with which she'd said it, the inevitability—it had been a promise, pure and simple.

Here Charlotte made no promises. And beneath the dignity of her words, did Livia detect a trace of apprehension?

To Charlotte, fear was but a word in the dictionary—or at least it had always seemed so to Livia. While Livia dreaded and fretted over a thousand ghastly possibilities, Charlotte dealt with only facts and actual events. What did she know, then? What concrete, undeniable particulars could make Charlotte Holmes, she of the nerves of Damascus steel, actually afraid?

"Is it really that bad?"

Charlotte looked at her for a moment. "Lord Ingram is not without allies. Not to mention he has resources of his own."

Again, an indirect answer. Livia's heart fell like a dropped stone.

Charlotte moved to the middle of the nursery. "Anyway, how was your interview with the police?"

"I met that Inspector Treadles you worked with on the Sackville case. What an awful, sanctimonious man."

Charlotte tilted her face in inquiry.

"The other inspector asked whether Lady Ingram might have been jealous of the friendship between you and Lord Ingram. I said that if she was jealous, it was over nothing, as you and Lord Ingram have always conducted yourselves according to the strictest rules of decorum. And guess what Inspector Treadles said?"

"Ah," murmured Charlotte.

"He said, in almost those exact words, that weren't you banished from Society because of something highly inappropriate with a different married man." Livia all but growled. "I despise him. I wonder how Lord Ingram can be friends with someone like that."

"No doubt Inspector Treadles wonders the same, how Lord Ingram can be friends with someone like me."

"I have some police inspectors in my Sherlock Holmes story. I'll change their portrayal, make them idiotic and incompetent, and call one of them Treadles."

"That might not be the best idea."

"Maybe not. But it's a most *satisfying* thought."

"I see you are all right," said Charlotte wryly, "which is what I came to see."

"I'll be fine. I'm only a bystander in all this. I hope Lord Ingram . . ."

Against the stark reality of the situation, her hope seemed too fragile to take shape.

Charlotte briefly settled a hand on her shoulder. "I'll do what I can. Now tell me, in some detail, what you discussed with Scotland Yard."

When Livia had finished recounting what had been said, to the best of her recollection, including her charge that someone was deliberately trying to frame Lord Ingram, namely whoever had set Lady Avery and Lady Somersby to uncover a "grand injustice" for Lady Ingram, Charlotte nodded and fell silent.

After a minute or so, she said, "I must go now. The police will wish to speak to you again. And when they do, will you do something for me?"

---

"Uneasy about something, Inspector?"

Treadles started—and realized that he had been rubbing his temples while pacing the parlor, his strides quick and agitated. The more he thought about it, the more complicated Charlotte Holmes's presence became. Despite Lord Ingram's denials, that he might wish to marry her was considered a potential, perhaps likely, motive for Lady Ingram's murder. If Treadles were to tell Chief Inspector Fowler that Charlotte Holmes was here on the premises, in close contact with Lord Ingram, how would that affect Lord Ingram?

Disastrously, to say the least.

Fowler peered up at Treadles. He looked owlish, but an owl was a predator and a damned good one at that. Treadles felt trapped between his professional obligations and his loyalty to Lord Ingram. And the longer he waited before he revealed what he knew, the worse it would look for him.

"I was thinking about the state of Lord Ingram's marriage in the past few years," Treadles said. "Must not have been pleasant living in that household."

"That's the trouble with putting women on a pedestal. You do that, and they always fall off—knocking you over on the way down," said Fowler.

Treadles might have laughed, if not for how aptly Fowler's observation described his own situation.

The next moment his fingers were at his temples again, pressing hard. His reaction to the crumbling of Lord Ingram's marriage had consisted primarily of a despondent sympathy. But now a terrifying thought struck. He had met Lady Ingram, not long before the latter allegedly fled with her lover. Granted the meeting had been very brief. But had he received any impression that Lady Ingram was the kind of woman to sacrifice everything for a man?

To the contrary, the more he thought about it, the more discordant Lord Ingram's account grew.

At times he'd considered Charlotte Holmes cold, when Miss Holmes was only unsettlingly neutral. Lady Ingram, on the other hand, had been truly cold, a glacial lack of warmth that made Treadles wonder whether she derived any pleasure from life. He could see her act out of spite, but not love.

Not love.

He became aware that Fowler was still observing him. No point pretending that he wasn't distracted, so he shook his head, as if to clear it. "A deuced business, this case."

Now to redirect Fowler's attention. He pointed at Sergeant Ellerby's notes on ladies Avery and Somersby, which Fowler had been reviewing. "Something to keep in mind, Chief Inspector: I fear Sergeant Ellerby might have a mistaken impression of Lady Avery and Lady Somersby."

"Oh?"

"He thinks them the town equivalent of a pair of village busybodies."

"Sometimes busybodies stumble upon crimes. You needn't worry that I wouldn't take them seriously as witnesses, Inspector."

"I didn't worry about it at all, Chief Inspector. But it behooves me to mention that during the Sackville case, Lord Ingram himself had consulted them for pertinent information—though of course he didn't tell them that he was the conduit through which the information would pass to Scotland Yard."

Fowler tapped his fingertips on the desk before him. "So they are to a pair of village busybodies what the Reading Room at the British Museum is to the typical lending library."

"Precisely."

The Reading Room at the British Museum walked in just then, a pair of alert women in their early forties. Unlike most other witnesses Treadles had faced in his career, Lady Avery and Lady Somersby were neither nervous nor reticent: They came prepared to impart every fact they knew and a few theories besides.

For most of the interview, what they said did not add much to Sergeant Ellerby's preliminary report—despite his doubts about their gossiping ways, he had taken copious and accurate notes. But Fowler's ears perked up when Lady Somersby brought up the encounter between Charlotte Holmes and Lord Ingram near the end of the Season.

Treadles had seen Lord Ingram and Charlotte Holmes together more than once this past summer. Judging by the location the meeting was said to have taken place, it would have been around the time he and they met by chance outside a house in Hounslow that happened to contain a dead body, a case that was supposedly solved, though never to Treadles's satisfaction.

He still didn't know what they had been doing there. But the ladies, well, at least they didn't insinuate; they said in so many words that it seemed a distinct possibility that Lord Ingram might have been keeping Miss Holmes as his mistress.

Treadles didn't think that had been the case. He thought of the tension between Lord Ingram and Miss Holmes the night of his and Lord Ingram's first visit to 18 Upper Baker Street. There had been a great deal of genuine disapproval on Lord Ingram's part. Perhaps sentiments other than censure also fueled that tension, but overall their interaction had not come across as loverly.

When he'd met them in Hounslow, after the conclusion of the Sackville case, he had been more than a little taken aback—and upset—by Miss Holmes's sudden and unexpected appearance at a murder site of which he had just been informed himself. But he should still have sensed the difference had they become carnally involved by then.

That said, he had no way of knowing whether that had changed since the end of summer, especially after Lady Ingram's departure, if the latter had indeed absconded with her own illicit lover.

"You wouldn't know how we could speak to this Miss Holmes, would you, ladies?" asked Fowler.

Treadles's conscience twitched. He exhaled, relieved that his colleague wasn't looking in his direction. But he knew that he was lying by omission—more so with every passing minute.

Lady Avery snorted. "Good luck with that, Chief Inspector. We have been trying to discover her whereabouts since she ran away from home."

Fowler glanced down at his list of questions. "Now, if you don't mind telling me, madam, did you immediately suspect that Lady Ingram's departure had something untoward about it, or was it only after you accidentally learned that Miss Holmes had met with Lord Ingram after she became an exile?"

"Well, to be perfectly honest, neither. Shortly before I set out for the Isle of Wight, where I would meet the maid who had worked at the tea shop in Hounslow, we received a note, asking why we, who have made it our business to inquire into situations that do not seem right, hadn't paid the slightest attention to Lady Ingram's absence. Scolding us, one might say, for that lack of animal instinct.

"We were of a mind to disregard it. We receive a great many anonymous tips concerning all manner of individuals. And we had become proficient at distinguishing those that deserve further investigation from those that are merely pranks—or worse, malice in written form.

"Lord Ingram was one of the few good ones, we thought, a man whose integrity we need not question, because he was vigilant about it and never self-indulgent. But the meeting with Miss Holmes changed everything. Now he had a reason to want to be rid of Lady Ingram. A reason that could pass for noble sentiments, even: Were he a free man, he could rescue Miss Holmes from her state of exile."

Chief Inspector Fowler nodded. He did not ask whether Miss Holmes needed—or indeed even wanted—to be rescued from that state of exile. "There seems to be a gap of a fortnight between when you verified with the maid that the woman with Lord Ingram had indeed been Miss Holmes and when you wrote to him about the matter. Were you further checking the facts during that time?"

"I wasn't," said Lady Avery. "As it so happened, my sister and I both fell ill. Even the most exciting exposé pales in importance when one's health is at risk."

"I see," said Fowler, a hint of incredulity to his tone, as if he couldn't believe that these two women would prize anything above gossip. "I hope you have both recovered satisfactorily."

"Yes, very much so."

"I'm glad to hear that. And if it's not too much trouble, I would like to see the note you received."

Lady Avery excused herself, left the room, and returned a few minutes later. The policemen inspected the stationery—good but not exceptional, postmarked near Euston Station in London—and the writing—done by a typewriter, every letter regular, crisp, and anonymous.

"We'd like to hold on to this, with your permission."

"You are welcome to it."

"And one last thing before I let you go, ladies. Have you heard, by any chance, of a man Lady Ingram might have loved as a girl, before she married Lord Ingram?"

"We have, but fairly recently. The first we heard was this past summer." The ladies each opened a large diary and found the record almost simultaneously. The last day of June, as a matter of fact.

"Do you believe it?"

Lady Somersby closed her diary. "That's difficult to say. We had thought, at first, that it made a great deal of sense. But now when we consider everything together, we ask ourselves, as much as it pains us to do so, whether Lord Ingram might not have had a hand in its dissemination."

Treadles stiffened, recalling his own doubt about the likelihood of Lady Ingram giving up everything for a man.

"To what end?" asked Fowler.

"Should people doubt the validity of the initial reason given for her disappearance—her health—he could then fall back on a different one. Much more embarrassing, granted, but believable—that she might have run off with the man she loved—with no hint of wrongdoing on Lord Ingram's part."

This was exactly the explanation Lord Ingram had given. It didn't mean that Lord Ingram had lied—Treadles prayed that he had not—but it now behooved Treadles to proceed with at least as much skepticism as did ladies Avery and Somersby.

Did Lord Ingram understand the uphill battle he faced?

Treadles remembered him standing outside the icehouse, staring off at nothing in particular, with only his cigarette for companion.

He understood. He understood better than anyone that he was in a fight for nothing less than his life.

"Since you are vocal about where your suspicions fall," said Fowler, "let me ask you, then, ladies, do you think anyone other than Lord Ingram might have wished Lady Ingram harm?"

"I know a number who would derive a certain satisfaction if he found grounds to divorce her, but frankly I can't think of anyone who would want her *dead*," said Lady Somersby.

"What about Miss Charlotte Holmes?" Fowler asked.

Lady Somersby grimaced. "I must say, Miss Holmes had never displayed the slightest interest, benign or otherwise, in Lady Ingram. She is a difficult one to understand, that one."

"Lord Ingram insists that he would not have proposed to Miss Holmes, even if he were a free man. He also insists that Miss Holmes would not have accepted any proposal from him, not even today. How do you assess those statements?"

"Well, it is true that Miss Holmes had turned down some highly eligible men in her time." Lady Avery frowned, but shook her head. "I can't predict with any accuracy what she would do, if she were presented with a proposal from Lord Ingram, as a free man."

"Even in her current state of ruin?"

"Even so. Miss Holmes is *odd*, Chief Inspector. And I don't mean eccentric. Eccentric is wearing two hats on your head because you like it. Miss Holmes's oddity is both different and . . . larger."

"The fact that no one can be sure she will accept a proposal from Lord Ingram—does it not undermine your claim that he would murder his wife to make that proposal possible?" Treadles pointed out.

He certainly wanted to believe that.

"Not as much as you would imagine, Inspector. First, Lord Ingram could very well be prepared for an initial rejection. As long as he remains an eligible man, he would be able to repeat the same overture and gradually wear her down. Second, Miss Holmes is in a difficult position. She has diminished her parents' standing and severely impaired her sister's chances at a good marriage. She knows it. And she knows that only by marrying a man in a position of power and prestige can she hope to undo some of the damage.

"And third, but perhaps most important, Lord Ingram might not be able to help himself on this matter. Part of the reason he was eager to marry Lady Ingram was because she appeared to require a knight in shining armor to rescue her from her penury. He could easily convince himself that he was the cavalry charge Miss Holmes didn't know she desperately needed."

"Lord Ingram does not seem to me a fanciful sort of man," countered Fowler. "In fact, he appears very much in control of himself."

"Lord Ingram is good at appearing so. But he is a man in love, and a man in love will do just about anything for the object of his affection."

Fowler's eyes widened. "You allege that Lord Ingram is in love with Miss Holmes?"

Lady Avery exchanged a look with her sister. "Why, isn't that obvious?"

## Twelve

The interview with Lady Avery and Lady Somersby did not conclude there.

Chief Inspector Fowler went on to ask the ladies who they supposed might have sent the note chiding them for not paying closer attention to Lady Ingram's disappearance. They had no good guesses but felt that the writer was unlikely to be a member of Lord Ingram's staff, because of its imperious tone.

"Even an upper servant, writing anonymously, wouldn't address a ladyship in this manner. Would have been more deferent."

Attesting to Sherrinford Holmes's skillful insinuation, Fowler concluded by asking whether the ladies knew anyone who might wish *Lord* Ingram harm. The question surprised the ladies and made them thoughtful but yielded no useful answers.

Treadles took good notes, as he should. But it was difficult to maintain his concentration.

Lord Ingram. In love. With Miss Holmes.

It shouldn't have shocked him. Hadn't he sensed something between the two, from the very beginning? He hadn't wanted to let his thoughts go down that direction, hadn't wanted to believe that Lord

Ingram, the very embodiment of manly virtues, could feel more for Miss Holmes than an exasperated friendship.

The exasperated friendship had most certainly been there. As well as a deeply frustrated protectiveness, a constant awareness, and a fierce and fiercely repressed yearning.

What did he see in her? Treadles supposed that one must admire Miss Holmes's mind. He himself still did, however reluctantly. And he supposed there were Miss Holmes's looks, which were not displeasing. But her femininity was only skin-deep. Underneath that . . .

Near the end of the Sackville case, Miss Holmes had sat calmly and unspooled one revelation after another, as he, the professional, reeled from the ugliness that came to light. The woman had no feelings. No horror at the vilest human deeds. No regrets about running away from home. No shame over the conduct that had brought her low.

And certainly no need for a man.

Lord Ingram might as well have fallen in love with a pretty dress—or an advertising poster featuring a woman with blond ringlets.

Lady Avery and Lady Somersby were leaving. Fowler rose. So did Treadles, a moment too late.

"I must confess," said Fowler, rather conversationally, after he thanked the women, "that I'm now highly curious about this Miss Charlotte Holmes."

Treadles's conscience chafed again. Why was he keeping this silence? And for how much longer?

"If you find her," replied Lady Avery in all seriousness, "please tell her we wish to speak to her."

When they had left, Fowler turned to Treadles. "Did you notice what she said? *If* we find her, not when. We are policemen, are we not? Let us find her."

---

The interview with the boy who first discovered Lady Ingram's body was a great deal less interesting, notable only for the confirmation that yes, the last time he'd been sent to fetch ice was indeed a while ago. But that ice hadn't been needed didn't mean he didn't visit the third antechamber, either to fetch or to store foodstuff, only that it hadn't been necessary to proceed all the way to the ice well.

In other words, the body could have been there for weeks without anyone knowing. Anyone, that is, except Lady Ingram's murderer.

Chief Inspector Fowler made quick work of the rest of the indoor staff, seeing them in groups. Most had little of value to impart. But the policemen did learn several interesting things.

First, there had been a minor fire in the house a little less than a month ago. Second, Lord Remington, the youngest of Lord Ingram's three elder brothers, had visited Stern Hollow not once, but twice in the recent past, the first time apparently incognito. He'd been met at the front of the house by Lord Ingram himself. They had then sequestered themselves in the library for most of the rest of the day, emerging just before dinner for Lord Remington to take his leave.

The head footman, who had delivered tea and food into the study and therefore had a good look at this visitor, was thoroughly surprised when Lord Remington had visited again, this time as the master's brother. Lord Remington, having lived abroad for most of his adult life, hadn't been known to Lord Ingram's staff. But he'd endeared himself to them when he came again.

The third oddity involved complaints from the French chef and the housekeeper. They had been asked whether they'd noticed strange goings-on in the household and had both mentioned small quantities of food going missing, for weeks on end, in a way that couldn't be easily accounted for.

"Once I went down to the stillroom late at night and saw the light on," said the housekeeper, Mrs. Sanborn. "I thought I'd catch the thief at last but it was only Lord Ingram, fetching himself a few extra ginger biscuits."

"Does that happen often?" Fowler asked.

"I'm sure it does sometimes. His lordship is very considerate of the staff. Unless there are guests, we are not expected to work after dinner. Anything he needs at night, he sees to himself."

Fowler moved on to other questions. But before he let the housekeeper return to her duties, he asked, "Does Lord Ingram like ginger biscuits?"

"Not particularly—his lordship doesn't care for sweet things. I keep some on hand because Miss Lucinda and Master Carlisle enjoy them, but Lord Ingram doesn't eat them very often."

At that answer, Fowler gave Treadles a delighted look. Treadles felt his stomach twist.

They went on to interview the rest of the guests.

A few of the gentlemen had returned from Scotland recently, having enjoyed some excellent Highland shooting while there. Another fancied himself an amateur astronomer and had actually set up his telescope near the icehouse one night but saw and heard nothing remotely useful to the police.

Most of the other guests, ladies by and large, had been at various other gatherings before they alighted at Mrs. Newell's. None of them seemed to have any cause for wanting Lady Ingram dead. Many knew her only minimally.

Mrs. Newell gave the reason. "She had never cared for me, nor I for her. You will excuse an old woman's pride, but I have always been a good judge of character and I knew from the beginning that she did not love him. That woman did not have his best interests at heart, not for a day of her life.

"I never invited her to my house and she returned that favor.

Our circles did not intersect very much. Lord Ingram always called on me here and in London, when I still went for the Season, but she never accompanied him."

Fowler glanced down at Sergeant Ellerby's notes. "You are related in some way to Lord Ingram, am I correct?"

"My late husband's sister was married to Lord Ingram's maternal uncle. It's hardly a close kinship, but I've always been fond of him. And Remington. Their two elder brothers, not so much."

Mrs. Newell then went on to berate Fowler for even harboring the slightest suspicion concerning Lord Ingram. "I don't know who killed her and I don't particularly care—if there weren't children involved I'd say good riddance. But her husband did not do it."

Fowler waited until she had finished testifying to Lord Ingram's general saintliness before asking, "Madam, you must have heard Lady Avery's report on the meeting between Lord Ingram and Miss Holmes in the summer, after she'd disappeared from Society. What do you think is going on between those two?"

"I will not stoop to speculations. But I will tell you this, Chief Inspector. That young lady knows everything. I've known her since she was a little girl—her father is my cousin—and it was the most disconcerting thing to hear her tell people things about them that she couldn't possibly have known in advance."

"What things, if you don't mind my asking?"

"Once she told the late Duchess of Wycliffe, Lord Ingram's mother, that she was sorry about the news from the doctor. Her Grace had just learned that she had a tumor—the tumor that would kill her—and she hadn't informed *anyone*. Not a soul, because she refused to believe it herself."

"Hmm," said Fowler.

"Precisely. Later she learned not to say such unsettling things to people—or at least to do so less frequently. But trust me when I tell you that her powers did not disappear when she came of age. If

Lord Ingram killed his wife, then he could never again appear before Miss Holmes. Even if no one else ever knew, she would. And I don't think she would countenance a cold-blooded murder, not even on the part of a very good friend."

—❖—

The policemen asked to see Lord Ingram again and were received in the library. This time, Lord Ingram was alone, the heavily disguised Miss Holmes nowhere to be seen.

Chief Inspector Fowler got to the point. "You mentioned, my lord, that Lady Ingram consulted Mr. Sherlock Holmes. We should like to speak with the detective as soon as possible."

Lord Ingram nodded. "Naturally. I will ask his brother to send a message."

"Excellent," said Fowler. "There is someone else we would like to see—Miss Charlotte Holmes."

"I'm afraid I have no idea how to get word to Miss Holmes," answered Lord Ingram, without any change in tone or expression.

He looked at Fowler, but Treadles felt himself at the center of Lord Ingram's attention.

He didn't know whether Lord Ingram and Miss Holmes had expected him as an emissary of Scotland Yard. Nor could he be sure whether Miss Holmes had been aware the exact moment he had seen through her disguise. But when Lord Ingram had made it known that Sherrinford Holmes was brother to Sherlock Holmes, who, as a fictional character, could have no flesh-and-blood brothers, he had announced to Treadles loud and clear that Miss Holmes was among them.

Had, in effect, asked him, out of friendship, not to inform anyone of her presence.

Because Chief Inspector Fowler was not the only one conducting a murder investigation at Stern Hollow.

Miss Holmes, despite Treadles's unease at her unchaperoned attendance, was not there to engage in an illicit affair with Lord Ingram—or at least not only that—but to find out the truth of what had happened to Lady Ingram.

For her work to continue unhindered, there could not be any challenge to Sherrinford Holmes's identity.

But this went against everything Treadles believed about how a man and an officer of the Criminal Investigation Department ought to conduct himself. He would be breaking so many rules that he might as well set Buckingham Palace on fire, too, while he was at it.

Not to mention, by allowing Lord Ingram to get away with this massive lie, he would open himself up to accusations of criminal misconduct, of a magnitude to end his career with the C.I.D.

"Are you sure about that, my lord?" he heard himself ask. "That you have no means of reaching Miss Holmes?"

Lord Ingram looked him in the eye. "I am sure."

*If Lord Ingram killed his wife, then he could never again appear before Miss Holmes.*

Treadles said nothing else.

Fowler sighed. "I do wish that were otherwise."

A knock came at the door. When Lord Ingram gave his assent, Miss Olivia Holmes walked in.

Her gaze landed on Lord Ingram first, a look full of concern and sympathy. Upon seeing Chief Inspector Fowler, her expression turned wary. When she realized Treadles was also present, her features twisted with loathing.

He had never done this woman any harm, never done anything except speak factually of her sister's misdeeds.

It should not matter that Miss Olivia Holmes detested him. Yet her animosity was like a bludgeon across the cheek and something inside him cracked with a flash of searing bewilderment.

She, who had never set a foot wrong, was now saddled with near-certain spinsterhood, because of her sister's reckless amorality. She should be angry at that sister—should blaze in the dark with the heat of her outrage. Yet if she could cause it with the force of her will, at this moment it was Treadles who would be flying out of the window in a spray of glass and wood splinter.

And she was not alone in her devotion to Charlotte Holmes.

Standing beside her in comradeship was Lord Ingram, a man of otherwise incorruptible virtues. A man who would, Treadles was beginning to see, never, ever repudiate Charlotte Holmes.

Not to his last breath.

Not even if that last breath was drawn with a noose around his neck.

"Ah, Miss Holmes," said Fowler, "just the person we wished to see."

"How may I be of assistance, Chief Inspector?" said Miss Olivia Holmes, her tone cautious—and more than a little prickly.

"We find ourselves in need to speak to Miss Charlotte Holmes and we were hoping you could help us."

"But I already told you that Charlotte has nothing to do with any of this."

"Nevertheless, we would like to ask her some questions."

Miss Olivia Holmes looked toward Lord Ingram, her gaze beseeching, as if a word from him would send the policemen packing.

"At this moment, it would be best if Fowler could speak directly to Miss Charlotte," Lord Ingram said with great gentleness. "I can offer no advice on how to locate her. If you can, it would be of help to me."

Still, Miss Olivia Holmes hesitated.

"Miss Holmes," said Fowler, his tone grave to the point of heaviness, "may I remind you that—"

"I know you are the law, sir. But I have no idea where my sister is. It is our agreement that I remain ignorant on the matter, so that I cannot inadvertently inform my parents of her whereabouts."

"I see," said Fowler, frowning.

"But before she left home, Charlotte told me that if I needed to contact her, I can put a notice in the paper, in a simple code of her devising. I will give you the cipher. Is there anything else you need from me?"

Fowler took a step in her direction. "You are not leaving, are you, Miss Holmes?"

"We are here because of an unfortunate mishap at Mrs. Newell's house. Now that her place is habitable again, Mrs. Newell has invited me to return there."

"And the other guests?"

"Most of them will leave directly from Stern Hollow to their next destination. Mrs. Newell expressed the wish that I should remain with her a little longer, and I will."

"Very good. We were hoping you will remain in the vicinity for some more time, in case we need to speak with you again."

Miss Olivia Holmes smiled, a smile at once brittle and icy. "I will, of course, render every assistance."

When she had left the room, Fowler said, "A very spirited young lady. Is her sister at all like her?"

The question was addressed to Lord Ingram, who said, almost as if amused, "I shouldn't think so."

"How would you describe Miss Charlotte Holmes, then?"

"She . . . rather defies description."

Fowler would not take that for an answer. "Lady Avery and Lady Somersby characterize her as odd, grandly odd. What do you think?"

Lord Ingram picked up a paperweight from his desk and turned it around in his hand. "If I were to think of it at all, I would be struck by how grandly and inhospitably strange the world must appear to Charlotte Holmes."

❊

Charlotte had originally planned to inquire at nearby railway stations as to whether any coffins had recently arrived. But by the time she reached the village, she had changed her mind.

A coffin coming to a small community invited questions. *Who was inside? Where would the burial take place? How was this person related to local residents?* All inquiries that those transporting murder victims on the sly would not want to answer.

She next thought to check with station porters for trunks that weighed more than a hundred pounds. But those might appear suspicious, too. Worse, they might prove memorable.

Crates, then. People expected crates to be heavy. Not to mention, so many things were shipped in crates they would arouse no more curiosity than a . . .

"Sir? Sir? May I help you?"

She started, but it was only the station agent. She realized that she had been standing four feet away from his window for several minutes, caught in her own thoughts. She stamped her feet—the train shed shielded the platform from the rain tapping at the roof, but not from the cold, which seeped in patiently, inexorably—and approached the man.

"Yes, you may, my good man."

"Excellent. Where are you headed? Miserable day to be out, isn't it?"

Perhaps he was loquacious by nature; perhaps sitting inside a small brick box all day long, on this not-at-all-busy platform, had given him a hunger for conversation. In either case, he was exactly what Charlotte was hoping for.

"Miserable day, indeed," Charlotte agreed heartily. "I wouldn't mind sitting by a fire with a hot toddy in hand, I tell you. Anyway, Sherrinford Holmes, at your service."

"Wally Walpole, at yours."

"I just came from Stern Hollow. You've heard what happened?"

Wally Walpole's eyes widened with both dismay and the anticipation of gossip. "Terrible, terrible thing. And she such a beautiful young woman, too."

"A tragedy, no doubt. But now we must find out what happened. I've been tasked by Lord Ingram's family to investigate on his behalf. I understand that some crates headed for Stern Hollow came through here recently."

Wally Walpole blinked, not quite seeing the connection between crates and Lady Ingram's sensational death. But that did not prevent him from answering Charlotte's query. "Yes, two large crates. I had to sign for them, since they were put into the station's care. But that really wasn't necessary. Lord Ingram's lads were already here, waiting."

"How did they know to come?"

"From what I understand, the London agent of the company that sells the equipment sends a note around and tells Lord Ingram when his orders are expected to arrive."

"So the lads show up and you have a chat."

"Not too long, since they do have work to do." Wally Walpole sighed with regret. "But yes, a bit of a chat."

Since he seemed in dire need of company, Charlotte related some of what had been going on at Stern Hollow, nothing any of the servants wouldn't have been able to tell him, had they come through the railway station. He listened with his mouth half open, his throat emitting occasional gurgles of disbelief.

When she judged that she'd given him enough, she paused, as if remembering something. "By the way, the two crates you mentioned, were those the only ones that came for Lord Ingram recently?"

Wally Walpole's eyes lit up. "Funny you should ask."

⊰⊱

One of the reasons Chief Inspector Fowler, the Bloodhound of the Yard, had come by that moniker was his legendary ability to sniff out a valuable witness from a mere bystander.

That ferocious instinct was on display when he and Treadles interviewed the outdoor staff. As he had done with the indoor staff and the guests, Fowler spoke to them in groups. This time, however, when he had seen everyone, he asked to see one particular gardener again.

The young man trudged back inside the blue-and-white parlor, and immediately glanced at Treadles, as if seeking reassurance. He appeared scared and, Treadles had to admit, guilty.

Of something.

"Mr. Keeling," said Fowler coldly, "I don't think you've told us everything you know."

Keeling looked to Treadles again. "Best answer the chief inspector's question," Treadles said. "No use trying to hide anything."

"I'm not. I don't know anything about how Lady Ingram died."

"Maybe not," said Fowler. "But you know something. And that something you know might prove useful to us."

Keeling, perspiration already beading on the tip of his nose, mulishly shook his head.

Fowler rapped his knuckles against the arm of his chair and looked meaningfully at Treadles. Treadles grimaced inwardly. Everyone always said he had a kind, trustworthy face, which meant that when hardnosed old coppers wanted someone to ease a witness into compliance, Treadles was their man.

He leaned forward in his seat. "A woman who hasn't been seen for months turns up dead on her husband's property. Whom would *you* suspect, Mr. Keeling?"

"I don't think it's Lord Ingram."

"I don't think it's him either. I know the man—we've been

friends for years. But this isn't looking good for him. If you know of something that might help . . ."

"I don't know anything that'd help. At least, I can't think how it would help. I only know something strange."

"Something odd would be a good place to start."

"But if I tell you, I'll get into trouble."

"I'm sure Lord Ingram will compensate you for that trouble, should it come to that."

Still Keeling hesitated. "I'm not the only person who'll get in trouble."

Treadles was beginning to understand his reluctance. "If something were to happen to Lord Ingram, his children would go to live with a guardian, and this place will most likely be shuttered until Master Carlisle comes of age. In which case, most of the staff will be let go. Have you thought of that?"

Keeling shrank. "Will that really happen?"

"I'm hoping to prevent that. You like it here?"

"I do."

"And you would like for things to stay as they are?"

"Yes."

"Then let me hear what you're holding back. I promise you won't regret it. And I promise to protect the other person who is involved in this story from any and all repercussions."

"That's a real promise?"

"A real promise."

"What about—the chief inspector over there?"

"My father was in service. I understand it's a difficult life," said the "chief inspector over there." "I am not here for you or whatever minor infractions you might have committed. I am here to find out what happened to Lady Ingram. That's it."

Keeling swallowed. "There is—someone who works in the house. We try to see each other, but it's not easy. Used to be I snuck into the house. It's a big house and most of the time, most of the rooms don't have anyone in them.

"But the last time we met in the house we were almost discovered. She said no more. I was scared witless myself, so I agreed. But then, one day, Finney came to see Mr. Dean, the head gardener."

"Finney being the kitchen helper who first discovered Lady Ingram?"

"That's him. There was going to be a dinner in the big house that night and he needed to get into the icehouse. But the French cook gave him the wrong key. He was afraid of the French cook, so he came to Mr. Dean to ask for his copy. Mr. Dean didn't know Finney—he'd just started that week—so he gave the key to me and I went with Finney to the icehouse and showed him how to chisel out ice.

"Later, I started to think that the icehouse would make for a good place to meet. The outermost chamber didn't feel any colder than outside."

"Still pretty uncomfortable in this weather for disrobing," Fowler pointed out.

Keeler flushed. "We don't disrobe."

"Ah," said Fowler.

"No, I meant, we don't do anything of the sort. We just want to be alone and talk."

"What do you talk about?"

"She can paint beautiful miniature portraits from people's photographs. And I—" He flushed again. "I write poems. We talk about the day when we can have a small studio. The portraits would be the main draw, of course, but I can write a few lines of verse for each picture, something the clients won't be able to get anywhere else. Those would make for one-of-a-kind engagement gifts."

Treadles smiled. Most of the time, a revelation such as Keeling's did not involve aspirations that were almost adorable in their wholesomeness. "I like that plan. Now go on, about the icehouse."

Keeling relaxed a little. "Day before yesterday, we were supposed to meet there after tea."

Not a bad time. Keeling's own work would have finished by then. Assuming that his sweetheart was a housemaid, her work would be behind her, too. And the work in the kitchen would be in full swing, any foodstuffs needed from the icehouse fetched hours ago.

"I always go to the icehouse first, to make sure no one is around. If it's safe, I tie a handkerchief on the branch of a nearby tree. But that day, when I tried to unlock the door, my key wouldn't go in. It was a bit dark by then, so I tried a few more times before I knelt down to take a good look. And it wasn't the same lock that had always been there."

Treadles's heartbeat quickened. "No?"

"No. My uncle was a locksmith—he died when I was fourteen and his widow had to sell the business. But even if I'd never been his apprentice, I'd have known that it was a different lock. Different shape, different weight, different everything."

"Did you try to open it?"

"No. Once I realized it was different, I got scared that we'd been discovered and this was a warning. I ran down to the tree. She was just coming then. I told her that the lock had been changed—that maybe someone knew about us. We agreed that we shouldn't meet for some time. She went back to the house and I went to my room above the mews."

"And there to spend a restless night?"

"Well, no, I saw her at supper in the servants' hall, but we didn't speak. And then a restless night."

"What did you think when you learned that Lady Ingram's body had been found in the icehouse?"

"I was confused. Nobody mentioned a new lock. This morning I got up early, picked the lock of the cabinet where Mr. Dean keeps his keys, and checked the copy I'd made against his. He still had the same icehouse key as from before. And I'm sure he'd have been given a new key if the lock change had been official."

Treadles glanced at Fowler, who did not seem remotely displeased by the news.

Any time his superior took pleasure in a development, it could only be bad news for Lord Ingram. And now that Treadles had tacitly yet indisputably sided with Lord Ingram, Fowler's pleasure felt like a punch in the gut.

"Thank you, Mr. Keeling," said Chief Inspector Fowler. "You have been most helpful."

## Thirteen

Sherrinford Holmes marched into the library at Stern Hollow.

Despite the direness of his situation, Lord Ingram had to suppress an urge to smile.

By and large Charlotte Holmes was unhurried in her ways. Unless one knew, for example, the fiendish speed at which she read or that she needed only three seconds of observation to extract all pertinent life facts from a stranger, it was easy to mistake her for a creature of languor, or even indolence.

The character she had created in Sherrinford Holmes, however, spoke at a rapid clip and walked with a bounce in his step. And was a far more affable soul than she had ever been. In fact, if Lord Ingram didn't know any better, he might not find the chap comical at all. A bit peculiar but obviously a man of intelligence, discretion, and unimpeachable loyalty.

"Already back?" said Lord Ingram, rising. "I expected you to be out for longer."

"Come with me," said Holmes.

Lord Ingram did not hesitate.

In the vestibule a footman waited with hats, overcoats, and

gloves. Mr. Walsh, the house steward, was also there, alongside Sergeant Ellerby.

"Do you remember the two crates of expedition equipment you received a few days ago?" asked Holmes, shrugging into a caped coat.

Lord Ingram nodded.

The crates had arrived on the day Charlotte Holmes and Mrs. Watson toured the grounds of Stern Hollow. While he and Holmes were walking about in the kitchen garden, she had asked why he hadn't gone on any digs. And he had pointed to the lavender house, where his staff had just finished stowing the crates, which he hadn't bothered to open and examine, archaeology being the last thing on his mind these days.

"Well, according to the very helpful gentleman at the village station, one more crate arrived for you the next day. Do you know about that?"

His heart thudded. "No."

She turned to the majordomo. "What about you, Mr. Walsh?"

Mr. Walsh's eyes widened. "Now that you mention it, Mr. Holmes, I do recall being informed about an additional crate. It was the day Mrs. Newell and her guests arrived. Carts and carriages were pulling up to the house one after another with guests, luggage, and food for the kitchen. When the crate came, the two men who brought it said that a mistake had been made on the part of the equipment company and that they'd forgotten to include a few items, which was why the crate was being delivered all the way to the house instead of the railway station."

"At what time did the delivery come?" asked Lord Ingram, his heart beating even faster.

"Toward dusk. Or perhaps a little later. Since your lordship hadn't wished to bother with the other two crates, I had someone show the men directly to the lavender house. I meant to inform you, but it was a bit of an uproar that evening. I did remember twice the next day, but the first time you'd taken the gentlemen out to shoot and the second you were resting and had asked not to be disturbed. And then—and then the matter with the icehouse, and I'm afraid the additional crate completely slipped my mind." Mr. Walsh's complexion had turned a thoroughly perturbed pink. "My apologies, sir."

"I would have paid no mind to the crate even if you had mentioned it," said Lord Ingram. "No need to dwell on it further."

He had no idea what he would have done had he been told, but no point saying anything else to the steward. He turned to the policeman. "Sergeant, Mr. Holmes and I are headed for the lavender house. Would you care to come with us?"

Sergeant Ellerby, in fact, had no choice but to come with them. When Lord Ingram had gone for his ride earlier, he'd discovered that henceforth either Sergeant Ellerby or one of his constables must accompany him every time he stepped out of his own front door.

"I would be honored, sir," answered Sergeant Ellerby, with great sincerity.

And gratitude.

This gave Lord Ingram pause.

Sergeant Ellerby had been mortified when he'd informed Lord Ingram of the curtailment to his freedom. And now he was relieved that an invitation had been issued, so that he didn't need to officially insert himself as an unwelcome minder.

Lord Ingram supposed he could be forgiven for thinking that deep down Sergeant Ellerby believed him innocent.

But Sergeant Ellerby didn't know him as a person. His faith might be nothing more than a reluctance to attribute true darkness to a man who lived in an earthly Eden. Or even a tribal allegiance to the local squire, against barbarian outsiders from London.

No matter the sergeant's reasons, Lord Ingram found himself grateful. From the moment Lady Somersby had barred him from descending into the ice well, he had understood that he would be the prime suspect in this murder. But intellectual knowledge was scant preparation for the reality of the investigation.

There was Chief Inspector Fowler, of course, all lupine ferocity behind his owlish mien. There was Inspector Treadles, radiating discomfort, vacillating between sympathy and dismay. But the worst was the collective uncertainty of his staff. More than anything else, their unspoken misgivings made the air in the house heavy and the silence oppressive.

They still believed in him—they desperately did not want him to be the murderer—but they were beginning to wonder whether they knew him as well as they had thought they did.

Had it been twenty-four hours since Finney, the young kitchen helper, had run screaming out of the icehouse? Already, *not* being a murder suspect felt like a mythical state of bliss for which Lord Ingram could only yearn in hopeless futility.

The rain was now an inconsistent drizzle, but the temperature continued to drop. A gloom had settled over Stern Hollow. What daylight still remained suffered from a watery pallor, a grayness that stripped all vibrancy from even the gaudiest stretch of autumn foliage.

They were halfway to the lavender house when Sergeant Ellerby at last asked, "If you don't mind, Mr. Holmes, why are we headed out to see a crate of expedition equipment?"

Holmes pulled down the flaps of her deerstalker cap—Lord Ingram's deerstalker cap, in fact. It fit her well and he liked seeing it on her. "If I may be frank, Sergeant, it's obvious that Scotland Yard suspects Lord Ingram."

"I'm sure it's far too early to come to any conclusions," protested

Sergeant Ellerby. "Lady Ingram's body was only discovered yesterday."

"We thank you for your impartiality, sir. And I can truthfully say that no one was more flummoxed by Lady Ingram's untimely death than my friend here. Set aside the fact that his house swarms with investigators and the papers in London are saying goodness knows what, the whole thing has been incomprehensible from an operational point of view.

"Lady Ingram did not return to Stern Hollow at the end of the Season. She hasn't been here this autumn. How did her body end up in the icehouse? If we assume that she didn't travel here under her own power while she was still alive, then somebody else had to have transported her body. How did they do it?"

"The crate!" cried Sergeant Ellerby, catching on.

"From the lavender house it's about a furlong to the icehouse. Still no small distance to move a dead woman but doable for two men, or even one very strong one."

"So if you are right, we should see an open, empty crate in the lavender house?"

"That is possible," said Holmes. "At the very least, we should see that the lavender house's lock has been tampered with."

And the padlock that had once secured the lavender house was indeed absent. Sergeant Ellerby exclaimed and went down on all fours. "I see bits of metal filings near the threshold—still new and shiny. The servant Mr. Walsh sent to accompany the men with the crate would have locked the door after the crate was put in. So when these men came back for the crate again, they must have used a bolt cutter on the lock."

He opened the door excitedly.

Alas, the lavender house contained no open, empty crate.

Sergeant Ellerby glanced uncertainly at Holmes. But it was Lord

Ingram, his heart thumping, who said, "There are only two new crates here—these two."

He set his gloved hand atop a stack of crates placed against the far wall, between sturdy metal shelves that held a number of boxes and other crates marked FRAGILE and THIS SIDE UP. "Everything else was already here earlier. If Mr. Walsh is right and a third crate came the day before Lady Ingram was discovered—well, that crate is gone."

"But . . . wouldn't it have been easier to open it here and carry only the body to the icehouse?" puzzled Sergeant Ellerby.

"Look at the floor," said Holmes, pointing down. "Ash, would your servants have been so untidy?"

Elsewhere a few pieces of straw and wood splinters would not have been considered untidy in a rarely visited outbuilding. But this was Stern Hollow, where meticulousness was not an aspiration but a minimum standard. Lord Ingram's heart thumped harder. "They wouldn't. All the senior servants believe that cleanliness is next to godliness, and they have trained those under them accordingly."

Holmes nodded. "So the men who came later did uncrate in here."

"Then what did they do with the crate?" asked Sergeant Ellerby. "The gatehouse keeper might not mind a crate coming in. But wouldn't he think it strange to see men *leaving* with one?"

Holmes turned to Lord Ingram. "When I first visited here, I was given a map at the gatehouse. I remember more than one entrance marked on the map."

"So they could have left a different way and not been seen," marveled Sergeant Ellerby.

"Normally I would say no," said Lord Ingram, doing his best to keep his voice even, "because the only other entrance that would let a cart through doesn't have a manned gatehouse and is almost always locked. But if those men had a bolt cutter and a willingness to use it . . ."

"Get us some horses, Ash. Let's ride out that way," said Holmes.

---❈---

The unused entrance, from a distance, appeared properly shut. But when the company drew near, they saw that the two halves of the gate had been fastened together with nothing more than a length of rope, the chain and heavy padlock that usually secured them nowhere to be seen.

Rain was coming down hard again. They had borrowed some mackintoshes from the coach house, but Lord Ingram's trousers were soaking wet. And he could barely feel the tips of his fingers.

"I'm no expert," Sergeant Ellerby shouted to be heard above the rain. "But I didn't see any signs that would indicate our quarries veered off the driving lane to get rid of the crate. Why do you think they took it with them?"

"They might simply be cautious," replied Holmes.

"Or perhaps they needed it for some other reason," said Lord Ingram, still searching the ground, his boots squelching in the mud.

"Maybe," said Holmes. "It's getting dark and the rain isn't helping. Let's go back to the house!"

As much as he would have preferred to pursue the men with the crate—or at least find some hints as to where they had been headed, she was right. It was too late in the day to see anything, and with cold, wet trousers plastered to his person, he might come across pneumonia first.

He helped her up her horse. "Good work," he said, in a volume meant for only her ears.

"Thank you, my lord." She leaned down and murmured, "And do you know what I want in return for all my good work?"

His heart skipped several beats. "What?"

"Three hundred quid in compensation." She squeezed his hand through their sodden gloves. "Mrs. Watson will send an invoice."

⁎

Chief Inspector Fowler spoke again to Finney, the young servant who first stumbled upon Lady Ingram's body. The boy was confused to hear talk of a different lock and insisted that he, in his short time at Stern Hollow at least, had ever seen only one lock on the icehouse, the one he opened every time he went there, including the day he found Lady Ingram.

The discrepancy made Treadles's palms perspire.

After Fowler dismissed the boy, he informed the house steward that he wished to tour Lord and Lady Ingram's private chambers. Mr. Walsh, not exactly in a position to deny him the request, reminded him that Sergeant Ellerby and his men had already looked through the rooms' contents.

"Nevertheless, we wish to examine them again."

Mr. Walsh led the way himself, his gait stiff with disapproval.

Lady Ingram's rooms, where they stopped first, felt as if they had never been occupied. Dust sheets covered everything, which, in the lamplight, seemed like so many bulky ghosts. Her dressing room, which should have housed a resplendent collection, was three quarters empty. Her clothes, like the woman herself, had never returned from London.

And the décor here had a different feel from the rest of the house, more opulent yet somehow, at the same time, stodgier.

"Empire style," mused Fowler, "while most of the other rooms we have seen are more modern."

Treadles recalled what ladies Avery and Somersby had said during their interview, that they suspected a secret oppression on Lord Ingram's part. They had given as example that Lady Ingram had not left any imprint on Stern Hollow—that it had seemed to belong wholly to her husband.

"Lady Ingram had very little interest in the decoration of domiciles. She was satisfied with how her rooms appeared and didn't want men traipsing through, changing everything," Mr. Walsh said with staunch loyalty to his employer, the one who was still alive.

Lord Ingram's chambers, in contrast, though of the exact same dimension as his late wife's, felt light and airy. Instead of Old Masters artworks, which populated the public rooms of the house, here on the walls were hung charcoal sketches of archaeological sites. Treadles recognized the one depicting the site on the Isles of Scilly, where they'd all enjoyed such a convivial time—and where he had first heard the name Sherlock Holmes.

The one that had pride of place—over the mantel—was labeled simply *Roman Villa*. Treadles recalled that Lord Ingram had written a small volume about the finding and excavation, when he was an adolescent, of a minor Roman ruin on his uncle's property.

"Inspector, if you would bring some more light here, please?" Fowler called from the dressing room.

Treadles brought in a seven-branch candelabra and lit all the tapers. Fowler was on his knees on the large, luxurious rug at the center of the spacious room. Before him lay a boot box that had been opened.

"I'm sure if you need to inspect any items from the dressing room, his lordship's valet will be more than happy to assist," said Mr. Walsh, his voice almost high-pitched with anxiety.

"Thank you but we are capable of helping ourselves," said Fowler, in a tone that brooked no dissent. Then, more quietly, to Treadles: "I found these at the very back. Take a look."

The boots were old and worn and seemed thoroughly unremarkable. But when Treadles lifted them up, he saw what Fowler had seen: The soles were encrusted with coal dust.

There had been coal dust on the floor of the icehouse.

Of course, this wasn't conclusive evidence that Lord Ingram had been inside the icehouse before Lady Ingram was found. Treadles would be surprised if the boy, Finney, didn't have some coal dust on his soles, from fetching enough coal to power kitchen stoves that daily must cook for a staff of eighty.

But again, this did not look good for Lord Ingram.

Treadles exhaled slowly, trying to contain a rising panic. Charlotte Holmes had better be quick with exculpatory evidence— Scotland Yard was proceeding at a blistering pace.

Fowler, satisfied that Treadles had understood the significance of the boots, went on to search the rest of the apartment.

They left with the boots, which Fowler gave to a constable, since Sergeant Ellerby, according to a most unhappy Mr. Walsh, had gone out with Lord Ingram and Mr. Holmes.

"I think it behooves us to examine the icehouse one more time, don't you think?" said Fowler.

They'd brought mackintoshes, but that did not make the walk to the icehouse much more pleasant. The constable stationed at the icehouse had retreated to inside the first antechamber, where he sat on a stool, huddled over a brazier that the house had provided.

"Chief Inspector! Inspector!" He leaped up and saluted.

"Why is it so wet in here?" asked Fowler. "Does the door leak?"

"No, sir. Sergeant Ellerby, Lord Ingram, and—"

The door to the second antechamber opened, and out came Sergeant Ellerby, Lord Ingram, and Miss Holmes.

"Chief Inspector, Inspector," said Sergeant Ellerby, his teeth chattering, "here to have another look at the icehouse? Us, too."

"Great minds think alike," added "Sherrinford Holmes," whose lips were quite blue.

Fowler's eyes narrowed. "Best get back to the house soon, Sergeant, before you catch a chill. Same for you two, my lord, Mr. Holmes."

"Thank you, Chief Inspector," said Mr. Holmes. "By the way, I have heard back from my brother. He will be able to receive us tonight, after dinner. Does the time suit you, gentlemen?"

Fowler raised a brow. "Yes, very much so. Thank you, Mr. Holmes. Though I must say, I had no idea Mr. Sherlock Holmes was in the vicinity."

"He has been rusticating in these parts for a few days," said "Sherrinford Holmes" cheerfully, despite her chattering teeth. "I am in the area to visit him, in fact. Of course I haven't seen much of him since everything happened. But there will be plenty of time for brotherly chats once all this unpleasantness is behind us."

Miss Holmes's nonchalance should have heartened Treadles, but the news that they were to see Sherlock Holmes so soon caught him flatfooted.

When a client called on Sherlock Holmes, Miss Holmes explained that his health kept him bedridden and all communications must go through her. From time to time, she would disappear into an adjacent room to consult him. In truth the room was empty and Sherlock Holmes only a front for Miss Holmes to exploit her own deductive abilities.

Chief Inspector Fowler, however, would not be satisfied with being told that Sherlock Holmes was in the next room. Where would Miss Holmes find an actual Sherlock Holmes on such short notice? And how could the act possibly fool eyes as sharp and suspicious as Fowler's?

"Shall we expect you after dinner, then?" asked Miss Holmes.

"Yes, of course," said Fowler, with a wolfish grin. "We are most eager to meet with Mr. Sherlock Holmes."

It was only after Miss Holmes, Lord Ingram, and Sergeant

Ellerby were on their way that a horrifying possibility occurred to Treadles. After he had stood by Lord Ingram, when the latter declared that he had no way of getting word to Miss Holmes, surely . . . surely she didn't mean to unmask herself tonight?

But what if that was exactly what she intended?

## Fourteen

"I have your tea here, Holmes."

Charlotte smiled a little: There was no better or more desirable way for a man to announce himself.

She emerged from her dressing room to find Lord Ingram already in the bedroom, standing with his back to her. He wore a blue-gray lounge suit, his dark hair still slightly damp, his fingertips grazing the lapel of Sherrinford Holmes's jacket, which she'd placed on the back of a chair.

Well, well. And here she thought she'd still need to push, shove, or otherwise cantilever him into her den of iniquity.

At her entrance he turned around. She thought he might comment on her attire—or lack thereof: She had on only a heavily embroidered dressing gown. But that was not what caused his jaw to slacken.

"What happened to your *hair*?"

She'd forgotten that he hadn't seen her without her Sherrinford Holmes wig. "I had it chopped off. There was too much. Wigs wouldn't sit properly."

"You chopped off everything!"

She hadn't. There were a good few inches left—Mrs. Watson

had absolutely refused to trim her hair any shorter. "I like it. Mrs. Watson says it brings out my eyes."

He shook his head, not so much in disagreement, but as if he still couldn't believe what he was seeing. "Anyway, come and eat something."

He had never complimented her looks—and he didn't need to. All she'd ever wanted from him was friendship.

And this, of course.

*This.*

She walked to the tea tray, which held an astonishingly beautiful French apple tart, paper-thin apple slices arranged in perfect concentric circles, glistening under an apricot jam glaze.

A decade ago, sitting at one of his digs with a book in one hand but, alas, nothing to eat, she'd pined for a French apple tart to try. He, a lover of Monsieur Verne's scientific romances, had pointed out, rather indignantly, that the French did things other than cooking. To which she'd replied that two of the foremost French inventions, canning and pasteurization, had to do with food and drink. And then she'd written a message in his notebook in Braille, another major French invention:

*You should have said, I'll ask my godfather's pastry chef to make it for you.*

She had no idea whether he'd ever bothered to translate the note. Certainly he had never obliged her on the French apple tart. Until now.

Too bad she didn't want any.

He looked at her. She smoothed the back of a spoon across the jam glaze on top of the tart, returning his gaze. He stood very still—no fidgeting for him. But in the rise and fall of his chest there was agitation. Inquietude.

"Why are you nervous?"

He hesitated. "You make me nervous."

"Why?" She was not nervous at all. "You must have done this hundreds of times—at least."

"Not with you."

"The process should be the same."

He glanced out of the window, his strong, sharp profile to her. "It's impossible to talk to you, sometimes."

"You mean, *all* the time? Or at least the vast majority? That's why we wisely did not bother with conversation when we were children."

He drew the curtains shut. It wasn't six o'clock yet, but it was almost pitch black outside. "What will we be to each other afterward?"

"What we have always been. Friends."

"And you think this"—the word was accompanied by a gesture toward the bed—"won't have repercussions?"

"So . . . you think we've had an easy, uncomplicated rapport and you don't want it to become thorny and convoluted?"

He snorted. "Can I want it not to become *more* thorny and convoluted?"

"Why does it have to be? Why can't things become simpler? Surely some of the difficulty we've experienced in our friendship could be attributed to the fact that we wanted to sleep together but you wouldn't permit it."

"Well, if you're going to put it like that."

"How would you put it, if not like that?"

He didn't reply but crossed the room, pulled out his pocket watch, and set it down on the nightstand. She liked the sight of it—his watch on her nightstand, his person leaning against the side of her bed. She went up to him and placed her hands on his chest.

"Thank you."

"For what?"

"For the apple tart, of course. For remembering it after all these years."

"I've never forgotten—and I absolutely will not have it said that Bancroft feeds you better than I do."

She smiled, cupped his face, and kissed him. He stood still and let her. And then he wrapped his arms around her and lifted her into bed.

Over supper, Chief Inspector Fowler and Treadles listened to Sergeant Ellerby's account of the missing padlock and crate from the lavender house, and the unused estate gate with its chain and lock gone.

Treadles, who had been picking at his food until Sergeant Ellerby joined them, experienced a surge of appetite—so Miss Holmes had been making some progress of her own, after all. Thank goodness.

He attacked his steak and kidney pie with renewed vigor.

"And then we returned to the icehouse for another look. And that's when Mr. Holmes asked me whether any bodies have turned up recently in these parts. I said no, not that I've heard of, and he asked me to keep an eye out for a well-dressed woman with her face bashed in and a man, not so well-dressed, who might have soiled himself before he died."

"Is that so?" said Fowler sharply. "Did Mr. Holmes say why?"

"I asked who they were and how they were related to Lady Ingram's death," said Sergeant Ellerby. "Mr. Holmes said that he didn't know enough to speak with complete confidence. Only that those bodies must be there—or at least the woman's must be there, according to his deductions."

Treadles remembered the strands of hair that Miss Holmes had found, some six feet away from where Lady Ingram had lain.

Fowler asked several more questions. When it became clear that the sergeant had nothing else to tell them, he thanked him gravely and wished him a good evening. Sergeant Ellerby saluted and left for his room at the constabulary, pushing open the door of the inn with some difficulty.

A high wind lashed. The night promised to be intolerable.

Treadles hesitated before he asked the chief inspector, "What do you think of the two bodies Mr. Holmes spoke of, sir?"

"A fishy thing to ask about, isn't it? I can't decide whether it's pure chicanery. Hard to think it could be anything else, when he must know word would get back to us."

Treadles did his best not to frown. Miss Holmes's methods might be incomprehensible to him but he could not argue with her effectiveness. Granted, Fowler hadn't worked with her before, but the competence "Sherrinford Holmes" displayed in the icehouse today should have earned her pronouncement a closer scrutiny. "And the rest?"

Fowler shook his head. "Too convenient that a crate that wasn't ever expected has by now disappeared. Not to mention, anyone could cut a padlock or two. Sergeant Ellerby is a good copper, but frankly, a little naïve."

But the arrival of the third crate was something that could be verified by interviewing the station agent, Mr. Walsh, and the man-servant Mr. Walsh sent to accompany the crate to the lavender house.

Would Fowler suggest, then, that all those involved must have been bribed by the rich and powerful local seigneur?

Treadles didn't say anything. It was clear that Fowler had his sights set on bagging Lord Ingram, who could prove a spectacular feather in the cap of an already legendary career.

Miss Holmes had better not help the chief inspector by revealing the truth of Sherlock Holmes tonight.

Treadles excused himself by saying that he needed to write his wife. He hadn't meant to actually do that, but before he knew it, he had already finished a letter.

*Dear Alice,*

*It's cold and miserable in Derbyshire. An interminable day, and it still hasn't ended yet.*

*I wish I could reassure you otherwise, but at the moment it isn't looking very good for Lord Ingram. The evidence that points to him is legion. Evidence to the contrary, despite some illogic and oddities, scant.*

*I hope tomorrow will bring better tidings.*

*Love,*
*Robert*

He found himself turning his pen around and around, wanting to write more. He used to dash off letters running several pages, telling her about every part of his day, major and minor. But now he felt like a rusted spigot that let out only trickles and irregular spurts.

He set down the pen and dropped his head into his hands.

———— ❖ ————

"Is there time to do it again?" asked Holmes, her eyes bright, her face flushed.

Lord Ingram reached for his watch on the nightstand. Three minutes to seven. They were to dine with Bancroft at half past. And even though he'd already told Bancroft they wouldn't be changing into tails and pumps, they were still running short on time. "No, not properly, in any case."

She sighed, the sound a sweet flutter. "I liked it. Did you?"

Did he? If he liked it any better, he would be stark-raving obsessed. "It was all right."

"I thought you'd be rusty, since it's been a long time for you—or so you claim."

It had been an age of the world. He ran his fingers down her arm, marveling at the softness of her skin. "Maybe it's like riding. Once you learn, you don't forget how."

"I have much to learn," she said happily. "I wonder if Mrs. Watson can impart any wisdom."

Good God. "How about I tell you exactly what I like?"

"Really?" She batted her eyelashes at him, needlessly long lashes that would have been a lethal asset had she any interest in flirting. "I'm astonished, my lord. You never tell me anything except what you don't like."

"In that case . . ." He placed his lips against her ear and whispered for some time.

When he pulled back, her eyes were slightly glazed. "I was rather hoping, given how starchy you are in public, that in private you might be a man of varied and somewhat depraved tastes. I must say I'm not disappointed."

He gave her a mock-glare. "I'm too young to be called starchy."

"You are too young to *be* so starchy."

"Fine," he said, laughing a little. "I deserved that. Now tell me, when you were talking about your inability to eat earlier, were you using impotence as an analogy?"

"What if I was?"

She took a strand of his hair and rubbed it between her fingers, a gesture the intimacy of which rather took his breath away—and made him forget, for a moment, what he was about to say. "Please, please make me very happy by informing me that your experience with impotence happened with Roger Shrewsbury."

"He managed to overcome it in the end," she said in her matter-of-fact way.

"I know that—no need for reminders. I just want to hear that he couldn't get it up for some time."

"Well . . . he told me that I intimidated him," said the most intimidating individual he had ever met.

"Ha!"

She placed a hand on the pillow, under her cheek, her expression genuinely curious. "Why are you so happy about that?"

"I don't know." He grinned. "Obviously, despite my starchiness, I am not a very good man. I've wanted to punch him ever since that day last summer—every time we came across each other."

"Why? You could have slept with me at any time since I was seventeen."

And therein lay the rub, didn't it? He'd been massively wrong about what he wanted—and needed.

"Maybe the one I really wanted to punch was myself," he said.

She gazed at him, a pensive look on her face. Silence enveloped them, not tense or heavy, but a shade melancholy.

He sat up and checked his watch again. "We must dress now. This moment."

She took his hand as he was about to leave the bed. "See, we're still friends. Nothing has changed."

He looked back at her, at the fulcrum of his life. She was not wrong. Nothing had changed.

Except him.

Mrs. Newell and her guests had left in the afternoon. The senior police officers had retired to their rooms in the village, leaving only a young constable in the entrance hall. The corridors echoed as Charlotte and Lord Ingram made their way to the drawing room.

Lord Bancroft was already there, studying a map of Stern Hollow. He rose. "You are late."

They were, by ninety seconds.

"My apologies," said Lord Ingram. "We must leave soon to fetch the policemen. Shall we dine?"

Lord Bancroft inclined his head. "I have requested service à la française. We won't have need of servants."

Dinner was normally service à la russe, with courses brought out sequentially, the reason Charlotte had sat through more than one three-hour dinner. Service à la française placed all the food on the table at once and the diners helped themselves.

They proceeded to the dining room, with its twenty-five-foot ceiling and a table capable of seating sixty guests. They occupied the merest corner of this table. The food took up more space: Lord Bancroft was not the sort of diner to accept anything but the finest efforts from the kitchen—and a variety of those, no less.

After soup was ladled, Lord Ingram dismissed the staff. Almost immediately Lord Bancroft asked, "Ash, what is this I hear about a page of your handwriting that might implicate Miss Holmes?"

"I think Lady Ingram had cut out some pages from my practice notebooks and sent them to Moriarty," answered his brother, "so that he and his underlings would recognize letters from me, should they intercept any, even if I'd written in a different hand."

Lord Bancroft loaded his plate with roast sirloin, lobster ragout, and oyster patties. "What woman would wander about with such a thing in her stocking? Can the police not fathom that it's a transparent attempt to point the finger at her husband?"

"It's obvious to *us*," said Lord Ingram. "But Scotland Yard sees only what it wants to see."

"Passel of idiots. Very well, what have you found out?"

The question was directed at Charlotte, so she told him about the extra crate that was put into the lavender house, and which later disappeared.

"So that's how her body arrived at Stern Hollow, I see," said Lord Bancroft, frowning. "When I was here last, I tried to ascertain whether other agents of Moriarty, besides Lady Ingram, had successfully infiltrated this household. I'd thought myself fairly satisfied on that account, but perhaps I was wrong."

"You are not the only one who has taken a hard look at the

servants," said Lord Ingram. "I spent weeks at that same task. They are not working for Moriarty."

Having spoken to all the staff, Charlotte was inclined to agree. "The men who came with the crate were lucky. The station agent is a talkative chap and probably told them everything they needed to know—and their arrival coincided with the mass migration of Mrs. Newell's guests."

"They seemed to know the estate rather well for strangers," Lord Bancroft pointed out.

"Mrs. Watson and I toured the grounds a few days ago, before the imbroglio with Lady Ingram. We were given a map of the entire estate and its walking paths, and on the reverse side was a smaller map of the house, the garden, and the outbuildings. Perhaps the men who put Lady Ingram in the icehouse had done a similar tour earlier, which would have given them all the familiarity necessary for their task."

Great country estates often permitted sightseers on the grounds—some even allowed the public rooms of the house to be viewed, when the family was away. And it was not uncommon to have maps at hand for the tourists, so that they would know how to proceed.

"But why did those men choose the icehouse? Why not dump her body in the gardens? And is the icehouse even labeled on this map you speak of, the one handed out to tourists?"

Lord Ingram and Charlotte exchanged a look.

"You are right. It may not be," said Charlotte. "I don't recall seeing the icehouse on the map."

"Then why?" Lord Bancroft murmured, as if to himself.

"You were out in the afternoon, did you find out anything?" Lord Ingram asked his brother.

"I went to see the body. Couldn't quite believe it until I'd seen it with my own eyes. The pathologist is arriving tonight—Scotland Yard wanted their own—and the autopsy has been scheduled for the morning. We'll see if we learn anything. What do you suppose she did to turn Moriarty against her?"

"I thought it was simply a case of his having no more use for her. But Holmes disagreed. She thought a woman such as Lady Ingram would be highly valuable, even after she had lost her proximity to you."

"I agree with Miss Holmes. Which makes the entire matter even more incomprehensible."

No one said anything else for some time. Charlotte ate doggedly. It was enough that her lack of appetite had struck fear in the hearts of Mrs. Watson and Lord Ingram. She didn't want Lord Bancroft also to wonder about her current state of mind.

Lord Bancroft broke the silence. "Those are excellent garments, by the way, Miss Holmes."

"Thank you, sir. Men's clothes are far more interesting than I first assumed. I have now made a rather thorough study. Do feel free to inquire," she said solemnly, "should you find yourself with questions concerning the latest fashions in gentlemanly attire."

"I will be sure to take advantage of your expertise, if and when the need arises," the perpetually stylish Lord Bancroft answered with equal gravity. "Have you been handling cases that necessitate dressing as a man?"

"Not yet. But Mrs. Watson and I both thought that it wouldn't hurt to be prepared. It would be only a matter of time before such a case arose."

"What made you think that you'd need men's garments for a two-week stay in the country?"

"I didn't think so, but they are rather like new toys. I didn't want to part with them."

"You've also had practice speaking and acting as a man."

"Mrs. Watson was a professional actress—and her butler had been on the stage, too. They make for excellent tutors."

Charlotte, who didn't have a high voice to begin with, had learned to pitch it much lower. She didn't need to drop it a whole octave for Sherrinford Holmes—no one expected that gentleman to have a gravelly voice—but she could, if necessary.

"Quite a bit of practice. I thought you were an odd fellow, but until Ash mentioned Sherlock Holmes, I didn't think you were Charlotte Holmes."

"Why, thank you, my lord."

"My point is, you didn't arrive overnight at this level of proficiency. And I can't see you putting in this much effort for a mere nebulous future need. What is going on that I don't know about?"

Charlotte glanced at Lord Ingram, who took a bite of his filet of leveret, and seemed to concentrate on only his chewing.

"Well, before this unfortunate incident with Lady Ingram, Ash and I were discussing taking a trip abroad after Christmas. While under my parents' roof, I rarely set foot outside of Britain— something I wish to rectify. And Ash, of course, could use some time away from Society.

"My reputation is beyond recovery, but he still has his to think of. And since the children would have come along, we must conduct ourselves with *some* semblance of propriety. If I could pass for a man, well, then, problem solved."

Lord Bancroft was in the middle of slicing through a vol-au-vent of chicken. He stilled. "Where were you thinking of going?"

This question was directed at Lord Ingram, who took a sip of his wine and said, "Warm places, since we would have left in the middle of winter. Spain, Majorca, Egypt, the Levant. By the time we reached India, it would probably have been unbearably hot in the plains, but the hill stations should still have been pleasant."

His eyes locked with Charlotte's, a small smile animating his lips.

"I see," said Lord Bancroft, whose courtship of Charlotte had twice ended without her hand in marriage, his tone remarkably even.

Charlotte served herself *oeufs à la neige*, poached quenelles of meringue in a bath of crème anglaise. "These are delicious. And not too sweet."

"They are made by the undercook trained by the pastry chef Bancroft poached from Stern Hollow," said Lord Ingram.

"Do you still have that pastry chef in your employ, my lord Bancroft?" Charlotte asked.

She had heard herself described as difficult to read. Lord Bancroft's face must be on a par with hers in its opacity. She could decipher little in his features beyond a concentration on his food.

He looked up. "I do. And before I left to present myself at Eastleigh Park, he made me a most excellent citron tart."

Charlotte turned to Lord Ingram. "I like citron tarts."

"Then you shall have them." His gaze again lingered over her. "Now if you are done, Holmes, we must be going. Enjoy your dinner, Bancroft."

❖

"Now why do you suppose Lord Bancroft didn't believe that I would invest some time and energy to gain the ability to pass myself off as a man?" asked Holmes, when she and Lord Ingram were alone in the coach. "It's a valuable professional skill."

"Because, for all that your mind is a thing of wonder—and terror—you are not particularly industrious. When need be, yes. Otherwise you could easily pass for a *Punch* caricature of a lady of leisure, eating bonbons and reading novels on the chaise, except you'd be reading *The Lancet* or a Patent Office catalogue.

"For you to set aside that book, get up from the chaise, put on the padding, the clothes, the wig, the orthodontia, the beard and mustache, and practice passing for a man—why should Bancroft believe this would have happened under normal circumstances?"

"Do you think he believed I would do it to travel abroad with you?"

He shrugged.

It was, as ever, difficult to guess what Bancroft might be thinking. But *he* would have liked to believe that. He could so easily see them standing shoulder to shoulder at the bow of a ship. It didn't matter what kind of seas they sailed, warm, cold, smooth, or choppy. It didn't matter where they were headed, empty wilderness or teeming metropolises. It mattered only that they were together at last.

She was right. He was still the same romantic he had always been. A bittersweet thought, more bitter than sweet.

He wanted to ask whether such a voyage might be possible, one of these days. But she was a woman who made no promises of the future. And he . . . deep down he still wanted all the promises.

Or at least clarity and certainty.

He glanced out of the window, at the murky night and the rain that seemed determined to drag on for the remainder of the year. After a while she placed her gloved hand on top of his.

Her words echoed in his ears. *Why can't things become simpler?*

No, no complicated relationship ever became simpler by the addition of physical intimacy. But at least now, when they ran out of words, he could turn to her—and kiss her.

So he did.

Treadles had not expected to see "Sherrinford" Holmes in the coach—he thought she would have already gone to their destination to prepare for her role as Sherlock Holmes's sister—or God forbid, Sherlock Holmes himself. But she—and Lord Ingram—greeted the policemen cordially.

Chief Inspector Fowler led the way with small talk. Treadles waited for him to steer the conversation to the bodies in which "Sherrinford" Holmes had expressed an interest. But whether he was genuinely uninterested or merely wished others to think so, he instead concentrated his questions on the running of a large estate.

Treadles had attended Lord Ingram's archaeological lectures. The man had no trouble keeping an audience spellbound. Here, although the topic was much more mundane, Treadles found himself fascinated by what he had to say about the myriad responsibilities that fell upon his shoulders.

"Do you enjoy it, your estate?" asked Fowler.

The question met with almost half a minute of silence, before Lord Ingram said, "My godfather, while he yet lived, had strongly hinted that Stern Hollow would be mine upon his passing. I liked the idea exceedingly well—the wholesome, peaceful life of a country squire seemed everything I could possibly hope for.

"But in truth, this life is taken up with more mundane decisions than I could have imagined. Stern Hollow has an excellent staff. Still, the staff deal with routine matters. Anything out of the ordinary gets passed up. And since Lady Ingram had very little interest in the running of the estate, everything eventually came to me.

"In the beginning I welcomed all the decision making. But after a while . . ."

The carriage turned. The lanterns at the front swayed. Light spilled across Lord Ingram's features, then he was sitting in darkness again.

"About eighteen months ago, I was informed that one of the estate's gates was in bad shape and should be replaced. I could barely recall such a gate—I had to be shown its location on a detailed map. It was in a remote corner, where the land was a great deal rougher, and inaccessible except by foot or on horseback.

"I said to go ahead and replace the gate. But my estate manager told me that it was the second time the gate had to be replaced in a decade.

"If we replaced one indifferent gate with another, warned my estate manager, we would need to replace it yet again in a few years. We rode out and looked at the thing. He was right; everything was falling apart, not just the gate. So we decided to improve the entire boundary, fences, gate posts, gate. And because wooden gates had proved useless, we agreed that a wrought iron gate would be a much more satisfactory option.

"But how should this wrought iron gate look? I fancied myself a proficient draftsman, so I set about creating designs, only to then learn that some were too fanciful to execute and others too easy to climb over. And while he had my attention on the matter, my estate manager brought up a whole slew of other deficiencies near the gate, everything from a derelict woodsman's cottage to footbridges that were too rotted for safe crossing.

"Before I knew it, I'd spent three weeks perfecting a part of the estate I would never visit again—not to mention creating and discarding dozens of sketches to finally arrive at an acceptable design for the new gate.

"When it was all done, I felt little gratification. Not even relief. By and large I was stunned that I'd spent so much time on absolute minutiae. On things that I didn't care about and which made no difference to anyone, except my estate manager, who derived a Calvinist satisfaction from scratching off every last item on his to-do list."

"Ah, I see," said Fowler, after a minute. "Undiluted joys are difficult to come by in life."

Lord Ingram inclined his head, as if in gratitude at being understood. "The chief draw of life in the country—or so my younger self had thought—was family and friends, away from the noise and distractions of the city. But at Stern Hollow, what family life there existed had been a divided one. And what functions we held never without an undercurrent of strain.

"As beautiful as my estate is, and as much as I take pride in looking after it, in and of itself it has given me very little joy and certainly none of the undiluted variety."

No one else spoke. Treadles squirmed on the inside. What could anyone say when a man laid bare the truth of his life?

Of course Lord Ingram needed, absolutely needed, to strike Chief Inspector Fowler as candid, with nothing to hide. But surely, this was going a little too far.

And then Treadles remembered the person sitting beside Lord

Ingram. He hadn't been addressing the policemen, he'd been speaking to *her*, specifically and entirely.

She had listened with the quietness of good soil soaking up the first drops of rain. And even now, when he had stopped speaking, she was still listening.

To the sound of his breaths?

All at once Treadles felt a pang of longing for Alice, for her slightly honking laughter, her sweet-smelling hair, and the wink she always gave him when she brought him a sip of whisky, because she would have brought herself a larger one at the same time.

He missed her. He missed her so much. He missed—

It occurred to him, with a reverberation of shock, that she hadn't gone anywhere. That she hadn't turned out like Lady Ingram, to have married him for any kind of gain. That she hadn't even been cold or distant—all the formality and aloofness had been on his part alone.

They were near their destination when Fowler spoke again. "When we questioned ladies Avery and Somersby earlier today, they said something rather interesting. They said, in so many words, that you are in love with Miss Charlotte Holmes. Are you, my lord?"

Treadles sucked in a breath, the sound mortifyingly loud in the otherwise impenetrable silence.

Did Lord Ingram tense? Did he brace himself for what he was about to say? "I have not thought in that direction."

"That is hardly something that requires thinking, is it? Either one is in love or one isn't. Are you, my lord?"

With no excitement or unease that Treadles could sense, Charlotte Holmes turned toward her friend, a man being forced to expose the deepest secrets of his heart.

He glanced out of the carriage, at the cottage they were rapidly approaching, golden light spilling from every window. "Yes, I am. I am in love with her."

# Fifteen

"Sherrinford Holmes" did not disappear into the bowels of the cottage, then to reemerge as her true self.

Instead, they met a gamine-looking young woman in the parlor. "A good friend of the family," said Charlotte Holmes, "Miss Redmayne."

Miss Redmayne cheerfully shook hands with all three men. "Good to meet you, Chief Inspector Fowler. I have heard of you from Sherlock, Inspector Treadles. And my lord, it is good to see you again."

"Always a pleasure, Miss Redmayne," said Lord Ingram, with a smile.

"How is the great savant?" asked Charlotte Holmes.

"Cranky, as usual."

"The Good Lord ought to consider making non-cranky geniuses, for a change."

"At least he *is* a genius. Plenty of men are cranky without the least bit of brilliance for excuse. Gentlemen, do please sit down."

A maid came in and brought a considerable tea tray. Miss Redmayne poured for everyone. Charlotte Holmes and Fowler each accepted a biscuit.

"If you don't mind my asking," Treadles heard himself say, "is Mr. Holmes's sister not here today?"

"She has been in Scotland, visiting friends. Part of the reason Sherlock is rusticating in the country, instead of solving cases in London."

"And part of the reason I came here," said "Sherrinford" Holmes. "Someone has to be the great genius's eyes and ears and able interpreter."

"Exactly," echoed Miss Redmayne. "This past summer Miss Holmes was also away from London for some time, and dear Sherrinford couldn't be spared, so I stepped in to help for a fortnight."

Fowler set aside his tea. "To help as . . ."

"I told clients I was Sherlock's sister," said Miss Redmayne. "I thought it would be something fun to do, a change from dissecting cadavers, and—"

"I do beg your pardon, Miss Redmayne. Did you say, dissecting cadavers?"

"Yes, I'm a medical student at the Sorbonne. I'm afraid by now I've more than a nodding acquaintance with human anatomy."

"I see," said Fowler, taken aback.

"As I was saying, I was home on holiday and thought it would be a lark to receive Sherlock's clients, pour tea, and listen to their problems. Little did I know Lady Ingram would turn up at our door, seeking help."

It made sense, using someone else in the role of Sherlock Holmes's sister, as Charlotte Holmes was known to Lady Ingram.

Lord Ingram rose. "I believe I will take a stroll outside."

Fowler waited until the door had closed behind Lord Ingram. "Mr. Sherlock Holmes did not refuse to help Lady Ingram after learning of her request, even though Lord Ingram is his good friend?"

"I was both astounded and a little dismayed, I must admit," said Miss Redmayne. "But Sherlock's view was very much that just as I wouldn't refuse to treat Lady Ingram, if she came to me bleeding and in need of medical help, he ought not to turn her down simply because she was the estranged wife of a friend."

"Lady Ingram bleeding to her death and Lady Ingram wanting to meet the man she once loved—those are not equivalents," Treadles said, less to Miss Redmayne than to the other woman in the room, the one calmly turning her biscuit on a plate.

After Lord Ingram had admitted that he loved her, Fowler had asked whether his sentiments were reciprocated. And Lord Ingram had said, after a moment, *I cannot tell. Sometimes I am not sure that she understands the full spectrum of human emotions.*

And here she was, demonstrating precisely that lack of understanding. Even if she'd felt nothing in the summer, shouldn't she be racked with guilt now, for going behind his back like that?

"Nevertheless," said Miss Redmayne, "we took on Lady Ingram as a client."

Her account accorded with what Lord Ingram had said, that they had been making progress when Lady Ingram suddenly called off the search. "We were relieved but also suspicious, which was why we finally decided to tell Lord Ingram, in case unfavorable changes were coming his way."

Treadles had no idea who Miss Redmayne was, in truth, but he found that he believed her. Had he been wrong about Lady Ingram not loving any man enough to run away from her entire life—or was there something else at work?

"How did he take it?" asked Fowler.

"As well as anyone could be expected to take such news."

"And this would have been . . ."

"The day before the ball in honor of Lady Ingram's birthday."

"During which she disappeared."

"During which she *departed*," corrected Miss Redmayne, amiably yet firmly.

"Did Sherlock Holmes predict this . . . departure?"

This question was addressed to "Sherrinford" Holmes, who said, "I wasn't on hand for the case, but I don't believe he was surprised that she left."

Fowler finished his cup of tea. "Would it be at all possible to speak with the great consulting detective in person?"

"Outside of his intimates, Sherlock hasn't received callers since his unfortunate accident," said "Sherrinford" Holmes. "But he understands this is no ordinary visit on your part. Please come with me and please excuse the dimness of his room—he cannot tolerate strong light."

So it would be a counterfeit then, passed off with the help of smoke and mirrors. Treadles breathed a sigh of relief.

He shouldn't have been so worried in the first place—until she had investigated Lady Ingram's murder to her satisfaction, Charlotte Holmes needed all the illusions she'd built around the character of Sherlock Holmes to remain intact.

Which begged the question of why he had fretted so in the first place.

*You are irrational at times—more so than you want to admit.*

He didn't pursue that thought—it was a discomfiting one. And because they had now arrived before Sherlock Holmes's room.

He held his breath. Would this deception pass muster?

The corridor already smelled medicinal. When the door opened, the odors of camphor and carbolic acid immediately rushed out. Inside the room it was indeed dim. Treadles's eyes were first drawn to a lamp that had been placed on a shelf, which was crowded top to bottom with bottles of tinctures and compounds.

And then his gaze came to rest on the man on the bed—and he very nearly gasped aloud.

The man's face was a horror, a crisscross of deep welts that made Treadles think of red clay soil that had been drunkenly plowed. One scar cut straight across his nose. Another pulled back his upper lip to reveal missing teeth.

Beside Treadles, Chief Inspector Fowler, who must have seen no end of disturbing sights in his life, seemed barely able to hold his revulsion in check. Even Treadles, who knew that it was all playacting, couldn't help some very real twinges of fear and pity.

This was powerful theater, not something pulled together without both forethought and expertise. It made Treadles wonder what else had Miss Holmes arranged.

What else had she prepared for.

"Sherrinford" Holmes went to the man's bedside. "Sherlock apologizes that he is no longer able to communicate except via touch, in a simplified Morse Code. He offers his greetings and asks whether there is anything he can do for you."

"We are most grateful that he has received us, and sincerely sorry to disturb his repose," Fowler managed. "If he has some insight he would like to share with us, we would be most appreciative."

"Sherrinford" Holmes took the hand of the man on the bed and waited for some time. "*Cisterns.* That was his message."

"Would he be referring to the cisterns at Mrs. Newell's house that broke, sending her guests to Stern Hollow?" asked Fowler.

"That is correct," confirmed "Sherrinford" Holmes.

"Thank you, Mr. Holmes," said Fowler. "Now, if I may ask one more question. We have spoken to both Lord Ingram and Miss Redmayne about Lady Ingram's case. But neither, thus far, has mentioned a name. Surely, Lady Ingram must have given you a name for you to begin your investigation."

As she had done before, "Sherrinford" Holmes took the man's hand. After half a minute, she glanced at him, a brow raised.

Then she turned back to the policemen and said, "According to Sherlock, the man's name is . . . Moriarty."

—❧—

"Sherrinford" Holmes bade the police good night in the parlor. "I will remain with my brother tonight."

When Chief Inspector Fowler and Treadles emerged from the house, Lord Ingram was waiting for them under the porch, in the company of a young copper who had been dispatched from the local constabulary. Lord Ingram was not smoking, but the scent of cigarette lingered.

"I apologize for keeping you away from your friends, my lord," said Fowler. "Will you care to say a few words to Sherlock Holmes? We can wait in the carriage."

Lord Ingram shook his head. "Sherlock Holmes is already doing what he can. He knows my situation and he knows my gratitude."

As they climbed into the coach, Treadles couldn't help but wonder whether, all things being equal, he himself would be as grateful. After all, would Lord Ingram be under as much suspicion if he hadn't been seen with Miss Holmes in the summer? If the fact that he was in love with her didn't carry such weight against his struggle to prove his innocence?

As if he heard Treadles's thoughts, Fowler said, "We have already sent a message to be published in tomorrow's London papers. We hope Miss Holmes will come forward promptly."

"I'm sure she will," said Lord Ingram. "When you meet her, do convey my regard."

"Have you, by any chance, confessed your more tender sentiments to Miss Holmes, my lord? Or have you any plans to do so in the near future?"

"No. And no."

Treadles winced.

"In which case, I must apologize," said Fowler, sounding not at all sorry. "It is unlikely that we will be able to keep it a secret, as we will be speaking to her on that very subject."

"I dare say she already knows," answered Lord Ingram. Then, more softly, "I dare say she's known it for years. For longer than I have, if anything."

———❈———

Charlotte, free of all disguises, regarded herself in the mirror.

"Oh, your skin is red from the glue." Miss Redmayne tsked, fussing over her. "Here, I have some rose water. Pat it over your face. That should calm it down. Some chamomile tea also wouldn't hurt."

Charlotte puffed up her cheeks and moved her jaw left and right. The worst wasn't the glue, but the modified orthodontia she'd worn for most of the day. If she never put them in her mouth again, she would consider herself blessed.

"I haven't had the chance to thank you yet, Miss Redmayne, for coming so swiftly."

After Charlotte had some time to think the day before—had it been only a little more than twenty-four hours since they'd received Livia's distraught note?—it had been easy to predict that several things would happen.

One, Lord Ingram would be forced to tell as much of the truth as possible, most likely relying on the surface version of Lady Ingram's search for her lost lover, in order to avoid touching on the fact that her perfidy had cost the lives of three agents of the Crown.

Two, the account of her search would lead to a call on Sherlock Holmes, the one who had undertaken the endeavor for her.

Three, the police would wish to speak to Charlotte Holmes, whose rapport with Lord Ingram would become a central line of inquiry in a case that gave them little else to go on.

Charlotte didn't mind speaking to the police, but Sherlock Holmes was a different matter. They would need to see a man. She could not meet them both as Sherlock Holmes's sister and later as herself. And Mrs. Watson, needed for other things, couldn't be expended on this occasion.

So among the tasks she had entrusted to Mrs. Watson to accomplish had been a cable to Miss Redmayne, begging the latter to make haste and return to England. Mrs. Watson, confident, capable Mrs. Watson, had of course executed everything perfectly.

"Don't thank me for coming," said Miss Redmayne. "I would have been upset if you hadn't informed me right away. And I would have caught the first train to Calais even if you'd told me I wouldn't be of any use here."

She sighed. "I wish I'd been able to speak more to Ash. Poor thing, he looked—I mean, he looked fine but he seemed . . . heavy-hearted."

There was the weight of his wife's murder—and the uncertainty of his own future. But was part of the heaviness there because he had been forced to speak truthfully of his sentiments to Charlotte, a woman he wasn't sure understood "the full spectrum of human emotions"?

"It will be all right, won't it, Miss Holmes?" asked Miss Redmayne.

Charlotte understood enough of human emotions to know that the girl wished for reassurance, from someone she trusted to get to the bottom of the matter. But if they'd learned anything from the debacle with Lady Ingram, it was that truth was sometimes no one's friend.

That getting to the bottom of the matter could shatter bonds and upend lives.

"Brace yourself," she said. "It will not be good. This is an ugly case that can lead only to an uglier end."

In the mirror Miss Redmayne's reflection was aghast.

Charlotte sighed inwardly. The problem was not that she didn't always understand the full spectrum of human emotions. It was that even when she did, she still gave those close to her the opposite of what they wished for.

———※———

Lord Ingram woke up to fog-obscured windows. His watch marked a quarter past nine o'clock, almost three hours later than when he usually started his day.

Was he already becoming less starchy by first becoming lazy?

He got up, dressed, and went up to Holmes's rooms. She wasn't there, of course, though he wished she were.

Pleasurable pain. Painful pleasure. He couldn't get enough of either. It would never be simple or easy between them. So he let himself luxuriate in all the gladness and all the complications.

While he still could.

All the pain and pleasure in his heart, however, did not prevent him from noticing that another person had been in the room. Not the servants—they had strict orders to leave those rooms alone unless otherwise instructed by either himself or Holmes.

Who, then? Bancroft? Or someone else?

He descended for breakfast and ate, staring at the writhing fog.

Footsteps raced across the marble floor of the entrance hall. Bancroft burst into the breakfast room, still in his overcoat, his walking stick hooked over his forearm.

Lord Ingram leaned back in his seat. He couldn't remember the last time he saw Bancroft in such agitation. "What's the matter?"

"When was the last time you bedded her?"

Lord Ingram stared at his brother, his mind stuttering at the baldness of the question.

Bancroft didn't seem to notice. "Your wife. When did the two of you last sleep together?"

Oh, with *Lady Ingram*. "Before I inherited."

More than three years ago, his interminable celibacy broken only yesterday evening.

"I just came from the autopsy," said Bancroft, tapping his walking stick on the floor for emphasis. "She was with child."

*Sixteen*

There were no signs of tampering on the cisterns at Mrs. Newell's house. A Mr. Jones, who had been hired to oversee the repair and rebuilding of the cisterns, showed Inspector Treadles and Charlotte Holmes, in her full Sherrinford Holmes guise, photographs that had been taken of the cisterns, right after the accidents had happened, as well as those of the pipes leading in and out.

"They weren't built well to begin with. Mrs. Newell got rid of her former estate manager several months ago, after it was discovered he'd been skimming from the top for almost as long as he'd been working for her, so I wouldn't be surprised if he'd got the cheapest everything and pocketed the difference. And he hadn't bothered with proper inspection and maintenance in the years since.

"The new estate manager seems to be a decent fellow. But his predecessor left things in such a state he hasn't got around to the cisterns—had to replace the boiler first. Me, I'm not surprised the cisterns flooded the house, only that they didn't do it sooner."

The dismantled parts of the cisterns indeed appeared shoddy, brown with rust and neglect, bulging and sagging alarmingly, and almost paper thin in spots. But there were no incisions, and no marks that had been left by a saw, a hatchet, or any other tools of sabotage.

The tampering of the cisterns, coinciding with the transportation of an additional and now unaccounted-for crate to Stern Hollow, would have made for a strong, if circumstantial, case that someone was trying to frame Lord Ingram.

But now that the cisterns had turned out to be an overdue accident, this elegant house of cards came tumbling down.

Treadles swore inwardly. Miss Holmes couldn't be pleased that her hypothesis had been proven wrong, but she gave no outward signs of disappointment, only rubbed her beard gravely as she thanked Mr. Jones.

Afterward, they found themselves alone in Mrs. Newell's foyer, both waiting for their next appointment, Miss Holmes having applied to see her sister, and Treadles, Mrs. Newell's cook.

"How is Lord Ingram holding up, if I may inquire?" he heard himself ask.

"I have never seen him not hold up," said Miss Holmes. "I expect he will continue to do so."

"But is he all right?"

Miss Holmes thought about it. "Sometimes he has hope. Other times he might be preparing himself for an unhappier future."

Again, that inhuman detachment, as if the hangman's noose were but a bit of a bother.

*You are irrational at times—more so than you want to admit.*

He recoiled. But was the voice right? What would he have thought had Miss Holmes displayed greater fear or distress?

*You would have considered her far too emotional to handle an investigation with your friend's life at stake.*

"I very much hope that an unhappier future will not come to pass," he said quietly.

Miss Holmes turned to him and inclined her head. "No matter what happens, Lord Ingram and I are both grateful to you, Inspector, for allowing us to search for the truth unhindered."

Sometimes he still couldn't be sure whether he'd kept his silence more out of loyalty or cowardice. But her words were clear and sincere and he was . . . touched to know that his inner struggle had not been completely in vain. That he had rendered a service to his friend.

Footsteps. Miss Olivia Holmes rushed down the grand staircase, her expression full of both anxiety and an anxious love. At the sight of Treadles, however, she stiffened.

"Good morning, Miss Holmes," he said as she approached.

She glanced at him, then pointedly looked away, her eyes for only her sister. "You wished to see me? Is everything all right?"

Treadles's face scalded. He had not realized that he had offended her to such an extent that she would choose to discard basic civilities.

Charlotte Holmes looked at her sister with gentle reproach, but before she could say anything, Chief Inspector Fowler strode into the foyer. After a perfunctory greeting to Miss Olivia Holmes, he said, "Gentlemen, a word please."

"I'll be a second," said Charlotte Holmes to her sister.

Her sister nodded. "I'll wait in the white drawing room."

"I didn't know you were acquainted with Miss Holmes, sir," said Fowler, when Miss Holmes had disappeared behind a set of doors.

Charlotte Holmes patted the ends of her mustache, which had been waxed to a high sheen. "I am only here as an emissary of Lord Ingram's. He knows Miss Holmes is fearful for him and wishes to let her know that he remains in tolerable shape."

"Most chivalrous of him." Fowler lowered his voice. "Now, this is strictly police business, Mr. Holmes, but since Lord Bancroft Ashburton was present at the autopsy, presumably you would soon have known what he has learned, namely that, at the time of her death, Lady Ingram was with child."

Treadles sucked in a breath.

Miss Holmes, in her imperturbable way, said only, "And the cause of death?"

This extreme sangfroid garnered her a wary look from Fowler. "The pathologist deemed likely your idea of death by excess alcohol, injected intravenously. He will be performing more tests to ascertain what substances might have been in her bloodstream."

Charlotte Holmes nodded. "Most prudent of him."

"I hope this will not come across as unseemly curiosity, Mr. Holmes. In your knowledge, is there any chance that the child Lady Ingram carried could have been Lord Ingram's?"

"Anything is possible but that is highly unlikely. Their estrangement was complete, and my understanding is that it marked the end of all affections, both of the heart and of the body."

"Thank you, Mr. Holmes. I mustn't keep you any longer from your meeting."

Charlotte Holmes inclined her head. "Good day, gentlemen."

When she was out of earshot, Fowler said to Treadles, "Do you realize what this means, Inspector?"

After Treadles's initial dismay, a sense of relief had washed over him. If the child truly was not Lord Ingram's, then Lady Ingram's pregnancy gave great credence to his assertion that she had defected with her lover. But Fowler seemed almost gleeful—never a good sign—so he erred on the side of caution. "Yes, sir?"

"It means that now we have a motive that is much stronger than Lord Ingram's desire to marry Miss Charlotte Holmes. What would your reaction be, Inspector, if your missing wife turned up carrying another man's child?"

Treadles blinked, unable to even contemplate the idea.

Fowler nodded with satisfaction. "My point exactly."

❈

Livia leaped up when Charlotte came into the white drawing room. "Have you learned anything?"

"Not enough yet. Have you been well?"

"I . . . I don't know, frankly."

This morning Livia had received two notes. One came from Lord Ingram, informing her that he had written to his solicitor to begin the process of looking into Moreton Close, the institute now in charge of Bernadine. The other one was unsigned and without a return address but had been postmarked at the nearest village post office.

It read, *I have been looking for the Sherlock Holmes story everywhere. Has it been published yet? If not, please hurry.*

She was terrified for Lord Ingram, worried about Charlotte, frustrated with herself, and yet, with the arrival of this second note, so extravagantly buoyed that she could have walked over a carpet of rose petals and not bruised a single one.

He knew she was at Mrs. Newell's. And he was nearby. Had he come to meet her? How would he make it happen?

She became aware that her sister was observing her. "What about you, Charlotte?" she said, her face warming. "Have you been busy?"

"Rather," said Charlotte. "You?"

Livia scoffed. "What does a near-spinster have to do?"

At least Mrs. Newell enjoyed her company, something that couldn't be said for Lady Holmes. She was grateful that Mrs. Newell had asked her to stay, knowing how much she disliked going home, but she also wished she didn't need to rely on someone else's goodwill for a respite from her own parents.

"What about your story?"

"Haven't been able to write a word since I saw Lady Ingram in that icehouse." She expelled a long breath. "But at least I heard from Lord Ingram. I asked him to help me look into Moreton Close and he's written his solicitor, as he'd promised."

Charlotte nodded. "I'm glad you referred the matter to him— that gives him something to do."

"I was surprised that I didn't need to tell him who Bernadine was—to the wider world she might as well not exist."

"I mentioned her in a letter. He was taken aback to learn that there are not three but four Holmes girls."

Livia sighed. "Poor Bernadine. I hope Moreton Close is exactly what it purports to be—a haven for women like her. But I can't stop worrying. If she's mistreated, she wouldn't even be able to tell anyone."

Bernadine had never spoken. And she certainly didn't know how to read or write.

Charlotte made no reply. Livia was used to these conversational lulls with her sister. She was probably assessing the chances of Lord Ingram's solicitors meeting with success at Moreton Close.

"Asylums, both public and private, are regularly inspected. That's the law," Charlotte eventually said. "Moreton Close is not operating in a vacuum. So let's hope for the best."

And that Lord Ingram's solicitors worked fast.

Charlotte gave Livia's hand a quick squeeze. "Look after yourself. I have some matters to investigate in London."

As Charlotte made her way to the door, it occurred to Livia that she wanted to ask her sister about the nameless young man who had pretended to be Mr. Myron Finch, their illegitimate brother. Who was he? And what did Charlotte know about him?

But by the time she screwed up her courage, Charlotte had already left.

<hr/>

The policemen's conversation with Mrs. Newell's cook was brief. Yes, a slab of ice had been sent. And it had been sent because Mrs. Newell had specifically requested so.

Now they were waiting to speak to Mrs. Newell again. Chief Inspector Fowler having gone to use the commode, Treadles was alone in the foyer when Charlotte Holmes came out from the white drawing room.

On her way to the front door she passed him and nodded. "Good day, Inspector."

"Mr. Holmes," he said. "A moment, please. I have a question for you."

"Yes, Inspector?"

He didn't know why he had stopped her. And now that he had, he had no idea whether he could condense all the whirling thoughts in his head into a single question.

"I have, or so it would appear, offended Miss Olivia Holmes greatly."

She waited for him to continue.

"I seem to have a knack for giving such offenses. Not to ladies like Miss Holmes usually, but to . . ." He paused, unsure how to phrase what he was about to say.

"But to women who are thoroughly lacking in respectability, with the very respectable Miss Holmes affronted on behalf of her disgraced sister."

He thought of Mrs. Farr, with the possibly dead missing sister. He thought of Mrs. Bamber, the publican he had encountered a few months ago. He preferred to believe that they were exceptions, and perhaps they were. The problem was, he could too easily think of others, scattered throughout his career, like sand in a bowl of grain.

"I am a police inspector. I will need to speak to many more women in the course of my work. A tendency to provoke is . . . not a personal asset."

She waited again. When it became apparent he had confessed as much as he could bring himself to, she said, "Should I assume that you do not entirely understand how—or why—your words give rise to such unfavorable responses?"

He nodded stiffly, already regretting the conversation.

"I can't speak for other women, but perhaps in the case of Miss Holmes, I can offer some explanation. Her sister Charlotte had always understood, from an early age, that she was ill-suited for marriage. She had an agreement with her father that if by her twenty-fifth birthday, she still hadn't changed her mind, he would sponsor her to attend school and receive training, so that someday she might become headmistress of a girls' school, a respectable position with respectable remuneration attached.

"When the day came, her father reneged on his promise. Charlotte Holmes was faced with the choice of either entering into a marriage she did not want or remaining forever under the roof—and thumb—of a faithless father."

Treadles had no idea of the circumstances surrounding her disgrace. He couldn't imagine any good reason for her to have done what she did, so he'd decided that she'd slept with a man as nothing other than an amoral lark.

"Neither was acceptable to her. So she strived to create a third alternative. She would get rid of her maidenhead and use that loss to blackmail her father into coughing up the funds for her education."

Treadles's shock and dismay must have shown in his face, for her expression became ironic. "Yes, a terrible idea, but she had no other resources to call on. Women of her class are molded to be ornaments. She was willing to work for her own support, but she had few skills worth mentioning. And she was not so naive as to think that she could toil her way up from the floor of a factory—factories don't pay women enough to live on, the reason many must prostitute themselves besides, to supplement that meager income."

Treadles couldn't stop his brows from rising. He knew about the likelihood of female factory workers also being prostitutes—but had always assumed that it must be because factories attracted a less chaste class of women.

"In the end, Charlotte Holmes went ahead with her plan, which had seemed to her the least terrible of all choices. Things went awry. She found herself faced with a new set of undesirable choices: to be confined for the rest of her life—or to run away and take her chances in the wilds of London.

"Thanks to the kindness of friends, she did not starve. Today one might say she is faring rather tolerably. All the same, what she did was a desperate gamble at a desperate moment, when she felt as if she would never again have any say in her own life.

"Miss Olivia Holmes does not blame her sister for either her initial choice or what happened subsequently, because she herself feels that same desperation daily, the sinking sensation that what will happen to her is entirely out of her hands.

"When you brought up her sister's sins before her, it was with an intention to shame. Perhaps you yourself were not aware of that— perhaps you thought of it as merely pointing out the facts—but it's nevertheless true.

"For Miss Olivia Holmes, who knows the entire story, to hear it reduced to one single choice, shorn of all context, and casually judged as degenerate . . . I believe to her it felt unjust. And acted as a painful reminder of the narrow confines of her own life: She can either continue to live in accordance with her parents' demands— and wither a little every day—or she can defy conventions and be called a shameless hussy for the rest of her life."

Miss Holmes spoke calmly, without rancor. But Treadles's ears burned—and his face, too. He wasn't sure he understood everything she said, but he did understand now why he had asked her the question in the first place.

*Not* to find out why the women had reacted as they had, but in the hope that she, with her uncompromisingly logical mind, would tell him that they were but being unreasonable.

Hysterical, even.

"Thank you," he said numbly.

"I'm sorry. I do tend to tell people exactly what they don't wish to hear." She sighed softly. "I might as well add, since we are on the topic, that perhaps some of the women's reactions have to do with your face. You have an open, amiable mien, which might lead those speaking with you to expect understanding. And yet your judgment is such a pointed, implacable thing, as if you are the personification of the larger world they have known, the one that has thwarted them at every turn."

He might have mumbled something in reply. She bade him good day and walked out of the front door.

"Was that Mr. Holmes?" said Chief Inspector Fowler a minute later, startling Treadles.

"Yes, that was."

"Hmm," said Fowler, studying Charlotte Holmes's retreating back. "There goes a man far more dangerous than he looks."

—◈—

Mrs. Newell did not pretend to be pleased that she must speak to the police again. Faced with her aloofness, Chief Inspector Fowler dispensed with small talk. "Ma'am, I understand that you yourself gave the order to send ice to Stern Hollow. Why?"

"Lord Ingram asked me to. He said that one of their freezing pots is missing, if I wouldn't mind sending one from my kitchen, so that my guests would be able to enjoy the cold dishes that they are accustomed to. And would I not mind sending some ice along with the freezing pot."

Treadles went cold. What reason could Lord Ingram have for requesting ice from a neighbor, when he had several tons of perfectly good ice waiting in his icehouse?

"Did he mention why he wanted you to send ice?"

"He didn't. But I was delighted to oblige, since he was doing me the far larger favor by taking in all my guests. My kitchen staff already had a block of ice in an ice safe and it was very little trouble to send it along with all the food that would have otherwise gone to waste."

"Why did you not mention this when we last spoke?"

"You didn't ask."

"Mrs. Newell, withholding evidence from the police, in the course of a murder investigation, is a serious offense. I didn't ask because I didn't know enough to inquire in that particular direction, but you knew the significance of what you were not telling us."

The old woman wrinkled her nose. "Why should I volunteer information that might send an innocent man to the gallows?"

"What makes you still think that he is innocent?"

"What makes you think he is guilty?"

"Simply from what you've told us, it's obvious that Lord Ingram was hiding something. He requested for you to supply the ice so that none of his servants would need to go near the icehouse."

There could be no other conclusion, yet Treadles still cringed to hear it said aloud.

*If Lord Ingram killed his wife, then he could never again appear before Miss Holmes.*

Mrs. Newell had said that, Mrs. Newell who was obviously biased in favor of Lord Ingram. But Treadles clung to that statement, to the implied integrity of Miss Holmes.

Mrs. Newell, unlike him, was not disheartened by Fowler's charge. "If that were the case, wouldn't Lord Ingram have made sure no one entered the icehouse the next day as well? Why would a servant be able to waltz in a mere twenty-four hours later?"

"Perhaps he underestimated how much ice the kitchen needed. Perhaps he thought the amount you supplied would be enough to last the entirety of your guests' sojourn at Stern Hollow."

Mrs. Newell scoffed. "Would you make such assumptions, Chief Inspector, if you had *your* wife's dead body lying in a structure that is sure to be visited at some point by members of your staff? Lord Ingram is not stupid. And any inference of guilt that starts with him doing something stupid is, by default, a line of reasoning that must be rejected."

———❈———

The fog was still rampant when they left Mrs. Newell's house but had begun to clear by the time they reached Stern Hollow. Instead of calling for an interview with Lord Ingram, Chief Inspector Fowler requested to speak to his valet, Cummings.

They had already spoken to Cummings once, when they had interviewed all the other servants. When Treadles consulted his notes, he saw that Fowler had already written, in the margins, *Need to question this man again.*

"Mr. Cummings, do you recognize these boots?"

Cummings, a small, neat man, examined the contents of the boot box, which had been taken from Lord Ingram's dressing room the evening before. "They belong to Lord Ingram."

"You have seen them before?"

"Yes. They are quite old, from before I came to work for his lordship."

"Are they usually kept in the dressing room?"

"No. Usually they are kept near one of the side entrances, along with his Wellington boots, for when he wishes to walk about the estate."

"Were you not concerned they were no longer there?"

"Boots that are never worn in public do not fall under my purview, Chief Inspector. The hall boy has the responsibility of cleaning them. I check on them once in a while, to make sure he has done them properly. But I usually inspect only one of the side entrances at a time, and there are several in this house. If I don't see a pair of boots at any given point in time, I assume that they have been stowed near one of the other doors."

"Why do you suppose these boots have been stowed in the dressing room?"

"I can't say, Chief Inspector."

"You are responsible for Lord Ingram's wardrobe, which means the dressing room should fall entirely under your purview. You didn't think to ask his lordship about the appearance of these boots at a place they didn't belong?"

"I might have, if they'd been put on my side of the dressing room," said Cummings. "The innermost quarter or so of the dressing room is where Lord Ingram keeps his letters, journals, portfolios, and such. I do not venture into that part of the dressing room. My instructions are clear. Even if I see something on his side that has clearly been misplaced, say, a necktie or a comb, that should have stayed on my side of the dressing room, I am to leave it alone and let his lordship sort it out in time."

"So you have seen this boot box in the dressing room but not gone near it."

"That's correct, Chief Inspector."

"How long has the boot box been in the dressing room?"

"Years."

"Years?" Fowler frowned. "I see, let me ask a different question. When did it move to Lord Ingram's side of the dressing room?"

Cummings bit his lower lip. "Two or three weeks ago. Three, most likely."

"And of course you didn't ask why."

"No, indeed."

"The boots have a great deal of coal dust encrusted on the soles. Where do you think they have been worn to?"

"I can't imagine. The coal cellar would be the only place in the house where there might be some coal dust to be found."

"If he goes to the coal cellar and comes back, surely you would have seen coal dust in the dressing room?"

Mr. Cummings hesitated.

"May I remind you, Mr. Cummings—"

"I understand I am to speak truthfully, Chief Inspector."

"Has Lord Ingram demanded otherwise of you?"

"No. When Sergeant Ellerby came, his lordship asked the entire staff to be forthright and helpful when questioned by the police."

"Then why the reluctance, Mr. Cummings?"

"I don't know, Chief Inspector. But you are right, I've noticed coal dust lately in the dressing room."

"Did you ask Lord Ingram about it?"

"No, I cleaned up and carried on with my duties."

"Now, Mr. Cummings, has there been anything else about his lordship's ambulatory habits of late that is out of the ordinary?"

Mr. Cummings hesitated some more. "About a fortnight ago, I checked on the boots by one of the side doors in the morning, instead of in the evening, as I usually do, and saw a pair of Wellingtons that were encrusted with mud. I had a word with the hall boy. He swore that he had not been neglecting the boots. That at the end of the previous day, they'd all been scrubbed, brushed, and set to rights.

"He told me that he'd been finding the boots used overnight. That he'd been cleaning them first thing in the morning. But that morning, Mr. Walsh had some other tasks for him and he hadn't got around to the boots yet."

"I see," said Fowler, a gleam in his eyes. "Anything else, Mr. Cummings?"

The valet shook his head.

Fowler dismissed him and studied a detailed map of the estate, an exact copy of the one that hung in the library. Then he looked up. "Inspector Treadles, care for a little outing?"

—❧—

Before they left, they spoke to the hall boy, who confirmed that indeed, every morning for the past few weeks he'd found a pair of Wellingtons that needed heavy cleaning.

The policemen rode out, accompanied by Mr. Platts, the estate manager. Treadles saw little of the passing scenery. Scotland Yard's progress was accelerating. What was Miss Holmes doing? Was she finding out anything that could save Lord Ingram?

They reached the gate Lord Ingram had mentioned the night before, the one the reconstruction of which had given him much trouble and negligible pleasure. From the gate, after five minutes on foot, they came to a clearing, with a cottage at its center. The cottage occupied only a little more area than a town coach, but it was two stories tall, with a gabled, deeply pitched roof, round dormers, and window boxes full of pink and purple sweet alyssums.

*And while he had my attention on the matter, my estate manager brought up a whole slew of other deficiencies near the gate, everything from a derelict woodsman's cottage to footbridges that were too rotted for safe crossing.*

Treadles had not seen any new footbridges, but the once derelict woodsman's cottage had certainly been restored to a state of glory. Had Treadles encountered such a scene as a child, he would have thought he'd wandered into a fairy tale. Even as a grown man, he would have felt a swell of wonder and delight—under any other circumstances.

Now all he felt was an inchoate panic. If this was the place Lord Ingram had visited at night, resulting in those muddy boots, then he was sure Lord Ingram wouldn't want Chief Inspector Fowler to know about it.

"Very nice," said Fowler to Mr. Platts.

"I concur," said the estate manager. "It's my understanding that the children quite adore it."

The children. Dear God, the children.

"May we see the inside?" asked Fowler.

"Of course."

The inside of the cottage was decorated with yellow gingham curtains, baskets hanging from ceiling beams, and rustic furniture built for small people.

Fowler examined every square inch of the interior. Treadles had no choice but to do the same.

To the experienced eye, there was no question that until quite recently there had been people inside. The policemen found strands of fine dark hair, in two different lengths, on the beds in the loft. The small stove on the ground floor had been used less than two days before, judging by the lack of dust on its surfaces. And a jar on the shelves above the stove contained several ginger biscuits, which according to the housekeeper—Treadles remembered this with a plummeting heart—Lord Ingram had been fetching from the still-room in the middle of the night, even though he didn't care for them.

As they started the walk to where they had left the horses, Fowler asked, "Mr. Platts, can you tell us if there is anything interesting or different about the coal cellar at Stern Hollow?"

"It's certainly an amply proportioned one. And I've always appreciated the dumbwaiter that Lord Ingram had installed, so that the servants needn't carry coal up and down the stairs. But beyond that—"

He stopped for a second. "How silly of me. I've become so accustomed to the estate's various oddities—all great houses have them—that I didn't think of it sooner. You see, Stern Hollow boasts a magnificent kitchen garden, one of the finest I've ever seen, and I try to visit them everywhere I go.

"The garden slopes downhill by design, to maximize exposure

to sunlight. Unfortunately, this meant that the glass houses, which are built halfway down the slope, are approximately six feet below the top of the north wall, behind which stands the boiler hut. To send hot water to heat those glass houses and to ensure that the water returns, the boilers had to be sunk to a spectacular depth, almost eighteen feet, to be exact, as the boilers themselves are the tubular sort the height of which must also be accommodated.

"Once the boilers are lit for the winter, and they should be any day now, one of them must be operating at maximum capacity all the time, which means they must be stoked three times a day, and one more time late in the evening on particularly cold nights. A hair-raising task, it used to be, going down a pitch-dark pit on a rickety ladder bolted to the side of the chute, with a heavy basket of coke on one's back.

"Some fifteen years ago one young man fell down the ladder and broke his limb. Lord Ingram's godfather, who had acquired the house not long before, told me to do something—he didn't want anyone else seriously injured in his service. How I was to accomplish this he left to me—he didn't want to be bothered about details—only that something must be done.

"I puzzled over the solution. It was Lord Ingram, in fact, visiting on his school holidays, who suggested that since there was already an underground tunnel connecting the kitchen to the dining room, why should we not branch out and intersect it with one going from the coal cellar to the garden boilers?"

Mr. Platts, warming up to his subject, described the construction of this tunnel. Then he assured them that it had been worth the time and treasure, having made it both easy and safe to heat the glass houses.

Treadles could tell that Fowler had no interest in the finer points of this tunnel, but was biding his time until he could see it for himself. Back at the house, Mr. Platts gladly unlocked a double trap door in the coal cellar and led them down a ramp.

With considerable pride, the estate manager flipped a switch. A bright, if rather harsh light flooded the tunnel, which was wider than Treadles expected, enough for three slender men to walk abreast.

"Electricity, gentleman—a wonder of the modern age."

"Is the rest of the house electrified?" asked Treadles. "I don't recall that being so."

"The staff quarters and the domestic offices are all electrified, but not the main part of the house—Lady Ingram had strong feelings against electricity, and her wishes were respected."

Finally, an assertion to counterbalance ladies Avery and Somersby's charge that Lady Ingram might have been made to feel unwelcome in her own home.

As if he hadn't heard, Fowler said, "With your permission, we would like to walk the length of the tunnel."

"Certainly. But you'll excuse me for not accompanying you, gentlemen. I can't spend much time in these confined, underground places without getting into a state."

"You have already been most helpful, Mr. Platts. We can look after ourselves, and we will make sure everything is in order before we leave."

Mr. Platts left for his regular duties. The policemen proceeded down the tunnel. By and by they came to a cross tunnel, which must be the one between the kitchen and the dining room. Then the tunnel began to slope downward noticeably. Treadles could feel grooves underfoot, to slow the descent of a wheelbarrow filled with coke, no doubt.

The fabled boilers came into sight, cold and silent, not yet lit for winter. Something else also came into sight: laden shelves.

The shelves must have been intended for the tools and implements necessary for the functioning of the boilers. But those had all been banished to a corner. Now the shelves were occupied by a thin, rolled-up mattress, toiletries, a row of foodstuffs from Swiss chocolate to tins of potted chicken and condensed milk. One section was devoted to picture books. There were also crayons and hand-sewn notebooks that contained children's drawings.

Fowler picked up a small mug and handed it to Treadles. The remnants of its contents had yet to dry completely. He sniffed. Cocoa. And no more than two days old.

Fowler looked around for some more time. Then he nodded. "I believe I shall now speak to Lord Ingram."

Treadles dreaded arriving at the library. Was this the beginning of the end? Was there anything he could do? Where was Miss Holmes—and had she prepared at all for this moment?

—✖—

Miss Holmes was nowhere to be seen in the library. But Lord Ingram was not alone: With him was another man, elegantly turned out yet blank in some ways.

Lord Ingram turned to the man. "Allow me to present Chief Inspector Fowler and Inspector Treadles of Scotland Yard. Gentlemen, Lord Bancroft Ashburton."

His brother, then. The newly met men shook hands.

"Lord Ingram, if we could have a word alone," said Fowler. "We have a somewhat delicate matter to discuss."

"Lord Bancroft is well versed in the situation," Lord Ingram answered firmly. "There is nothing here that needs to be kept from him."

"Very well, then, my lord—"

The door burst open.

"Chief Inspector! Inspector!" cried Sergeant Ellerby. "We found another body on the estate, a man's body!"

# Seventeen

"It was Mr. Holmes's idea. Remember he told me that I should be on the lookout for the body of an indifferently dressed man?" gushed Sergeant Ellerby, as excited as a child who had discovered a cache of sweets. "He also told me that the body could very well be located not that far from the icehouse. So this morning, as the fog cleared, I thought to myself, why not conduct a search? And lo and behold, we found it within the hour."

The dead man's clothes were shabby, not so much those of a vagrant but more those of a ne'er-do-well. He had been strangled, the marks on his throat still vivid. And though the smell was fading, he had indeed soiled himself before he died, as Charlotte Holmes had predicted.

The spot he lay on was fifteen minutes' walk from the icehouse, longer if one were pulling a body—his still-damp trousers showed tears consistent with having been dragged.

Chief Inspector Fowler's expression was unreadable. He sent a constable to inform the London pathologist to delay his departure. Then he examined the body and the surrounding area. Lord Bancroft walked about slowly, taking in everything. Lord Ingram leaned against a tree, smoking, seeming to pay no attention to the goings-on.

Half an hour later, they were back in the library.

Fowler wasted no time. "Lord Ingram, why don't you tell us who that man was."

"He told me his name was George Barr."

"Why did you kill him?"

"Last I saw him, he was perfectly alive. I had nothing to do with his death."

"Very well, then. Tell us how you came to know him at all."

"It was the day before Mrs. Newell's guests came to my house, or perhaps I should say the day of, since it was approximately one o'clock in the morning. I was in the tunnel going toward the glass house boilers when he appeared at the end of the tunnel. The electric lights were on and the entire tunnel was lit. He saw me and immediately turned around and started up the ladder.

"I chased after him. Near the icehouse I caught up with him, overpowered him, and tied him up."

"You carried rope on you?"

"Some good cord."

"Why?"

"Perhaps you've learned from my staff that there had been a fire at Stern Hollow some time ago?"

"I was made aware of that."

"I am almost entirely certain the fire was started as a distraction—that same night there was an attempt to kidnap my children, which I managed to foil only because I didn't run toward the fire but in the direction of the nursery."

"You didn't tell me, Ash," said Lord Bancroft, his voice low.

Lord Ingram shook his head. "You had enough to worry about. I didn't want to add to your burden."

"So you were already concerned that your children might be abducted?" asked Fowler.

"I did not think Lady Ingram was above such machinations."

"And that was the reason you sent them away with Lord Remington. You thought they would be safer away from Stern Hollow," said Treadles.

"Yes. I trusted Remington to be able to evade anyone Lady Ingram might send after him."

But if the children were far away, then who had slept in the fairy tale cottage? Who had drunk the hot cocoa in the space that housed the boilers? And what had Lord Ingram been doing there past midnight?

Fowler apparently had the same questions. "My lord, why were you in the tunnel in the first place, late at night?"

Lord Ingram shrugged. "I don't sleep very well these days. So I sometimes walk about the estate at odd hours."

"All right. You subdued this man and tied him up. Then what?"

"I tried to question him. At first he wouldn't say anything. Then he told me that his name was George Barr and he lived outside the village, mainly on money his sister sent him. He'd heard that Stern Hollow housed a valuable collection of art. He'd also heard that art theft was both quick and easy.

"A few weeks ago he met a footman from Stern Hollow at the village pub, having a pint on his half day. During their chat he said he'd heard that the manor was locked up nice and tight at night, with no way for anyone from the outside to get in. According to him, the footman, having already had a few pints, declared that if he were trying to break in, he would get into the boiler hut, climb down the ladder, and take the tunnel to the coal cellar. And Mr. Barr decided that he would do exactly that, for instant riches.

"He seemed a genuinely stupid man. But I didn't dare trust my first impression. So I decided I would verify his story first, before I did anything else. Since we were already near the icehouse, that seemed as good a place as any to stow him.

"I tied him to a tree, gagged him, and went to the head gardener's shed and took his key to the icehouse. While I was in the shed, I saw that he had a pile of padlocks and decided to take one. I didn't want the kitchen helper to accidentally come upon Mr. Barr before I could find out whether he was truly the village idiot.

"I put him in the second antechamber and secured the icehouse with the other lock. In the morning I meant to take him some water and food, but the outdoor staff were working nearby and I couldn't get into the icehouse without being seen. And then the cisterns broke at Mrs. Newell's and I was faced with an influx of guests who must be looked after. I was unable to get away for the rest of the day. And when I managed to do so after most of them had gone to bed, one of the gentlemen decided to set up his telescope twenty feet from the icehouse.

"I waited for an hour. He showed no intention of leaving. I came out again at three in the morning. He was gone by then. But so was the lock on the icehouse door. This alarmed me to no small extent. I went in and all that remained of the man was a foul smell he had left in the second antechamber.

"You didn't go deeper into the icehouse?"

"No. My first—and only—thought was that he *had* been sent by Lady Ingram—and that he had not been sent alone. His partner must have set him free. Since it would profit them not at all to venture farther into the icehouse, I never thought to check the inner chambers."

"And then what?"

"Then it didn't matter anymore whether anyone came into the icehouse; I put the old lock back on, returned the spare key to the head gardener's place, and went back to the house." He tapped his fingers once against the top of his large mahogany desk. "And that afternoon Lady Ingram's body was discovered twenty feet from where I'd stood that morning."

---

Beyond the windows the sky was blue—the fog had cleared entirely; the day promised to be cold but crisp. The brilliance outside only made the interior of the library, despite its many lamps and sconces, appear somber and unlit.

In the wake of Lord Ingram's confession, silence reigned—even the fires barely hissed. Chief Inspector Fowler polished his spectacles. Lord Bancroft finished one slice of cake and picked up another. Lord Ingram took a sip of tea, his hand steady, his expression detached, seemingly unaware of his impending doom.

Treadles held on to the edges of his notebook so that his fingers wouldn't shake. Where was Charlotte Holmes? And where was the exculpatory evidence that he and Lord Ingram had trusted her to unearth?

Fowler, satisfied with the clarity of his glasses, set them back on his nose. His owlish gaze landed on the master of the manor. "Lord Ingram, this is what I believe happened: You killed this man."

Neither Lord Ingram nor Lord Bancroft betrayed any reaction. Treadles gritted his teeth, wiped his perspiring palms with a handkerchief, and resumed his note-taking.

"It could have happened under two different sets of circumstances, both involving your children," Fowler went on. "I do not believe your children left with your brother, Lord Remington Ashburton. I believe they are still somewhere here on this estate. George Barr happened to stumble upon one of the places where you keep the children, and possibly their governess—namely, the tunnel between the glass house boilers and the coal cellar. Little wonder, then, that his presence so alarmed you.

"You chased him down and subdued him. This is where possibilities diverge. It's possible you killed him on the spot. But I am of the opinion that you didn't. That you told the truth about locking him in the icehouse while you sought to discover whether he truly was the moron he appeared to be.

"And then Lady Ingram arrived in secret. Perhaps things had gone awry with the man of her dreams. Perhaps her return was only for the sake of her children, all three of them. But she knew that you'd explained her absence as a visit to a Swiss sanatorium, which could be easily enough reversed. And she wished now to come back home, mother her children, and raise her future infant in respectable circumstances rather than ignominious exile.

"This enraged you, you who were beginning to consider letting the truth be known, so that you could petition for divorce on grounds of desertion. So that you could carry on with the rest of your life, preferably with Miss Charlotte Holmes as the next Lady Ingram. You pretended to be amenable to Lady Ingram's plea, gave her a quantity of laudanum—the pathologist found that in her as well—and then injected her with absolute alcohol.

"Now that the deed was done, you wondered how to turn the situation to your advantage. It would be best if you could manipulate things so that it would appear to the general public that she had passed away while abroad. For that you would need her body to be shipped back in a casket and a funeral held.

"But how to get her to the Continent to be shipped back? Arrangements must be made. In the meanwhile, she must be preserved, in a way that would be convenient to whatever chronology of events you chose to fabricate. You remembered the fellow in the icehouse. The icehouse, you realized, would be the perfect place to keep her from spoiling—or spoiling your future.

"Which then, of course, means that poor Mr. Barr, who witnessed you dragging in Lady Ingram, must now be forever silenced."

It was with great effort that Treadles didn't stare at Fowler with his mouth open. This was a ghastly interpretation of the known facts, but the worst thing about it was that he could see a jury being convinced of such a scenario.

"I had no idea Scotland Yard employed novelists these days," said Lord Bancroft coldly. "Of the penny dreadful variety, no less."

Treadles, who until now had felt only a respectful wariness toward his friend's brother, began to harbor warmer sentiments. Lord Bancroft was no doubt the kind who had no reservations about eviscerating men he considered his lessers, but at least now he'd done it on behalf of someone Treadles wished to defend but couldn't.

Fowler was not chastised. "Truth is often stranger than fiction, my lord."

"If everything happened as you claimed, Chief Inspector, then why would I put back the original lock on the icehouse, with an estate full of guests and a kitchen that was certain to require ice?"

Lord Ingram's tone was calm, far calmer than Treadles's would have been, under the circumstances.

"Sir, with all due respect, we have no evidence at all that you are the one who put the original lock back. It could very well have been someone else who discovered that the wrong lock was on the door and rectified the situation."

"Ridiculous," said Lord Bancroft. "You are saying that my brother did all this while the estate swarmed with guests?"

"It is a great deal less ridiculous than the version of events peddled by Mr. Sherrinford Holmes, which would have me believe that *outsiders* did all this while the estate swarmed with guests."

Against that, even Lord Bancroft had no proper retort.

Treadles glanced toward the door of the library. Why was Charlotte Holmes not marching in, the true culprit following meekly in her wake? He would declare Sherrinford Holmes's stupid mustache the most beautiful sight he'd ever beheld if the damned thing would only materialize.

This very moment.

Lord Ingram, too, gazed at the door. Then he looked back at his nemesis. "Are you here to arrest me, Chief Inspector?"

"No, not yet, my lord," said Fowler, the barest trace of smugness to his voice. "But I ask that you will please remain in the manor, pending further notice."

———※———

Mrs. Watson read Miss Holmes's telegram, changed in record time, and rushed out of her house. Luck was with her. She encountered no congestion of carriages on the way to Somerset House, where she employed every last ounce of her charm and finished her search in what must also be record time.

She next traveled with breakneck speed to Paddington station, where Miss Holmes was already waiting on the platform.

With her Sherrinford beard on, it was difficult to gauge how close—or far away—she was from Maximum Tolerable Chins, the hypothetical limit at which Miss Holmes began to watch how much she ate. But Mrs. Watson very much suspected that her appetite had not recovered. She didn't look very different, but she felt slighter—and very, very weary.

They clasped hands briefly.

"Are you all right, ma'am?" murmured Miss Holmes.

Mrs. Watson, who tended to fret even in the normal course of events, had been lying awake every night, well into the small hours, trying to wrestle her mind into some semblance of tranquility. Alas, every time she succeeded, a few minutes later she would find that she had but started down a different path of contemplating how everything could go horribly, irrevocably wrong.

"Well enough," she said. And that was a truthful answer. Compared to Lord Ingram, they were all faring spectacularly well, cocooned in good luck and blessings.

But perhaps the tide was about to turn for him as well. Certainly the work Mrs. Watson had put in this day must rank among some of the most worthwhile of her life.

"How did you know?" she asked Miss Holmes. "How did you know what I would find at the General Register Office?"

"I didn't. I didn't think in that direction until this morning, after I learned that the pathologist, in the course of the autopsy, discovered that Lady Ingram was with child."

Mrs. Watson gasped. "What—what does *that* mean?"

"That's what I hope to find out in Oxfordshire."

As if on cue, the waiting train whistled.

Mrs. Watson was still reeling. "Does Lord Ingram know? What does he think of it?"

"I imagine he must, by now—Lord Bancroft attended the autopsy. But I have not met him since I heard the news from Scotland Yard."

"Oh, the poor boy. What an intolerable situation."

"Well," said Miss Holmes. "That situation will change soon."

"I hope so!" Mrs. Watson said fervently.

"Be careful what you wish for, ma'am," said Miss Holmes, a hint of apology to her voice. "It could change for the worse."

—✳︎—

The past summer, while in Oxfordshire trying to find the whereabouts of one Mr. Myron Finch, Charlotte had passed by Lady Ingram's ancestral estate. At the time, she and Mrs. Watson had peered in at the gate but not called upon the inhabitants.

Now she did, or at least Mr. Sherrinford Holmes did, on behalf of Lord Ingram.

The house struck Charlotte as well maintained, well decorated, but lacking a sense of history. She could imagine Lady Ingram's parents, upon being lifted out of decades of penury, getting rid of all their old things in a hurry—the ones they hadn't been able to pawn, in any case—in order to acquire new and more presentable possessions.

As she waited for the master of the house to be informed of her arrival, she closed her eyes. She was both weary yet uncomfortably alert, an awareness that flooded her with too many sensory details.

This was something she'd learned from a very young age: Her senses sharpened on an empty stomach, occasionally to such an extent that she needed to cover her eyes and stick her fingers in her ears; but a small degree of overeating dulled those senses to a more tolerable level.

As a toddler, she had despised raisins. But the family cook had specialized in plum cakes, which required half a pound of currants apiece. And such had been the palliative effect of an extra slice of plum cake that over time she had come to associate raisins with a feeling of comfort and relief.

After her adolescent years, the oversensitivity had become less intense. A day or two of water and very small quantities of plain toast would not reduce her to a quivering mass of frayed nerves. Still, she had reached a point when a fifteen-course meal would be a pleasure from beginning to end.

If only her stomach would cooperate.

Even plain toast made it mutiny. And along with a sharp nausea would come waves of fear—the dinner with Lord Bancroft had been an exercise in misery.

The fear was utterly unnecessary, she'd told herself. She had prepared; she understood the circumstances; she was determined to be careful and vigilant. She didn't need any additional fear to channel or guard her.

The fear had roiled on, irrational but palpable. And the only way to reduce its impact was to keep her stomach as close to empty as possible.

She hoped this meeting would help. If it didn't, the mountain she must climb would become much higher.

"Mr. Holmes," said the footman, "Mr. Greville will see you now."

Charlotte shoved aside her discomfort and donned Sherrinford Holmes's jollity. "Ah, excellent."

Mr. Alden Greville, the older of Lady Ingram's two younger brothers, received Charlotte with an anxious keenness. "Please tell me my brother-in-law is carrying on tolerably. I wished to go to Stern Hollow right away after I learned the news, but he specifically instructed me to stay put. He thought it would be too distressing for me to be there. But it's been awful sitting here biting my nails and waiting for a word, with the papers printing every sort of unkindness imaginable."

Charlotte accepted a cup of tea, which she drank black—a lump of sugar and a spoonful of cream would have been enough to set off a fresh revolt in her stomach. "He is holding up all right. But I must warn you, any day now he could be charged with your sister's murder."

Mr. Greville turned a deathly pallor. "No, that cannot be! He would never have done such a thing."

"Alas, the body of circumstantial evidence is overwhelmingly not in his favor. And the police will very much desire a conviction in such a prominent case. Our only hope is that they won't wish to make a mistake in the matter—which would result in a prominent debacle. For that reason and that reason alone, we might still have a little time."

Mr. Greville knotted his fingers together. "I cannot tell you what a blow that would be. Obviously, it would be catastrophic for Ash and the children. But for Hartley and myself, it would be— I can't overstate what Ash means to us. I know the one we should be grateful to is Alexandra, who married him to better our lives. But to tell you the truth, my sister never much cared for us, and it was always Ash who took the time to listen and to help, with money yes, but above all with kindness.

"My brother worships Ash even more than I do, if that's possible. He would be devastated if anything was to happen to him. We were both horror-struck at the rupture between Alexandra and him, when we thought we would lose his affection. It didn't happen, of course, thank goodness. But to think that now he might lose his—"

Mr. Greville swallowed, unable to continue.

"As Lord Ingram's friend, I share your concern," said Charlotte. "I want to make sure that the worst doesn't happen to him. That's why I came to you, Mr. Greville. Will you help me?"

"Of course! What can I do? Please tell me. I will do anything in my power."

His eyes shone with a desperate wish to help. Despite the seriousness of the situation, Charlotte felt pleased for Lord Ingram. He had been unable to spark love in his wife, but the affection he inspired in others was deep and genuine.

"There are some things I need to find out about your late sister. Most likely you will not be able to offer the answers yourself, but somewhere in this house we should be able to locate what I need."

Mr. Greville leaped up. "Then let us proceed!"

As he led the way to the study, Charlotte asked when Lady Ingram had last visited. Apparently it had been after their parents passed away, to go through some records.

"Once she left, she didn't come back very often. Almost not at all," said Mr. Greville, a little apologetically.

And that absence translated into scant traces of Lady Ingram in this house. Charlotte had caught sight of an oil portrait and several large photographs of Lord Ingram—and only one picture of Lady Ingram, as part of a group. It was almost as if he was a favored son of the family and she only a distant cousin.

Mrs. Watson had once relayed to Charlotte an opinion on an adolescent Lady Ingram, by a woman who had worked for the Grevilles. Her main impression of Lady Ingram at that age was one of frustration. A frustration that approached rage, at times.

Lady Ingram hadn't been angry because she'd wished to marry

a different man, as Mrs. Watson had thought at the time, but because her life hadn't been her own.

Charlotte did not pity Lady Ingram—the woman played no small role in her own fate. But she sometimes thought of the former Miss Alexandra Greville, brought to London and told to smile, told to be happy that an eligible man loved her, told that upon marriage she would have everything a woman could desire.

When it should have been obvious to all who knew her that such a life would unravel her. Yet they'd pushed it on her with all their might—and made it plain that for her to do anything else would be a gross betrayal to her family.

Perhaps she had always been a monster, but even the lady monsters of the world couldn't escape the expectations that came of being women.

❖

It was past eleven o'clock when Charlotte's train pulled into Paddington station again. She hailed a hansom cab to take her to a small house in St. John's Wood, the address of which Mrs. Watson had given her earlier in the day.

Mrs. Watson herself opened the door. "I think we have done it," she said in a whisper.

"This house looks exactly the kind of place for a kept woman," Charlotte whispered back.

Mrs. Watson smiled. "Glad to oblige, my dear."

Behind Mrs. Watson stood Frances Marbleton, Stephen Marbleton's sister, though Charlotte had never been entirely convinced that they were, in fact, siblings.

"Come," said Miss Marbleton.

In the parlor, a woman sat rigidly in a high-back chair, dressed in somber clothes that were neither new nor fashionable but hardy of material and well made. At Charlotte's entrance she looked up: One of her eyes was an ethereal blue, the other milky and blind.

In the first days after Charlotte ran away from home, she'd come across a beggar woman and her child and had been so moved by their plight that she'd given them some of her scant coins. Only to realize later that her pocket had been picked during the encounter.

This was that woman.

Stephen Marbleton, who had been seated across from the woman, rose. "I hope your journey has been a pleasant one."

Charlotte found her voice—or, rather, Sherrinford Holmes's voice. "It has been, thank you."

Even so the woman stared at her, as if trying to recall where she'd heard her before.

Charlotte was not very often unnerved, but she sensed in herself a strong quiver of apprehension.

"This is Mrs. Winnie Farr," said Mr. Marbleton.

A notice had gone into the papers the evening before, seeking those with a young, dark-haired sister or daughter who had been missing for more than a fortnight. And Mrs. Winnie Farr had answered, Mrs. Farr, who had already written Sherlock Holmes for help with her missing sister.

Except Sherlock Holmes had been too preoccupied of late to take on any other case.

"Sherrinford Holmes, at your service, Mrs. Farr," Charlotte said to the woman who stole a solid pound from her. "How do you do?"

"Your man said you can find out what happened to my sister."

Her voice had a heavy quality, as if words had to be dredged up from her larynx. Her expression was almost as heavy. But her good eye was alert and piercing, and Charlotte found herself having to take a deep breath.

The reverberations of alarm were only partially brought on by Mrs. Farr's presence. They were echoes of a difficult time, of the closest Charlotte had come to the edge of desperation. The loss of one pound had been disastrous; the loss of hope, far worse.

But she was in a different place now. And this was no time to lose her concentration, because a primitive part of her mind was too busy wallowing in old fears. She owed Mrs. Farr her undivided attention. She owed Lord Ingram her utmost effort.

She owed herself the clarity to know when she was in danger and when she was not.

"We *may* be able to help," she answered. "Did you bring photographs?"

Mrs. Farr opened a shabby handbag and took out two small pictures. When Charlotte held them in hand, she realized that they were not photographs but postcards—or, rather, a young woman's face cut out of postcards.

Postcards came in many varieties: some scenic, some sentimental, and others highly risqué. There was no need to ask which category these ones fell into.

The young woman in the postcard was full of vitality, her eyes mischievous, her hair shiny even in the grainy print.

"How old was she at the time these photographs were taken?"

"They were taken this year. She's twenty-five. Twenty-six January next."

Which made her close in age to Lady Ingram. "And you said she has been missing a little more than three weeks?"

"I last saw her almost a month ago. She told me she'd be out of London for a day or two, but that she'd be back in time for my daughter's birthday. I didn't want her to go. Sometimes, postcard girls are invited to stag parties in the country—and those parties don't always go well for the girls.

"She said it would be nothing of the sort, that she'd already helped this gentleman before. She said he thought well of her ideas—which worried me even more.

"She was tired of depending on men to photograph her, you see. They don't pay much and some of them want favors besides. She was going to buy her own equipment and learn how to do everything herself, from pulling the shutter to developing the negatives. She wanted to have a stable of the best girls in the business. And someday she wanted to own a printing press, too."

Mrs. Watson looked uncomfortable. Charlotte felt no particular dismay. Pornography would exist as long as the human race did. If a woman didn't mind appearing on a risqué postcard, she might as well maximize her control over—and profit from—the entire process.

"I see," she said. "Commendable entrepreneurial spirit on her part."

Mrs. Farr had looked defiant as she narrated her sister's plans. But Charlotte's comment seemed to have rattled her, as if she'd expected anything except a compliment. "I—I thought so, but I didn't believe her gentleman thought the same. When a man first claps eyes on a girl on a postcard, the chances of him ever seeing her as anything other than flesh—" She shook her head. "Anyway, we had words. I told her she oughtn't go. And she told me that she looked after herself just fine and didn't need a one-eyed old woman ordering her about.

"When she didn't come for my daughter's birthday I thought maybe she was still angry with me. But the next day I thought, no, that's not my Mimi. She doesn't hold a grudge. And she loves her niece and thinks the world of her. I went 'round to her room, but her landlady already let the room to someone else because she'd been gone more than a week and hadn't settled her account.

"Her friends didn't know what to think. She promised them that she'd start her own studio as soon as she returned, and she wasn't some flighty girl who made promises she didn't keep. I went to Scotland Yard and begged to speak to somebody. And this hoity-toity inspector told me that it was hardly unheard of for girls like Mimi to hole up with a man and not be seen for a while.

"I told him that maybe he knew nothing about girls like her.

Because girls like her have family and friends they see on the regular, and rooms and appointments to keep. Girls like her have mementoes that mean something to them—she knew her landlady would sell her belongings wholesale to some rag dealer, if she left them behind. And what kind of arrangement with a man wouldn't give her half a day to come back to see to her things and tell her family and friends that she now had an arrangement?

"But I might as well have talked to a statue—men like that have ears but nothing goes in. I kept going back, but it was no use. There was one nice sergeant who told me I ought to write to Sherlock Holmes. I did but he was out of town and I still don't know anything more about Mimi."

"Sherlock is my brother and I'm here on his behalf. For the past few days I have been occupied with a difficult case, but it would seem that you and I are fated to meet after all."

"Is that so?" Mrs. Farr sounded doubtful.

"That is so. Have you or any of your sister's friends seen this gentleman of hers in person?"

Mrs. Farr shook her head. "None of them. And not me either."

Charlotte asked a few more questions, but Mrs. Farr could tell her nothing else about the man. And she was becoming impatient. "I've told you everything I know. Now what can *you* tell *me*?"

Her question was a near growl. Surprising how much authority a woman who begged on the streets at least some of the time could pack into a few words. Then again, Mrs. Farr was not an ordinary down-on-her-luck mendicant—Charlotte had already deduced that after their first meeting. She might exist on London's underbelly, but she was not lost in it. In fact, she might have carved out her own small fiefdom there.

Charlotte did not recoil this time. "I'm afraid all I have concerning your sister is bad news."

"I'll take bad news. I'll take any news."

Since she'd become Sherlock Holmes, consulting detective, Charlotte had made her share of unwelcome announcements, but this might be the most brutal one yet. As hungry as Mrs. Farr was for news—any news—hers was a despair still shot through with strands of hope. Now Charlotte would snip every last filament of that hope.

"Unless there are more than one young brunette with a beauty mark who's been missing for exactly as long as she has, your sister is most likely dead."

On an otherwise blandly pretty face, the beauty mark had served as a punctuating feature, bringing focus to Mimi Duffin's pert chin and bow-shaped mouth. And it had been the cause of her misfortune. Mrs. Farr was right; the gentleman hadn't been in the least interested in Mimi Duffin's ideas or ambitions.

Mrs. Farr clamped her fingers over the arms of her chair. The veins on the backs of her hands rose in sharp relief. "What happened? Where is she?"

"Her body hasn't been found yet. It might take some time to surface, as there was incentive to move it some distance from the site of the crime. As for what happened, she bore a resemblance to someone else, someone the gentleman wanted others to think of as having been murdered.

"He probably saw her face on a postcard and realized she could make for a fairly decent approximation to the body he wanted. He found her, cultivated her, and then had her transport herself to where he intended to kill her."

"And where is that?" Mrs. Farr's voice turned harsh.

"At the moment I'm not at liberty to divulge that. I apologize, but the man who did this is wily and dangerous and I have put everyone here at risk in seeking Miss Duffin's identity. The less you know, the better. But I promise you that as soon as possible, I will tell you more. And I will not consider the matter finished until your sister's body has been found and returned to you."

Mrs. Farr sat still and silent. Mrs. Watson brought her a glass of brandy. Mrs. Farr drank with shaking hands. When she was done, she set down the empty glass, rose, and walked out.

Mr. Marbleton got to his feet. "I'll see that she reaches home safely."

"Thank you, sir," murmured Charlotte.

Only then did she allow herself a moment to deal with the memories the sight of Mrs. Farr had brought to the fore—and the associated panic that still rippled in the back of her mind.

<hr />

Mrs. Watson left with Mrs. Farr and Mr. Marbleton. She didn't say why, but if anyone could give comfort to Mrs. Farr right now, or at least not have her presence despised, it would be Mrs. Watson.

"There's food in the larder," said Miss Marbleton, rather standoffishly. "And an Etna stove that you can use."

"Thank you," said Charlotte. "And thank you for all your help, Miss Marbleton."

Miss Marbleton pursed her lips. "You know I'm against our involvement, Miss Holmes."

"And I have told your brother I will speak no kind words on his behalf to my sister."

"She would not last a minute in the kind of life we lead."

"You might be surprised at the strength of the fragile. And for some people, it is ordinary life that is most challenging, not so much the extraordinary."

In a way, Livia's greatest strength was that she was so overlooked and underestimated. Within seconds people decided who she was, and what she was and wasn't capable of. But no one was so easy to sum up, least of all a someone like Livia, who yearned to be more with every fiber of her being.

"That said, I hope she never decides to find out for herself. I expect you heard from your father that he and I met?"

"I took a few days to recuperate and everyone decided to throw all caution to the wind," said Miss Marbleton, who was clearly the enforcer of rules in her family.

"Did he tell you that he introduced himself as Moriarty?"

Miss Marbleton shrugged, a gesture almost French in its resigned disapproval. "He was born a Moriarty. It's his prerogative to introduce himself however he pleases."

"It must gall James Moriarty to no end that his wife absconded with his brother."

Miss Marbleton only shrugged again, an even more eloquent gesture.

"If I may be so forward, is Mr. Stephen Marbleton your brother or your cousin?"

"We are not related. Mr. Crispin Marbleton is my stepfather."

A neat sidestepping of the question. Did she know the truth of his parentage? Did Stephen Marbleton himself know? In either case, it would be highly dangerous for Livia to become better acquainted with him.

Charlotte sighed. "Your brother should stop sending my sister gifts and messages, but I'm sure you have already wasted your breath saying the same."

"He has been needlessly obstinate, refusing to make any promises not to contact her again. Would you please tell her that he's too young for her?"

Charlotte could scarcely admonish Livia about a man she had never admitted to having met, let alone having fallen in love with. "I will see what I can do. Before you go, there is something else I need to ask."

"Yes?"

"Last night, when Mr. Stephen Marbleton played the part of Sherlock Holmes, he told Scotland Yard the man Lady Ingram was involved with was Moriarty. Other than the fact that Lady Ingram did not have romantic feelings for Moriarty—as far as I can tell—that claim was largely correct. But all the same I was surprised that the name Moriarty came up and that he wanted the police to hear it."

Miss Marbleton shrugged into her coat. "On that front, at least, Stephen did not do anything rash. We discussed this as a family and the decision was unanimous. If Scotland Yard does not know Moriarty's name, they should learn it. If they already do, then it is high time they pay him more attention."

# Eighteen

*Departing Oxfordshire. A. Greville sends his regards. Holmes.*

There were hundreds of things Lord Ingram needed to keep in mind and dozens of tasks to finish, but he stood in place and read the cable again and again, thoughts of Holmes overriding everything else.

They had not spent a great deal of time together, not in years. Even when they had been much younger, passing long stretches of silence in each other's company, he occupied with some minor excavation, she burrowing through two brick-like books in a single afternoon—those had not been regular occurrences, but had come only when they both happened to be at his uncle's or Mrs. Newell's estate at the same time.

He had a very clear memory of the day she told him to write her. It was the summer of the Roman villa ruins. She had blackmailed him into kissing her—and afterward had visited the ruins as she pleased, with him by and large ignoring her. Or, rather, he had not spoken to her, but had furtively observed the utterly incomprehensible girl.

And had remembered the kiss more often than he wanted to, when he lay in bed alone at night.

*I'm leaving in the morning,* she'd said one afternoon, with no preamble. *Here's my address.*

Out of politeness, he'd taken the slip of paper, while thinking ferociously, *I won't.*

But two months later he had, from his room at school, with cricket practice canceled and a thunderstorm raging outside. And it had been a far longer letter than he'd intended. Nothing personal, a rather dry encapsulation of the lessons he'd learned from working on the ruins of the Roman villa, and the improvements to both record-keeping and excavation methods that he intended to make.

Her reply came sixteen days later—yes, he'd counted—and was almost identical to his in tone, a summary of books she had read in recent months on pedagogical theories and practices, and then the casual conclusion that she believed she would make a fine headmistress at a girls' school.

He wrote back and told her that he'd never met any girl who made him think less of a headmistress, followed by his observations, only partially related to the subject, on how boys in a resident house organized into factions and cliques.

She admitted in her next letter that she wanted to be a headmistress less out of a desire to influence young minds than because a headmistress could command up to five hundred pounds a year. And by the way, she did not understand people as well as she ought to and found his anthropological account of the behavior of boys very helpful.

After that they wrote weekly. It had come as a minor shock, when he'd met her in person again, to realize that their regular and sometimes voluminous correspondence would not translate into conversation, that silence would still be the order of the day. But sliding back into silence had not been difficult or uncomfortable.

That correspondence continued without interruption—even when they were together, they would hand each other letters—until their quarrel over the future Lady Ingram, with Holmes warning darkly against believing in the illusion of the perfect woman. He'd stopped writing until he'd returned from his honeymoon, euphoric in the knowledge that he was about to be a father.

In subsequent years, their epistolary exchange remained regular as clockwork, but without a single reference to his inner turmoil, not through the disintegration of his marriage, and certainly not with the suddenly piercing understanding of what he felt for Holmes— what he had always felt for her.

The correspondence faltered again when she ran away from home. And after Lady Ingram's departure. He had stared at a blank page many times, with no idea what to write, now that his hesitation was the only thing that held them back from becoming more than friends.

Now they were more than friends.

Now every hour without her was an eternity.

*Wait*, he told himself, staring into the night. *Patience.*

But he had already exhausted a lifetime's supply of patience. Had already held himself back for ages beyond count. And he had no more restraint left, no more willpower.

Only need.

It was past midnight, when Inspector Treadles arrived in London. The house he walked into was dark, silent. Lately it had not seemed quite his own, as if it no longer belonged to him, or he it. But tonight— tonight he felt as if he'd come home.

Alice was already in bed, asleep. He lay down beside her and stared up, Charlotte Holmes's words echoing in his ears. *You have an open, amiable mien, which might lead those speaking with you to expect understanding. And yet your judgment is such a pointed, implacable thing, as if you are the personification of the larger world they have known, the one that has thwarted them at every turn.*

Did this also happen to his own wife? Frustrated with her father, who, though a good man, an excellent man, had refused to ever entertain the idea of giving her the reins to Cousins Manufacturing, she had fallen in love with a man she believed to be different, only to realize that of the two, her father had, in fact, been far more broad-minded.

*When had she realized that?*

It struck him that she had known it for a while, for a long time, possibly since before she married him—and *that* was the reason she had never mentioned her erstwhile ambitions.

Then why had she married him?

*She loved you, you idiot*, said a voice inside him.

Perhaps she'd convinced herself that they could still be happy together. Perhaps she'd believed that since she would never helm Cousins Manufacturing, he would never see—or disapprove of — of that side of her. Or perhaps she'd thought that if they dealt well for some time, he would come to trust her enough to see that ambitions or not, she was still the same woman he loved.

But she had been mistaken.

And how had she lived with his judgment, which he'd thought he'd kept to himself, but which, as Charlotte Holmes had pointed out, was anything but discreet or subtle?

His misery was like shards, cutting through every organ and nerve. He felt as if he didn't know anything anymore—as if he'd never known anything at all.

In despair he turned to Alice and placed an arm around her.

She had her back to him. They used to sleep all entangled in each other, but as distances had grown elsewhere, the same had happened in bed, until they each slept facing a wall, a trench of empty space between their backs.

He laid his forehead against her shoulder and breathed in the scent of her skin. Alice, who had realized he was not the man she had hoped he would be, and loved him anyway.

264 · *Sherry Thomas*

She sighed and turned toward him.

The next moment they were kissing, as wildly as if this had been their wedding night.

And everything that followed was just as untrammeled.

※

Livia was an early riser. Though it was still dark outside, she'd already been at her desk for hours, wrestling with the second part of her Sherlock Holmes story.

The nameless young man's eagerness to read her work didn't make the work any easier. But it did make her more willing to bash her head on that particular wall a few more times.

She'd just finished a new précis of the plot when a commotion erupted on the floor below. Mrs. Newell herself came knocking on her door.

"Oh, my dear, I'm afraid that I'm once again the bearer of ill news."

Livia's ears rang. *Lord Ingram. No!* "What—what's going on?"

"You will not believe this, but they discovered a bomb in the coal cellar."

"A *what?*"

"Not to worry, we aren't in any immediate danger. The bomb is in the kitchen's coal cellar and that's a fair distance from the house."

"Oh," said Livia, but her hands still shook.

In the past few years, Irish republicans had placed dozens of time bombs all over Britain, especially in London—explosions as a form of political expression seemed a permanent fixture of modern life. But all the ones Livia had heard of, whether they'd gone off or been defused, had targeted places of strategic importance. Military barracks, railway stations, newspaper offices, and such. In the only instance she could recall of a private home as a target, the home had belonged to a member of parliament who strenuously opposed Irish Home Rule.

"But why? Why would anyone put a bomb *here?*"

"I know!" cried Mrs. Newell. "If I could vote I'd have cast my ballot for Mr. Gladstone, to give the Irish their Home Rule."

"Oh, I'm so sorry this happened, Mrs. Newell!"

Mrs. Newell patted her on the arm. "I've sent someone to fetch the police. They'll probably need to cable the Special Irish Branch to come, for all I know. But I'm afraid in the meanwhile we must decamp again."

And not to Stern Hollow.

An idea came to Livia fully formed and requiring immediate implementation. "I—I really mustn't impose anymore. I've been enough trouble to you and should have gone home directly from Stern Hollow. I believe I'll do that now."

"Nonsense. Come with me to the inn, my dear. I know you don't wish to go home."

Livia didn't, but sometimes one did what one must. "I'll stay an extra week next year, if you'll have me. You know I love it here, Mrs. Newell. But now I really must go."

In the morning, Treadles almost couldn't face his wife across the breakfast table. His cheeks kept flaming as he ate his toast and fried eggs. They had made love three times during the night and done things to and with each other that he hadn't even known were within the realm of possibility.

But they had not spoken, not a single word.

She, after sorting through the early post, broke the silence first. "I didn't expect you home so soon, Inspector. Has the case already been solved?"

That she sounded tentative gave him some much needed courage. "No, not yet. We are in London to speak to Miss Charlotte Holmes."

News had come the previous day that Miss Holmes had responded to the notice the police had put in the papers. She was amenable to meeting them this morning at eleven, at the tea shop in Hounslow where she had been seen with Lord Ingram.

Treadles had been incredulous. Lord Ingram was under house arrest, for all intents and purposes, and Miss Holmes thought it necessary to travel to London for the express purpose of meeting with the policemen? He'd tried to convince himself that perhaps at the appointed time she would present them with the all-important evidence that would clear Lord Ingram's name but such hopes were beginning to wilt.

"Ah, the mythical Miss Holmes." A small frown marred Alice's forehead. "Her name has been all over the papers—along with Lord Ingram's. Some are portraying her as quite the Jezebel."

And some were saying far less kind things.

*Our fallen young lady certainly has plenty of cheek,* Chief Inspector Fowler had commented, his jolly mood an agony to endure. *Well, let us be on the next train bound for London.*

*But if you are certain, Chief Inspector, that Lord Ingram killed his wife because she had turned up carrying another man's child, then is there still any need to question Miss Holmes?* Treadles had asked.

He had wanted to stay behind. He might yet uncover something that would be useful to Lord Ingram—or at least give the latter some company.

*It will be a change of scenery, at least, wouldn't you say?* had been Fowler's answer. And the implacability beneath the seeming agreeableness of his tone had told Treadles it would be useless to protest.

"I'm more than a little curious about this Miss Charlotte Holmes," Alice continued. She smiled a little. Was she feeling as jittery as he? "Will you still be here in the evening to give a juicy account?"

"I was rather under the impression that we would be headed back to Stern Hollow this afternoon. But everything could change between now and then."

He was afraid that Fowler had left Stern Hollow to make it easier for Lord Ingram to escape. All the evidence against Lord Ingram was circumstantial. Should he take to the witness stand in his own defense, there was a chance that the jury would prefer to believe him rather than the prosecution. But if Lord Ingram ran from the police, it would automatically brand him as guilty in the eye of the public and make the trial's outcome far less uncertain.

Surely Lord Ingram was too intelligent to fall into that particular trap, no matter how hopeless his situation appeared at the moment?

"And how is your work, by the way?" he asked his wife.

Her fork stopped in midair.

In all the months since she took over from her late brother, he had never once inquired into what she did with Cousins Manufacturing. Had no idea who served as her advisors or who opposed her ideas every step of the way. Had treated this very large part of her life as if it were something that concerned only her and was beneath his notice.

"Are you certain you have the time for it, Inspector?" Her tone was unsure.

She was giving him a chance to say no.

He set down his knife and fork and said, "Yes, I have the time."

———— ❊ ————

After she'd left Stern Hollow, Lady Avery had put herself up at Claridge's hotel in London.

The calling card brought in just now announced the wishes of one Mr. Sherlock Holmes to pay his respects. Sherlock Holmes had made his name in a case involving the death of three prominent individuals; it took Lady Avery no time at all to deduce that he must be here to discuss Lady Ingram's murder.

But when her caller was shown into the sitting room of the suite, she proved to be a beautiful woman of similar age to Lady Avery, perhaps even a few years older.

"I am Mrs. Hudson," she introduced herself, "here on behalf of Sherlock Holmes. Mr. Holmes has an unfortunate condition that prevents him from departing his sickbed. His friends and family must therefore perform the legwork for him."

Under any other circumstances, Lady Avery would have immediately inquired as to how exactly Mrs. Hudson was related to Sherlock Holmes, whether she was a friend or a family member. But this morning she was too impatient. "Of course, Mrs. Hudson. I take it you are here on Lord Ingram's behalf?"

Sherlock Holmes had consulted for the police before, but Chief Inspector Fowler didn't strike Lady Avery as the sort to tolerate much input from anyone else on his investigation.

"Indeed. I would like you to take a look at this young woman and see if you recognize her."

She handed over two images which, after a second, Lady Avery realized were portions of postcards.

"This—" She was so astonished she couldn't speak for a moment. Postcards! And judging by the girl's languorously flirtatious expression, what had been on the rest of the postcards would have proven too indecent for public consumption. "This girl saw to me at my hotel in Cowes, on the Isle of Wight."

"She was the one who recognized Lord Ingram from a photograph in the paper that she was using to wrap some mementoes you had purchased, am I correct? And who then went on to tell you about the encounter she had witnessed between Lord Ingram and Miss Charlotte Holmes at the tea shop in Hounslow, where she worked during the summer?"

"Yes. How did you find her? And why is that germane to the case?"

"I am not at liberty to speak further on the matter. Your confirmation is all I need for now." The woman rose. "Thank you, my lady."

Lady Avery shot out of her chair. "But you must tell me more!"

Mrs. Hudson turned around and regarded Lady Avery with pity, as if the latter had been had. "I recommend that you remain in town for a few days, ma'am, if you wish to learn more. You will hear from Sherlock Holmes again."

---

Sergeant Ellerby rushed into the magnificent entrance hall at Stern Hollow and immediately asked to see Lord Ingram.

"His Lordship hasn't come down yet," said the footman who received him. "And we aren't to disturb him when he's in his apartment. But I can ask Mr. Walsh if it's all right to knock, since it's for the police."

Lord Ingram didn't strike Sergeant Ellerby as the sort to linger in his rooms, nice as those were, until almost ten o'clock in the morning. "He hasn't taken ill, has he?"

"Not when I last saw him."

"And when was that?"

"At half past seven. Yesterday he asked for a citron tart from the kitchen. This morning I delivered it to the apartment. He looked fine to me."

"Well, go ask Mr. Walsh, then. Tell him I have news for his lordship—news he'll want to hear."

News that would make him downright ecstatic, in fact.

The bomb that had been discovered at Mrs. Newell's had looked awful enough, but was a dummy that would have never gone off—instead of saltpeter and phosphorus, it had been packed with soot and what most likely would turn out to be baking soda.

Mr. Holmes had suspected that the cisterns had been tampered with. When they turned out not to have been, it had rather knocked a hole in his theory that someone was trying to frame Lord Ingram.

But with the dummy bomb, which couldn't possibly have been a coincidence, that theory had roared back to life.

His mind buzzing with ideas, Sergeant Ellerby paced in the entrance hall, under the startled gaze of the constable who had been left on guard. He ought to send out a bulletin to nearby constabularies and enlist their help in locating the other missing body. He could interview all the staff members again and ask if any of them had put the original lock back on the icehouse door. If none had, then it would bolster Lord Ingram's testimony that he had been the one to do so. He could—

"Sergeant Ellerby."

The speaker was the very grand Mr. Walsh, who made Ellerby far more nervous than did his master. "Yes, Mr. Walsh?"

"I regret to inform you that Lord Ingram is not in his chambers," said Mr. Walsh. "Nor anywhere else in the house."

Sergeant Ellerby stared at the house steward, who stared back at him—and swallowed.

It occurred to him for the first time that even Mr. Walsh could turn a nervous wreck, under the right circumstances.

"Are you sure, sir? His lordship was given specific instructions not to leave the manor."

"Unfortunately, I am sure. I have spoken to the outdoor staff. Lord Ingram requested a horse saddled a little after quarter to eight this morning. And neither he nor the horse has returned."

But Ellerby had such good news! If only Lord Ingram had been more patient. If only he'd had more faith in the universe.

And now he was a fugitive. If he never got caught, then perhaps he might be all right. But if he did—

If he did, he was headed for the hangman's noose.

# Nineteen

Chief Inspector Fowler and Treadles arrived at the Hounslow tea shop a quarter hour before the appointed time. But Miss Holmes was already there. Treadles felt his superior's momentary disorientation. He was a little surprised himself, because Miss Holmes, for this particular interview, had dressed with considerable simplicity.

No excessive rows of bows on her skirt, no acreage of lace trailing from her sleeves. To him, who had only seen her in splashes of riotous color adorned by a surfeit of trimming, as if her dressmaker had been paid by how much spangle the latter could attach to a garment, her russet jacket-and-skirt set seemed as austere as a nun's habit.

Were he to view her from Fowler's vantage point, however, he would see a young woman attired with tremendous propriety, her eyes clear and somber, her demeanor hinting at a gravitas well beyond her years.

Another woman, twice her age but still ravishing, had accompanied her to the tea shop. She was dressed with greater flair but in a way that spoke of wealth rather than wildness.

Treadles was slightly uncomfortable with sitting at a table in

public with a woman—or two, for that matter. Things were changing, of course, but for men and women to dine together in public—
suffice to say he had never been at the forefront of such changes.

But it would be worth any amount of discomfort if Miss Holmes
would give him a sign that all would be well. That Lord Ingram had
not entrusted his fate to her in vain.

Not a flicker of recognition, however, crossed Miss Holmes's
features—Treadles remembered that by formal rules, they had never
even met. The parties presented themselves. Miss Holmes introduced the older woman as Mrs. Watson. "My patroness, for whom
I serve as companion."

The men exchanged a look. What lady would have a fallen
woman as a companion?

Mrs. Watson smiled and said, "I was an actress and as such, not
a very good fit for the very respectable young women who usually
seek positions as companions. Miss Holmes and I, on the other
hand, are a perfect match."

Miss Holmes inclined her head toward her "patroness."

Treadles had to marvel at the number of associates Miss Holmes
could lay claim to. How did a young woman who ran away from
home manage to establish a reliable network in such a short time?

Tea, sliced cake, and finger sandwiches were swiftly served. They
spoke for a few minutes about the weather, and then Fowler got to
work.

"Thank you for meeting with us, Miss Holmes. You have heard
of Lady Ingram's passing, I imagine?"

"What the papers had to say, yes."

With a start, Treadles realized that until she gave this answer, he
had not thought of her as Sherrinford Holmes, who had studied
Lady Ingram's body in the icehouse alongside the police.

"You didn't hear directly from Lord Ingram?" asked Fowler,
sounding dubious.

"He and I are not in regular contact."

Miss Holmes was an extraordinarily efficient liar, every word delivered with naturalness and calm conviction. Gently but firmly, she fended off Fowler's questions.

Yes, the meeting with Lord Ingram the past summer, at this very tea shop, had been a coincidence.

How likely was such a coincidence? No more unlikely than that the waitress who served them should in turn serve Lady Avery at a place hundreds of miles away.

Hostility on Lady Ingram's part? Nothing to it. Not being liked by her was the norm—her antagonism was a broad and catholic entity, aimed at no one in particular.

Did Miss Holmes not feel distraught that her old friend was a prime suspect in the murder of his wife? No, she had complete faith that Scotland Yard would discover the truth.

"And if that truth should be unfavorable to Lord Ingram?"

"Then what could anyone do?"

Treadles could only hope this was not her true sentiment. As delivered, her words fell with a disheartening detachment.

Fowler leaned forward an inch. "Are you aware, Miss Holmes, that Lord Ingram is in love with you?"

Mrs. Watson sucked in a breath.

Miss Holmes, who had known this for days—if not years, as Lord Ingram had declared—remained unmoved. "He has something of a preference for me, certainly. But love? I would have thought he'd had enough romantic love to last a lifetime."

Fowler sat back in his chair and regarded her, no doubt recalling Lady Avery's comment on her oddness. Oddness, what an anodyne term for a woman who might not be entirely human.

"You are in difficult circumstances, Miss Holmes," Fowler began again.

"Am I?"

This question gave Fowler even greater pause. She did not conduct herself as a woman in trouble. That extraordinary poise, for one thing. For another, Mrs. Watson, her patroness, was clearly a little in awe of this "companion."

"As a result of your choices, you can no longer be part of your family."

"You have not met my parents, Chief Inspector. I do not know of many who would want to remain a permanent part of their household."

"What about your sister?"

"You contacted me via a cipher I created for the two of us, specifically. I assume you have already met her?"

"We have."

"Did you receive the impression that she blames me for what happened?"

"No, I did not."

"Then in what way am I in difficult circumstances, sir?"

Fowler couldn't answer that.

"No doubt it will be challenging for you to understand, but my fall from grace has opened an entire new world for me. I enjoy my life far more than I ever have. I have the freedom to do as I wish. And I do not suffer from a lack of funds, thanks to dear Mrs. Watson here. Indeed, by my own estimation, I am a woman in an enviable position."

Fowler gave his tea a stir. "Very well, then. But would your position not become even more favorable, were you to marry Lord Ingram?"

"How so? I do not care for Society. I have little interest in household management and even less in childbearing. I am my own mistress right now; why should I take on a lord and master in the form of a husband?"

"Does Lord Ingram himself not present any attraction for you?"

"He does, most assuredly. I have propositioned him three times."

Even Fowler's jaw dropped. "Not proposed, but *propositioned?*"

"Correct. I thought then and I think now that it would be a fine idea if he were to become my lover."

"But you will not marry him, the surest way to turn him into your lover?"

"No. I want him for one thing and one thing only. That is no reason to marry a man."

"And Lord Ingram knows that?"

Lord Ingram knew it emphatically, but Treadles was breathless to hear how *she* would answer that.

"He knows it better than anyone else. But it's a moot point, whether I will marry him. He will not marry me."

"Because you have propositioned him three times?"

Miss Holmes smiled slightly, as if she found Fowler's question risible. "Because he does not trust that I will love him. And he is correct in that regard. I find romantic love a difficult concept to grasp—at least with regard to marriage. Men and women change. Sentiments change. Yet we are expected to make lifelong contracts based on fleeting emotions."

"That isn't what marriage is about," Treadles found himself saying. "One goes into a marriage knowing that changes are always afoot. The point is to weather the vicissitudes of life together."

"Is that so, Inspector? Or does one go into a marriage expecting everything to remain as it is on the wedding day? Most of the marriages I have seen close up do not inspire confidence, because always, at least one spouse rues the changes that have been brought on by the passage of time."

She looked squarely at him, as if she already knew about the fragile new bond between him and Alice. As if she already perceived his fear that he would not be able to nourish this new bond as he ought to. And that it, too, will someday fray and snap.

He looked away, ashamed that he couldn't say more to defend either his own marriage or the idea of wedded bliss as a whole.

Her gaze returned to Fowler. "No, Chief Inspector, Lord Ingram will not offer for my hand—not even for love."

She paused and considered a moment. "Especially not for love."

—⚜—

"Three times? *Three* times?" Mrs. Watson exclaimed, once they were inside her carriage.

Charlotte shook out her skirts. "Two and a half times, strictly speaking. The second time I needed only an instrument for the riddance of my maidenhead. He wouldn't oblige."

Roger Shrewsbury had obliged instead, in his largely incompetent manner.

Mrs. Watson let out a breath, as if she couldn't quite believe what they were talking about, even as she herself drove the conversation. "If you'll pardon my incurable nosiness, what about the other two times?"

A murder investigation was truly a unique phenomenon. Now there were two policemen in London with intimate knowledge of the amorous history—or the longtime lack thereof—between Charlotte and Lord Ingram. And here was Mrs. Watson, quite justified in wanting to know a bit more about her friend and protégée than did a pair of coppers.

"The third time was at 18 Upper Baker Street—before you had your brilliant idea to monetize Sherlock Holmes's gifts. He proposed to sponsor me to emigrate to America, where no one knew me, and where I could go to school and find respectable employment. I told him I would agree to those terms if he would take me as his mistress. He refused."

Even though at that point he no longer needed to worry about compromising her, since she was already hopelessly compromised. The man could be needlessly stubborn.

"And the first time?" Mrs. Watson sounded a little breathless.

"Shortly before I turned seventeen. We'd known each other for a while by then, and I decided that he would make for a good—or at least interesting—lover."

"But you were so young, practically children!"

For someone who had led a rather scandalous life, Charlotte reflected, Mrs. Watson was rather easily scandalized. At least by Charlotte.

"It's hardly unheard of for girls to be married at sixteen. And he had already lost his virginity, so it wasn't as if I threatened him with imminent deflowering."

Mrs. Watson giggled. "And he said no to this nonthreat."

"After I wooed him with a beautifully wrapped French letter, no less."

Mrs. Watson covered her mouth with both hands, scandalized anew. "Where did you even find such a thing?"

"I believe I have told you that my sister and I snooped in our father's study whenever the opportunity presented itself?"

Mrs. Watson nodded.

Sir Henry and Lady Holmes had never told their children anything of true importance, such as the family's near bankruptcy. Their two youngest daughters, who had always been each other's greatest allies, had formed the habit of finding out everything on their own.

"I always read my father's diary. Once he recorded the name and address of a store where he had been sold a condom. I wrote to the shop and asked whether they conducted any business by post. They were happy to assist. So I sent in a postal order and picked up my purchase at our local post office."

"You did this when you were all of sixteen?"

"No, the year before. I was fifteen."

"I'm surprised—and relieved—that you didn't proposition his lordship *then*."

"I thought about it. But decided I wasn't yet curious enough."

"Even though you'd already purchased a condom?"

"A condom, a sponge, and a syringe for flushing out any semen that hasn't been blocked by the condom and the sponge—if you want the itemized list. For my expenditure, the shop sent me a copy of *Fanny Hill*, gratis."

Mrs. Watson gasped. "And what did you do with *that*?"

"I read it. Then I sold it to Roger Shrewsbury, for twice what it would have cost him to buy."

Mrs. Watson's lips moved, but no words emerged.

"I know," said Charlotte, shaking her head. "Mr. Shrewsbury was never the most enterprising of fellows."

"Did Lord Ingram know that?" Mrs. Watson sounded slightly choked.

"He brokered the deal—and took a cut of the profit." Charlotte smiled. "He wasn't always as stuffy as he later became."

She wasn't sentimental about some mythical past version of him—he might have been more adventurous, but he'd also been naïve and arrogant. Adversity didn't improve everyone—or the world would be filled with men and women of flawless character and sublime insight. Lord Ingram, however, had endured his misfortunes with grace and forbearance and had chosen to become a better man.

When Charlotte commented on his stuffiness, it was never about returning him to his former self—she liked him as he was—but from a deep-seated wish that he would let himself be happy.

Or at least less burdened.

And she had no idea if that would ever be the case.

"Does it really not make any difference that he loves you?" came Mrs. Watson's soft yet fervent question.

Charlotte sighed. "It isn't that love makes no difference; it's that what he and I want out of life are diametrically opposite. It's far easier for people who want the same things to fall in love than for people who want different things to *remain* in love."

Mrs. Watson's breath caught. "Are you—are you saying, Miss Holmes, that you *are* in love with him?"

Charlotte made no reply.

She'd already given answer enough.

——✄——

Livia was proud of herself. Downright, heart-poundingly proud.

She had taken advantage of Mrs. Newell's general distress about the bomb to refuse the offer of her maid for the way home. "You need her more than I do. I have traveled this route more times than I can count. There has never been any trouble in the ladies' compartments. Don't worry. My parents won't know a thing."

And she had prevailed, for once.

But as her hired trap drew abreast of Moreton Close, her warm self-confidence began to turn into something less sustaining. The garden had faded since her previous visit and little resembled the sunny, trim place she remembered. All the windows were shuttered—in the middle of the day! And not a bit of light seeped out from around the edges of the shutters, the way it would have if candles and lamps had been lit, as they must have been on this cold, gray day, if anyone at all were inside.

No one answered her summons. She pulled the bell cord again and again and made enough of a ruckus to rouse even Sleeping Beauty.

`Still no one came.

Remembering the path that led to the wrought iron gate, she ran down that way, pushed open the gate, and knocked on the door of a cottage. At last someone answered, a woman with flour-covered hands.

"Afternoon, miss," she said tentatively.

"Good afternoon. Can you tell me where all the people in the house went, Missus . . . ?"

"Garnet. Everyone went to the south of France for the winter."

The south of France, which Livia had always wished to visit. For a moment she was terribly envious of Bernadine, until she asked herself how likely was it that for the pittance her parents paid, Bernadine would receive trips abroad, above and beyond the already miraculous bargain of Moreton Close.

"All the ladies who can't look after themselves went to the south of France?"

Mrs. Garnet looked confused. "There's only one lady in the house and she looks after herself just fine."

"Only one lady?"

"There are her husband and her sons, but she's the only lady."

Livia's ears rang. "But I was here last week and I saw with my own eyes a houseful of ladies."

"Last week the mister and I went to see our grandbaby. Maybe miss went to a different house?"

Mrs. Garnet's tone was sympathetic, but that only made Livia's voice rise faster. "It was this house!"

"Well," said Mrs. Garnet apologetically, "the family went two weeks ago. I don't know how the house could have been full of ladies last week. I really don't know."

Charlotte alit in front of the bijou house in St. John's Wood where she'd met Mrs. Farr the evening before and stayed the night. She waved good-bye to Mrs. Watson, now headed to her own destination.

Inside the house she took off both her hat and her wig—a woman's wig, this time—and sat down in front of the vanity table to massage her scalp. In the mirror she seemed thinner. Was she already down to only one point two chins?

Another face appeared in the mirror. "Counting your chins?"

"Me? How dare you accuse me of such rampant self-absorption!"

Lord Ingram smiled. "How was your meeting with the police?"

"It went as you would expect." She turned around. He was very close to her, her favorite place for him to be. "You shouldn't be here."

"I know."

She exhaled. "Tell me what has happened since I left—I assume you didn't come just to sleep with me."

He stepped even closer. "And you would be wrong about that."

—◆—

"I'm still unsettled to find myself in bed with you," said Lord Ingram.

"I just find it strange that I'm abed in the middle of the day," answered Holmes. "But I don't mind."

She was looking at him rather fondly—and that made his heart beat fast. They lay a few inches apart, he propped up on an elbow, she with her head on a pillow, a hand under her cheek. He brushed a strand of her hair back from her forehead, taking care not to touch her elsewhere.

"Is it true, what I once heard your sister say, that you don't like to be embraced?"

She took some time to think. "Sometimes Livia needs to hold someone, and I'm the only suitable person nearby. When I was little, I used to wriggle out of her arms and escape to a corner of our room. But it wasn't so much that I couldn't stand being held as that I didn't want to be held indefinitely. Later I taught myself to count to three hundred to mark five minutes—which helped me to realize that she needed only about half that time. I can take two to three minutes of being held. But Livia remains hesitant to this day—she's still scarred by my bolting away from her embrace."

He would be, too.

In fact, sometimes he felt scarred by her, even though she had never done anything except be an excellent friend.

She lifted her hand and hesitated for a moment—as if she expected to be brushed aside—before she reached across and touched the back of her hand to his jawline. "I know I've said this, but you shouldn't have come."

"I know. I've lost my mind."

She tsked. "But I guess I can't be entirely displeased, especially given that . . . What do you call that thing you did?"

"Madam, I did more than one thing to you."

"You know the one I mean. I don't think they did that even in Sodom and Gomorrah."

"You should give Sodom and Gomorrah more credit: After living there, Lot's daughters thought nothing of incest."

She laughed—and giggled again after a moment. "My, you are a wittier man in the vicinity of a bed."

Now it was he who grinned. "Maybe I'm just more relaxed after a good roll in the hay."

"Which reminds me . . ." She climbed above him. "Is there time to do it again?"

---

"I did not," protested Charlotte.

"Yes, you did," insisted Lord Ingram, half-laughing. "You told me I was odd-looking. Said Roger Shrewsbury had the perfect face but mine was just odd."

"No, I wrote that everyone's face was odd to me. And Roger's was odd, too, because it possessed near-perfect symmetry, which is highly unusual."

"And how is that different from saying that he has the perfect face?"

She studied his face with pleasure, because it was so much more arresting and magnetic than Roger Shrewsbury's. "Have I told you lately, my lord, that, compared to you, Mr. Shrewsbury is a sadly inadequate lover?"

A beatific smile spread slowly across his face. "I apologize, but a thousand gardens just bloomed in my soul."

She returned the smile. "I'm not sure why, but I'm beginning to wallow in this particular pettiness of yours."

She wasn't sure that she wanted to understand the full spectrum of human emotions—everything that remained seemed dire to one degree or another. But this warm, silly, mutual delight, *this* she wouldn't mind experiencing until she comprehended its place in the world.

Alas, they could not cocoon themselves off for much longer from the realities they faced. Soon her lover honored her request from earlier and recounted what had happened at Stern Hollow, culminating with his departure.

"Things have progressed faster than I thought," she murmured.

"If I hadn't left when I did, the next time you saw me would have been in jail."

She traced a finger along his brow. "Chief Inspector Fowler is convinced that you would have killed a wife who came to you carrying another man's child. But what would you have done if Lady Ingram had indeed returned in such a state?"

"The thought alone gives me nightmares."

"But you would have taken in the child, in the end."

He expelled a breath. "Of course. I was such a child."

It was hardly analogous. His parents had had that tacit understanding Chief Inspector Fowler had referred to, with none of the acrimony that had characterized his own marriage. But he would never have blamed the child. Would have done his best to make sure that it was treated with kindness and generosity.

She settled a hand on his arm. "Let me tell you something. I met Roger Shrewsbury a year before I met you—and idly thought that perhaps someday I'd kiss him to see what it was like. But then I saw you and immediately knew that it would be you and never him."

"Never?"

"Never. I didn't permit him to kiss me at any point in our acquaintance. But that's not all I'm going to tell you."

He kissed her slowly. "Frankly, Holmes, I don't know how you can possibly improve on what you have already told me."

"Have some faith, Ash," she admonished. "Now, when I said someday, at the time I thought that meant when I reached twenty, or some similar ripe old age. And then, do you remember the ink incident at your uncle's estate?"

"What ink incident?"

"Two boys rigged up a device that could squirt ink a fair distance. They decided to try it on a girl. But things went awry, and they splattered ink all over themselves instead."

"Oh, that ink incident. Yes, I remember."

"I'd observed ink stains on the boys' hands, in quantities too large to be attributable to any normal writing. And then, just before the ink incident, you, on whose hands I'd only seen traces of dirt from working on the Roman villa, also sported visible ink stains. And when the incident happened, when the boys were flailing about in shock and confusion, you were the only one, other than me, who didn't laugh."

"You didn't admire my restraint?"

She had been rather lost for a moment, riveted by his aloof silhouette, of the gathering yet very much apart. "I was busy studying the device to see which girl they had targeted. Did you know it would have been Livia?"

"Had it been you, I wouldn't have taken the trouble—re-engineering their device ruined my shirt." He sighed. "I didn't think Miss Olivia would have cared for the experience."

"No, she would have been humiliated and traumatized. In any case, when I woke up the next morning, I found myself in an unholy hurry to kiss you. I couldn't wait another week, let alone another seven years."

He gazed at her for a while. And, with a murmured "Thank you," wrapped his arms around her.

For precisely two minutes and not a second more.

❧

"Stay awhile longer," she said. "Don't go anywhere yet."

Lord Ingram wasn't sure he'd ever heard Holmes speaking in such a tone. She sounded almost . . . anxious. He snapped his braces in place and reached for his waistcoat. "I came with a citron tart and the shirt on my back. Somehow I don't think Sherrinford Holmes's clothes would fit me."

"I can send for Dr. Watson's—Mrs. Watson still has plenty of his things."

He shook his head. "You didn't even ask where the citron tart is. Who are you and what did you do with Charlotte Holmes?"

She came off the bed and threw on a dressing gown. "So where's the citron tart, then?"

"In the pantry."

"Thank you."

"You don't need to thank me for the citron tart, since my motives are impure: I'm aiming to overtake Bancroft's place as your favorite procurer of fine cakes and pastries."

"Lord Bancroft's motives were no more pristine than yours. And I wasn't thinking of the citron tart, but the thing that they didn't— or perhaps did—do in Sodom and Gomorrah."

Her words might be interpreted as flirtatious; her tone, however, was anything but. Her expression, too, was tight and shuttered.

Briefly he cupped her face. "Still scared witless?"

Of course she was—he'd had to remind her that there was a citron tart on the premises.

She did not answer but only wandered about the room as he finished dressing.

"It'll be all right. I'll bring something back for supper. How does a basket from Harrod's sound? Or would you prefer that I visit a greasy chop shop?"

She remained silent and followed him to the vestibule. They stood there for some time without speaking. Her silence became less tense and more wistful; he let out a breath.

"I'll be back before tea time," he said. "How would you like to try the kind of tea public school boys made for themselves—scrambled eggs, tinned beans, and slices of toast covered with their weight in butter?"

Her lips curved down slightly. "Bring back a basket from Harrod's, too, in case I don't care for your cooking."

"I will. And you, Holmes, has anyone ever told you that you are romance writ large and personified?"

With that, he kissed her and walked out of the house.

—⚬—

Ah, London. Noisy, malodorous, overcrowded London. He didn't always care for the great metropolis, but today he could write a sonnet, no, a five-canto ode, to its noisome vapors and grime-streaked thoroughfares.

The multitudes that thronged the streets were a much-needed antidote after the sometimes unbearable solitude of the country. And after the fishbowl Stern Hollow had become, he couldn't get enough of this blessed anonymity, just another bloke hurrying about his business, one face among millions.

He reached Abbey Road and raised his hand to hail a hansom cab. Someone tapped him on the shoulder. He turned around. A stricken Inspector Treadles stood there, next to a broadly smiling Chief Inspector Fowler.

"My lord," said Chief Inspector Fowler, sounding like a fox still spitting out a mouthful of chicken feathers, "I'm sorry to interrupt your stroll, but you will need to come with us."

## *Twenty*

"Be careful what you say to me. I have not in the least eliminated the possibility that you are the one who killed Lady Ingram, accidentally or intentionally, when she came to abduct the children."

Silence.

How far he had fallen, thought Lord Ingram, that Holmes suspected him of manslaughter—and possibly murder.

Then again, for her, nothing was unthinkable.

"She did not come to abduct the children and I did not kill her."

"Where are your children?"

"They are exactly as I'd told you, with Remington."

She studied him. He held her gaze: He had nothing to hide from her. Except, if he must be completely honest, certain sentiments—and that was only for the sake of his pride.

"I was in your apartment earlier tonight. There was a pair of boots hidden in a corner of your dressing room that have coal dust encrusted in the soles. Years ago, in one of your letters, you wrote

about a tunnel that was opened up under the house at your sugges-
tion, between the coal cellar and some boilers for the glass houses in
the gardens. What were you—"

She paused.

"I see. You want *somebody* to think that your children are still
here. Why? Has there been an attempt at abduction?"

He let out the breath he had been holding. Until her suspicions
lifted, he hadn't realized how heavily they had weighed on him. "The
would-be abductors set a fire as a diversion, but they didn't succeed."

"When was this?"

"A month ago."

"When did Remington come?"

"A few days later. He'd actually visited Stern Hollow earlier, but
this time he came at my request."

She propped her chin on her hand. "I had trouble believing
you'd actually let your children out of sight. I'm sure others might
have had the same doubt."

"That's what I've been hoping for. I've been keeping both the
story cottage and the tunnel appearing as if they've recently housed
children."

She nodded slowly, swirling her spoon in the Bavarian cream
from the charlotte russe. Then she broke apart the sponge cake
base. Bad enough that she wasn't eating her dessert, but dismantling
it? The relief he'd felt evaporated.

*You should be terrified*, she'd told him earlier that evening. *I am.*

He had already been swimming in anxiety and distress; her statement had perhaps not made quite the impact it ought to have. Now it
dawned on him that although his life was at stake, it was possible he
still had only the most superficial understanding of the situation.

She looked up from the disassembled charlotte russe. "There's
still something you aren't telling me. Livia wrote about the ordeal
of meeting with you this afternoon. At first she could only bring

herself to mention the icehouse. She reported that you appeared weary but steady. It was only when she brought up Lady Ingram's name that you became stunned. Which leads me to ask, did something else happen at the icehouse?"

Trust her to be able to deduce something like that from nothing more than her sister's account of how he had reacted. He told her then about the man who called himself George Barr, who might or might not have been a common thief, and whom he had kept in the icehouse, pending an investigation into the man's true identity.

"Lady Ingram must have already been in the ice well when I stood in the second antechamber, wondering how George Barr had managed to escape. But I didn't go forward because outside each inner door there is a large latch, and the one on the next door was perfectly in place. When Miss Holmes first started to stammer about the icehouse, I thought to myself what an idiot I had been not to check more thoroughly. If Barr had an accomplice, and if that accomplice thought Barr had become a liability, there was every chance that he would kill the man and put him deeper into the icehouse to delay discovery. Instead . . ."

She pressed down at the ruins of the charlotte russe with the back of her spoon. He grabbed her wrist. "Stop that. I *am* terrified now."

He felt the tension in her arm, as if she might yank away. But a long second later, she set down the spoon and flexed her fingers.

He exhaled and let go. "I've told you everything. Now you tell me what *you* have kept back."

"Me?"

"Yes, you. Of everything that's happened today, the most inexplicable has been your reaction. You are never so terrified that you are unable to eat. What is going on?"

"Can I not simply be concerned for you?"

"Holmes, you ate half a dozen macarons while you told me that my wife had become an agent of Moriarty's."

"Yes, I did, didn't I? They were excellent macarons."

"And this"—he pointed at the dessert carcass—"was an excellent charlotte russe, something you would have had two helpings of, on any other day, *after* you'd had the cake Mr. Walsh served."

She stared at the blight on her plate. "Very well. There are a few things I don't understand yet, but I would say, on the main, that someone is trying to frame you. Had it been anyone else in the icehouse, the suspicion would have immediately fallen upon Lady Ingram—at least among those of us who know the truth. In fact, even though you tell me it's Lady Ingram herself in there, I daresay that a part of you is still convinced that she has somehow masterminded all this."

She was exactly right about that.

"I know you wonder whether she hated you enough to spite you this way. I am more than convinced that she wouldn't have minded seeing you dead, but not enough to throw her own life into the bargain. So we must take her out of the role of the mastermind.

"She was a pawn—the most important piece on the board, perhaps—but this is someone else's game. Which leads me to ask, what is the ultimate objective of this game that *Lady Ingram* was used as the opening sacrifice?"

He had been eating as she spoke—he hadn't had any food since luncheon. But now the game pie congealed in his stomach, as heavy as a cobblestone. "What?"

She rose from the table. A kettle of water had been provided for the room. She swung it into the grate. "That it's Lady Ingram in the icehouse muddies the waters. But if I must name a motive for this scheme, I would say it's Mr. Finch."

"Your brother, Mr. Finch?"

She nodded.

Mr. Myron Finch had once been an underling of Moriarty's but had chosen to leave the organization. Lady Ingram, pretending to be Mr. Finch's star-crossed lover, had asked Sherlock Holmes to find him, knowing that he was Charlotte Holmes's illegitimate half brother.

"Don't you think this is a bit extreme, simply to get back a renegade?"

She came back to the table. "It depends on what he stole from Moriarty."

Holmes had told him that according to Stephen Marbleton, when Mr. Finch left, he had taken something of great value from Moriarty.

"What can it be? Plans to assassinate the queen at next year's Jubilee celebrations?"

"Mr. Finch was Moriarty's cryptographer. I think he left with something he was deciphering, which might have been more personal in nature."

She took a strand of her hair and let it fall through her fingers. At its current length, her hair was just long enough to begin to curl. He would have thought, if he were asked to imagine how she looked shorn of most of her locks, that she would appear somewhat boyish. Instead, the paucity of hair only seemed to emphasize her eyes and her lips.

"I didn't have the opportunity to tell you this yet," she went on, "but on the day I last saw you in summer, I also met Mr. Finch."

"You found him after all?"

"You and I were, in fact, both in the same room with him a few days prior, but at the time I hadn't realized his true identity yet."

A few days prior he had met her at the office of her father's solicitor. Four other men had been present, their goal to forcibly abduct her and return her to the high uncomfortable bosom of her family. "You mean the groom your father brought? The one who had been helping you and Miss Olivia pass letters to each other?"

"Mr. Finch, in the flesh. I asked him about what he took and he declined to tell me."

"You are sure he remains free to this day?"

"I have reason to believe so. Although on the night we met, he was almost taken. If it weren't for Mr. Marbleton's timely appearance, I'm not sure what would have happened."

"You don't mean to tell me you were accosted by Moriarty's people? My God, Holmes—"

"I'm fine. Nothing happened to me. Mr. Finch is still on the loose—that's the most important thing."

"What about since? Have Moriarty's agents plagued you since?"

"I don't believe so. But"—she pointed at her hair and her men's clothes—"I began to learn, with some urgency, how I may pass myself off as a man. Mr. Marbleton came to us dressed as a woman—most convincingly so. And we all went on our way that night in some form of cross-dress."

"I was wondering how—and why—you had come by this proficiency, since you aren't—" He stopped. "I must have missed something. Why would anyone frame *me* for a murder to get their hands on *Mr. Finch*?"

She didn't say anything.

After a moment, he said, "You mean to tell me that they think *you* know, and that by placing me in jeopardy, *you* will somehow deliver Mr. Finch into their keeping?"

Again she said nothing.

"Are they correct?"

"No," she said, "I don't know where Mr. Finch is."

"You know what I mean. Are they correct in pressuring you via me?"

This time her silence lasted even longer. "Our unseen opponents are counting on that to be the case. So we must do two things. First, we must further bolster their belief that they are correct in that assessment. For that we should become lovers as soon as possible—and please believe me, I am not proposing this solely, or even mainly, to take advantage of you."

He snorted, but the somberness of her voice prevented any other attempts at levity.

"Two, we might have to sacrifice you at some point. In fact, we must. Not your life, no, but your freedom—at least temporarily. I don't believe our opponents would show their hand unless and until you are in police custody for the murder of your wife and possibly that of the poor village idiot."

He felt a haunting need for a cigarette, to clear his head and steady his nerves. She, whose head never needed clearing and whose nerves never needed steadying—or so he would have still believed, if only she'd polished off the damned charlotte russe—observed him, as if she could hear the pounding of his heart and the rushing of his blood.

"I have been worried for a while that something like this would happen," she went on. "I didn't anticipate Lady Ingram's death, nor that the pressure would come from your direction. Only that somehow this pressure would come, because I was careless enough to reveal Mr. Finch's location, however momentarily. That if those seeking him did not find him on their own, I would become the last lead they had on his whereabouts.

"What I feared most was that they would get hold of my sisters, especially Bernadine, who cannot defend or even look after herself. To that end I poached her from my parents, by creating the illusion of a secluded private asylum, with help of Mrs. Watson's friends in the theatrical profession, including one who had married into respectability and loaned us the use of her country house as setting."

Even given the magnitude of the day's news, this astonished him. "*You* have Miss Bernadine now?"

"At the cottage. And I must not be away from her for too long—she has deteriorated considerably since I left home."

"Does Miss Olivia know?"

"Not yet. If I told her the truth about Bernadine I would have also needed to warn her that she herself might be at risk for abduction. Livia is anxious as it is; I didn't want to overwhelm her."

The water in the kettle boiled. He made tea and poured for them, his hands not yet shaking. Not yet. "But in the end, they didn't choose to hold your sisters over you."

"Or Mrs. Watson, for that matter. Which tells me that our opponents do not value friendship or sisterly bonds. But at least they seem to have experienced romantic love—or perhaps even sexual obsession."

He recalled what she'd told him, that Moriarty was still on the hunt, all these years later, for the wife who'd had the temerity to leave him. "And Moriarty is the sort who becomes obsessed over a woman?"

"Mr. Finch told me Moriarty has been thrice married. When a man volunteers himself for the altar that many times, either he has absolutely no idea what to do with himself—or he does value romantic companionship to some extent."

They drank their tea in silence.

"What do you think of what you are being asked to do here?" she asked, tenting her fingers underneath her chin.

It took him a moment to grasp the thrust of her question. "Oh, I will go to jail before I give up my virtue, you may depend on that."

She smiled a little, a sight that never failed to do worrisome things to his heart. He set aside his tea. "That said, I still don't think you have told me everything. Far from it."

She gazed at him for some time. "You are right. I have not told you everything."

## Twenty-one

"So . . . you have sacrificed me in your opening gambit," said Lord Ingram to his extravagantly mustachioed visitor. "How is your game progressing?"

"Patience, my lord," she answered. "I nearly starved, by the way, waiting for you to return with tea and supper. Had to go to Harrod's myself for a basket."

She'd known, of course, that once he stepped out of the house he would be nabbed by the police—he had timed his departure from Stern Hollow so that Chief Inspector Fowler would be informed in time for her carriage to be followed, after she left the interview. At first she thought he had come too soon—their original plan had called for him to remain in Stern Hollow for as long as possible. But once he explained everything that had taken place, she had agreed that he had chosen the right time.

And now here he was, behind bars, the basket from Harrod's his only companion for the long night to come.

He had been in worse surroundings—the jail cell, out of consideration to his station, was not too filthy; even the smell in the air was not too foul. But he had never been in worse circumstances, even if he had allowed himself to be put up as bait.

He had trusted his fate to her. But if she was wrong . . .

"Don't worry," she went on. "I brought two other baskets for the guards, so they should leave yours alone."

As if he would worry about a food basket at a time like this. "They can have mine."

"So speaks a lordship who's never had to dine on *cuisine de prison*. You will be denied bail. Guard your basket with your life."

He set a hand on the basket, his fingers digging into its wicker exterior. He wanted out of this place. He wanted to see his children. He wanted a wall behind which to hide, damn it, and not be exposed to every passing guard's curiosity.

"Come here," she said.

He rose and went to her. "I'm afraid."

Terrified.

"As you should be. As am I. But don't forget, sir"—she reached through the bars and took hold of his hands, her own hands steady, her gaze clear and calm—"that I am a queen upon this board—and I do not play to lose."

❊

Livia grabbed the envelope.

It was the day after she'd made the devastating discovery at Moreton Close. She'd arrived home in numb despair and had to spend the rest of the day fending off her mother's angry comments about Mrs. Newell's inconsideration at not providing a maid to accompany Livia on her trip.

She wrote Charlotte a letter, begging her sister to do something. Anything. She hoped to be able to post it away from Lady Holmes's prying eyes—and feared it would be just like a peevish Lady Holmes not to let her out for a day or two.

But the early post had brought a letter from Charlotte. The short note was written in the code that they'd devised for themselves—not the one Charlotte had made up for her to give to the police, but the modified Caesar cipher they had been using since childhood.

Translated, the message read,

*Dear Livia,*

*My apologies. B is with me and has been all along. Please do not worry anymore. I will explain everything when I see you next.*

*C.*

*P.S. Until then, please make no decisions with regard to Mr. Moonstone.*

※

Inspector Treadles had done his best to ensure that Lord Ingram was put up in a clean cell and treated with due respect and courtesy. But still he felt guilty, as if it had been his machinations that had put his friend behind bars, and not Chief Inspector Fowler's.

"You mustn't abandon hope, my lord," he said.

Lord Ingram did not look worse for wear—yet. It had been only a day. "I have not. I have friends working on my behalf."

"Sergeant Ellerby is seeking the other body specified by Sherlock Holmes with all his might," said Treadles, feeling more than a little stupid. He wasn't sure how that would help Lord Ingram.

"You must thank him on my behalf until I can do so in person. He has been very kind." Lord Ingram smiled a little. "And how are you, Inspector? How is Mrs. Treadles? Cousins Manufacturing running smoothly under her stewardship?"

"I think so. Or as smoothly as can be expected now, since she is still relatively inexperienced. But I'm quite astonished at how much she has learned." There was a lingering sweetness on his tongue. It took Treadles a moment to recognize it as pride—he always used to speak of his wife with pride and now he was once again doing so. "I would find the management of such a large organization over-whelming, but she enjoys herself immensely."

"I'm happy to hear that. I hope to have you both to Stern Hollow someday soon."

He imagined his friend, free again. The Treadleses, walking arm-in-arm on that beautiful estate, talking and laughing. And himself, bathed in forgiveness and understanding, neither of which he de-served, but he hoped to.

Someday.

"I will be most gratified to have that come to pass."

Lord Ingram smiled slightly. "Holmes is on the case. We have nothing to fear."

---

Lord Ingram was in custody for more than thirty-six hours before the message Charlotte had been waiting for came, typed on plain paper, posted from one of the busiest corners of London, in an en-velope addressed to Sherlock Holmes.

*Hand over Mr. Finch and exculpatory evidence will be offered for Lord Ingram. You may post your reply in the papers as a +10 Caesar cipher.*

She immediately sent in her reply. *Hand over exculpatory evidence first.*

The response came two hours after the morning editions be-came available, this time delivered to the mail slot at 18 Upper Baker Street itself. *You are not in a position to negotiate. Give your answer as a Vigenère cipher. Keyword: STERN.*

She took a deep breath and dispatched her next message to the evening papers, coded as specified: *22 Compton Lane, Hampstead Heath.*

---

The man in the parlor of 22 Compton Lane had become accus-tomed to making himself at home in different surroundings. He always carried the same Darjeeling tea and the same pair of house slippers wherever he went, so that there would be some sense of familiarity and coziness, no matter how strange and inhospitable his new dwellings.

This house was not so bad. Close enough to London to be convenient, but with slightly cleaner air and somewhat less clogged streets. There was a bookstore nearby he enjoyed browsing—in fact, he'd spent too much money there—and the food at the tea shop on the next street was downright decent.

He had just settled into his chair, a glass of Armagnac at his side, a Mrs. Braddon novel in hand, when he heard suspicious sounds at the front door. He rose and extinguished all the lights in the parlor. The firelight from the grate couldn't be helped, of course, but he did take the poker in hand, before he secreted himself behind the grandfather clock.

Men came into the house. Two of them. One went deeper, ascending the stairs. The other came toward the parlor.

He recognized those footsteps.

The intruder walked into the parlor. He glanced at the glass of Armagnac and the hastily cast aside book—and cocked his revolver.

The occupant of the house stepped out from behind the grandfather clock.

The intruder raised his firearm. Then his expression changed.

The firelight was not brilliant, but it was illumination enough in such close quarters.

"Remington," said the intruder coldly. "What are you doing here?"

Lord Remington shook his head. He'd thought he had steeled himself, but still he was close to tears. "I had hoped it wouldn't be you. Even after everything I've learned, I still hoped that we were wrong and that it wouldn't be you, Bancroft."

# Twenty-two

STERN HOLLOW
EARLIER

"What do you think of what you are being asked to do here?" murmured Charlotte.

"Oh, I will go to jail before I give up my virtue, you may depend on that."

She couldn't help smiling a little. With everything spinning out of control, at least his defense of his virtue was a familiar refrain, even if this time it was uttered with a hint of mockery rather than as an outright refusal.

He set aside his tea cup. "That said, I still don't think you have told me everything. Far from it."

He sat sprawled in his chair, one shoulder lower than the other—she rarely saw him with less-than-perfect posture. Fatigue was writ deep across his features. Dread, too. A desire *not* to know radiated from him. He must hate these serious conversations with her—they had never held one that didn't strain their friendship or, far more unhappily, upend his life.

"You are right," she said reluctantly. "I have not told you everything. I have not told you whom I suspect to be behind all this."

He straightened, his expression incredulous, almost disbelieving. "Someone other than Moriarty?"

"When I made arrangements to remove Bernadine from my parents' house, I wasn't thinking of Moriarty."

"Then who?"

"When Mr. Finch left Moriarty's service, why do you suppose he didn't turn to agents of the Crown?"

"He must have known that there was at least one informant among our ranks."

"He could have gone straight to the top, bypassing the ranks."

Now he only looked confused. "You aren't implying that *Bancroft* is working for Moriarty?"

"No, not that. Bancroft would never put himself in the hands of someone like Moriarty. I would even posit that he despises the existence of Moriarty's organization: It isn't affiliated with or dependent on any sovereign nation, but forms mercenary alliances as it sees fit. In an already complicated landscape of competing powers and loyalties, it is an agent of chaos."

Lord Ingram exhaled, his relief palpable.

But a man did not need to work for or with Moriarty to have done something reprehensible. She bit the inside of her cheek. "However, it's possible—in fact, I would put it as probable—that what Mr. Finch stole from Moriarty concerns Lord Bancroft and that Lord Bancroft knows it."

He braced his hands against the edge of the table. "I'm willing to cede that as a possibility. Bancroft doesn't have the cleanest hands. And if worse comes to worst, I can believe that he might have slept with someone unsuitable, an agent for a foreign government— or from Moriarty's organization.

"But Bancroft wouldn't have passed along secrets to women he dallied with. And empires are not built with clean hands. I fail to see how Mr. Finch's illicit knowledge could possibly damage Bancroft to such an extent that they would fear each other."

She considered what she was about to say. "What did you think when you received Lady Avery's letter, the one that detailed our meeting at the tea shop in Hounslow?"

"I thought it was a remarkable piece of bad luck that someone who served us in a random tea shop should also serve, in a random hotel counties away, the one woman who would listen, take note, then broadcast this all . . ."

His voice trailed away—he was beginning to see.

"Indeed, an extraordinary coincidence. Which begs the question. What if it hadn't been a coincidence? What if someone deliberately wished Lady Avery to know about our encounter? Besides the two of us, who else knew that we were there that day?"

"I know you want me to say Bancroft, since he sent his man Underwood to fetch us. But why couldn't Moriarty also know?"

As soon as he said it he grimaced.

She knew exactly what he remembered. "Moriarty wouldn't know because we shook off his minions when we set out that day. I'm certain you were vigilant even afterward, making sure no one else followed us—I know I was. Not to mention that, on the night Mr. Finch was almost caught, it wasn't Moriarty's men who stopped my carriage. It was Mr. Underwood, Lord Bancroft's man."

Granted, she had then run into Mr. Crispin Marbleton, Moriarty's brother. But that had been an amicable meeting, focused more on Mr. Marbleton's concern for his son Stephen—and Charlotte's for Livia. The worries of two parties who weren't ready to become in-laws yet—who feared that the unexpected attraction between their loved ones could lead to dangerous complications.

She didn't burden Lord Ingram with this particular development—they had more pressing problems.

He frowned. "But you know Bancroft was also looking for Mr. Finch at the time. That it was Mr. Underwood who tried to nab him doesn't mean anything."

"But since it wasn't Moriarty that night, Moriarty couldn't have any idea that I knew, however briefly, where to find Mr. Finch. He wouldn't have had any reason to pressure anyone else in my orbit to get to me."

He gripped his teacup, as if needing to extract what remained of its warmth. "Still, what could Bancroft possibly have done that he would need to orchestrate such a diabolical trap, to get the evidence from Mr. Finch?"

She finally took a bite of the charlotte russe. It was beautiful, cool and velvety on the tongue—but her stomach convulsed in protest.

She waited for the spasm to pass. "Who made this?"

"An acolyte of Bancroft's pastry chef—who once worked in this house, of course."

"When we were talking about Lord Remington, Mrs. Watson mentioned that Lord Bancroft had in fact been the family's black sheep."

"I have heard that—my father mistrusted him because he spent too much money. But that was long ago."

She pushed away the dismembered charlotte russe at last. "What kind of a man keeps a pastry chef in his employment?"

He stared at her, his eyes wide with dread that was beginning to congeal into understanding. "What do you mean?"

She took a deep breath. "I mean, how much income would you estimate he has? Lord Bancroft is a second son. He works for the Crown, which doesn't pay extravagantly. And he doesn't have, as far as I can tell, a wealthy godfather who has settled a magnificent fortune on him."

He didn't speak.

"I knew very little of men's clothes before this autumn. But now that I do, I can see that his garments are, if not vastly, then at least noticeably superior to yours. Not that yours are inferior by any means, but his are *superlative*.

"And let's not forget the house near Portman Square, which he bought and kitted out in anticipation that I would marry him. We joke about how he threw all taste and refinement to the side to please me, but have you ever thought of how much such a venture—a house in a desirable location, filled to the brim with exotic and extravagant furnishings—would have cost?"

He pressed his fingers against his temples.

"When Mrs. Watson mentioned his spendthrift ways, she kindly posited that no one should be judged on their adolescence. But we are not judging Lord Bancroft on old habits. We are looking at how he lives now. Where do you suppose he obtains such a sizable income?"

Now he covered his entire face.

"You may know something of how he directs the day-to-day operations of his agents. Do you have the impression that they are being shortchanged in terms of remuneration or other necessary funds?"

Behind his hands, he shook his head.

She was breathing fast. Her hands were clenched together. She flexed her stiff fingers and forced herself to exhale slowly, quietly. "Whatever possibility remains, then, no matter how terrible it is, must be the truth."

❖

Lord Ingram shot out of his chair.

For a man in Bancroft's position to have so much inexplicable income—if he wasn't stealing from his office, there was only one other possibility.

He was selling state secrets.

Lord Ingram wanted to deny it. He wanted to shout that it was beyond absurd that such an accusation could be levied at his brother.

But truth, however absurd it seems at first, always possesses undeniable weight and solidity. Yes, Bancroft had been a valuable asset to the Crown. He was extremely competent and handled everything under his purview with aplomb. But he was also a man without true loyalties, except to himself. Lord Ingram wasn't certain, now that push came to shove, whether Bancroft could even be called an honorable man.

Dear God, all this time, all this time when Bancroft had asked his subordinates to risk their lives for Queen and country . . .

He didn't know whether he wanted to weep or to smash things. All he knew was that he gripped hard onto the mantel, feeling as if he'd never be warm again.

"I'm sorry," she murmured next to him.

"It's not your fault," he said by reflex. "But what am I to do?"

"You protect yourself. And you protect me. Can you imagine what would happen if he were to guess that we suspected his worst secrets?"

He shivered, chilled from head to toe.

"There is still, of course, a chance that I've read too much into everything. That he is a bystander in all this. If he is innocent, he will do as he usually does, remain in the shadows himself and let others take care of everything.

"But I think he has something to do with what happened in that icehouse. He visited Stern Hollow five weeks ago. What reason did he give—that he wanted to make sure that there are no other traitors in your household?"

He gave a small, grim nod.

"While he was here, he would have familiarized himself with the geography of Stern Hollow—that's how the abductors he'd sent knew to head directly for the nursery. Had he succeeded, had he your children in hand, he would have been in a stronger position to demand Mr. Finch in exchange. But that attempt failed and he knew that you were vigilant. So he switched to his contingency plan, and made it appear that you had murdered Lady Ingram."

"But surely I would have learned of it, if he or his men had found her."

"I don't think he found her. I suspect the 'maid' who told Lady Avery about our encounter in the tea shop was involved in more ways than one. If I must guess I would say that she was of the same approximate height and build as Lady Ingram, with dark hair and a beauty spot in a similar position on her face. Bash in her face, put her in your icehouse, and who would that beauty spot identify her as?"

"But that wasn't the body your sister—or I—saw in the icehouse."

"That part puzzles me—I can only assume something went awry. But the important thing is, if my suspicions are correct and Lord Bancroft indeed orchestrated the icehouse incident—or part of it—then he would not stay away. He would send Mr. Underwood—and possibly even come himself to investigate. There are many questions to which he would need answers. How did the actual Lady Ingram end up in the icehouse? Where had that decoy gone? Who else was at work? Who knew enough of what he was doing to mock him so?"

The fire in the grate crackled. She sighed softly. "Should he or even Mr. Underwood arrive, you must take it as an admission of guilt and be careful. Above all else, do not let him guess that you know."

Now he understood, viscerally, why she couldn't eat. Now he was as afraid as she. Moriarty was a distant specter. But his brother, a man with just as much power and menace, was right here, moving among them.

She fell quiet. Exhaustion battered him—he could scarcely remain upright. But he knew what he needed to do.

He would protect himself.

And he would protect her.

The policemen vacated the library. Now he and Holmes were alone with Bancroft, who had been watching them from the recesses of the gallery.

Bancroft looked even worse than Lord Ingram remembered from his recent visit. But now he knew that this deterioration was not due to the loss of Holmes's hand for a second time, but because Mr. Finch, in possession of his secret, was still at large—and his schemes to pry the man's whereabouts out of Holmes had not gone as planned.

Lord Ingram's eyes met Holmes's. She rubbed her bearded chin. "By the way, Ash, you bowdlerized my pangram. I'm devastated."

"I don't know why you believed I would have ever committed the original in writing, in any of my scripts."

He could scarcely feel a single muscle in his body, only a palpitating fear that somehow Bancroft would take one look at him and know everything.

He took a deep breath. "Will you come down, Bancroft, or should we join you up there?"

*And so it begins.*

## Twenty-three

"And so it ends," murmured Lord Remington.

Society still remembered him largely as a wild young man, but in his years abroad, he had risen high in the Crown's service. Lord Bancroft, he had told her, was being held in a secure location, pending a thorough investigation of everything he had done during his tenure.

And now Lord Remington and his men—who occupied a separate compartment—accompanied Charlotte on what she hoped would be the final journey for this case. She was bone-tired. And the sandwich she'd wolfed down before she boarded the train—Lord Bancroft being put away had restored most of her appetite—contributed a lethargy in addition to the fatigue that had accumulated for days.

The countryside sped by in the darkness, the train's wheels thudding rhythmically. Before she knew it, Lord Remington was shaking her softly by the shoulder. "Miss Holmes, wake up. We have reached our destination."

Outside the railway station, the company climbed into waiting carriages. She was almost about to doze off again when Lord Remington said, "Forgive me, Miss Holmes, I've only just now remembered the bomb. Was that also Bancroft's doing?"

Charlotte rubbed her eyes and sat up straighter. "He chose the ice well as the place to leave Mimi Duffin's body because he'd learned that in Lord Ingram's household, not a great deal of ice was consumed. The icehouse must have seemed perfect—the body wouldn't be discovered immediately after he left. But when no one came across it for days on end, I imagine he grew impatient.

"He and Lord Ingram had called on Mrs. Newell together, so he knew that Mrs. Newell was expecting guests. If he put a bomb in place, then her guests would need somewhere else to go. Stern Hollow, of course—its master could always be counted on to do the right thing. And once the guests arrived, the kitchen boy would be digging out ice from the ice well."

"I see," said Lord Remington. "What I still don't understand is why did Moriarty choose to get involved? And how did he even know what Bancroft was up to in the first place?"

"I've been pondering the same question. Perhaps Moriarty knew that the code Mr. Finch was breaking concerned Lord Bancroft but not exactly what it entailed. Perhaps he had other informants who learned that Lord Bancroft was still ardently seeking Mr. Finch's whereabouts, with more intent and focus than he was putting into the search for Lady Ingram.

"And if Moriarty had someone observe Mr. Underwood, he would have seen that Lord Bancroft was up to something irregular. As for why Moriarty interfered—in the end, it might have been nothing more than malice. Lord Bancroft was a powerful opponent. Why not throw a wrench in his plans? Why not see if this was his Achilles' heel?"

"Moriarty killed a woman for *that*?"

"He killed someone he believed to be utterly without value. As did Lord Bancroft."

The asylum came into view. At night, it would have been easy to mistake it for just another isolated country manor, if it weren't for the walls that surrounded it on all sides. They drove through the gates into a courtyard. The main building was large and ivy-covered; behind several of the dark, barred windows, curtains fluttered.

A nervous-looking man of about fifty-five introduced himself as Dr. Connelly and conducted them inside. After a quick cup of tea, they were taken down long corridors to one wing of the house.

Dr. Connelly unlocked a door and lit a sconce. "Miss Greville, we have some visitors for you."

The room was spartan. The woman inside sat at the edge of the bed in her dressing gown, holding a sharpened pencil as if it were a knife. She gave a look of pure loathing to Dr. Connelly but recoiled as her gaze landed on Lord Remington.

"Would you mind coming with us, Lady Ingram?" said her brother-in-law. "We have need of your help."

———※———

"How did you find me?" demanded Lady Ingram, once she, Charlotte, and Lord Remington were all in the carriage together. "How did you know about this place at all?"

Charlotte had first believed, as had everyone else, that the woman in the icehouse had been Lady Ingram. But that woman had turned out to have been pregnant. Lady Ingram had never been interested in romantic love. How likely was it that she would take a lover when she was on the run for her life?

For a moment, Charlotte's mind had moved toward darker possibilities—a woman didn't need to be a willing participant in her own impregnation. But then she remembered what she herself had said, when Lord Ingram had expressed his disbelief at the sight of his dead wife.

*Maybe that's her secret twin sister in the icehouse. And the real Lady Ingram is waiting in the wings, cackling with anticipation.*

He had said immediately that if she did have such a sister, no one knew about her.

But such sisters existed—Charlotte had one. She'd told him about Bernadine, but prior to her meeting with Mrs. Watson, he had been the only outsider with whom she'd ever broached the subject. To the rest of the world, there were only three Holmes sisters, Henrietta, Olivia, and Charlotte.

And this was true for a woman who had lived under the family roof until Charlotte had poached her away. What if Lady Ingram's twin sister had a worse condition, one that required her to be institutionalized from an early age? Parents didn't mention such children. Eventually, even their own siblings forgot about them.

Mrs. Watson had verified the existence of one Constantina Greville at the General Register Office, headquartered at Somerset House: There was a birth certificate for her, showing that she was born on the same day as Lady Ingram, but no death certificate. Lady Ingram might have discovered the existence of this twin sister when she had gone through some of the family papers after her parents' deaths, or even known about her all her life. And when she'd needed a safe refuge this summer, a place to hide from Lord Bancroft's wrath, she must have remembered this sister no one had ever heard about.

"We know because Miss Constantina Greville, who lived here before you displaced her, is now dead," said Lord Remington.

"You are lying!"

Lord Remington handed her a newspaper. "It's a long story, but in essence Moriarty killed her to frame your husband for murder."

Charlotte did not fail to notice that Lord Bancroft's name had been omitted.

"But he promised to look after her!" Lady Ingram cried, even as she yanked the paper from Lord Remington.

She read in the light provided by Lord Remington's pocket lantern, her breathing growing more and more agitated. At last she crumpled up the paper and threw it aside.

The silence was harsh.

"Did Moriarty himself promise to look after Miss Greville?" asked Lord Remington.

"I've never met Moriarty. I dealt with a man named de Lacy."

Charlotte remembered the name from her investigation this past summer.

"De Lacy wasn't impressed when I went to him," Lady Ingram continued, speaking as if through clenched teeth. "I was supposed to look after myself, he told me, not needing to be sheltered. Lord Bancroft was always going to be after me, how would I deal with that? In the end he challenged me to last six months out there by myself and I agreed.

"I thought it would be a brilliant idea to take Constantina's place in the asylum. No one would ever find me. And when I told de Lacy my plan, he agreed to get me in and bring Constantina out, and to look after her in the meanwhile, in exchange for my emerald necklace."

She laughed bitterly. "Maybe there really is no such thing as honor among thieves, and I'm just the last person to learn that."

---

They spent the night at a railway hotel, with Lady Ingram carefully guarded by the men Lord Remington had brought. In the morning they took the early train into London and went to Lord Ingram's town house, where Lady Ingram's wardrobe, left behind when she'd fled, was still in her dressing room.

Charlotte, ironically enough, had served as Lady Ingram's chaperone since the latter had been taken into custody. The interaction between the two women had been almost entirely silent, but as Charlotte helped Lady Ingram into a handsome travel gown, the latter said, "It's your idea, isn't it, to make me the scapegoat?"

"No," said Charlotte. "You have Lord Remington to thank for that."

She believed Lord Bancroft should be exposed for his crimes, but the Crown did not want the failings of its clandestine servants made known.

Perhaps Lady Ingram was getting her just desserts. Mr. Underwood would pay, too. But Charlotte wasn't so sure Lord Bancroft himself would suffer the fall of the hammer. A man such as he, who dealt in secrets, could have easily set things up so that other powerful men's shameful dealings became at risk of exposure, unless his own safety was assured.

"As it stands, you can't touch de Lacy or Moriarty," Charlotte went on. "But there is something you can do for your late sister. It was kept from the papers and, out of delicacy, Lord Remington hasn't mentioned it either. But Miss Constantina Greville was with child at the time of her death and I think you have a fair idea who must have done it to her, she who could never have given consent."

"That bastard," Lady Ingram growled. "Connelly."

"Did he try anything with you?"

"Oh, he tried. But one jab of the pencil and he ran out crying."

A man who only preyed on the weakest of the weak.

"Here's what you can do," said Charlotte.

After she gave the contours of a plan, Lady Ingram scoffed. "You want me to speak to *those* hags?"

"I wouldn't overlook potential allies simply because they haven't been my allies before. But if you find that too distasteful—"

"No," said Lady Ingram. "I'll do it for Constantina. She deserved better."

Charlotte nodded. "Should I tell Lord Remington that you are ready?"

One side of Lady Ingram's mouth curved down, the side where her beauty mark had been. A woman on the run couldn't afford such a distinguishing characteristic; now there was only a slight dent. The dent on Constantina Greville, at the same spot, must have been to disguise the fact that *she* had never had a beauty mark.

"Are you not going to thank me?" Lady Ingram said, her voice slightly less strident than it had been. "You only look good to him compared to me."

"I can thank you if you need me to," Charlotte said. "But really all he needed was time to grow up."

Lady Ingram set a severely sleek hat on her head. "You have a very high opinion of yourself."

She regarded her reflection with the scorn of someone who did not have a very high opinion of herself. Who had, in fact, never cared for the person in the mirror.

Into Charlotte's lack of a response she said, "He will disapprove of you. You know he will."

Of course he would—he'd always made it plain when he disagreed with her. But disapproval was not the same as obstruction and he would never stand in Charlotte's way.

She smiled a little. "I'll let Lord Remington know you are ready."

———※———

The invitation from Sherlock Holmes had filled Treadles with a strangely elated presentiment. *I think Chief Inspector Fowler is going to suffer a public debacle,* he'd told Alice over breakfast. *I just don't know how yet.*

The discovery of the bomb should have given Fowler pause. But he was adamant that the bomb was irrelevant, that they had enough to get a conviction in court. Treadles had found his excuse repugnant. Their first commitment should be to the truth, not to whether their evidence could be spun into a hangman's noose.

He was hampered by both his lower rank and his friendship with Lord Ingram—anything he said could be construed as a display of personal bias. Nevertheless, he had made a carefully deferential argument for more police work, which Fowler dismissed in its entirety. So one might say that Treadles rather wanted for his superior to suffer a public debacle. And how oddly fitting that Sherlock Holmes should be the one to administer that dressing down.

They arrived to their rendezvous with the consulting detective at a St. James's tea shop only to realize they were to be seated at the same table as Lady Avery and Lady Somersby.

"Chief Inspector, Inspector, what an unexpected pleasure," declared Lady Avery. "Are you also here at Sherlock Holmes's invitation?"

Fowler eyed her warily. "We are, my lady."

"Excellent. Now I'm even more excited for what we are about to learn."

Treadles's pulse accelerated. Whatever it was, Sherlock Holmes meant for the news to be splashed all over town before the end of the day.

A man came and sat down at a nearby table. He looked familiar, somehow. Like a bigger, more rough-hewn version of Lord Bancroft. Could he possibly be another one of Lord Ingram's brothers?

Before Treadles could ask the gossip ladies, Lady Somersby made a choked sound. "Oh my—my goodness gracious! Caro, look. *Look!*"

She was pointing at the door. Lady Avery glanced up. The policemen turned halfway around in their seats.

Lady Ingram was headed directly for them. Lady Ingram, not a corpse, but a woman very much alive, if rather pale and tense, with an expression of distaste on her face.

*Her antagonism is a broad and catholic entity,* Charlotte Holmes had once said, *aimed at no one in particular*. Even so, Treadles wished he were out of its swath.

Too late. She came to a stop next to him. Remembering that they had been formally introduced by her husband, he scrambled to his feet.

"Lady Ingram, I am—I am overjoyed to see you in good health." She nodded regally. "Inspector."

"May I present my colleague, Chief Inspector Fowler, the lead detective on your murder case."

Fowler remained where he was, agape. Treadles had to give the man a nudge on the shoulder for him to come out of his chair. Even then he was capable of only a haphazard bow.

"Charmed, I'm sure," said Lady Ingram coolly. "Lady Avery, Lady Somersby, we meet again."

Lady Somersby's recovery was quicker than Fowler's. "Lady Ingram, we thought your husband had killed you."

Lady Ingram rolled her eyes. "That man is so sanctimonious he probably wouldn't even let himself think of such a thing. No, I had left him for another man. But the situation was . . . complicated, so I decided to take my twin sister's place at a private asylum in Gloucestershire. She was removed from home at four and committed to an asylum eight years later.

"Moriarty, the man I left my husband for, had taken on the care of Miss Constantina Greville. But he chose to murder her to frame Lord Ingram, and that is something I cannot countenance."

Lady Avery blinked. "You left Lord Ingram for a *murderer*?"

"It would appear that I did," answered Lady Ingram, seemingly unmoved, but Treadles caught sight of her hand tightening into a fist. "Anyway, I thought the police should know. And as enjoyable as this meeting has been, I regret I cannot stay much longer. Now that I've exposed Moriarty, I myself am no longer safe."

"Wait, we need to—" Fowler began.

Lady Ingram cut him off. "Ladies, by the way, this may not have been in the news but the police can confirm that my sister was with child. I understand you take an interest in exposing and righting injustices. In which case, allow me to point you in the direction of one Dr. Connelly at her former asylum. Good day."

She turned and marched out.

———※———

Lord Ingram embraced his children again and again.

He took them to the park, bought them boiled sweets, and had both tea and dinner in the nursery. They, of course, excitedly told him about seeing their mother earlier in the day, even as they were saddened that she had to leave again.

Remington had promised her that the Crown would no longer pursue her for her earlier collusion with Moriarty, which had led to the death of three agents, and see her safely out of the country, if, in exchange, she took responsibility for her sister's death. She had asked to see her children in addition, and there had been a harried reunion before she set off for parts unknown.

But Remington had been surprised by the choice she'd made to point the finger at Moriarty. He was one of the true culprits, of course, and she had not been forbidden to mention his name. But still, by speaking the truth she had announced her break with Moriarty and put herself at risk.

*We may not see her alive again,* Remington had warned.

*I hope you are wrong,* he'd replied.

She was still the mother of his children and, for their sake, he wished her well.

"I will still be here," he promised them. "Mamma will come when she can, but I will always be here."

After they went to sleep, he would have liked to call on Holmes. But she was no longer in London: Mimi Duffin's body had been found, and Holmes and Mrs. Farr had left for Derbyshire together.

So he made a less pleasant visit.

Bancroft had been put up in quarters much superior to Lord Ingram's jail cell. But no one had brought him a basket from Harrod's. And judging by the plate of half-eaten food he'd set aside, the cooking was not to his taste.

"In my shoes you would have done the same," said Bancroft, without any preamble.

He wouldn't. He wouldn't have sold state secrets in the first place.

But that one sentence from Bancroft let him know that he would get nowhere with his brother, this stranger. So he asked only, "When you proposed to Charlotte Holmes this summer, after her exile, I'd thought you more enlightened than I'd given you credit for. But it was only so that you could get close to Mr. Finch through her, wasn't it?"

Bancroft said nothing.

No denial on that front, then. And when he had withdrawn that offer, it would have been because he realized that his secrets would be far less safe, if he were, in fact, married to Holmes.

Without another word, Lord Ingram rose and saw himself out.

—❖—

Lady Ingram's revelations—and the fact that she wasn't dead—shocked Society. No less breathtaking, however, was Lord Ingram's subsequent petition for divorce. Livia was most astonished, however, to receive an invitation to Stern Hollow: Lord Ingram was hosting a small gathering of family and friends, Mrs. Newell would be present to serve as her chaperone, and a suitable woman would be sent to accompany her on her travels.

Who turned out to be Mrs. Watson in glasses and a sack of a dress, speaking in a broad Yorkshire accent, devoid of all glamour—but still warm and delightful, once they had a train compartment to themselves.

Livia asked about what had happened with Lord and Lady Ingram, and the answers she received astounded her. Lady Ingram had become the eyes and ears of a dangerous man named Moriarty. She'd had to leave when Charlotte found out what she was doing. Lord Bancroft, fearful of what secrets Mr. Finch might know, had done everything in his power to apply pressure to Charlotte, including via Lord Ingram—and that Moriarty had played the spoiler in his plans.

It was almost too much to take in. Almost.

But not so much that she didn't eventually get around to the one participant in the drama that Mrs. Watson had not mentioned yet. "The young man who pretended to be Mr. Finch, ma'am, do you know who he was? And why he had tried to pass himself off as someone else?"

"About him, your sister plans to speak to you herself. But between you and me"—Mrs. Watson winked—"I find him rather adorable."

Livia prayed that she hadn't flushed a splotchy shade. "Do you also know him then, ma'am?"

"Not to any great extent, I'm afraid."

"But he isn't a confidence artist or anything of the sort, is he?"

"I would say not."

"Then . . ." Realization struck Livia; as always, a slap of dismay. "He is this Moriarty's man."

Mrs. Watson leaned forward and took Livia's hands. "Not in the way you think, my dear. Not in the way you think."

But what did that mean?

After they reached Rampling Cottage, Livia was taken to see Bernadine, who looked rounder and happier, and almost acknowledged her presence. Charlotte was also in the room, looking not very different from how she had when Livia had last seen her at the cottage. The two of them sat side by side without speaking, watching Bernadine, who was completely absorbed in her own world. After a while, Charlotte signaled to Livia that they should repair to the parlor, where they took tea by themselves.

Charlotte asked Livia how much she'd been told. And when Livia had rattled through the major points, Charlotte added, "Mott is Mr. Finch."

Livia leaped out of her chair. "What?"

But as flabbergasted as she felt, the news was not unwelcome: Her illegitimate half-brother had turned out to be someone she liked and cared about. And from time to time she'd thought of him and hoped he was all right.

"Goodness! Last I saw him, he was running away from some people."

"From Lord Bancroft's men. He's still safe, as far as I know."

"That's a relief."

"And your young man is Moriarty's estranged son."

Livia fell back into her chair with a thud.

"His mother left Moriarty for the latter's brother, and Moriarty has been hunting for the entire family ever since. He is also at least five years younger than you, in case that matters. Mrs. Watson's late husband was eleven years younger than her, by the way."

Livia blinked. "So do you or do you not approve of his age?"

"It is not my place to approve or disapprove. I am here to tell you everything that I know about him, so that you do not make up your mind in a vacuum."

"Make up my mind? What is there to make up my mind about? He sends an occasional memento. That's all."

"All I can tell you is that his father—not Moriarty, but the man who raised him—was concerned enough to arrange for a face-to-face meeting with me, months ago."

"About me?"

"And him. Yes."

Livia didn't know whether to blush in delight or tremble with fear. "This is—this is—"

"I know," said Charlotte, handing her a plate of sandwiches. "Life never takes a gentle turn; it always swerves."

Livia ate two sandwiches without knowing what they had for fillings. "What should I do?"

"What you would like to do, I hope."

Livia set down her plate to throw her hands in the air. "But I don't even have any means of contacting him, to tell him that I don't want any more notes or presents."

Charlotte popped a fancy-looking tartlet into her mouth. "You can tell me. I'll pass the message along."

Livia had been gathering herself up to launch into a tirade about how the young man had never requested permission to write her, how he had never even apologized for misrepresenting himself, and how she really couldn't care at all if he disappeared off the face of the earth.

Charlotte's answer punctured all that blather.

"Oh," said Livia—and couldn't think of another word.

Charlotte poured Livia a fresh cup of tea. "You don't need to make up your mind until you are ready. And you don't need to consult me on the matter, unless you wish to. And if you have any more questions, I'll be happy to answer them, but I'm almost sure you'd prefer to pose them to Mrs. Watson instead."

Livia took a sip of tea and shook her head to clear it. "When— ah—when do I need to arrive at Stern Hollow? Mrs. Newell must be expecting me."

"If you start from here in half an hour, you should be in good time," Charlotte said, picking up another tartlet. "And by the way, I know him as Mr. Marbleton. Mr. Stephen Marbleton."

She bit into the pastry with relish.

❧

Lord Ingram called upon Rampling Cottage the next afternoon, during Mrs. Watson's nap time.

"My, the prodigal lover returns," murmured Charlotte as she offered him a seat.

He gave her a look.

"Very well," she said with a sigh. "The constant friend returns."

She had severely underestimated his unwillingness to give up his virtue, even after she had explained that to misdirect Lord Bancroft's attention, they must become lovers in truth. *He would check the sheets. You know he would.*

*I can contribute to the sheets by myself,* he'd said stubbornly.

*And you think he wouldn't be able to tell the difference?*

Frankly she'd had no idea whether that was a valid argument, her experience having been too scant on that front. Lord Ingram had, however, grimaced—and, finally, yielded. But not without further conditions.

*It will be only for the sake of keeping us safe from Bancroft. It ends the moment I am arrested. And it doesn't count: I have not agreed to become your lover, either for now or for the future.*

*Goodness gracious, you are a stick-in-the-mud.*

*And you clearly have a weakness for sticks-in-the-mud, since I'm constantly fending off your advances.*

She'd sighed. *I am no longer a woman anyone can compromise. You are no longer a married man. Not to mention I have at my disposal every manner of contraceptive known to woman. Why do you still object so?*

*Perhaps my body in bed is enough for you. But the reverse isn't enough for me. I have already endured years of unhappiness because I wanted more than what a woman could give. I will not put myself through that again—especially not with you.*

And what could she have said to that?

Present day Lord Ingram accepted a cup of tea from Charlotte. They chatted about his guests, Bernadine's progress, and his
plans to host another house party at Christmas, this time for his
fellow devotees of archaeology, including Inspector and Mrs.
Treadles.

Half an hour later, he rose to take his leave. "If you are still in
the area by Christmas, Sherrinford Holmes and Mrs. Watson are
more than welcome to the archaeologists' party at Stern Hollow."

She shook her head. "Thank you for the very kind invitation,
but we probably will not extend our stay at the cottage again."

"Of course," he said, "Sherlock Holmes's livelihood is in London."
Silence fell.

A weight pressed down on her lungs. She was . . . reluctant to say
good-bye. As reluctant as she had been the afternoon he headed out
to be arrested.

*And you think this won't have repercussions?* he had asked her before
they'd made love for the first time.

At the time, she'd responded with something breezy and blithe.
But perhaps his had not been an idle concern. Perhaps for her the
repercussions were only now making themselves felt as regret and a
sense of loss.

"I have something for you," he said, holding out an envelope and
peering at her at the same time.

She raised a brow. "If it's payment for Sherrinford Holmes's services, you will need to speak with my bursar, Mrs. Watson."

"That will be seen to. But this is not pound sterling."

"Oh?"

She took the envelope, unfolded the piece of paper inside, and,
after a moment of stunned silence, burst out laughing.

On the paper he had copied, two dozen times in his own handwriting, the original and unsanitized version of the pangram she

had composed for him years ago, which referred to an act that most certainly had been known in Sodom and Gomorrah, pre–fire and brimstone.

"So you did commit that to paper—repeatedly, too," she said, still smiling.

"Several of my pens burst into flames, my library smelled strongly of sulfur, and I am frankly scared," he said, also smiling.

She folded the paper carefully. "I will treasure this token of your regard," she said, meaning every word.

He inclined his head. "Good day, Holmes."

When he was already at the door, she heard herself call out, "Wait!"

He turned around.

For a moment her mind went blank—and then she knew exactly what she wanted to say. "I have my sisters to think of, and you your children. But if—if someday the conditions should be conducive, would you like for all of us to go away together? Spain, Majorca, Egypt, the Levant? By the time we reach India, it will probably be unbearably hot in the plains, but the hill stations should still be pleasant."

He gazed at her, as if he couldn't be sure he'd heard her correctly. And then a smile slowly spread across his face.

"Yes," he said. "I would like that."

# Epilogue

Alas, Lord Ingram's gathering lasted only three days. All too soon Livia found herself back home, where no one paid her any attention except to point out her numerous shortcomings.

Chief among which, according to her mother, was her inability to attract a husband.

But an "opportunity" was at hand. The Holmeses were hosting Sir Henry's new business associate for dinner. Lady Holmes lectured Livia on and on about the importance of making a good impression.

"He and his family have been abroad a long time so they don't know about . . . our scandal. If you have an ounce of sense, Olivia, you will try to get yourself noticed by this gentleman. Goodness knows I'm tired of taking you to London Season after Season."

Whenever her father tried a new venture, the family grew poorer. Sir Henry possessed no judgment at all—it would be a miracle if this new associate wasn't a swindler. Abroad, her arse. That he didn't know about Charlotte's scandal only meant that they wouldn't know anything about him either.

And she was supposed to smile at and flatter *him*?

Lady Holmes made Livia don her most fashionable dinner gown and spent an hour fussing over Livia's hair, unhappy with every style Livia tried. By the time Livia sat down in the drawing room to wait for this man's arrival, she was convinced she was at the beginning of one of the most execrable evenings of her life.

And then the drawing room door opened and in walked Stephen Marbleton.

# ACKNOWLEDGMENTS

Kerry Donovan, Roxanne Jones, and Jessica Mangicaro, who are wonderful to work with. The art department at Berkley, who creates a more splendid cover for every new Lady Sherlock book.

Kristin Nelson, for whom I'm running out of superlatives.

Janine Ballard, who pushes me to do my very best.

My husband, who has been a tireless salesman for these books.

And you, if you are reading this, thank you. Thank you for everything.

Photo by Jennifer Sparks Harriman

*USA Today* bestselling author **Sherry Thomas** is one of the most acclaimed historical fiction authors writing today, winning the RITA Award two years running and appearing on innumerable "Best of the Year" lists, including those of *Publishers Weekly, Kirkus Reviews, Library Journal,* Dear Author, and All About Romance. Her novels include *A Study in Scarlet Women* and *A Conspiracy in Belgravia,* the first two books in the Lady Sherlock series; *My Beautiful Enemy;* and *The Luckiest Lady in London.*

She lives in Austin, Texas, with her husband and sons. Visit her website at sherrythomas.com.